Chasing Rainbows

Finding the End of Your
Rainbow Is Not Always Simple.

By Pamela Le Bailly

Strategic Book Publishing and Rights Co.

Copyright © 2012
Pamela Le Bailly. All rights reserved.

No part of this book may be reproduced or transmitted in any form or by any means, graphic, electronic, or mechanical, including photocopying, recording, taping, or by any information storage retrieval system, without the permission, in writing, of the publisher.

Strategic Book Publishing and Rights Co.
12620 FM 1960, Suite A4-507
Houston TX 77065

www.sbpra.com

ISBN: 978-1-61204-777-5

Other books by Pamela Le Bailly:
Pressed Flowers
Second Time Around: Ideas and Recipes for Using Leftovers
Simply Single: No Fuss Recipes for Single Cooks
Available on Amazon.

For my late husband Louis, who gave me my first computer and encouraged me to use it.

To my three daughters who encouraged me, my friends who were asked to read my first stumbling efforts, and to all those who search for their own Rainbow's End.

St. Wraich cannot be found on any map of Cornwall, but friends living in one small village may recognise it as their own although all characters are fictitious. I have drawn from personal memories of living in South Africa during the last War and in America after the War. A few episodes are taken from my own experiences, such as the encounter with the black mamba.

For those who have never been fortunate to visit South Africa:
Stoep is the covered veranda usually surrounding a house, providing much needed shade and shelter.
Rondevals are small round huts built near the main house, used as guest rooms, sometimes quite lavishly furnished.

In 1940, Jean Shapwick is evacuated from her home in London as the bombing starts and finds herself growing up in the West Country. This story of love and betrayal, set in Cornwall, South Africa, and America, follows her family through many twists and turns as they seek to find their own Rainbow's End.

England

Prologue

Unexpectedly, it was a beautiful day. Sometimes in March the sun comes out, and all of a sudden everyone feels spring may be coming at last, after the miserable winter. This was just such a day and James felt a kind of relief, a small lightening of the gloom that had engulfed him for so long. The house, which had seemed like a suffocating prison for the past few months, was breathing again. The windows were opened and the curtains drawn back to welcome the sun, and there was no longer an aura of ill health dominating all the rooms. James had insisted on the light being let in, although the housekeeper Ellen had resisted any attempt to deny the hushed and dismal atmosphere which she felt ought to prevail after her Master, who she had served so diligently, had 'passed away' as she called it. James felt it was the most blessed relief he had experienced for a long time.

He had been busy, organising the church service, alerting the newspapers, solicitors, undertakers, relations and last but not least, certainly in Ellen's mind, the funeral meats as they were so quaintly called. These were now all laid out in the dining room, ready for the numerous mourners coming back to the rectory after the burial. So many would come. After all, the older ones had known his father for many years, some of the really ancient crones since he was a baby. They would come in to the room they had known all their lives, sit down as near to Ellen's famous sponge cake as they could, and spend some time saying, "what a wonderful man he had been"; and "how he will be missed"; and "no-one will be able to take his place"; when all the time James would have to nod, and be polite and gracious. Little did they know of the real man they had come to see buried, a man who had ruined his life.

James' sister Elizabeth and her husband Robert had arrived late the day before, and the old house was filled with life again, and even laughter when Ellen was out of earshot. They came downstairs now looking suitably sober, dressed in black which suited Elizabeth, making her look so like their mother that it gave him a little jolt of nostalgia.

"Ellen has done wonders considering." She said, looking round at the display of refreshments. Before her father had died, he had asked her to place a little sealed box in his coffin, which she felt was rather strange, but the contents had obviously meant a great deal to him, and so she had taken it to the undertakers and placed it beside him, wondering a little just what memories it contained.

"Time to go;" said James, looking at his watch for the umpteenth time. "Has everyone else gone?"

"They went over about twenty minutes ago." Elizabeth's husband Robert said impatiently, feeling the odd one out, with James and Elizabeth seeming so close at this time of their lives.

It wasn't far to walk to the church. Although their grandfather, a former Rector of St. Wraich had died in 1960, Elizabeth had been married there. She had walked to the church and the wedding reception had been held in the rectory. Of course it was The Old Rectory nowadays, a modern one having been built in the Glebe field. Their father had bought the old house when Grandfather had retired, and they all considered it their home.

They could hear the gentle strains of the organ as they approached the church. James tried not to think of those other funerals he had attended, all more tragic than this one. The Reverend Catherine was waiting at the lych-gate with the undertaker and bearers by the coffin; it looked extraordinarily large, dominated by the obligatory flowers (family only) placed on top. James took one look, arranged his face to look solemn, and took his place behind the Rector, alone now as head of the family. He beckoned to Ben to walk beside him, putting his arm gently round Ben's thin shoulders for a minute, in a small gesture of comfort for his younger brother.

The organ began, the bidding words read as they walked up the aisle. James heard a little rustle as the waiting congregation stood up and then they were there in the front pew, where over many years he had been made to sit through endless, meaningless sermons. Those Sundays, when all he could really think about was the river waiting for him, or his bicycle or the wide open beaches with the surf coming in.

Now he was there to honour his father. A man he had hated and despised for so long that he could hardly bear the eulogies, the praise and memories people seemed to experience as they knelt in prayer. Perhaps once he would have felt the same, but today, when he knew the truth of it all, the whole ceremony seemed a farce.

It was over now, and they followed the coffin out to the cemetery across the road. There seemed so many determined to see the man they knew laid to rest.

He looked up for the first time, seeing his brother and sister, and several strangers gathered round. One small person moved into his sight and a sickening shock hit him. He took a step backwards and felt Elizabeth's hand steady him.

"What on earth? It can't be. It just can't," he breathed.

And time stood still.

England

Chapter 1

The letter lay on the table between them. Mrs Shapwick had been the first home, and Jean had rushed up to her as she always did when she heard her mother's key in the lock.

"Mummy, I've got a letter from Miss Herbert. She said you have to open it as soon as possible."

"Heavens, Jean, give me a chance to get my coat off." Mrs Shapwick leant down to give her daughter a kiss, and handing Jean her gloves, she hung her hat and coat on the hooks by the door. "Now, let's get the kettle on; your dad will be home in a minute, and you know he likes a nice cup of tea as soon as he gets in. Go and lay up the table...Oh, I see you've done that."

"But Mummy, Miss Herbert said it was ever so important and she wants an answer by tomorrow so..."

"Don't be so impatient my pet. It will keep for another hour till after your Dad's had a nice sit down and a cup of tea."

Now it had been opened. They both felt a sense of shock, and a dawning realization that the war, a shadowy worry until now, had become a grave problem, which would affect all their lives. A decision had to be made, and made before the morning.

Miss Herbert had written to every parent explaining that the Government was sending all the children out of London to protect them from the bombing, which was expected to escalate before too long. She had to have their permission of course, but she strongly recommended that they allow Jean to be evacuated to the country. The children would be safe, be able to continue with their education, and generally have a better life away from the dangers of wartime London. The train would leave in two days' time, and the group of children, (Jean attended quite a small school), would be escorted by Miss Hull, who would see that they all were integrated into suitable homes. They must agree to these arrangements by the next morning, and instructions would be given to the parents at once. Miss Herbert hoped they would understand the urgency etc. etc...

Of course, Jean had been told. They did not usually keep things from their only child.

She had gone quiet but she had felt a sense of excitement inside. After all, it would only be for a few weeks, just like a holiday really. But, her parents explained, they would not be able to go with her. Her father was just about to become a soldier, and her mother had important work, helping to win the war as she put it. Jean had become a latchkey kid, and she did not much like it.

Then Jean had been sent up to bed, and now her parents had to make a decision.

Mr Shapwick reached forward and picked up the letter to read once again, although by now he knew it by heart and felt as if each word was a knell of doom. How could England have come to this, when parents had to send their children far away to protect them from the follies of the people who were supposed to know better? This tinpot dictator Hitler, what did he think he was doing, sending weapons of destruction raining down on cities and towns, so that children had to be evacuated, without their parents, in hope they would find safe sanctuaries? He sighed deeply, and when his wife looked up, he could see she was quietly weeping.

"How can we let our Jean go off, all on her own, without knowing where she will end up?"

He got up and put another lump of coal on the dying fire.

"Maybe it will be warmer, wherever it is." He sighed. "She's got to go, love, we both know that. There were bombs dropped in the East End last night. Suppose it's our turn next and she was here all alone. I've got to leave next week, and you can't always get back in time. It would be good to think whatever happens she will be safe in the country, having good food and fresh country air."

His wife dabbed her eyes, and took up the letter again. "I know. Shall I write an answer then and we'll both sign it?"

She went over to the cupboard and collected a pad of paper and an envelope. Taking a pen out of her handbag, she wrote their permission for the school to whisk away their only beloved child, out of their arms, out of their lives, for goodness only knew how long. Each word seemed more laborious than the last, and when she had finished she silently passed it over to her husband. He read it, took the pen and signed it, giving a sniff and pulling his large handkerchief out of his pocket, blew his nose loudly.

His wife got up, and as she passed him she placed her arms round his bony shoulders for a moment. Putting her cheek against his she whispered, "Our little girl will be all right," before going slowly up the stairs to say goodnight to her treasured daughter.

***

The station was huge, bigger than anywhere Jean had ever seen. Even bigger than Olympia where the family had gone to see the Ideal Home Exhibition before the war. It was so noisy too, people rushing around and shouting and loudspeakers blaring, which made it all rather scary.

She clutched her mother's hand, and the warmth of it made her realize that in a little while they would have to say goodbye. Daddy had told her this morning to be very brave.

"We are not sending you away because we want to get rid of you, but the nasty Germans are trying to bomb London, and we think you will have a lovely time in the country." He said.

"Can't you and Mummy come too?"

"Oh we'll be fine, don't you worry about that. Think of all the nice things you can do down in Cornwall; and we'll come and see you when we can get time off, you'll see." He tried to reassure her.

Jean sort of understood. They both worked in quite important jobs to do with the war, and were not always home when she got back from school, and Daddy was going off to be a soldier quite soon. It was a bit lonely letting herself in the back door with the special key which hung round her neck. Even if she was nearly nine years old, she understood about air raids, and was quite scared to be on her own sometimes. When the council lady had come round the school, and told all the children they would be going to live in the countryside for a while, she had, like all her friends, got quite excited.

Mummy and Daddy had seemed pleased too, and said it would not be for very long anyway; just like going on a holiday with lots of friends.

But now the moment had come to get on the train the feeling of excitement abruptly disappeared, and she felt slightly sick, clutching her mother's arm and gulping.

"Now, dear, don't cry. That would never do. You must show all the little ones how brave and grown-up you are." Her mother gave her a hug and pushed her up the train steps. Miss Hull, her teacher, told her where to sit, luckily next to the window. She waved and waved to her mother as the train gave a lurch and a chug and started moving, gently at first, but quickly gathering speed. Her mother ran alongside for a little way, but the train went faster and faster and all at once she couldn't see Mummy any more.

***

She heard a little sniff beside her. One of the other girls from her school sat hunched and crying gently into her handkerchief, which was pretty sodden.

"Annie, don't cry." Jean put her hand out and stroked Annie's arm.

"I don't want to go away and leave Mummy all by herself," she sobbed. "But she made me."

"My Mum," replied Jean, "works in a factory making things for the war, and my dad is going away in the army, so they couldn't really look after me. What does your mum do?"

Annie gave a sniff. "She doesn't do much, but she's always going out and she said I'd be alone too much and it was a good thing that the council was sending all the children away from London."

"What about your dad?"

"I haven't got a dad now. He went away when I was a baby, and Mum is all alone and..."

Jean thought the waterworks was starting all over again, and she looked over to Miss Hull. "Please, Miss, can we have our sandwiches now?"

"Why don't we all wait until one of you can see a cow in a field?" suggested Miss Hull with a smile. Jean thought this was a splendid idea, although it seemed to be some while before any fields appeared. She and Annie gazed at the rows of houses and factories and wondered if they would see any cows before they became too hungry.

The journey seemed endless, not helped by the constant hold-ups waiting for more important trains to go by. At last the cows were spotted and the sandwiches unpacked and an aura of contentment reigned for quite a while. They had each been given a packet of sandwiches and a slab of cake by the kind ladies at the station, and the novelty of a sort of unexpected picnic quite diverted their attention from the fact that they were gradually being transported miles away from their homes to a completely alien and unknown future. Jean was almost asleep when one of the other girls in the carriage interrupted her daydreams.

"Please Miss, I want to go to the lav," piped up Mary, a little tearaway at times, but strangely on her good behaviour at the moment.

Of course this meant that they all wanted to go, and so the next half hour was spent escorting them down the corridor. (Fortunately it was one of the trains that had corridors these days), and initiating them into the odd sort of arrangement that the Great Western Railway had for dealing with customer's needs. Miss Hull would not let them lock the door, afraid they would be unable, in a sort of panic, to extricate themselves, so she waited outside for each child to emerge, refreshed and giggling at the novel experience.

"Soon we'll be able to see the sea!" Exclaimed Miss Hull, once they had all returned to their seats. Actually it seemed ages, not at all 'soon' to Jean. But there it was at last, right beside the train, little white waves rolling in from a grey sea. Some of the children had never seen the sea at all, and they all clambered up on top of each other, to get to the window and gaze at this new part of the world which they were experiencing. All too soon black rocks hid the water and suddenly everything went dark, as the train entered a tunnel.

"Are we under the sea, Miss?" whispered one terrified little boy.

"Heavens no, Jack, only going through some cliffs, and now here we are, out the other side!"

It was the most exciting time of the whole journey. They were starting to get tired and a bit sleepy, when Miss Hull told them to get their coats on and collect their bits and pieces. The train started to slow down and finally stopped.

"Come on, out we get. We have to get another train to take us on." They followed Miss Hull with a meekness she had never witnessed before.

The next train was much smaller, but all managed to scramble into it with only one of Annie's gloves getting left behind. This time they gazed out of the window as the train crawled over a huge bridge that spanned an enormous river, which Miss Hull told the children was the River Tamar, and they were now in Cornwall.

"Is Cornwall where we are going?" Mary asked.

"Yes and when you get to Wadebridge we will find a lot of nice ladies who will take you to their homes and probably give you supper." Miss Hull just hoped her predictions were right. She had been given such vague instructions about the reception that they would receive when they finally arrived at their destination; she tried not to worry too much about what was awaiting them.

When the train huffed and puffed into Wadebridge station, juddering to halt with a screech of brakes, they collected all their little suitcases and clambered out. Miss Hull led them into a building and told them to sit on the benches each side of a huge room. They saw a group of ladies who seemed to be looking at them.

Miss Hull was talking to them, and after a bit she came over to the children and said, "I'm afraid you can't all stay in the same place. Some of you will be going to stay here in Wadebridge, but three are going to a village called St. Wraich. You Jean, Annie and Harry come with me." And she led them over to three ladies waiting by the door.

One lady came forward and Jean looked up. She saw blue eyes and a halo of grey hair with a kind face, and all at once she felt a bit happier.

"You are coming to stay with me, and your friends will be going with someone else, but you will all be in the same village. Isn't that nice?" said the lady, bending down a little.

Jean would have liked to stay with Annie, (not Harry), but she felt too shy to say anything except "thank you," as she had been told by her mother. At that point the thought of her mother overwhelmed her and bursting into tears, she sobbed, "Mummy! I want Mummy!"

The lady bent down, gave her a hug, and whispered, "Oh my pet, I'm sure your Mummy is thinking of you too, but just now you are coming with me. Come on, we'll get in the car and drive home."

That was the first time Jean thought of the Rectory at St. Wraich as "home."

England

Chapter 2

The Rectory was a big rambling house with trees and shrubs lining the drive. Jean, who had never been out of London before felt smaller and smaller as Mrs Bretton drove up to the front door.

"Out we get," she said, and helped Jean and her little suitcase get out of the car. They went into a big hall with some old chairs against the wall, and a large round table taking up space in the centre. Mrs Bretton helped Jean off with her coat and hat, and flinging them down on one of the chairs she led the way into a light airy kitchen with a huge stove on one side. Jean felt everything was enormous after the small terrace house in London.

"Tea I think, or would you like a glass of milk?"

Jean wondered if she dared say "milk," as Mrs Bretton had the kettle boiling on the hob. But she did, and was rewarded by the most delicious glass of anything she had ever tasted. It was cold and creamy, and when Mrs Bretton also handed her a slice of cake she felt a little bit of contentment creep back into her.

But she was so tired, she felt her eyelids droop and her arms ache as she slowly sipped and chewed. She put the empty mug back on the table, finished the last crumb and allowed herself to be led upstairs. Mrs Bretton took her into a small bedroom, gently took off her outer clothes and tucked her up in the bed. She drew the curtains and tiptoed out of the room.

"No point in trying to give her a wash or undressing her properly," she told George, her husband, later. "She was so tired I don't suppose she really knew where she was. At least she was clean, unlike some of the children I saw at the station."

George Bretton, the Rector of St. Wraich, gave a small sigh of relief. He had felt it was his Christian duty to take in an evacuee from London, but some of the stories he had heard, (lice-invested, rude, and dirty), had made him apprehensive. He led a peaceful existence, looking after the souls of the Parish, and in his spare time researching the meaning of science in relation to God. They only had one child, a son David, who was away at school. Nancy, his wife, helped with all the village activities, and looked after him and the Rectory in spite of increasing arthritis. Neither of them was young, and the thought of a small child in the house again was somewhat daunting.

"Well, as long as it is not too much for you; and of course she will go to school."

***

Jean did, in time, go to the village school, which was only across the road from the Rectory. But that first morning when she woke up she felt so strange and lost, that Mrs Bretton noticed and decided that Jean should have a few quiet days to settle in to her new life.

When Jean woke the sun was shining in, and a girl who was drawing the curtains turned round, and seeing she was awake, said, "I'm Violet. Ma'am said I should come and 'elp you wash and dress before breakfast."

"I can dress myself, I'm nearly nine, you know."

"Yes, I can see you're a big girl. Just show you where the lav and the bathroom are, though," said Violet, as she turned away and led Jean down the passage.

"I'll be about when you're ready love. Just call out "Violet" and I'll take you downstairs."

That first day was a kind of magical interlude for Jean. It was all so different. No traffic was rushing past the window, only a quiet garden with trees and flowers as well as space; bags and bags of space. Mrs Bretton said she could go anywhere in the garden or house, but she must be quiet as Mr Bretton was writing his sermon.

She spent the whole morning exploring. She met an old man digging a long trench, and stood watching him for a bit.

"And 'ow are you, little maid?" he said, in a funny sort of voice. "I be diggin' for vict'ry, that I am. See 'ere, I've got them tatties to put in," and he handed her a small rather dirty potato and showed her where to put it in the trench. "That's right, cover 'en up, and we'll mark 'en with a stick, so we will, so we know 'tis your own tatty."

Jean did as he said, and put the stick just over the place with great care.

"Now you can come and see 'ow 'tis growin' so you can, whenever you want."

She watched him for a little while, as he filled the rest of the trench with potatoes, and covered them up, so that all she could see was her stick standing up alone in the row. Then she wandered away across the big lawn.

She made friends with a cat. Violet later told her he was called Jumble, as when he was a tiny kitten he had been found on a rubbish heap in an old box, and he was now part of the family. He purred when Jean stroked him and rolled on his back to have his tummy tickled. Jean, who had never had a pet, or in fact had never been nearer to animals than the zoo, was entranced.

Jumble followed her while she walked to the end of the garden, and sat beside her when she looked over the gate at some cows that were grazing in the field. She wished her mum and dad were there to see all this too, and started to feel sad again. But Jumble purred loudly and rubbed against her legs, as if to say "I'll look after you," which cheered her up, and she started to feel hungry. She found Violet in the kitchen, stirring something on the stove which smelt delicious, and made her even hungrier. Violet, who had several small brothers and a sister, gave her a biscuit "to keep you going till lunch."

"What's 'lunch?' asked Jean.

"I think that you'd call it 'dinner', but 'ere t'is 'lunch' served in the middle of the day. They call 'tea' 'dinner' and have it later, though I expect you'll have your tea earlier because of your bedtime," explained Violet, which muddled Jean more than ever.

She met Mr Bretton at lunch. He smiled at her in a vague sort of way and said he hoped she would be happy in the Rectory, and she would soon be going to school and make some friends.

"I believe you have two friends already, who came from London with you," said Mrs Bretton.

"They were at my school, but we weren't really friends. Annie was one, and the other was a horrid boy called Harry. I suppose he will be at the school too."

"Well" said Mr Bretton, "I expect he will settle down. I believe he has gone to live on a farm."

"Am I going to school soon?" asked Jean.

"We thought you might go tomorrow for one day," Mrs Bretton told her. "As it is Friday you can go, and have a day to find out which class you are in and everything, and then start properly on Monday."

Jean spent the afternoon getting to know the house. She started right at the top. She discovered some stuffy attics which were reached by a tiny narrow staircase, and were filled with all sorts of old boxes and suitcases. I'll explore those on a wet day, she thought. There seemed to be lots of bedrooms. She knew the one which belonged to Mr and Mrs Bretton, and her room the other side of the passage. She then found three or four tidy bedrooms which were obviously not used, and one big room full of boy's books and toys and models. Mrs Bretton had told her they had a son called David, who was away at school. The bed had a cover on it with a picture of a boat, as well as a model boat on the shelf, and lots of books piled up on a wooden chest. She would have liked to have looked in the chest, but she was afraid Violet or someone would come along and discover her, so she shut the door quietly and went downstairs.

Jumble met her in the hall, and led her to a little room tucked away behind the dining room. She found several bits and pieces there; an old fishing rod, two cricket bats, a football and a comfy looking armchair piled with old coats and scarves. She cleared them to one side and sat down snuggling into the aged softness, and Jumble followed and curled up on her lap.

And that is where Mrs Bretton and Violet found her, after a slightly frantic search, fast asleep with Jumble in her arms.

Dear Mummy and Daddy,
I hope you are well. This is a nice house, and Mr and Mrs Bretton are nice. I have a new frend. He is called Jumble, and he is a cat. He has black fur with wite paws and he purrs a lot. I put a potato in the grownd and old Mr Trewon said I can eat it when it grows. Dont wurry I have lots to eat.
Lots of love from Jean.

***

Violet woke Jean early the next day. "School today!" she said brightly, "You'd better hurry and get dressed, and mind you put that jersey on," pointing to a bright red jersey lying on the chair.

Jean could not eat much breakfast as she was so excited, but also anxious at what it would all be like. She needn't have worried; Annie rushed up to her as Mrs Bretton took her into the classroom.

"Jean, Jean ... I'm so glad to see you, where are you staying? Whe..."

"Now, now," a small lady advanced. She seemed very young to be a teacher. She indicated where they should sit, had a word with Mrs Bretton and went to stand behind a big table. Mrs Bretton gave Jean a little wave and an almost wink, and left.

The teacher looked at them all and said; "We must welcome our new pupils, Annie, Jean and Harry, who have come all the way from London to live here. We hope they will soon settle in and be happy, and we must all help them, as they have had to leave their parents behind and do not know any of our country ways, but I am sure they will soon feel at home and make lots of friends."

Annie looked across at Jean, and then at the row in front. Jean followed her gaze and saw Harry, looking extremely pleased with himself as if he already knew everyone and therefore was vastly superior to them.

"My name is Miss Norton," the teacher told the new pupils, "but you can just call me "Miss" when you need to speak to me. Now...," and they started on reading.

Jean found the work fairly easy. The school she had been attending in London was quite small and the tuition good. But being a little shy she only answered when Miss Norton asked her questions, and went quite pink when she was told she had answered correctly. The morning passed quickly and soon it was break time. Then they were allowed to run about outside in a sort of courtyard and those who wished, to let off steam, Harry already showing leadership in that direction. She and Annie huddled together on the side, until two other girls came up and asked their names and could they come and play, so that the time went very quickly.

Jean discovered that Annie was staying with a couple who lived the other side of the village, and Harry was indeed with a farmer. As he was mad on animals, and already had shown he was keen to help, he had lots of jobs he had to do when school was over.

"You see, I have to go and find the eggs, and then help to round up the cows. I can't do the milking yet, but Mr Pipton is going to teach me, *and* all sorts of other things. Soon I'll be too busy to come to school," he said grandly. Jean and Annie wondered what Teacher would think of that!

Mrs Bretton was waiting for her outside the school at the end of lessons. She explained she was only doing it today as it was her first time, but Jean could easily walk back by herself to the Rectory, which was only a little way down the road from the school.

"Did you have a nice day?" she asked, as they walked back.

"Oh yes" Jean replied, "The lessons were quite easy and I met loads of boys and girls, and I like Miss Norton too."

"She was a pupil at the school not long ago," said Mrs Bretton, "but because of the war she has been asked to come back."

"I hope she stays," said Jean. She thought so many things changed because of the war, she wanted everything to stay the same forever and ever.

Dear Mummy and Daddy, I hope you are well. I go to school now, which is very close, so I walk there by myself. We have a nice teecher called Miss Norton. She is not quite so nice as Miss Hull, and she is very small. We all wear red jersys. The school has a garden and we all get a bit, and teecher gave us some seeds to sow. I had lettis and carrots.

Lots of love from Jean.

***

Jean settled in to her new life quite quickly. She enjoyed going across the road to the school and she easily made friends. Annie did too, and although they saw each other almost every day, the friends they made were from different groups. Annie's group was a somewhat giggly lot, always comparing clothes and hair, and sometimes, boys. They did not see much of Harry, who was rather rough and inclined to pull pigtails, and put out his tongue behind the teacher's back. Jean's group was quieter, a little serious, and fond of animals. They all had pets of some kind; a hamster, two guinea pigs, a couple of dogs, and quite a few cats. Naturally Jean was pleased and relieved that she could relate the antics and history of Jumble. In fact he sometimes followed her to school and had to be repulsed when they got to the door, much to the admiration of her friends.

She found the work easy, except for Natural History, which they had not really studied in London. In St. Wraich they often had a nature walk when the sun was out. Miss Norton was knowledgeable about the local wild flowers and plants, and Jean's favourite school project was collecting and pressing the flowers and leaves, then making a picture with them, which she presented to Mrs Bretton one day.

"How lovely!" she exclaimed, "why don't you make one and send it to your mother?"

Dear Mummy and Daddy, I hope you are well. We go on Natcher walks with Miss Norton and she helped me make this card with the leaves and flowers we picked. You have to put them in a book first so they dry. I made Mrs Bretton one too. Jumble came to school with me today but I had to tell him to go home as Teacher said cats were not aloud. He only has to go across the road.

Lots of love Jean. X X X

***

When Jean had been at St. Wraich for several weeks Mrs Bretton told her she had some very exciting news. It was the half term holiday, and Jean was wondering how she would spend the day. Mrs Bretton had a letter in her hand and she said, "Your mother is coming to stay for two or three days! She's coming tomorrow afternoon and we'll go down to the station to meet her. Isn't that lovely?"

Jean was so excited she jumped up and hugged Mrs Bretton, something she had never done before, and then did a little dance round the room.

"We must get the bedroom next to yours ready, and you can try and find some flowers in the garden to put there. I'll tell Violet to dust the furniture..."

"Oh! But can't I do the dusting," exclaimed Jean, "I will get it all ready for Mum if you like."

In the end Jean and Violet had a lovely time getting the bedroom all 'bright and cheerful' as Violet put it.

Jean found some primroses and put them in a little glass jug which she found in the kitchen. That night she could hardly sleep with excitement, and was up early the next morning, gazing out of the window to see what the weather was like. Luckily it wasn't raining, the clouds were chasing each other across the sky, and a shaft of sunshine was peeping through. She was early down to breakfast, even before Mr Bretton. She knew he liked to have his breakfast 'in peace' as he called it, so she went to find Jumble and tell him what was happening today.

She had to wait a long time, as the train did not get to Wadebridge until three o'clock in the afternoon. She went up to her mother's room, as she thought of it now, to see if the primroses were all right. They looked slightly droopy, so she picked some more. Jumble tried to jump on the bed so she had to haul him off, which he didn't like at all and stalked off with his head in the air and his tail twitching with indignation. But for once she didn't mind. The thought of her mother coming, and all the things she would tell her and show her, overrode any other feelings she had.

They took the car to the station. Mr Bretton decided that he had enough petrol to spare, and "it is a special occasion after all."

The train came chuffing in and drew to a halt with a whistle of steam. The doors flew open, and people came pouring out. Mrs Bretton had Jean firmly by the hand, but when Jean shouted, "There she is!" she let go and felt a lump in her throat as Jean hurled herself at a well-dressed woman just alighting from the train. They hugged and hugged, laughing and crying at the same time, till Mrs Shapwick said, "Hold on, I must get my things," and she hauled a suitcase and two boxes out onto the platform. Then, "Heavens you've grown," as she hugged Jean again. Looking up she saw Mrs Bretton smiling gently at them both. "I'm so sorry, how do you do," she said, holding her hand out and smiling. "You are so kind to come and meet me. Oh it's lovely to be here, with Jean and in Cornwall after all this time."

"You have been to Cornwall before then?" asked Mrs Bretton.

"Oh yes, my grandmother lived near Wadebridge and we used to visit her in the summer until she passed away about ten years ago. We were so pleased to think Jean had ended up so near to her home."

"Mummy, you never told me that," Jean interrupted, pulling her along towards the car.

"Well, we never thought we'd ever come down to Cornwall again. And now here you are, living here!"

By this time they had reached the car, and were piling the luggage in the boot. Mrs Shapwick got in the front and Jean climbed in behind her and hung over the back of her mother's seat so that she would be as close to her as possible.

The visit went by far too quickly for them all. Her mother and Mrs Bretton seemed to have plenty to say to each other, and Jean was happy to listen and watch them talking and laughing as if they had been friends for years. They all went on expeditions together, and sometimes the sun was shining so warmly that she and her mother could just sit in the garden and chat. Jumble was included then and lay purring by Mrs Shapwick's chair while she tickled his tummy. Jean took her round the village and introduced her to her friends, both from school and in the little village shop, where she bought her weekly ration of sweets. Mrs Bowman, who kept the shop, even found a spare chocolate bar "which didn't belong to no one," for her and her mother to share.

"What a lovely place to live in," exclaimed Mrs Shapwick once, while they were walking back from looking at some newborn lambs, "You are a lucky girl."

"Yes," agreed Jean, "but I wish you and Daddy were here too."

"Well, perhaps one day we'll all live here, after the War."

All too soon the time came for Mrs Shapwick to go back to London. Before she left she and Jean went for a last walk round the garden.

"Mrs Bretton and I have been talking and we decided that, if you agreed, you should call her "Aunty Nancy" and the

Rector "Uncle George." It is very kind of them to suggest it, isn't it?"

Jean thought for a moment, and then nodded.

"It would be nice, and more, well, more friendly than always saying Mister and Missis. Violet calls them Ma'am and Sir, but I didn't really know what to say."

"That's good then. I feel better leaving you with such good people who seem to love you so much."

"I love them too, but I love *you* better" and she put her arms round her mother, as tight as she could, and buried her head in her mother's skirt. She wanted to keep it there forever and ever.

Mrs Shapwick disentangled herself gently and said, "I must go and get my case now. It's time to catch the train. I'll soon come down again, and you must be a really good girl while I'm away, and work hard, and help the Brettons..." She could not go on; she had such a lump in her throat at the thought of missing her little girl growing up without her.

***

Jean settled back into the school routine quite quickly. There always seemed something to do, and sometimes it was quite exciting. Easter was approaching, and the Shapwicks had not been regular churchgoers, so that the festival celebrations were new to Jean.

Of course, living in the Rectory Jean was expected to attend the Sunday school, and join in the various events connected to the Church. St. Wraich was a Church school and was therefore involved in many activities around the Christian calendar.

As it drew near Easter Jean found it particularly enthralling. The Sunday school always decorated certain windows with wild primroses, and an expedition was planned to go and pick them on Easter Saturday morning, and arrange the flowers in the afternoon. Jean looked forward to joining the other children, gathering the flowers and helping to make the Church beautiful for Easter.

But a few days before that, she had noticed an air of anticipation in the Rectory. Aunty Nancy rushed about, planning meals, making lists and rushing Violet off her feet with ideas of what to do next.

Jean asked Violet what all the fuss was about.

"My goodness, 'as no one said? David will soon be 'ere for the 'olidays, and then we'll 'ave some fun, I can tell you."

"Why?"

"Well, what David wants, David gets, if you know what I mean," answered Violet. Jean didn't, but she entered into the spirit and helped dust the room with all the boats in, and tried not to feel jealous of the boy who seemed to mean so much more to the household than she ever would.

***

Mrs Bretton was not at all sure what David would think, when he realized there was another child in the home he had been used to thinking of as his sole property. She had written to him at school to tell him that they had acquired a small girl who had been evacuated from London, but she had not told him how fond they were of Jean, or that Jean now thought of them as Aunt and Uncle. They had not consciously spoiled David, but he had been the only one for so long, in spite of many hopes that she and George would be blessed with more children. Now he would have to accept he'd have someone else with whom to share the holidays. He had always felt these days were his own, to do what he wanted and to go where he fancied.

They were having breakfast when Mrs Bretton decided to smooth the way, "Jean dear, I imagine you realize that David is coming back for the holidays today?"

"Oh yes, Violet told me, and I have been helping her dust David's room, but I didn't quite know when he was coming."

"Actually, it is today. His train gets in the same time as your mother's did, so shall we take the car and go and meet it?"

"Ooh, yes please." Jean thought life could not hold any more pleasures than it did at the moment. She now felt so much part of the Bretton family, in a way which she had not experienced before, and it gave her a feeling of happy belonging to be included.

The train was slightly late, but Jean did not mind. She loved seeing all the other people waiting with their suitcases, and wondering where they were all going and if they did not have luggage, who they were meeting.

Just then she heard the chuff chuff of the engine as it made its way up the incline into the station, and the hiss of steam as it drew to a halt. An air of bustle and excitement intensified as the travellers picked up their luggage, and others scanned the doors opening to see who was descending on to the platform.

This time it was Mrs Bretton who gave a little cry of welcome, and ran forward to greet a tall fair boy in a blazer and cap who had just descended from the train.

Jean held back, a small lump in her throat as she remembered not so long ago, when she had met her mother off the train. Mrs Bretton turned and put her hand out, drawing her in to be part of the welcome.

"This is David." she said.

Chapter 3

He always had that faint sense of anticipation as the train approached Wadebridge Station. He went to a school in Surrey, and it was a long journey, with two changes before climbing into the little train which meandered down to Cornwall, stopping at every station it passed. He watched the people getting off at the various halts, laden with luggage or parcels, waiting for the porters to retrieve their larger items from the Goods Van, or simply striding off in a purposeful and familiar fashion, as if they probably did the journey every day, which more than likely they did. He hoped that 'the child', about whom his mother had told him, would not be there to meet him. In fact he was dubious about having another individual in the house during the holidays, especially a little girl. He had always been the only one, and everyone had done pretty much what he wanted while he was at home.

His mother rushed up to him as usual, and he managed to avoid being kissed, fearful that someone might be watching and think of him as a 'mummy's boy'. Then she turned and put her arm out, and said to the little girl standing there, "This is David."

She was quite small, with short mousy hair cut in a fringe. In fact she looked rather like a mouse caught in the full glare of a car's shining headlights, shrinking back from his polite outstretched hand.

"Hello," she whispered, and stepped back. With horror he saw that she did not realize the edge of the platform was just behind her, and she was about to topple over backwards onto the rail, when he shot forward and grabbed her arm, pulling her to safety.

"You fool!"

"I'm sorry, I didn't see," she almost sobbed, and Mrs Bretton, thoroughly shaken, just said, "Are you all right?" and then to David, "That was very quick of you, David; now we'd better gather your things up and go home. Violet has your favourite cake waiting for you. She's been saving up the rations I know, to make it for your first day of the holidays."

They piled into the car, Jean managing to squeeze into the back with all David's things. She kept as quiet as possible and hoped no-one would notice if she rushed in when they got back to find Jumble, and tell him how this God-like boy had rescued her from a terrible accident.

Alas for her, when they got back to the Rectory Mrs Bretton made it quite clear she was part of the family, and as such, would join them for tea. Mr Bretton was there too and was regaled, (much to Jean's embarrassment), with the story of David's splendid rescue. She looked up briefly and caught his eye; he gave a small wink as if to say "Parents!" which cheered her up no end.

In spite of his fears, David found Jean did not intrude much on his life. His parents had decided she should be part of the family, and were obviously extremely fond of her. But she had her own friends in the village, and was so much younger than him, that their paths did not often cross. He did not appreciate that Jean deliberately kept out of his way, terrified she would do something stupid again. Only once did he suggest she should join him on a fishing expedition in the nearby stream at the bottom of the hill. She longed with all her heart to go but felt so shy and unsure, and hesitated so much that he said, "Oh well, it doesn't matter, just thought you'd like to come," and left it at that.

Jean, mortified, crept out to her favourite hiding place, a large rhododendron behind the garage, where she found Jumble and spent the next hour regretting her decision, and hugging Jumble so hard he protested by wriggling out of her arms and stalking off, his tail waving in disgust.

David had a good many friends in the area, and was quite happy finding things to do and other boys of his age to do them with. The first day of the holidays was always spent exploring his domain, and making plans. He was also aware that his mother, having missed him during the school term, liked to have his company at first. He was terribly conscious of the war; in fact was longing for it to go on long enough for him to take part, preferably in the Navy. His father had hoped he would go into the church, but David wanted to travel, to see the world, above all to make some money. He had seen his mother scrape by on a rector's salary, and he always felt there could be a much better way of making a living. To a certain extent the War had spoilt all his plans, but the next best thing was to join one of the Armed Services.

"You see," he said to his best friend Tom, as they lay under their favourite chestnut tree in the garden, "In the Navy you do at least go to all sorts of places abroad, even in the war."

"Yes, I think you can get to America or South Africa, although you'd have to dodge the U-boats going across the Atlantic." They had made a map, in fact several, of all the places they would like to visit, and poured over it depending on the News at the time.

"Easter in a day or two, and I suppose I'll have to go to boring church, and listen to Dad being boring, with a boring sermon."

"At least," said Tom, "we'll get a jolly good lunch that day."

"Do you know we've got an evacuee now? A stupid little girl called Jean, from London."

"I know, my cousin goes to school with her, and says she is awfully quiet like a frightened mouse, but quite nice."

"If we hang around we'll probably meet her. She's batty about our cat. He follows her all over the place." David sat up suddenly. "I know, let's try and make a go-cart; I think I can find some old wheels. I saw them in the shed last hols."

They rummaged in the shed behind the garage, and found a battered old pram; then managed, with difficulty and a few grown-up swear words, to remove the main part of the pram from the wheels. Tom said he had a large box at home which would do for the body, and they went off to his home over a couple of fields. When they reached the house, they could smell delicious foodie sort of smells, so they gravitated to the kitchen where they found Tom's mother, Mrs Truckle, just removing a casserole from the bottom oven of the Aga. Being farmers, they were never short of ingredients, and always generous to Tom's friends.

"Just in time boys," she said, mopping her forehead; "I was hoping Tom would turn up, and now here he is with you, David. First day of the holidays?"

"Yes, Mrs Truckle. That does smell super."

"Lucky I've made a good big stew then, isn't it? I hope you can stay."

"I'd love to," David's mouth was watering at the thought of one of Mrs Truckle's delicious stews; "but perhaps I'd better let my mother know."

"I'll give her a ring, while you boys wash your hands. I can see they need it."

"Thanks awfully, she does rather worry if I don't turn up for meals."

Fortunately, the Truckles had installed a telephone just before the war, and the Brettons had followed suit, although in their case it was inclined to be a mixed blessing, parishioners often calling in asking to use the telephone for some reason or another. Mrs Bretton was quite relieved to hear that David was being fed by the Truckles, as she was only just getting used to rationing and she knew David's appetite was insatiable.

After tucking in to the aromatic stew and a mountain of home-grown vegetables, followed by apple tart and custard, David and Tom felt ready to tackle the Go-cart project again. Tom found the box; it was not too deep and just large enough for them both to sit in with a squash. But as it was quite heavy David suggested going to collect the wheels. On the way back they met Jean, sitting forlornly on a bank.

"Oh, hello," said David. Waving his hand he reluctantly introduced her. "This is Jean."

"I'm Tom." Tom held out his hand and Jean hesitantly shook it.

"Come and see what we're doing," he said. David looked rather cross at the idea of 'the child' joining in their activities, but he needn't have worried. Jean smiled and said, "I'm waiting for Penny." As Penny was just coming round the corner at that moment, and David didn't particularly like her, the two boys drifted off quite quickly.

"Phew! That was lucky," exclaimed David, "I mean, Jean's OK, but that Penny, She's so boring."

They managed to fix the box onto the wheels at last, and David found a rope in the garage. "If we tie this to the bar in front, we can more or less steer it."

Eventually the job was done and they proudly pulled it out.

"You get in first and I'll push it," Tom said.

The box was somewhat uncomfortable, so David went and got an old cushion out of his room. They dragged the cart to the top of the hill outside the Rectory, and Tom climbed in behind David, giving it a little push with his foot as he got in. It was not enough to start the cart, so they both put their hands out and propelled it. Gradually their contraption began to move. As the hill got a little steeper, so they gained momentum, and suddenly they were away, hurtling down the hill, travelling faster and frighteningly faster. David hauled on the rope to try and keep a straight course, praying as he perhaps had never prayed before that no vehicle would be travelling on the road, or even cattle or sheep, which were often there, being transferred from field to field. They had quite forgotten even to think of the idea of a brake; but the problem was solved when they came to a slight curve in the road, and the wheels clipped the side of the bank and rolled over, spilling its contents with abandon, and careering on to the bottom of the hill.

Tom had landed heavily on his left arm, and let out a string of oaths that he didn't even know he knew, picked up from the farm workers no doubt.

"Dad will kill me if I can't help with the milking tonight," he moaned,

David had got off rather more lightly, grazing one hand and cutting his chin, which proceeded to pour blood dramatically. He mopped it with his handkerchief, and then tried to help Tom, who seemed unable to get up.

"Gosh! What a mess. We'd better go and find Violet and get cleaned up before Mum and Dad see us."

At that moment the two small girls arrived, dragging the Go Cart up the hill between them.

"It would be them," said David, ungratefully Tom thought. He felt it was decent of them to rescue the contraption.

"I say, thanks awfully," he said, and managed to get up at last, holding his arm which hurt dreadfully.

Violet was in the kitchen when the little procession arrived.

"Lordy me, what a mess!" she exclaimed and ran some hot water to mop up the various wounds. David's chin was soon cleaned up, and a plaster put on the cut, but she could see Tom was in quite a lot of pain. She examined his arm, but felt it was actually only bruised.

"Your dad won't be pleased if you can't help him tonight," she said, merely repeating Tom's thoughts. But after she had put a bandage (made from an old sheet torn up for that very purpose), it felt a lot better.

"A nice cup of tea wouldn't be a bad idea," she said, putting the kettle on the hot plate of the Aga. When she had made a pot of tea, and produced a plate of buns, life looked much brighter for all of them; and when Mrs Bretton appeared ten minutes later there was nothing to worry her, and a dramatic story to tell, and even the go cart to show her proudly. Jean and Penny's part in the adventure was acknowledged by Tom, which pleased the girls out of all proportion to the deed.

***

As soon as Tom was sixteen he would leave school, much to David's envy, and work full time on his father's farm. He had plans to join the RAF as soon as he was seventeen. This was not discussed with his parents, who felt he was doing an important job on the farm and therefore would be exempt from any call-up. So he bided his time, never telling them his ambitions, but he discussed them with David in the holidays. Even then he could not spend many carefree hours with his friend as he was expected to work "Twenty-four hours a day, seven days a week," as he ruefully told his friend.

Meanwhile David was destined to stay at his Public School until he was eighteen. He felt as if it was an eternity, and he would never get into the Royal Navy. When Tom was unavailable for company he found himself more and more relying on Jean's companionship during the holidays. Especially after the sad day when she became an orphan.

Chapter 4

Dear Mummy and Daddy,
I hope you are well. We had a lovely time at Easter. The Sunday school decorated the Church on Saturday. Miss Norton took us to a wood and we picked masses of primroses and lots of tiny dafodils, and put them in jam jars on the window sills. On Easter day we had to go to church. David he is Aunt Nancys son who is 15½ was very bord but I quite liked it. After we had a GINORMOUS lunch as the farmer had given Aunt Nancy a big chicken and things called gooseberries which are like small green plums with heers on but the heers disappeer when they are boiled. We had cream too. And an Easter egg made from cardbord, with little biscits in it, as Aunt Nancy could not get any more chocolate.
Lots of love from Jean.

Many years later Jean would remember that first holiday in St. Wraich as a golden time. She was allowed to roam the village, and found a great friend in Penny. Penny lived in a big house up the road, with a long drive. Her father was in the Army, like Jean's father, only he was an officer, whereas Jean's father was a corporal. But it didn't seem to matter, and Jean was as welcome at Tremoran as Penny was at the Rectory. Penny was almost the same age as Jean, their birthday's only being a couple of weeks apart in July. So it seemed sensible in the days of rationing and shortages to celebrate them together. As Penny's was on the twelfth of July and Jean's the twenty-fifth, Penny's mother Mrs Treleaven and Aunty Nancy decided they should have a joint celebration on the day of the Church Fete, which was always the Saturday nearest to July eighteenth. Held in the Rectory garden the Fete was a popular event, even in the War, and a happy fundraiser for the Church. After the trauma of the evacuation of the Army at Dunkirk it seemed particularly important to have something to celebrate, therefore to add the two little girls' birthday parties to the event was hugely popular with everyone, especially the other children. The mothers all contributed what they could to the tea, and somehow a cake was contrived, made by Violet. She had found nine small candles forgotten in a drawer, which produced cries of delight when they were lit and blown out.

Earlier old Mr Trewon had called her out to the garden, and helped her dig up her potato. She was so surprised to find there were nine other potatoes underneath the leaves.

"Look, it's had babies," cried Jean with delight, "and I'm nine today so it must have known, 'cos there are nine potatoes!"

Mr Trewon was as pleased as she was, and went all red in the face when she threw her arms round him and kissed him.

"Oh Thank you thank you, it's a lovely birthday present," and she took them in to the kitchen to show Violet, who cooked them for lunch and they all agreed they were the best potatoes they had ever tasted!

David was home for the holidays too, and helped organise the games with Tom, both of them approaching their sixteenth birthdays later in the year.

But most exciting of all, Jean's mother and father were there. Corporal Shapwick had been given a week's leave, and Aunty Nancy insisted on them staying in the Rectory. Jean thought it was the most wonderful birthday she had ever had; her parents were so relieved to see her so happy, with lots of friends, and the Brettons obviously so very fond of her. They had to go back to London after four days, and it was a sad parting, made more so by the cheerful time they had all had together.

"I'll try and get down again soon," promised her mother. Her father just hugged her very tight, knowing it might be many years before he saw her again.

"Be a good girl," he murmured, thinking how lucky they were that Jean had landed with such nice people, after all the stories they had heard from unhappy evacuees.

A few days later Jean came in from school, flushed with pride at having been given a star for arithmetic. This had been her weak point, and Miss Norton told her she had done so well in the last test that she could have a coveted star. She rushed in to the drawing room to show Aunty Nancy, to find her and Uncle George sitting there looking very worried.

"Jean dear, come here. I... I've got something to tell you."

Jean crossed the room, wondering if she had done something naughty, or put something away in the wrong place, or.....

Nancy put her arm out and pulled Jean to her.

"I'm awfully afraid that your Mummy and Daddy have been in an air-raid...."

"Oh," Jean couldn't say any more, the picture in her mind was too awful to contemplate or put into words, except she had to, "Are they alright?"

"I'm so sorry my dear, the.... Your house was hit by a bomb last night, and they were both in it, and there was no hope of anyone being rescued."

The world about Jean suddenly exploded into a thousand pieces, and she fell, luckily into Nancy's arms, with the world whirring about her and then, blessed nothing. When she woke a little later she was lying on the sofa, Aunty Nancy holding her hand and stroking her forehead in a comforting sort of way.

For a moment she couldn't remember why she was there, and when she realized what she had been told she burst into floods of healing tears. Even then she could not completely grasp that her whole family life had been completely destroyed.

Nothing seemed real for a few days. The sun came out and she felt happy, only for the truth to hit her all over again, and she would suddenly break down. She wondered what had happened to her little desk, which her parents had given her for her eighth birthday. She had put all her tiny treasures in the drawers, and her set of china animals on the top. She imagined them all shattered, and that brought pictures in her mind of her mother and father. Could people be shattered like toys? George Bretton could hardly bear it when she broke down, but Nancy told him to let it happen.

"Much better than bottling it all up," she said to her husband. He felt, as a priest, he should be able to cope with the situation better. But he had never had to deal with a small child losing their parents. The other way round, yes, but this was somehow such a tragic burden for such small shoulders.

As it was still the summer holidays David was home, and strangely enough he was the person who was able to give Jean some comfort by suggesting various projects and expeditions, sometimes with Tom and Penny, and sometimes on their own. Occasionally they lay on the grass under the big chestnut tree in the far end of the garden, often not talking much. Jean confided to David she had seen a bombed house and it was "all gone," and David told her as gently as he could that her parents would not have known anything.

"They wouldn't have hurt you know, just gone to sleep in bed and not know what happened, so don't worry or be sad for them."

Jean swallowed and bit her lips to stop the ever present waterworks, which she knew David hated.

"I just wonder," she said quietly, "what will happen to me, now I haven't got a home or...or anything."

David reported this conversation to his mother that evening. "Poor thing, it must be awful to feel there is no one there."

The Brettons had wondered themselves about this. Under gentle questioning there did not seem to be any other relations. A friend who had lived near the Shapwick had told them of the tragedy, and later had written in a letter to the Brettons that she did not know what would happen to Jean, there being no other members of the family. They spent many evenings discussing the subject of Jean's future. In the end they called David in when Jean was out with Penny, and asked him whether he would mind if they adopted Jean.

"You are our dearest boy, and she wouldn't take your place in any way, but we are very fond of Jean and could give her a settled home and family."

Not quite to their surprise David rather willingly agreed. Jean was not the 'silly child' as he had feared. She was quiet and obviously hero-worshipped him, which made him feel protective and grown-up. He quite liked the idea of a sister to brag about at school. Pity she wasn't pretty, but perhaps she would grow up better looking, and he could then show her off to his chums on Sports Day, and she did have a dramatic life story, which he could embroider a bit.

When they told Jean they would like to adopt her she was rather bewildered. They explained she was already part of the family, and they would still be Uncle George and Aunt Nancy, but they loved her so much she would be the daughter they had always wanted. Jean was a little confused, wondering why, if they had always wanted a daughter they had not already got one, but perhaps they couldn't find just the right baby, and she accepted that she was now going to be called Jean Shapwick-Bretton.

***

She and Penny discussed the situation for hours. Penny was all for it, as now St. Wraich was Jean's home she would not suddenly be whisked away, and they could stay friends for the rest of their lives.

Jean was quickly absorbed into the life of St. Wraich, and equally soon recognised as the Rector's daughter.

The months went by, dominated by the various festivals and events which had been part of the village's life since time immemorial, and it seemed would go on into the future forever, although war-time restrictions curtailed any lavish hi-jinks; Christmas and Easter of course; Sports Day and the Sunday School outings; hay making and harvest, with Harvest Festival a great event with so many farmers in the area; the Carnival which was tremendous fun; and always the Church Fête, with Jean and Penny's birthdays celebrated as they had been that first year. As Jean grew up, she found her birthday memories of 1940, when her mother had been visiting, easier to forget.

"Do you remember when my mother had been there?" she used to say to Penny, and Penny felt sad for her friend. But Aunty Nancy largely had taken her mother's place, and she was so loved by her new family that she had no regrets about being adopted. "Chosen" as Nancy Bretton used to say; "You are our chosen daughter."

Chapter 5

David, too, was growing up fast. Mrs Bretton found herself looking at him, almost willing him to remain a child as the prospect of him going off to fight in some capacity became closer and closer. David of course, like many of his contemporaries, could not wait to get into uniform.

He longed for adventure. St. Wraich seemed a dead end, his mother and father rapidly becoming part of the older generation. When he arrived back for holidays he felt smothered by the comfortable existence they seemed to lead, punctuated by services on Sunday and good works. The wireless dominated their lives, listening to the News and discussing the progress of the War, and Tom's parents were also riveted by the news bulletins every evening.

He and Tom, now a fully-fledged worker on the farm, discussed the future endlessly. "I can't think how they can live such a narrow life. I haven't told anyone this Tom, but last week I filled in a form from the Naval Recruiting Office!"

"Have you had an answer yet? I did the same for the RAF, but they turned me down as I was working on a farm. But they did write and tell me they were hoping to replace me with a Land Girl sometime soon, and then I'd have a chance."

"What do your parents think?"

"Well, they have no idea I want to leave the farm of course, but I think if I don't get into the services soon the war will be over, and I'll just be milking cows for the rest of my life."

David sighed. "I'll be eighteen in November, and then I'll have to do something. If I don't get into the Navy I believe Mr Bevan is making the boys leaving school become Miners, and I think going down a mine would be the worst kind of hell."

"Gosh, I didn't know that."

"It was in the paper the other day. When I showed it to Father he was shocked, so maybe he will be quite pleased if I can get into the Navy."

"When will you hear, do you think?" asked Tom, rolling onto his front. They were lying in a corner of the meadow out of the hot July sun, sheltered by the hedge. The sound of bees visiting the blackberry flowers, and the flutter of a few Red Admiral butterflies as they darted in and out of the hazel branches lulled them into a post-lunch torpor. David was just starting his holiday, but Tom would have to get back to work in a short while, and they were catching up on their news since they had seen each other last.

David picked a blade of grass to suck. "I hope soon. I might even be able to go in as a Junior Officer, as I have passed all the necessary exams. But whatever, I don't really mind, as long as I get away and see a bit of life."

Tom grinned and turning his head away said quietly, "and what about Jean then?"

"What about her?"

"She's getting to be a super girl, hadn't you noticed?"

"I've hardly seen her since I got back. But now you mention it, she is getting to be quite a looker isn't she?"

"Always busy with Penny, though. I heard she was going away to boarding school next term; somewhere in Somerset."

David was half asleep, and gave a grunt. Tom shoved him and they wrestled for a moment, but it was too hot for a real fight, and in any case they both felt they were getting a little old for the kind of good-natured tussles of previous holidays. Tom untangled himself.

"Back to work then I suppose," and he ambled down the edge of the field towards the farm.

David closed his eyes and went back to his favourite dream world, when he would be rich beyond his imagination. The family had always had to pinch and scrape. Because his father was a rector the money was always tight, and if they had any to spare there were so many deserving causes deemed much more important that the needs of the family. Even Jean had acquired the ethos, David had noticed. She really could do with a decent haircut for a start. Tom's remarks had made him see her in a different light. Although she had for all intents and purposes become his sister, he still felt a little apart, especially as he was away at boarding school, while she was at home all the time absorbing his parents' outlook on life far more than he ever had done. Thinking about her he got up and went back to the Rectory to see what she was up to, and perhaps talk to her for a bit, now Tom was working all the time.

Jean was not in, but he saw a letter on the hall table addressed to him. It looked official and he slit it open with his thumb, tearing the envelope in the process.

It contained a form some three pages long, inviting him to complete within three weeks in order that he might be considered for entry into the Royal Naval Volunteer Reserve for the period of five years. He gazed at it for a few minutes hardly daring to think that at last some of his dreams were about to become true. He was nearly eighteen and had endured enough of school. He could easily miss the autumn term, and be ready for whatever their Lordships ordered. Now, the main obstacle would be to win over his parents, as being under the age of twenty-one he had to have their consent.

He waited until after supper, when they had settled in the drawing room and seemed relaxed, to broach the subject as gently and firmly as he could. To his surprise they did not seem unduly upset, almost as if they had been expecting it. Which without a doubt they had. In fact they had hardly stopped thinking about what David would do if he was called up. It was so much better to volunteer, and the thought of him being a member of the Royal Navy, however lowly, pleased them immensely. How much better than being made to join the "Bevan Boys" and be sent down the coal mines, or even be conscripted into the Army and be sent to fight anywhere in the world.

From the forms David discovered he was to be sent to a place called H.M.S. Royal Arthur, where he would be given basic training for six weeks. Then he could, with his qualifications, apply to be awarded a commission, or work his way up from the ranks. Either way, he would be in the Royal Navy in some capacity or other, and would be contributing to the war effort.

"You realize," he said to Jean when he finally tracked her down, "I have to get away from Cornwall, and I want to travel, so it really is the answer, don't you see?"

Jean did not understand the idea of wanting to leave Cornwall, but she always felt that David had a restless streak, and perhaps after seeing a bit of the world he would want to return to what she felt was the best place on earth. So she was enthusiastic for him and helped him get ready for his big adventure.

The papers came sooner than he thought. Evidently the Navy was keen to recruit those under eighteen, and so in September David bade a tearful farewell (at least his mother was tearful) to his family, and took a train to Skegness, to join H.M.S. Royal Arthur.

This happened to be a training establishment for new recruits, and was a complete shock to the system for most of the young men arriving with stars in their eyes. The language was appalling, a real eye-opener for the country boys particularly, and the living hard and rough. Long route marches were the order of the day, strict discipline, and the basic living conditions came as an unforeseen surprise to many, especially those who had visualised glamorous uniforms and a life on the ocean wave, with a girl in every port.

However, David thrived on it. Although he had been an only child he had not been pampered, and there never had been money for luxuries, although his mother had done her best to indulge him whenever he was home. He revelled in the male companionship and the camaraderie that existed as they were all thrown together, mostly united in hatred of their superiors. He was quite sorry when the six weeks training were up and they all went their separate ways.

He was delighted when he received his orders to go to a training establishment in Plymouth for a further six weeks, after which he would possibly be able to apply for a commission as a midshipman. He found himself on a train en route to the West Country once again.

Dear David,
How are you? It was nice seeing you in your sailors uniform. I thought it looked OK. Aunt Nancy was sad you couldn't stay longer but Uncle George said you had to obey the Navy now and jump to it. I'm not sure what that means but I expect you do. I dont think you could jump very high in those funny wide trowsers. Violet has got a new friend. He works on Toms farm and they go out for walks when she has time off and seem very lovey dovey. Mrs Bowman says she hears wedding bells but they are not allowed to ring them til the end of the war so I don't know how she can hear them.
Penny is going to bording school soon. I don't know where Im going yet. Love from Jean.

***

The excitement of David's brief leave over, Nancy and George Bretton found they were, indeed, pondering over Jean's future. Miss Norton had told them that Jean was above average in class and suggested she would benefit from a boarding school. They had a small legacy from the Shapwicks which they could use on her education, and they made enquiries about other suitable schools. Penny was leaving the village that term to go to a school in Gloucestershire but that place was beyond their means, and in any case Nancy and Penny's mother thought temporary separation of the friends might help them both to develop. Finally they decided to go and look at a school called Glen Marten, in Somerset, and one day they all set out to visit it.

"You see, my dear," Nancy told Jean, "I am sure your parents would have wanted something better for you, as I know they were very concerned about your education."

"Can't I go with Penny?"

"I'm afraid Penny's school is too expensive, but from all accounts Glen Marten is a lovely school. Anyway we will see. We won't make up our minds till we have all seen it. Then you can tell us if you really don't like it."

But Jean did not just like it, she loved it. From the moment they drove through two fields, past a wooded area and drew up to a large old house covered in ivy, she felt, apart from St. Wraich, she didn't want to live anywhere else. Meeting Miss Harper, the Headmistress, and then Miss Cuddras, (who explained everyone called her "Cuddles"), confirmed her first feelings.

It was arranged she should start in September, at the start of the autumn term, and they left, satisfied they had found the right place for Jean to continue her education.

"I don't really want to leave St. Wraich, but Glen Marten looks awfully nice." Jean told Penny the next day.

"It will be dreadful going to different schools at the end of the holidays, but we can tell each other all about it, and it means we'll have twice the adventures to share, if you know what I mean."

"I suppose. But it will be odd going to school without you. Do you have to wear uniform too?"

They were in the attic above the stables where they often went if it rained. They had managed to find a few odd bits of furniture, and had made a den so they could be entirely by themselves sometimes. Penny's mother had even found them an old sofa and Aunt Nancy had given them some cushions that she had found, destined for the next Church Bazaar. David had not been inclined to want a pony, and so there was no use for the stables, except as a convenient place for storage.

Jean had discovered the hide-away not long after she went to live in St. Wraich, and after she had made such friends with Penny it became their own place, and, if missing, they could usually be found there.

"Yes, we have grey skirts and blue jerseys. In fact everything seems to be grey and blue; rather boring. What's yours?"

"Actually, it's quite pretty. We have sort of browny-green skirts and green jerseys. Cuddles (she is the Matron), has a lot of second-hand stuff, and so we don't have to use coupons much."

"I think we do the same," Penny said, "Though Mummy said we would have to go to a shop in London called Peter Jones to get quite a lot of stuff. They sent a huge list the other day. Things like twelve handkerchiefs!"

Having a lot of new things was exciting for them both. Rationing was fairly tight, but neither of them had used many of the clothing coupons allocated, and with second-hand items readily available, everything on the lists were soon collected, tried on for size, and then marked with special name tapes. They helped a bit, but sewing was not one of their favourite occupations, and so, in the rectory, Violet and Aunty Nancy marked most of Jean's uniform.

About a week before the start of the new term Mrs Treleaven suggested they have a special tea-party to show off their new uniforms. Rather bashfully they dressed up in their skirts and jerseys, and paraded in front of the grownups, giggling as they walked up and down.

Violet, and Doreen (the Treleaven's maid), had been asked to help them dress, and watched proudly from the doorway.

"Next time," said Doreen, "we'll be getting them dressed for their weddings, I don't doubt!"

***

Jean thrived at Glen Marten in a way that the Brettons had not anticipated. She was not scholarly, but enjoyed learning, and seemed to absorb more than merely the schooling. She quickly made friends and soon became the 'mother' of her group, caring and thoughtful for others, and reliable, which her teachers appreciated. She was by no means a goody-goody, and got into her fair share of scrapes. But the worst were usually the result of helping those less fortunate, or perhaps less skilful at avoiding detection than she was.

"You see," she was telling Penny in the first holidays; "We have always managed to get out of trouble, haven't we? So I sort of know, but sometimes I'm not quite quick enough!"

Penny wanted to know everything about Glen Marten, which sounded so much more fun than her school.

"What's the worst thing you did?" she asked.

"Well, I suppose the night we had a dare to get right round the dormitory without touching the floor."

"What happened?"

"A girl called Julie got practically the whole way round, and then she slipped and fell, pulling a picture down, which made the most awful row. I rushed over to help her, and fell over a chair, and Cuddles came dashing in and found us and was furious. She thought it was my fault for egging Julie on, and as Julie was crying, she didn't say anything..."

"How mean."

"Actually she is a bit of a namby-pamby, and was so upset I couldn't say it was her fault, 'specially as we had all been in the dare. Anyway we were both made to run round the playing field three times before breakfast as a punishment. I quite like running so it wasn't too bad in the end!"

"You do seem to have fun. We have so many rules; I sometimes don't know what I am supposed to do. I just wish I could leave and be at home all the time, or go to your school or something." As she said that she burst into floods of tears, saying, "I just hate the whole place."

Jean had not realized Penny was so unhappy at her school, and she told Aunty Nancy, who said she would have a word with Penny's mother, but couldn't really interfere too much.

However, some weeks later Penny came rushing into the rectory her face flushed with excitement. She hugged Jean and danced round the room.

"What on earth...!"

"Guess what, I'm coming to your school next term. I just can't believe it. Mummy asked me if I was happy at school, so I told her I could hardly bear the thought of going back, and the girls were horrid, the teachers were beastly, and I felt sick all the time."

"Gosh, what did she say?"

"She told me she had been in contact with Glen Marten, and they actually had a vacancy next term, and so...Whoopeee! I'm going with you."

Jean shouted "Whoopeee" too and they both made for their Den to make plans, which kept them occupied the rest of the holidays.

Contrary to their mother's fears, they were not too much together at school. Forewarned, the headmistress had put them in different dormitories, and they studied different subjects. Penny was keen on Maths, while Jean thrived on the domestic arts and crafts. But travelling to and fro from Glen Marten together gave them enormous pleasure, and in the holidays they were as inseparable as ever.

***

The war dragged on, with intervening periods of drama, when the Nation held its breath. At school they were allowed, even encouraged, to listen to the six o'clock News bulletins. There were some moments of sadness, as when a girl called Anna was told, with great sympathy by Miss Harper, that her beloved father had been killed fighting in France. She went home at once to be with her mother, but came back the following term.

"It was awful, as Mummy only has me now, but she decided I must go on with school. We are going to have to move to a smaller house, and I can't have my pony anymore and..." she hugged her anguish to herself. Jean was able to comfort her a little by saying, "At least you still have your mother."

"Why, what do you mean?"

"Well, my mum and dad were both killed in the blitz in London, and I still think about them; but I actually think more about my new mother, Aunty Nancy, who is the dearest person in the world, so I am very lucky really." She gave Anna a big hug, and the tears stopped for a bit.

Glen Marten was right in the depths of the country, and so food was fairly plentiful, and danger seemed far away. The school routine was hardly changed, except they were encouraged to take an interest in world affairs, and also knit socks and scarves for the troops. They had first aid classes, and the emphasis for the more senior girls was on future careers. Penny and Jean spent hours trying to decide what they would do when they left school.

Chapter 6

Penny felt she would do a secretarial course, possibly in London. Jean had no desire to go back there. She felt her home was St. Wraich, and she wanted to learn to cook 'properly' and perhaps run a restaurant or something.

Subconsciously, perhaps she had another reason for the attraction of staying in or near St. Wraich. As the years had gone by she began to think about David more. He had been so like a brother to her for many years. Now when he came home on leave, especially dressed in his naval uniform, she felt almost shy with him, and the old brother and sister relationship gradually developed into a strange tingling anticipation, which, unknown to each, affected them both.

Tom also had begun to notice the way Jean was growing up, blossoming as she did so into an extremely pretty young lady. But he had other, more pressing things on his mind than thinking about girls. After a couple of years fretting to leave the farm, the first Land Girl had arrived. He felt he could then be able to apply to join the RAF, and his papers arrived shortly afterwards. His parents were shattered, as he had given no inkling of his intentions.

But he argued forcefully that Rosie was now perfectly capable of taking over most of his work.

"In any case, they are sending another girl next week, and Rosie can show her the ropes. You have no idea how dreadful I feel with all my friends in uniform, and here I am, sat on my backside in a cushy job which the girls have proved they can do."

His father understood Tom's feelings, having been in much the same position in 1917, but his mother was more apprehensive, worrying about all the usual things, food and warmth for her only beloved child, who was suddenly a man wanting to go and fight for his country.

And so, quite soon, Jean was saying "goodbye" to David's best friend. She was only twelve, but Tom seemed to have been part of her life for so long that his absence was quite a wrench.

They both came back on leave at intervals, and always found time to talk to their "little sis," telling her of their adventures and escapades. Tom was always more serious and truthful, David exaggerating and over-glamorising his life in the Navy. Eventually he was appointed to a Cruiser, HMS *Nymph*, and his infrequent letters home were cheerful. Too cheerful, his mother thought.

"It's almost as if he is trying to convince himself that the whole war is fun," she said to Tom's mother.

"I know, Tom is the same. They don't realize we read the papers and hear the news, and we know everything is not quite as bright as they make out."

"We must just pray that they both come back in one piece when the war is over."

But one of them did not. At least not in one piece.

Unknown to his mother Tom was flying as part of a bomber crew. After a particularly difficult sortie dropping bombs over Germany, several of the planes were hit. Luckily the pilot of Tom's plane was very skilful, and managed to get them down as soon as they reached England, but the navigator had been pretty badly wounded when the plane belly flopped as they landed. The gunner managed to haul him out quickly before the sparks caught fire, and dragged him clear just in time.

The navigator was Tom. He was not badly burned, but his left leg was broken, which meant a long stay in hospital, and then an even longer convalescence at home. Not at all what he had envisaged when he joined the Service.

"I might as well never have joined up," he said to Jean, who had popped down to the farm to get some eggs, but really to see him.

"Well, I like it, I hardly get to hear about anything. It's really nice to have someone to talk to in the holidays."

"Isn't Penny around?"

"Yes, but I see her all the time, She's now at the same school as me,"

"Tell her to come and see me soon. I get so bored sitting here with my leg up, and all the farm business going on all around me."

After that Penny often came, sometimes with Jean, sometimes on her own, and although thirteen-year-olds were rather young to talk about the war, they were good company, and often made him laugh with stories of the village and parochial activities.

With good country air and plentiful farm food, Tom's leg healed far too quickly for his mother's liking, and soon it was time to say goodbye all over again.

***

By 1943 David had been at sea for nearly 6 months as a Midshipman on board HMS *Nymph*. They were part of the Fleet patrolling the Atlantic, acting as convoy to supply ships taking essential supplies to England from the United States, which by now had entered the war. The trips were hazardous, but being young and adventurous David was enjoying naval life, and like most young people the thought of anything happening to him was inconceivable. A few of the ships in the convoys which they escorted were sunk, and they were not able to stop and pick up many survivors. This distressed some of the members of the *Nymph*, especially those on the Bridge who could often see their hopeless struggles in the water. 'Always others, never them', so the thought ran through the crew. They felt lucky; HMS *Nymph* had the reputation of being a lucky ship, and she certainly seemed that way for many months of running gauntlet to numerous hazards.

"*In fact,*" David wrote to his parents, "*it is a dull life most of the time. We go on watch, which is fun, particularly at night, with all the stars so bright you feel you could almost touch them; and then you go below, and have a bite to eat, and a bit of sleep, and then you go on watch again. Quite boring really."*

Actually the reality was pretty grim at times, with the cold penetrating even their greatcoats, and sometimes rough seas causing the convoy to scatter and become easy targets for the lurking U-boats. Occasionally, too occasionally, they were able to locate a U-boat and use depth charges to varying effect, the icy waters of the Atlantic claiming as many victims as the missiles. The greatest disaster was when a supply ship was sunk, and the precious cargo and crew lost in the deep black inkiness of the sea.

HMS *Nymph* was too large to take part in the invasion of Europe in 1944, and after a short time in Portsmouth they were to be sent to the Mediterranean. David was given a brief spell of leave and rushed down to Cornwall, to be met with joy and relief that he was in one piece after the hazardous sea time in the Atlantic.

***

Rationing was very tight in England, but being the Rector of a farming community the Reverend Bretton was often slipped an extra egg or two on his rounds, and the Rectory managed a good many treats for the returning hero. Jean became his willing slave, giving up her sweet ration to help with the trifle, and her Sunday breakfast egg found its way to David's plate without anyone noticing, except perhaps Violet,.

David had become weather-beaten but extremely fit after his long exposure to the elements, but this had done nothing to detract from his good looks and he received many admiring glances from the older girls in the village.

They all noticed that one in particular, Judith Grange, the daughter of the doctor from the next village, obviously seemed to be smitten, and hung around the Rectory whenever David was about. She was just seventeen and Jean thought she was beautiful, and encouraged her to come in and visit. Very soon the whole village was involved in the "romance" as they thought of it. Wartime made all liaisons especially intense as they had so little time, and David made the most of it, engineering stolen moments of privacy with Judith, much helped and encouraged by Jean. She felt it was so romantic for David to have such a lovely friend, never feeling any jealousy, especially as David would always show his gratitude to her when she let him know the times and places when the grown-ups would not be around.

However his leave did not last very long, and the kisses and fumbles in the long grass did not go any further, and he left St. Wraich again with promises of undying devotion to Judith until he came home once more. Judith was sent to a secretarial school in Truro, and soon met another good-looking young man, this time in the RAF, who was stationed nearby, and her letters to David dwindled bit by bit, as her teenage passion faded.

Dear Jean,

Have you seen anything of Judith lately? I haven't heard from her for ages. I wonder what she is doing? How are you? I gather from Mum that you are taking over the Sunday school! Brave you! I heard from Tom the other day. I am glad he has recovered and is back with the RAF. I am having a rather boring time, and getting very hot!!! Please write, as it is nice to get letters. If you can find out anything about Judith I would be very grateful.

Love from David.

Dear David,

Thank you for your letter. I asked Aunt Nancy if she knew what Judith was doing and she said she was in Truro, doing some sort of typing. Then a friend of hers in the village called Patsy told me she was engaged to an officer in the RAF. I haven't seen her for ages, as she doesn't come home much now. Tom has been home on leave and said he was disappointed you couldn't have been home at the same time. It was lovely to see him, but I wish you could have been home as well. Uncle George said yesterday I have grown so much I was like a bean!!! I only help in the Sunday school, but it is quite fun. Mostly we don't get into the Church 'til after the sermon! (Please don't tell your father I wrote that). Come home soon!

Love from Jean. X X X X X

***

HMS *Nymph* had sailed for Gibraltar and on to Alexandria, and this proved a fairly quiet period for the crew after the traumas of the Atlantic convoys. David found he had plenty of time to think what the future held after he had left the Navy. He was by now a Sub-Lieutenant, albeit with a wavy stripe on his arm, and by 1949 he would be a civilian and having to make his way in the world.

Chapter 7

For some time now David had been chewing over the idea of some way of promoting a shopping card. He had heard of such a scheme in America, and he felt, with Great Britain emerging from the scarcities of post war, there would be an explosion of spending, on the home particularly. He spent his leisure hours at sea researching the most likely items which people would want, and then looking up all the possible shops they would visit to obtain them. He felt if a small discount could be arranged for anyone owning a card that could be used in those outlets, it would be an attractive proposition for retailer and shopper alike. If he could supply the cards for a small subscription they would all benefit.

By the time he was demobbed at the end of 1949 he had designed the distinctive card, and set about making contact with various big furniture and household stores all over the country, going to see the managers and endeavouring to 'sell' his idea. Some were dismissive of this, as they thought, a slightly American way of doing things; but he won over enough to begin collecting members for 'Focus' as he called the scheme.

***

By now he was living at home again, and he enlisted Jean to help in finding enough people who would be willing to pay for a card and the firms and shops who might be interested in giving discounts to owners of the cards. He used his small final gratuity from the Navy to pay for the cost of printing the cards, stationery and postage, and the necessary telephone calls.

He was immensely grateful to his parents, who allowed him to take over one of the spare rooms in the Rectory as an office, and he managed to pay them a small rent from his savings. Jean turned out to be a natural secretary, and after a few weeks he also insisted that she should have a wage. By now she was seventeen, and trying to think how she could earn her own living.

"You know this is your home, and we are your loving parents," Nancy told her, "and you don't have to pay us anything for living here. In fact, we would be very sad if you ever left us, and got a job somewhere else."

This is exactly what Jean felt. The Rectory had been an anchor in her life for so long, she couldn't even visualise leaving the Brettons for any reason. But she did feel she should contribute to the household, and so, when David handed her what he called "your wages," she went straight to Nancy, and gave her the envelope.

Nancy respected her wish to pay her way now she was no longer a child, and she accepted half, deciding privately that this would go into a trust fund for Jean to have when she got married, or finally flew the nest. She was so happy to have both Jean and David at home, and in her prayers she asked that one day, perhaps, they would marry each other, and stay in St. Wraich forever, although at the moment they only seemed especially good friends.

***

David was staggered to find that his idea of a loyalty card was becoming extremely popular. A few firms even contacted him for details, and very soon more and more were signing up, even sending details to their customers, to encourage them to spend more with the discounts they gave, when using the Focus card. The cards were all numbered, and quickly rose to hundreds, each earning him a small remuneration. One day he realized they were sending off the one thousandth card.

Jean brought it to him, her eyes shining with pride and enthusiasm.

"Look, David, I just can't believe it. You've sold one thousand already, and there are loads of queries in the box."

David gave her a brotherly hug, suddenly feeling very protective of his 'little sister', as he had always thought of her. Strangely, it also felt very right to have his arms round her, but Jean, somewhat embarrassed, disentangled herself, and turned away to hide the blush which was beginning to spread all over her face.

"I was going to keep this for your birthday, but I think this is the right moment to give it to you," said David, as he handed her an envelope.

She looked at him shyly, not used to any surprise gestures from her 'big brother', and tore open the envelope. Inside was a Focus Card.

"Look at the number."

It was No. 1. At least it said 00001. Jean felt it was probably the most valuable thing she would ever own.

"Oh David!" she whispered, "I just can't believe it. Number One of all the cards we've sent off. I'll keep it forever!"

"I know you don't really want to buy anything, but it may come in useful one day, and anyway I wanted you to have something special for helping me, and.... and, well, for being so patient with me all this time."

Jean didn't think, she just threw her arms round him and after a bit David gently disentangled himself and handed her his large hanky.

"I'm so sorry, I don't know what came over me." she gulped, mopped her eyes, blew her nose, and gave him a huge rather watery smile, which turned his heart over, making him feel quite differently about this lost waif who had come into his family, and, seemingly, won all their hearts.

"Anyway," she struggled to sound matter-of-fact, "this is the best present I have ever had!"

Mail Order was just beginning to take off in Britain, after the years of austerity. People needed new clothes, household goods and garden supplies, and it was so easy to be tempted by the discounts offered through Focus. But David was already thinking ahead, and he felt transactions would be simpler still if they could pay with a card instead of writing cheques, or handling cash. He approached his bank with the idea, and knowing his success with the Focus Card they asked him to set up a blueprint for what they called a cheque-card.

Once again, the initial take-up was slow, and quite often David almost felt he was swimming in thick treacle. But Jean, feeling anything David did was marvellous, kept him going with her enthusiasm, working all hours following up contacts, addressing envelopes, and trying to interpret David's more hare-brained schemes into reality.

He became aware quite early on that other banks would soon jump on the bandwagon, and it would be much better if a consortium of people could own cards that shoppers could use instead of cheques, and the shops or firms would then claim the money from the consortium, forfeiting a small fee for accepting the card payment.

It was just about then when he realized he would have to team up with what was now becoming known as "Entrepreneurs." Most of these young men with money to spare lived in America, so, greatly daring, he flew to New York in the dark days of November 1951 to investigate the possibilities.

***

America was a cultural shock, and he felt he had been plunged into another world. After becoming used to the drabness of post-war Britain, the vibrancy of New York galvanised him into contacting all sorts of people who might be able to help him. Armed with a few introductions from his Bank and Focus clients, he found that in the brave new world nothing was unachievable. His head whirled with possibilities, and he received so many invitations he hardly had time to think.

A good-looking Englishman, unattached, was a great draw for all the social hostesses, especially those with daughters.

Once or twice he found himself attracted rather too much to some of the bevy of beautiful girls who were asked to partner him at dinner parties, and had to remind himself just why he had come to America in the first place, and extract himself as gracefully as he could from the lure of one or other particularly amorous glamour girl or predatory mother.

Dear Jean, Just thought I would drop you a line and tell you how I am getting on. This is the most amazing place, and I am meeting masses of people, <u>some</u> of whom will be useful. There is a young man I have met, about my age, though he wasn't in the war, who seems very interested and is prepared to help with the new IDEA! I am seeing him tomorrow, and hope he will come up with the money to set the scheme going.

 I hope to be home in a week or two, although I will quite miss New York. It is simply buzzing, and everyone seems so enthusiastic about everything! I have met lots of nice people, and seem to go to a party every night, so it will be quite nice to get home for a rest!

Love to you all, David.

***

"I had a letter from David this morning." Jean was sitting in the Truckle's kitchen having a coffee with Tom who had come in from mucking out the pigs.

 He had seen her approaching the farm, and came in shortly afterwards, making the excuse he needed a coat. The January weather was colder than usual for Cornwall, and he even had to break the ice on the troughs for the cows to drink.

 Jean was now getting on for twenty, and was a very pretty girl, much noticed by the boys of the village, although Tom hoped she liked him the best. That is, the best after David. He half hoped that David would stay in America, and then he might have more of a chance with Jean. He looked at her now; a little flushed after her walk through the fields to the farm, her hair windblown and her cheeks gleaming with the heat from the Aga. But she had a sort of glow, which Tom noticed always came when she was speaking of his best friend, and he felt resigned to be second-best in her eyes. His mother was always going on about him finding a wife who would help with the farm settle there and raise a family, so that she and her husband could find a little cottage somewhere near and retire. But so far she noticed that Tom only had eyes for Jean, and Jean only had eyes for David.

"Do you think David will settle down here after all his travels?" he asked.

"I do sometimes wonder that. It rather depends on how this card business goes. He does love a bit of excitement; I just don't know."

She sounded somewhat depressed, so Tom, with great daring, asked if she'd like to go to the cinema in Wadebridge with him that evening.

"Oh Tom, that would be lovely," she said, cheering up at once. It was quite a boring existence for her in the Rectory, much as she loved her adopted parents, they were fairly set in their ways, and without David at home one day seemed just like another.

She got up to go and Tom helped her on with her coat.

"I'll walk a little way with you," he said, and off they went, leaving Mrs Truckle smiling thoughtfully. She knew that Nancy Bretton hoped that David would one day marry Jean, but she, also, had hopes that Tom would win Jean's heart. A nicer girl you couldn't hope to meet, as she said to her husband sometimes.

"David seems to be enjoying life at the moment then?" he asked Jean later, as they waited in the queue for the cinema to open.

"Well, yes, I think so. He is very excited about this new card idea. He has joined up with a friend he has made in New York, who has pots of money and apparently wants to find something to do with it."

"All right for some, eh? Just hope he doesn't get his fingers burnt, that's all."

At that moment the queue began moving forward and all thoughts were for the film. After sitting down Tom put his arm comfortably round Jean's shoulder and she felt happy with her old friend. If he wanted to do more he resisted. He knew he was trampling on David's territory but he wished with all his heart it was his own.

Afterwards, when the bus had dropped them back in St Wraich and they were outside the Rectory, Jean kissed him warmly. "Thank you so much for a lovely evening, Tom, it was the greatest fun."

Tom walked back to the farm, his heart singing, feeling that, perhaps, he had a chance with Jean after all.

But two days later, David returned.

Jean could not believe the difference in David. New York seemed to have had a galvanising effect on him, and he was so full of enthusiasm and energy he left them all breathless. He could not stop talking about the friends he had made and the plans that were already in the process of completion. A large firm had been approached and was willing to bankroll the initial launch of the "credit card" which was to be called "The Focus Account Card." The firm, which owned several large furniture outlets, had plans to offer extra points if money was spent in their stores. Otherwise points earned by using the card would all add up to credits which could be spent in various shops. There was to be widespread publicity for the launch of the card, with initial discounts for members joining in the first few weeks.

Brad Pitman, the young man in New York who had encouraged David's idea, and had found many contacts for him, was organising the American end, while David was set to introduce this newfangled way of shopping to the British public.

Needless to say, while it proved difficult to persuade the British to realize the huge benefits, the Americans took to it like ducks to water. New ideas were like nectar to them, and Brad was soon sending glowing reports of progress to David.

"I do feel," he wrote, *"that you will have to get the British Banks involved; they seem to be very enthusiastic this end, and as most of them have a tie-up with the Banks in Europe, I would suggest you ask them to contact the American branches, to see how well they are doing out of the Focus Account Card."*

David immediately set out for London, to persuade the big Banks they need have no worry of bankruptcies or bad debts from their customers using the card. He was only partially successful, but one of the major Banks was particularly helpful, and asked him to attend a meeting with the Managing Directors. He was closely questioned, and left feeling he may have made some progress.

Meanwhile Jean, acting as his secretary, had been dealing with so many interested enquiries and applications for cards, was relieved to see him home again.

Chapter 8

"I really think that we are going to have to get some more help." Jean told him when she had finally pinned David down on his return.

She showed him the pile of letters in the so-called "In box," which she simply had not had time to answer. In addition to that she was getting dreadfully worried about Aunt Nancy. She knew that Nancy had not been well for some weeks, picking at food, and obviously exhausted, when previously she had been a ball of energy.

"I do think, Aunt Nancy, that you ought to go and see the doctor. Perhaps he will give you a tonic or something."

"Perhaps I should, Jean dear. I must say I have been feeling slightly like flu, but I don't think there is anything about at the moment, is there?"

"I haven't heard of any bugs going round, but I'll make an appointment for you." She picked up the telephone and managed to arrange an appointment the next day.

Jean had learnt to drive while David was in America, and was pleased to pass her test the first time, so she insisted on driving Nancy to see the doctor. Doctor Howard was a family friend, having been in practice in Port Isaac for many years, and had brought David into the world and attended many ups and downs of the Bretton family.

Nancy seemed to spend ages with him, but eventually they came out of the surgery, with Dr Howard looking particularly serious, and Nancy looking beaten. Jean went to her at once, seeing she needed support. No one else was in the waiting room, and so Dr Howard nodded at Jean and said, "I'm so glad you are here, Jean. Your Aunt is not at all well, and she will need a lot of help from you. She will tell you all that I have said when you get home."

Jean managed to get them both back to the car, and after they were settled Nancy seemed to crumple in her seat before turning to Jean with a deep sigh.

"My dear. I have had rather bad news I'm afraid." Jean leant over and put her arm round Nancy's shoulders.

"Tell me," she said.

***

Nancy had Cancer, the dreaded Big C as it was known, and a particularly virulent form. She had to return to the doctor for all sorts of tests, but all they showed was that Dr Howard had been right to worry. To begin with Nancy and Jean had successfully hidden the devastating news from George and David, but as she became progressively worse it was left to Jean to break it them that Nancy had not much time left. Even with all his faith George felt it could not be true, and he insisted Nancy should see a specialist; but the diagnosis was merely confirmed, and Nancy went downhill very fast.

She had always been so full of fun and energy that it was distressing for her friends and family to watch the light, not so gradually, going out of her life. Jean was distraught. Her anchor was being pulled from under her. Nancy had been her virtual mother for so long, she felt she couldn't envisage life without her.

"You will be such a comfort to George and David," said Nancy, one afternoon when Jean was sitting with her. They had moved her bed near the window, so that Nancy could see her beloved garden. She could watch the birds on the lawn, and occasionally Fluffy, (Jumble's successor), pretending to stalk the blackbirds. But the light hurt her eyes and most of the time she lay with them closed, willing herself to remember better times.

Jean gently squeezed her hand. In her matter-of-fact way she had accepted the outcome, and because of that Nancy found her a great comfort. Many of Nancy's friends had visited, but always assured her in a put-on cheerful voice, that 'she would soon be feeling better.' Jean instinctively knew that Nancy would prefer to be told the truth, and face what was coming with all the faith she could muster.

After a bit she gave Jean's hand a little squeeze.

"I'd like to see David if he's about," she whispered.

"Of course, I'll go and fetch him." Jean put Nancy's hand gently back on the bed, and went to find David who was in his office. They all seemed to know instinctively not to stray far. He went up the stairs two at a time, but slowed when he got to the door, half dreading to go in and face his mother. She seemed the same, but all at once he realized he was looking at what seemed to be the face of a skeleton, not the plump-cheeked mother he had taken for granted all his life.

"Ah, David," she opened her eyes and looked at him with love. "I'm afraid I'm not going to be with you much longer. No, don't be too upset. I know where I'm going, and I'm really happy about it. It's just that I worry about you sometimes."

"Oh Mum, I promise you I'll be alright, and I'll look after Daddy, so you mustn't worry."

"I'm not so much worried about Daddy, it's Jean..." she took a deep breath and held his fingers; "I know Tom is terribly fond of her, but I wondered if you, well, felt anything for her?"

David was rocked back for a moment. Jean was so much part of his life that he thought of her as a permanent fixture, rather like eggs for breakfast or church on Sundays.

"I don't really know, Mum; I love Jean, she's always there and we get on tremendously well. But Tom...All three of us are such friends; we'll all stick together I'm sure."

"I think she is in love with you, David, so I don't want you to hurt her when I'm no longer there for her."

"Don't concern yourself, Mum. I promise you I will look after Jean. You've made me think about her in quite a different way now, so you never know."

Nancy felt she had pushed the subject far enough.

"I'm a bit tired now, dear. I think I'll have a little sleep. Give me a kiss."

David bent over and kissed the bony cheeks, and managed to control his tears until he was out of the door. He met Jean in the hall, and seeing his face she just put her arms round him and held him until he had stopped shaking. She took a clean hanky from the pile of washing on the chair beside her and silently handed it to him, then went on her way with the laundry.

Nancy died quietly, as she had lived, about a week later. George had to summon up all his faith to accept the fact that she was no longer there. They had been married for many years, and had rarely been apart. He did not feel strong enough to conduct her funeral, but the neighbouring Rector from St. Madron, the Reverend John Parton, being a long-term friend of the Brettons, stepped in to take over all the arrangements. Quickly realising that Jean was a calming influence on George and David, he involved her in everything. Nancy, knowing that there had been no hope of recovery, had written out a list of her favourite hymns and prayers, and Jean helped George and David to arrange the service. On the day of her funeral, in spite it being the beginning of December, the sun shone in a clear blue sky, and the air was crisp and clear, after a long period of gloomy clouds and rain. The church was packed, with many more standing outside unable to find a pew. In spite of the sadness, the singing was joyful, all wishing to express a feeling of thankfulness for a well loved lady, who had quietly helped so many of her husband's parishioners in their sad and difficult moments. George and Nancy had both been born and raised in Cornwall and most of George's ministry had been in St. Wraich. She was one of theirs, and they had come to thank their Lord for her goodness to them.

Helped by Violet, Jean had arranged a good tea in the Rectory, and most of the village came to partake of the delicious fare and talk of all the good and bad times Nancy had shared with them. Those closest to her had watched while her coffin was gently lowered into the grave, (which she would share with George when his time came), and walked the short way back to meet their friends, and greet their guests. They were silent on the walk home, but David tucked his arm under Jean's, and kept her close, trying to comfort her. Jean leant against him a little to gain strength to cope with the next hour or two.

"It's such a perfect day, isn't it? Just what she deserved." She felt the tears hovering on the surface. David looked down at her, his heart giving a strange little lurch, and handed her a large clean hanky.

***

The next few weeks were a great strain on Jean. All at once she seemed to be expected to take Nancy's place in the household. To cap it all Violet decided to drop a bombshell.

"If it's all the same to you, Jean, I'd like to give my notice in." As Jean gasped with dismay she went on hurriedly,

"My chap Colin, well he's getting rather impatient like, and he wants us to wed. He's got a good job as Gardener in the big house at St. Madron you see."

"Oh Violet I do see, but what on earth can I do without you?"

Violet had been so much a part of Jean's life, ever since she came to St. Wraich. Before the Brettons had even adopted her, Violet had taken her under her wing, nursed her when she was poorly, and generally acted as her prop and stay for over twelve years.

"It's not as bad as all that," Violet said, "you see, my young sister Ellen is willing to come and help. I know she's only seventeen, but Mum brought us all up right, and I can spend a little time showing her what to do."

Jean hugged Violet.

"Trust you to come up with a solution. And, of course, you must go and get married and you will make Colin a wonderful wife, I know."

Later on, she broke the news to George, but he was very apathetic these days, and just said, "Well, Jean, do what you think is right. They are a good family, and I just hope Ellen will be as good as Violet has been all these years."

They were all sad to see Violet go, but equally happy that she was getting married to the faithful Colin. Jean decided, with the Brettons' permission, they should pay for the wedding breakfast, which was held in the new Village Hall, and was an especially cheerful occasion, and a kind of closure to the mourning for Nancy. Ellen proved to be a marvellous addition to the Rectory, and a great support to Jean.

Jean was becoming more embroiled in David's affairs. The Focus Account Card business was burgeoning in a way which no-one could have predicted. The money coming in to David's Bank was staggering. He was working very hard, and also flying to New York every two or three months.

***

One time when he had been gone two weeks, Tom asked Jean out. A new Restaurant had opened quite near, and he suggested they should go and have a meal there one evening. He felt she deserved a break, and also felt the Brettons were taking advantage of her generous nature, never giving her time off from the household cares, as well as the secretarial work she did for the business.

Jean was pleased to be going out; she did not often have the opportunity to dress up for something a bit frivolous.

"You really look a treat," Ellen said, when she popped her head in to see if Jean wanted any help.

She was quite glad she had decided on a pretty dress when she saw Tom. He had put on a suit, (she knew he only had one, for special occasions). Obviously they were going to somewhere quite smart.

"Actually, a friend of mine has just opened his own restaurant down by Tregareth, and he is having a special evening for his friends. We are supposed to let him know what we think."

"That might be quite difficult if it's awful," Jean said, giggling.

The restaurant was set on a hillside overlooking Tregareth Bay, with a fantastic view from the wide windows. Tom's friend Pete showed them to a table by one of these windows. Of course they could not see much of the view as the winter evening had drawn in, but they could imagine what it would be like in the summer, looking out over the bay. There were candles on the tables, and the silver and glass gleamed in the glow. Jean glanced up at Tom and smiled shyly.

"Gosh, I hope this is not too expensive."

Tom reached across and took her hand, giving it a little squeeze.

"Don't worry, you're worth it, and you deserve a treat."

They settled back and looked at the menu, trying to decide what to have. There were so many choices, but Jean chose Smoked Salmon to start.

"I've never had that, and I think I'd better try all new things I don't have at home," she explained.

"Anyway it's a good idea. I'll have the same, and then I think I'll have the steak, and perhaps Peach Melba, because I don't know what that is but I like peaches!"

Jean thought for a minute. "I'm going to have chicken; no, perhaps the lamb as I have lots of chicken at home. Then I'll have the Peach Melba too!"

It was all a huge success. Greatly daring, Tom ordered a half bottle of wine, which they both enjoyed, and they never stopped chatting the whole meal. Pete noticed from the moment they sat down they seemed to be enjoying themselves. He hoped that meant that the restaurant was a winner. Other diners were equally cheerful, and complimentary about the food and service, so that he felt vindicated. So many people had told him a restaurant like that would not take off in Cornwall, especially in the winter. But some of his guests had told him they would be coming again very soon.

Jean was sipping her coffee when she became aware that Tom had become rather silent and seemed to be nervous about something. Help, she thought, perhaps he finds he can't pay the bill. It must be quite a lot.

He leant towards her, "Jean, I can't sit here any longer without saying what has been on my mind for ages. I do so love you, and I wondered if you..." he hesitated, then drew a deep breath, "I just love you so much, and I wondered if you would marry me?"

Jean was temporarily speechless. She was such a close friend of Tom. He had been part of her life forever it seemed, but she knew who she wanted to marry, and it wasn't Tom.

"Oh Tom, I do love you, but..."

Tom gave a wry little laugh. "There's always a 'but' isn't there? I think in this case the 'but' is David, isn't it?"

She looked at him, at his dear dependable face, and wished with all her heart it was him she loved. Life would be so simple. A small country wedding, life as a farmer's wife, a brood of children, and the whole scenario of her life being played over again. It was tempting, but not enough. David had shown her a life of excitement, of living on the edge, never quite knowing what was coming next; but not only that. It was David who she had loved since the day he had rescued her from falling into the path of a train, all those years ago, and she had never wavered. Of course, she had realized Tom was growing fond of her, beyond the childish friendship, but she had always hoped he would fall in love with one of the Land Girls, or even one of the WAAFs he must have met when he had been in the RAF. It was a surprise to everyone when he returned to a life of farming quite free of any romantic attachments. Now Jean realized the reason why, and she was desperately sad to disappoint him by refusing his proposal of marriage, especially after such a lovely evening.

"Well, I suppose so, But I don't think he feels the same about me, so there we are." she answered.

Tom was not so sure. He knew David was absolutely dependant on Jean, both in the office and in the house, but whether love came into it he didn't know. Now he knew how

Jean felt, he reluctantly decided to tackle David at the earliest opportunity. If David had no intention of asking Jean to be his wife, then he, Tom, would do his darndest to win her hand. Meanwhile, this was supposed to be an evening out for Jean and he mustn't spoil it for her. He felt in his pocket for the little velvet box that he had hoped to give her if she had said "Yes." He would keep it just in case; things might change.

When he dropped her off at the front door of the Rectory she gave him a hug.

"It really was a lovely dinner, Tom. Thank you so much," and they parted with completely different thoughts.

Chapter 9

David did not return from America until the beginning of March. The daffodils were beginning to flower in profusion, and as the train pulled into Bodmin Station he wondered why he ever left this lovely county that was his home.

He had not told anyone he was coming back; in fact, he had not known until two or three days before. But when the deed was done, the contracts signed and handshakes given, he felt he must get back and sort out his life at home. Jean had kept him in touch with the news, some of which was worrying. George had gone steadily downhill since Nancy's death, and Jean had written to tell him that the Bishop had suggested retirement. He had become apathetic about his future which he felt held nothing without Nancy, and he was becoming increasingly forgetful. His parishioners understood, but it did not lead to a very contented village, when he forgot so many meetings; and even once he forgot a sermon, leading to the embarrassment of the Church Warden, who gently had to remind him what he was doing in the pulpit.

Now David felt he would be able to sort it all out, and he couldn't wait to get home and help his father.

Jean heard the taxi in the drive and rushed out of the front door, hesitating a little as she saw who it was. David threw down his suitcase and hugged her so tightly she had to remonstrate.

"Heavens, what's all this about then?"

"Let's get inside and I'll tell you," he said, turning to Mr Crossdon who had been their taxi man for many years. "How much do I owe you?"

"I'll go and make some tea. You go and see Uncle George and I'll bring it in. It's Ellen's day off," she explained, rushing off to the kitchen, thankful to have an excuse to calm down a little. David seemed to have grown hugely since he was home last. "I always feel that," she thought, putting the kettle on the Aga.

David was having a somewhat stilted conversation with his father when she returned, and seemed pleased to be interrupted. George never had been particularly close to his son. He had always left that kind of thing to Nancy, and after drinking half a cup of tea and crumbling a biscuit he went back to his study. David looked at Jean.

"Is he always like that?"

"Well yes. Anything happening suddenly, like you coming home, throws him off balance I'm afraid."

"I'm sorry, but I had to get back and tell you the news. It is just so stupendous."

"What is?"

"I've just sold, or rather we've just sold, the Focus Account Card Business!"

"But David, why on earth, when it was doing so well?"

"That is the whole point. Pete was approached by some millionaire, who wanted to develop it, and he offered us the most amazing amount of money for it."

"Well, it is worth quite a few thousand I should think," said Jean, worried that David had got into debt and had let it go without thinking it all through. She got up to clear the tea things.

"Quite a few million, you mean!"

To say Jean was flabbergasted was an understatement. Nearly dropping the tray she sat down abruptly and David came to sit beside her on the sofa.

"Actually, after the American side have had their share and expenses and things, we should have about two million pounds in the bank."

Jean only heard one word out of that sentence,

"What do you mean 'we'?" she asked.

"Who do you think? Oh Jean, I do so love you and I think you love me. I've been waiting for all this to settle, but now it has, will you marry me?"

Could there be any more shocks for one afternoon she felt, but flung her arms round David and said, "Yes, yes, yes!" After that they both felt nothing but bliss as they embraced.

Later on, when they had both calmed down a little, David told her that he had got in touch with the Church Authorities and suggested to them that he should buy the Rectory, and pay towards a new, modern one being built on the Glebe field.

He could also afford to buy a smaller house for his father to move into. But here Jean intervened.

"David, darling" (how lovely to be able to call him "darling" out loud, instead of only in her dreams). "I really don't think your father could bear to leave here, and go and live somewhere by himself."

David agreed with a laugh. "Perhaps you are right, as usual! There is plenty of room here to make him a sort of flat."

There followed an interval when the kissing began again, and only stopped when Ellen appeared to tell Jean she was back, as she had heard Master David had returned.

"Ah, now, Ellen, you can be the first to hear our good news! Jean has consented to be my wife! Isn't that wonderful?"

Ellen went bright pink, and was immediately given a hug by both of them.

"Oh Miss Jean, how lovely. I'm so glad, that I am." She rushed out of the room, quite forgetting what she had come in for.

"I suppose I should ask someone for your hand in marriage?" David said thoughtfully,

"Well, there's only one person and that's Uncle George!" said Jean with a twinkle in her eye.

Of course, George was delighted. "Your mother always hoped this would happen, I just wish she could have been here to celebrate with us." Jean had a strong feeling that Aunt Nancy was with them, and silently acknowledged her blessing.

David recalled what his mother had said to him just before she died.

"I know, Dad. Mum did say she sort of hoped Jean and I would get married one day, and her words really made me realize I did love Jean. Also Dad, I realized I had kind of taken her for granted! But I wanted to tie up the business side of the Card before I asked her."

"Gosh, I wish you'd said something to *me*," laughed Jean.

After that they had a jolly evening, and George even came out of his depression, and began to take an interest in all their plans.

"Of course, I will marry you, it would really be such a pleasure."

"But who is going to give me away?" asked Jean, rather anxiously. She knew she had no other relations as her parents had no family. The dilemma was quickly solved when David suggested Tom's father Mr Truckle.

"Actually, I was going to ask Tom to be Best Man."

"And perhaps I should ask Mrs Truckle if I could stay the night before the wedding at the farm," and so the plans went on enjoyably until it was time to retire, and certainly in Jean's case, to dream of unknown pleasures to come.

David went to see Tom the next day. Jean felt it would be best if she did not go with him, and made an excuse. She wanted time to gather her thoughts, and perhaps go and see Penny, who happened to be home for a few days from her job in London.

Tom was delighted to see his friend.

"Goodness, David, you do look as though you had won a sweepstake or something."

"Amazingly Tom, I have sort of done that. Yesterday I asked Jean to marry me and she said Yes!"

Tom was expecting this, in fact had been for some time. Only he knew from things Jean said that she did not think he ever would. Now his heart sank a little, as he realized he would now never have a chance, and would have to make the best of it.

"The thing is, I wondered if you would be my Best Man at the wedding?"

"Of course, I'd be honoured. I'm so glad for you. I know Jean adores you and you are a very lucky chap."

"I realize that. I wanted to get the card business all sewn up before I asked her, and now that's done, well ...all systems go!"

Mr and Mrs Truckle had to be told, and congratulations given all round, and even though it was mid-morning a bottle of wine was produced and health's drunk, David promising to bring Jean over tomorrow.

"I know she wants to talk to you. I think she would like to have Mr Truckle give her away, as Dad is marrying us."

"In fact, she'd better come and spend a night or two here before the wedding," said Tom's mother.

"I do know that is what she was also going to ask you. Having no mother or my mother either, I think she needs you more than anything; I expect she'll pop over tomorrow. She's seeing Penny at the moment."

***

Jean and Penny were having a lovely talk. Penny had remained heart free, in spite of being especially pretty and full of fun. She had told Jean she met masses of nice young men in London, but all they wanted to do was to jump into bed with her, and she did not want that until she was married.

"I think we are a bit old-fashioned," Penny said. "So many of my friends seem to sleep with any man who asks them, but I want it to be special the first time, don't you?"

Jean agreed wholeheartedly, although in St. Wraich the problem had hardly ever occurred, at least for her. Maybe being a Rectory daughter had somehow shielded her from that sort of dilemma, for which she had been thankful. Tom had kissed her quite often, and once or twice his embrace had become a little enthusiastic, but he had been easily deterred. The only person she would have willingly given in to had never, until now, wanted her in that way; and now the miracle had happened, and she felt she would do anything David asked her.

Jean smiled to herself at the memory. "I do hope that you will be my bridesmaid?"

"I'd love to, but I don't really want to be the only one. Are you going to ask anyone else?"

"I thought I ought to ask Annie. Although she's not a great friend, we did sort of arrive in St. Wraich together."

Annie's mother had married after Annie's father had been killed in France, and Annie no longer felt she was welcome in her old home in London. Her stepfather had tried to 'interfere' with her when she had gone back at the end of the war. She did not, in any case, feel at home in London after all those years in Cornwall, and she had written to Mrs Nicholson, who had cared for her so well in St. Wraich and poured out her troubles to her. It nearly broke Mrs Nicholson's heart when she read the letter. Annie had become so much part of the Nicholson family that it had been a wrench when she had to return to London. She wrote off at once, telling Annie to jump on the next train and enclosing money for her fare. The reunion was all they both could have wished for, and Annie settled into her country life as if she had never left. She had managed to get a good job in the local Baker's shop in Wadebridge which was expanding, and needed well-spoken young ladies to serve in the enlarged premises. Now she was a friendly face to all the customers, and was 'walking out' with a nice young man who worked in the Estate Agents next door.

She was thrilled to be asked to be one of Jean's bridesmaids. Like most of St. Wraich, she had watched the emerging romance in the Rectory. In fact it had been a constant source of speculation. Will he? Won't he? And now, like everyone else, she was delighted with the happy news.

"We've come such a long way from that train journey, haven't we? So much has happened in our lives since then." She exclaimed to Jean.

They were both silent for a moment, each thinking of the journey they had taken through the years, and what it had brought them, both joy and sadness.

Then the talk turned to dresses, the big day, and all the arrangements to be made. David and Jean had decided to set March the twenty seventh as the date, and a great deal had to be organised, (mostly by Jean), before then.

***

March had come in "like a lamb," and they all felt some anxiety about the unpredictable weather. Tom would look anxiously at the rooks, to see if they were flying high. Now Jean had made up her mind to marry David he had decided it was up to him to make sure her wedding was everything she had dreamed (for so long) it would be.

Needless to say the girls all worried about the dresses and their hair, as the idea had been to proceed to the church in a decorated farm cart. Mrs Truckle soon firmly but gently suppressed that wild plan, and arranged for Mr Crossdon, the local taxi man, to put ribbons on his car and drive the bridesmaids to the church, while Mr Truckle would proudly convey her and the bride in the family car.

George decided that they should have the reception at the Rectory, and Penny's mother, Mrs Treleaven, offered to arrange all the catering. This proved quite easy, as everyone in the village wanted to contribute something. In the end the St. Wraich Women's Institute suggested they should co-ordinate the refreshments, and the result was an amazing array of every kind of delicacy imaginable. Annie's employers, Barton's Bakeries, offered to make the wedding cake for a special price, and Mrs Nicholson told Annie it was to be her wedding present to Jean. In the end Jean was so overwhelmed by the kindness and generosity of the people of St. Wraich that she burst into floods of tears.

"I c-can't b-believe how kind everyone is being," she sobbed on Mrs Truckle's ample bosom.

"My dear, they just love you, of course. You have always been there for them, and it is their way of saying "thank you." So cheer yourself up and help me with this batch of scones." Ever practical, they both got over that emotional moment.

Many more occurred before the big day dawned. But on March the twenty seventh Jean woke early, with the unfamiliar noises of the farm coming through her window. She jumped out of bed and drew back the curtains, and wished she hadn't. It was misty and grey, and thoroughly horrible she thought. Not a bit like she visualised her wedding day to be. At that moment she heard a knock on the door, and Mrs Truckle put her head in.

"Are you decent? I just wondered if you wanted your breakfast in bed today?"

"Heavens no! Give me a minute and I'll be down. Oh, it's such a horrible day!"

"Well, you know what they say "too bright too early"; it'll be better later, you see if it won't. Just put on your dressing gown, there's only Father downstairs and he's just off to do the milking."

Mrs Truckle was right. At about eleven o'clock the misty rain blew off and gradually the sun came out, warming the hearts of everyone involved in the wedding, and that was almost the whole of St. Wraich.

Everyone agreed that Jean made a lovely bride. She certainly felt beautiful for the first time in her life. She had experienced a quiet moment while she was waiting to leave the farm when she thought of her own parents, and how different it might have been if they had survived the war. But she was determined nothing would mar this wonderful time in her life, and she said a little personal "thank you" to them for the life she had been given by their unselfishness at sending her away in those dark days of the war. But as soon as she was carefully handed into the car, with her pale cream dress carefully arranged, and Mrs Truckle beside her, she felt nothing but the utmost joy. Walking along the church path and seeing the flowers arranged round the porch; hearing the organ burst into joyful sound; and then, with Penny and Annie behind her in their new coral silk frocks, walking up the aisle on Mr Truckle's arm, she felt more and more sure that this was the happiest day of her life. She saw Tom first; he looked round and gave a little wink and nudged David. Jean had eyes after that for only one person, who looked surprisingly well-scrubbed and tidy. As Jean came up beside him he turned to look at her and gave a little gasp. Had he been expecting to see the somewhat grubby little girl, or even the young lady who had seemingly produced meals and organised the Rectory for so long, with untidy hair, and sometimes a smut on her cheek? Whatever, this was a princess, and a beautiful one at that, and it momentarily took his breath away.

The rest of the day passed in a blur for Jean. The solemn promises she made, hardly able to take her eyes off the plain gold wedding ring which David slipped on her finger; the glorious hymns which seemed to her to be sung especially for them; the smiles and loving looks of the congregation as they walked back down the aisle, now "man and wife together"; and the fun and laughter in the Rectory afterwards. Soon it was time for the speeches, and surprisingly, Tom gave the best one of all, reducing the audience to gales of merriment as he recalled various episodes in their youth, involving both Jean and David.

He ended with a wistful plea, "Jean, you've got the best; but if you ever get tired of him, remember, I'm willing!"

It was meant as a joke, and everyone laughed, but Jean, remembering a certain evening not so long ago, felt it was a coded message to her, and she gave a little private nod of acknowledgement as they raised their glasses to drink the health of the bridesmaids.

Soon afterwards, she was hurling her bouquet behind her, and was gratified to hear the cheers as Annie caught it. "You next!" everyone shouted, as Annie's young man put his arm round her.

David had decided to take his bride to Torquay for their honeymoon, and they were soon boarding the train at Bodmin, with Mr Crossdon driving them to the station. Soon they were alone in their compartment, (Jean noticed it was First Class), and David put his arm round her and gave her a hug.

"Amazing, isn't it?" he whispered into her ear. "I just can't believe, after all that palaver, we've made it. Mr and Mrs... just think of that!"

Jean had been thinking of little else for the past hour or so. She had dreamed of this moment for so long, and she felt the rings on her finger to remind herself that this was now real life, and she really was Mrs David Bretton.

"Jean Bretton," she whispered to herself.

***

David was so accustomed to staying in hotels, that he was not overawed at the grandeur of the Royal Parks Hotel, as their taxi drew up to the imposing entrance, and an enormous gentleman in a top hat handed them out of the car and beckoned a younger man to carry their bags. They had to register, and Jean held back a bit as David confidently signed them in as Mr and Mrs David Bretton. Then following the porter with their luggage they travelled up in a large lift and shown into the biggest bedroom Jean had ever seen. To avoid having to look at the bed, which seemed huge, Jean went straight over to the window. The view, although by now dark, was magical. Little lights all the way down a pier, and more lighting up the boats moored in the harbour, and she thought she could just hear the soft swish swish of the waves as they broke gently on the shore.

David tipped the porter, who gave a gratified murmur as he realized the gentleman's generosity, and then came over to Jean. "Like it?" he asked, putting his arm round her.

"Oh yes, it is amazing, and you are amazing too, darling David, in the way you deal with all these people and...and... things."

"Well, I'm sort of lucky, having stayed in places like this quite often in America. Now, would you like to have a drink downstairs before dinner?"

Jean nodded and he tactfully went and sat in one of the armchairs facing out to sea, while Jean unpacked her things and went to the bathroom to have a wash, and wonder what she should do next.

"Do I change, do you think?" she asked.

"I think most women do put on a sort of dress in the evenings, so I'll go down and order the drinks, and you come down when you're ready."

Jean was thankful to hear him say that; she was not quite sure how she was going to take off her travelling clothes in front of him. She knew she would have to sometime, but not just yet!

On an impulse she threw her arms round David. "I won't be long, Thank you so much for all this,"

David disentangled himself as gently as he could. He felt if he didn't they may not get downstairs at all, and he felt he needed a stiff drink to recover from all the celebrations and the journey.

Apart from having the odd meal out, Jean had never experienced the grandeur of a hotel restaurant. The food looked delicious, and David had ordered Champagne, but Jean felt more and more apprehensive about what Ellen had called, in a hushed voice when helping to pack Jean's suitcase, "Your Wedding Night." She tried to eat at least part of the appetizing dishes placed before her by the waiter, usually with a great flourish. David, who had not noticed her nervousness, kept up an amusing account of all the other guests.

After they had drunk coffee, David could not help noticing Jean's eyelids begin to droop and he suggested she should go up to their room and he would join her in about half an hour. He took her to the lift and kissed her gently on the cheek.

"I think we've both had enough for one day. You get into bed and snuggle down; I'll come up in a bit."

Jean took his advice, and was soon half asleep in the big bed. She was worried at which side she would sleep, and decided to get in the left side; in fact she was, in truth, too tired to think much about anything, and when David came up half an hour later she was fast asleep. He was quite relieved, as he was pretty well worn out, and was not quite sure how easy it was going to be to lead her into the joys of loving. He undressed quickly and slipped in beside her, gazed for a minute at her innocent face, now devoid of make-up and looking more like the Jean of his youth, and fell into deep oblivion, dreaming of credit cards tumbling down a mountain, and Tom at the bottom trying to catch them as they fell.

They both woke at the same time, with the spring sunshine piercing the curtains. Jean looked across and started to giggle.

"This is the first time I've been in bed with a man!"

"I should hope so, and this is why." David reached across and drew her into his arms. He gave her a long lingering kiss and began to stroke her gently. She had an extraordinary feeling of yearning towards him, her limbs melting as he began to touch her in places she did not know she had. She wanted to give in completely to whatever he asked, and a drowning feeling engulfed her, carrying her along unimaginable rivers of pleasure until she felt nothing could ever stop this ecstasy.

Afterwards they lay together, not able to believe that such happiness could be theirs, until they both dozed off again, waking a little while longer with one thought in their minds... hunger!

"Let's have it brought up here," suggested David, and he rang down and ordered everything he could think of, and when it came they feasted as if they had never eaten before. Jean felt they were like children having a picnic.

"I couldn't eat another thing. What a wonderful breakfast. The first we've had together in bed!" They both rolled around in laughter, trying desperately to avoid upsetting the cups and plates onto the floor. It wasn't long before they were in each other's arms again, losing all sense of time and place.

A discreet knock on the door woke them some time later, making them realize it was halfway through the morning, and the maid was trying to come in and clean their room. David called out to come back in half an hour, and they quickly got dressed, deciding to go for a walk down to the harbour.

The sun was shining and they felt full of energy as they strode along, hand in hand. Jean felt as though she had gone to heaven, life was as perfect as it ever could be.

David glanced down at her, and was amazed at the transformation from the rather scruffy little girl he had known for so long, to this lovely sparkling young woman dancing along beside him. He had not known if he was doing the right thing in asking her to be his wife. He had never really thought of it until Tom had put the idea in his mind. He enjoyed his entrepreneurial life, and was not sure, even now, whether he wanted to be tied down to domestic bliss. But her aura of happiness affected him, and he felt he had, perhaps, been correct after all. She would be able to look after his father, and keep the home going as it always had, and it would be satisfying to come back from his trips to find a loving wife eager to cater for his every need.

But now was now, and he basked in her adoration, and was also faintly surprised at her ardour in bed, which he had not expected, and was a bonus indeed. "By God," he thought, "Tom knew what it was about, and that's for sure."

The week passed in a haze of happiness as far as Jean was concerned, but even so, she was surprisingly glad to get back to the Old Rectory again.

***

David plunged into his work, retiring to his father's old study to work on all the mysterious money-making deals in which he was embroiled, emerging at meal times with his hair ruffled and a light in his eyes, which Jean instinctively knew was not on her account. He was still loving and attentive, but had his mind on his growing business and could think of little else. Jean did not know so much about it as she had done in the past, and David did not confide in her as he had at the beginning. When she asked him questions he was inclined to brush them aside, saying, "It is all so complicated, and changes so much from day to day," and she wisely refrained from questioning him further.

Once he said to her, "The main thing is that there is plenty of money in the bank, and I hope to build up still more, so we never have to worry again."

She hoped he was right.

America

Chapter 10

Life at the Rectory continued much as it had before. If Jean had expected everything to be different she was mistaken. She found the usual routine continuing, only enlivened by the presence of David, and sometimes not even that. He was inclined to announce at breakfast that he was off to London, or Paris, or Manchester for a couple of nights. Jean gathered it was always to do with money, and generally David came back with some expensive trinket for her, and was even more loving when they finally retired for the night. But Jean would much rather have had his company than this endless and restless search for greater wealth. He opened a bank account for her and paid in generous amounts every month, which she used for running the household. Her own personal needs were quite meagre so that she never ran out of funds; but when David discovered, quite by chance, she was using money from this account for housekeeping, he immediately doubled the amount.

"Darling, I've got quite enough already for everything," she told him.

"But I want you to buy pretty things, and not do so much yourself. Anyway, you must get some more help with Dad, especially as I thought you might like to come to America with me in May. I have to go over there, and I'd love to show you all the sights."

New York! After all she'd heard about America she couldn't wait. It would be an adventure of a lifetime for her. She set about finding more help, and fortunately Ellen produced a young cousin May, who turned out to be a treasure, and was soon part of the Old Rectory family.

George was becoming more and more forgetful and needed constant vigilance; he had to be reminded to get up in the morning and to be fetched for meals. He seemed in remarkably good health, thanks to Jean's care. She made sure he ate well and regulated the visitors he received. After so many years as their priest he had many friends in St. Wraich, who were always popping in to see him and have a cup of tea and one of Jean's delicious homemade biscuits, or a piece of Ellen's famous sponge cake. He was a gentle and courteous man, but the light had gone out of his life when Nancy died, and he was simply waiting patiently to join her. The 'new' Rector was also a constant visitor, for which Jean was grateful.

David viewed all this activity with satisfaction, as he had dreaded having to cope with his father when he had so many other interests. Sometimes he felt a little spasm of guilt when he saw what a lot Jean had on her young shoulders. Occasionally in the evening she was so tired she fell asleep as soon as she had climbed into bed, and he lay beside her wondering why he was there. She had been so full of life on their honeymoon, totally devoted to him; and now... now he had to share every moment with the minutiae of domestic life as she struggled to cope with running a large house, an aged father, and all the demands that were expected of the Rectory, as had been accepted when Nancy was alive.

"I do wish," he said to her one evening, "you would remember to be a wife sometimes and not always be running after everyone else's problems."

It cut her to the quick, and she put aside the list of meals she was trying to plan, and went over to him, putting her arms round his neck and kissed him.

"Oh David darling, I'm so sorry. There always seems so much to do, and everyone comes to me to know the answers, and I don't always know what to do,"

David felt a stab of remorse, but could not help thinking that she should try a little harder and devote more of her time to him. His mother had always managed not to let domestic chores impede her time with him, whenever he was home, and he still thought Jean could emulate her. He did not realize that times had changed after the War, and everything was that much more difficult. He hoped they might regain a little of their honeymoon happiness with the trip to America.

***

This time they flew across. The large liners were gradually being turned over to cruising, and David did not feel like spending five or six what he felt as 'wasted' days at sea. Jean, on the other hand, had visualised a lovely lazy crossing, which would have given her the rest she so badly needed. However, anything David organised must be right, so she carefully packed the correct weight of suitcase, with essential belongings.

"I really don't know what sort of things I'll need," she said to David when he came into the room as she was gazing at a pile of clothes on the bed, "and I know you can't have more than a certain weight of suitcase..."

"My dear girl," he said, sighing, "you can have as much as you like, I can always pay for any extra weight. In any case, when you get there I will be quite busy, so you can go and buy anything you need; the shops are marvellous."

Jean could never get used to the idea that David seemed to have unlimited funds. She gave a little sigh, and went back to sorting and folding. This idea of having more than enough money was quite alien to her. All her life she had been brought up to be 'careful'. Even after she had been adopted by the Brettons, she felt she should not spend their money unless absolutely necessary, as she knew that a Rector had only a modest remuneration, and living in a large and draughty house took quite a large chunk of their income. Now, apparently, she never need think about money again except how to spend it, and this did not come easily.

At least Ellen was reliable to be left in charge of the house while they were away, with May to help her. Jean asked Mrs Truckle to look in from time to time, and Tom offered to call and see George two or three times a week.

She left lists of menus and shopping, and at last began to feel relaxed about their departure.

"You just go and enjoy yourself," said Ellen. "Goodness knows, you deserve a break. You and Mr David go and have a good time. Don't you worry 'bout nothing. Me and May will manage just fine."

Although travelling by air was a completely new experience for Jean, and she was determined to enjoy it, she found the airport dirty, the miles they had to walk to get to the plane extremely exhausting and the rush and hurry that everyone seemed to be in tiring. When they finally were settled in their first class seats she felt sick and headachy. She tried to perk up for David's sake, but even he noticed how pale she was.

"Are you feeling OK?" he asked. "Don't be nervous. These planes are very safe, you know."

"I'm fine; perhaps I could have some water or something?" she replied, swallowing hard.

The stewardess brought a tray of drinks, and David tried to induce her to have something a bit stronger. Taking one look at her the stewardess suggested a small brandy would be the best cure, and Jean managed to sip it, which did indeed, help a bit. Then there was a roaring noise as the plane revved up the engines for takeoff. David took her hand and squeezed it.

"Our second honeymoon begins," he whispered, grinning. Jean smiled shyly at him, and with the brandy warming her she squeezed his hand back.

The flight was uneventful, apart from David getting a little too merry with the flow of drinks which kept appearing. Jean closed her eyes and wished for oblivion. In fact she did sleep a little and woke feeling much better, smiling at David flirting with the stewardess. He noticed, and felt relieved that she had recovered.

"We're going to have a super time when we get there. I think Brad is going to meet us in New York, and his wife is all set to show you the sights."

"Won't you be able to do that?"

"Well, some of the time no doubt, but I haven't come all the way over to have fun, you know. I've got quite a lot of work to do as well."

Brad and his wife Kirsty were there at the barrier with a huge bouquet of flowers for Jean, and a welcome which Jean felt was rather over the top. Throughout their stay she was to feel that many times. So used to restrained British manners, she was shattered by the sheer exuberance of the Americans. Everything seemed to be bigger than she was accustomed to; the welcomes, the food portions, the choice. She felt totally bewildered by it all. For once David noticed and reassured her.

"I remember when I first came to America, feeling the same, particularly at the end of the War when everything was in short supply in England, and here they had too much. It seemed wrong somehow, but then I decided to simply enjoy it all while I could!"

Kirsty was a sweet person, about the same age as Jean. She had been married to Brad for three years, and they had a little boy of two, and, she confided in Jean, were hoping soon to have another baby.

She smiled at Jean. "I think it's best to get having babies over as soon as possible. Are you hoping for a boy or girl?"

Jean looked at her with amazement. She had been feeling a bit sick for the last few days, and she put it down to excitement over the trip, but now she suddenly thought of other signs, which she should have noticed, but in the flurry of packing up she had quite forgotten her period was overdue.

"Goodness, do you think I'm pregnant?" she gasped.

"Well, I thought you didn't look too special, and as you haven't been married all that long, I thought you might be. I feel awful, speaking out of turn. I'm so sorry; I kinda put two and two together. Do hope I haven't put my foot in it!"

"Oh Kirsty, how do I find out for sure?"

"You could go to my Gynea man, but I think it would probably be OK to wait till you get home and see your own doctor. David seems pretty sensible, does he know?"

"I shouldn't think so, he never notices much about me, except to give me brandy when I felt ill on the plane coming over. I don't want to spoil the trip, so I think I'll just wait till I get home."

Kirsty reckoned this was sensible, but also felt there could not be much intimacy between the two of them if David had not noticed. Brad knew exactly when her 'difficult' times were, and always made a point of spoiling her rotten for a day or two. But perhaps English people were much more 'stiff upper lip' than the outgoing Americans. She gave Jean a few tips on combating the sickness feeling, and proceeded to give her a little cherishing and saw that she had plenty of time to rest. She took her shopping and noticed that Jean was longing to buy some of the gorgeous baby clothes, but naturally hesitant in case it was all a false alarm. Kirsty decided as soon as she heard from Jean confirming her pregnancy, she would buy them and send them over to England. They found some pretty dresses, which were loose enough to do when (and if) her 'bump' began to show, and Jean went wild in the household departments for kitchen equipment, and attractive linen and towels.

"Really," she said to David after one shopping expedition, "I think I'll have to buy another case to take all the stuff I've bought!"

"Just what I meant you to do. Also, you'd better get presents for everyone at home while you are at it!"

"I've seen some lovely things which you can't get in England so I think I will, if that is all right with you?"

"It's just fine; I'm so glad you are having fun, you are looking better too. I think the break is doing you good."

Jean smiled inwardly, hugging her secret to herself for just a little while longer.

All too soon the fortnight was over, and they had to say fond farewells to several new friends they had made, and particularly Kirsty and Brad.

"You must come over and stay with us soon and see our beloved Cornwall," they said as they hugged farewell before boarding the plane.

"We will, we will!" they called back as they waved goodbye.

England.

Chapter 11

Plunged into the minutiae of life at The Old Rectory, Jean found it was nearly ten days before she was able to see Doctor Howard, who confirmed her pregnancy, but told her to come back in a month. She then waited until she had a quiet moment to tell David her news. She was beginning to feel less nauseous, and more able to face David's reaction when she broke it to him that he was going to be a father. His initial shock was so predictable she almost laughed, but managed to keep a straight face.

"Surely you realized that this is what could happen when we love each other?" she said with a smile

"Yes, but, I don't know, somehow I thought it would take longer," and he put his arms round her and hugged her tight, snuggling his chin into her neck and kissing her ear, which was one of his most loving gestures.

"Are you feeling all right? I mean, some of my friends' wives seem to feel sick when they are having babies."

"Well, yes I am now. Do you remember I didn't feel well in New York?"

"I noticed you were a bit 'off' now and then. I thought you found it a bit overwhelming after the backwaters of St. Wraich."

"Actually, it was Kirsty who bowled it out! She asked me if I was 'expecting' and I was slightly taken aback. But when I thought about things I realized I might be; but I didn't want to spoil everything for you, when it all seemed to be going so well."

David thought 'typical Jean,' and gave her another big hug before going back to his office.

Jean made an appointment to see the doctor again, who merely confirmed she was three months pregnant and that everything seemed fine, but she should think of getting a bit more help in the house and garden, and someone to take more care of George, and she should put her feet up every afternoon for at least an hour. Jean was appalled at the thought, but promised to do her best and arranged to see the district nurse every month until nearer the time.

David had also been busy and announced that, if Jean agreed, (had she ever not!) he would make enquiries about a maternity nurse to live in when the time came and to help for the first two or three weeks after the baby had arrived.

Although Jean did not mention her pregnancy to anyone outside the family, except of course to Mrs Truckle, the 'village' soon knew all about it, and kept a beady eye on the increasing bump.

"In fact, they seem to know a lot more than I do sometimes." Jean confided to David,

"Oh well, it keeps the old biddies happy," remarked David, who early on, had become somewhat bored with the whole proceeding. He told Tom, of course, but soon became aware that Tom was slightly more interested than he was. The latter kept asking after Jean's health, and being so concerned that David soon dropped the subject and hastily introduced other, more interesting topics.

Tom managed to pop in to the Old Rectory as often as he could, with little gifts of brown eggs or a jug of cream "from Mother," and the odd bunch of flowers that "I happened to pick early this morning." Jean appreciated all the attention, but was aware of a bit of tension between the two boys (as she still thought of them), and it was a little awkward sometimes.

"Tom, that really is good of you. Thank you so much, David does love a nice brown egg for his breakfast!"

But Tom instinctively knew what she really meant, and was satisfied just to have seen how she was getting on.

Actually, pregnancy suited Jean, and, with her hair gleaming and her skin glowing, people remarked how well she looked.

"They make such a lovely couple," the parishioners remarked one Sunday, when Jean managed to persuade David to go to church with her. This did not happen very often; memories of endless sermons given by his father, sitting on the hard pews and longing to be out in the fresh air, had put him off church for many years.

He also engineered quite a few visits away from home, mostly business, but sometimes he made up a story about meeting 'a fellow' to work out some deal or other, simply to get away from the whole pregnancy scenario.

Jean sailed through Christmas, much helped by the Truckles. She suggested they come up to the Old Rectory for Christmas lunch, and Mrs Truckle and Ellen between them produced the usual feast, pushing Jean off to church, and making her put her feet up when she got back. After lunch she was made to lie on the sofa in the drawing room while the rest of the party cleared the table; everyone was ready and waiting to listen to the King's Christmas message at three o'clock. He sounded so old and his voice was somewhat scratchy, they all felt a little pang of sadness after listening to the broadcast.

"He did so much during the war, and now he is always getting colds and infections on his chest." Murmured Mr Truckle,

January came and went, and Jean could hardly move, and she longed for the day when whatever 'it' was would make his/her appearance.

"If only it would hurry up, I'm sure I'm having twins," she grumbled to David one evening as they were getting ready for bed.

"Not half as much as I do, I can't wait to have you back without that huge encumbrance between us."

Jean felt it was not said in a kindly manner, and she was a bit hurt, but decided men did not view childbirth in quite the same way as women; a sort of excited anticipation, with a little anxiety mixed in.

Tom would have understood, she thought, and then was horrified that she could even compare the two of them in that way.

Tom was not his mother's child for nothing; he felt so much compassion for Jean, seeing her struggling with her bulk, and seemingly David making all his usual demands on her time. He tried to talk to David once or twice, suggesting ways in which he should take over some of the chores in the house, but David just replied, "Oh Jean loves doing all that sort of thing, and won't let anyone help her."

"Have you ever tried?" reflected Tom, but felt he should not pursue the matter, as he might only make it worse.

February the thirteenth dawned cold and grey, with flurries of snow, (unusual enough in Cornwall), and Jean began to suspect her time had come at last. It started with niggles of pain in her back, and soon became rather more like the shooting aching pains she had been plagued with every month, only these were definitely stronger. She telephoned Mrs Truckle as they had arranged, who dropped everything and rushed up to the Old Rectory as fast as she could.

The nurse, who David had retained, was booked to arrive the next day, and Jean was quite relieved that Mrs Truckle was in charge until then. David was told to telephone Dr Howard, who had just finished his morning surgery, and so was able to come straight to St. Wraich.

"Well, young lady, I can see you are on your way. I'll just have a look, but I'm sure everything is going fine." At that moment Jean had a shooting pain and couldn't speak. She clutched onto Mrs Truckle, who helped her lie on the bed as the pain gradually subsided. Dr Howard nodded wisely, and said,

"I'll give you something to ease it, but you will have a few more, and you'll have to ride the pains. Remember, your little baby is starting on a long journey, and you mustn't hold it back. Just relax as much as you can when the pains come and that way you can help your baby as well as yourself."

Jean smiled wanly, and looking up she saw Mrs Truckle give her a sympathetic grin, as if to say "what do men know about these things!" which made her feel better.

Dr Howard, having gently examined Jean, told them it would be a while yet, and he would come back later to see how everything was getting on.

It did take a long time. The doctor had left a little gadget which Jean gathered was gas and air, to help when she felt the pains were getting stronger. She was worried that David would not get his usual seven o'clock dinner, but was again reassured by Mrs Truckle that this had been taken care of. She had brought up a casserole, and an apple tart, and Ellen was coping with everything.

Actually Tom had come over after milking, and was sitting with David downstairs,

"God, what a bore all this is," David grumbled, "Why can't women have their babies like cats do, purring and then producing one kitten after another without all this paraphernalia?"

Tom smiled to himself. Animals did seem to 'do it' better, but he had known one or two cows that had had great difficulty giving birth, and it was harrowing to watch. He hoped Jean was not suffering too much.

"We do put them through it," he said.

"Ah, but what fun it is!" thought David, and momentarily visualised the time when Jean would be all his again.

The clock struck midnight, and a few minutes later they heard a noise from upstairs; just a squeak, but they both held their breath before Tom whispered "The baby?" David leapt to his feet, and was out of the door like a rocket. Tom found himself taking a step before he restrained himself. This was David's moment and he must hold back, however much he wanted, oh so strongly, to have the right to be first just then.

David ran up the stairs two at a time, but hesitated outside their bedroom door. Unexpectedly he felt shy and hesitant, not a bit like his normal self, who was always first to put himself forward.

The door opened and Mrs Truckle appeared. "Ah, David, come in and see what we've got for you."

He gazed across to where Jean was sitting up in their bed, looking dishevelled, her hair all over the place and her cheeks flushed. But she was smiling, and holding a bundle in her arms. She looked up at him with pride and love in her eyes.

"See darling, look what we have got!" She parted the towel and he found himself confronted by two blue eyes shining brightly at him. He felt weak at the knees and sat down on the edge of the bed and put out a finger, which was immediately grasped by the smallest fist he had ever seen. His heart turned over and his eyes filled with tears as he leant over and kissed Jean tenderly. "Thank you darling, it looks wonderful."

Jean chuckled, "It is a 'he' now, darling, we have a little boy!"

"And a very healthy son you have, David," said Dr Howard. "Now we'll just tidy things up and let Jean have a bit of sleep. She's had a hard time of it, so you go down and have a glass of something to wet the baby's head, and I'll soon be down to join you."

***

James David, as the baby was christened, thrived lustily. David began to feel very left out, surrounded as he was by his son's doting admirers. There seemed to be no other conversation and he longed to escape from it all. Jean was busy once again, with all her previous chores and caring for their baby son as well. One day, when Jean was stirring something in the kitchen he put his arms round her.

"Darling, couldn't you leave that and talk to me for a change? I never seem to get near you these days and you know, I need you too."

She turned round, stricken. "Oh David, my darling, you are always the first with me. I thought you knew that. I'm sorry if you feel I'm neglecting you, but there always seems such a lot to do and...."

"Now, my darling, don't take it so much to heart. I thought we would ask Ellen if her young sister May could come in all the time, and she could look after young James and give you a hand with other things. You could teach her various jobs. She comes from a huge family, and looking after one baby would be easy for her and take the weight off your shoulders."

Suddenly the thought of help seemed like heaven to Jean, and she couldn't imagine why she had not thought before of training up May. Ellen would probably leave to get married eventually, and May would be able to take over. Ellen always seemed to have plenty of young relatives, all willing to help in emergencies. She felt an enormous load lift as she hugged David. The hug was returned with great enthusiasm, and when he whispered "Come on upstairs," she took the saucepan off the stove, and went upstairs with him in a sort of a dream. The dream went on, as they fell into each other's arms and all the loving they had known in the past came flooding back, and they drowned in the pleasure of it all.

Neither of them thought for a moment what the future would hold. Jean had given up breast-feeding James when he was about four months old, and had forgotten, or perhaps it had not occurred to her (or David), that she could conceive again so quickly. For the next week or two they recaptured their honeymoon joy, and David hardly left her side, a fact which was noticeable to those close to them.

"They are like a couple of kids again," observed Mrs Truckle to her husband. "I thought David was going off married life a bit, but it seems to be suiting him after all!"

But it couldn't last.

The morning came when Jean was violently sick, and emerged from the bathroom with panic written on her face.

"It couldn't be," she whispered, and David, hearing the unpleasant sounds coming from the bathroom, felt his heart sinking at the thought of all the troubles connected with pregnancy facing them again.

"Oh Lord, do you think you really are having another baby?" he asked, putting an unkind emphasis on the 'another'.

Jean swallowed. "Perhaps it is just something I ate," she said.

But it wasn't.

She did not sail through this pregnancy. She was dreadfully sick almost every morning, and felt queasy and weak and tired. When she visited Dr Howard however, he pronounced that all was well.

"Perhaps it was a little too soon after James, and you must rest a lot. However you seem healthy enough in every other way, and therefore I expect you will soon be feeling better."

May was taken on, and proved an invaluable and natural Nanny to James and helpmeet to Jean. She was also quite a good cook, so that David did not suffer when Jean could not do any work in the kitchen. The smell of most foods sent her rushing to the bathroom.

Except, that is, kippers. Ellen bought some in Padstow on her day off, and when Jean smelt them cooking she yearned for them, and demolished two at one breakfast. Ellen was delighted, and arranged to have a regular supply to tempt Jean.

"I wonder if the baby will look like a kipper?" Joked David, delighted that Jean was sitting at the table normally for once.

***

James' first birthday came. They had a little tea party, and Jean waddled round admiring the other three babies, and envying her friends with flat tummies and plenty of energy. David appeared and was the perfect husband and father. He put his arms round Jean and gazed proudly at James as he was encouraged to blow out the one candle on his cake. He admired all the other babies, and everyone thought Jean was a lucky girl to have such a wonderful husband.

Only Jean knew how difficult he could be sometimes. He hated her being pregnant, almost blaming her for not being able to rush about with him whenever he wanted her to attend some function or other. Several times in the last few months he had taken himself off without an explanation. Just a few days each time and Jean did not like to probe too much. He always said it was business, and she believed him as she always had. She knew how he hated baby paraphernalia, and she tried to understand.

Tom was there whenever he could spare time from the farm. He seemed to know when David was away, but never pushed himself forward, seeming to appear naturally with a message from his mother or a few eggs or creamy milk remarking, "Mother said this would do you good."

The daffodils were all blooming, spreading a golden carpet under the trees in the garden, their heads nodding in the gentle breeze, when baby Elizabeth made her appearance.

This time the birth was quite straightforward and very quick, with no complications. Perhaps the fact that David had gone up to London for the night calmed Jean, and she felt as if she was able to relax.

"You haven't had any signs yet, I'll be back tomorrow in plenty of time to hold your hand," he had said before Mr Crossden appeared with the taxi.

It had been more and more of an effort to appear cheerful and well in front of David, and when she saw the car going out of the gate Jean visibly relaxed, and almost immediately felt the telltale pain start. She had a mad brief urge to run after the car and call him to come back, but quickly stifled it and lumbered inside to ring Mrs Truckle.

Only five hours later it was all over and she was sitting up in bed, gazing at the tiny bundle in her arms. The telephone rang and Ellen answered it.

"Ellen, this is David. Can I speak to Jean please?"

"Oh sir, there's been such a commotion! The baby's come an' all."

David sat down abruptly on the hotel bed.

"Can...I mean, is Jean alright?"

At that moment Mrs Truckle took the telephone from Ellen's shaking hands.

"David, Mrs T. here. Jean is fine and you have a lovely daughter. I should do whatever you want to do and come home as planned tomorrow. There is nothing to worry about, and Jean will have had a nice rest by the time you get home."

David put the telephone back on the stand and turned round to face the scantily-clad girl lying on the bed. He reached into his pocket and drew out some notes, thrusting them into her hand, saying "I'm sorry, I think you'd better go now. My wife has just had a baby girl, and I must go home as soon as I can."

Gloria (if that was her real name) shrugged and started to get dressed.

"Just as you like, but get in touch again sometime, won't you? For a little relaxation you know!"

David hardly noticed her as she gathered up her things and left. His mind was full of remorse. The problem was that Jean was such a very good wife, and he liked a bit of adventure and hanky-panky sometimes. He felt nothing much had changed since he was a small boy being tucked up in bed by his mother. At the beginning Jean had surprised him with her passion, but their romantic sessions had become so routine he felt he could almost have set a stopwatch for them. Jean seemed content enough, and obviously loved him, as she always had; but to a red-blooded chap like him it was not enough. Hence the occasional trips to London and the invigorating romps with Gloria and other glamorous girls, prepared to have fun and get paid for it.

He reached home by lunchtime the following day, remembering to stop and pick up a bunch of flowers from a shop near the station on the way.

"Darling, I'm so sorry I wasn't there when it all happened." He bent over Jean and kissed her, trying not to flinch at the milky odour from Jean's nightdress.

"Oh thank you, David."

Jean took the flowers and buried her nose in the blooms, but they had no scent. Why was it that bought roses never had any perfume?

"Look what we've got this time," she pointed to the little Moses basket, where the baby was sleeping peacefully. She was a beautiful baby, and David gazed at her pink cheeks and rosebud mouth, making little sucking noises in her sleep.

"She certainly is pretty. We decided on "Elizabeth" didn't we? Do you think that suits her?"

"I've thought of her as Elizabeth for such a long time, so I think she's already got that name. We can't change it now, do you mind?"

"Not a bit, I think it becomes her. James and Elizabeth make a good pair!"

He leant over to kiss her again and went downstairs to thank Mrs Truckle and Ellen for their help, and pour himself a large gin.

***

Jean could never pinpoint the moment when she realized that David was no longer contented with his life in St Wraich.

Just after Elizabeth's first birthday party they had a blazing row, something she had never allowed to happen before. David often upset her, but somehow she always managed to 'love him round,' as she thought of the efforts she made to keep the peace. The problem was that he wanted Jean for himself, and had no idea what it would be like to have to share her with the children. It had been bad enough before the babies arrived on the scene, with all the work that running a house, keeping his father contented, and the numerous jobs which living in the centre of the village entailed.

Only the week before he had come into the kitchen as she was preparing the children's supper. "Why can't you come up to London tomorrow?" he asked, knowing perfectly well that she had a coffee morning planned for the Toddlers Group;

which would mean clearing the sitting room, doing the flowers and cooking dinner for the family as well.

"If only I could," she answered, "but I must know in advance, so I can avoid arranging other commitments."

David flung out of the kitchen, muttering "no-one thinks of *me* anymore."

Jean blinked back tears, wondering how she could fit in all that David wanted when she could barely keep up with looking after two babies, an old and frail gentleman, and a large house and all it entailed, even with Ellen and May to help.

"Other chap's wives manage to turn up for these dos." David had returned to the kitchen for the mug of tea which he had left behind in his fury. "We've got plenty of money for help. Why don't you ask May to do more for the children or something, and let Ellen do all the cooking?"

But Jean loved being at home, being a real mother; making up for the fact that she had lost her own at so young an age. Hard work though it was, she revelled in looking after people and the Old Rectory, so much her home that she never wanted to leave Cornwall, to join those ghastly parties which David revelled in when he was in London. The 'Bright Lights' held no attraction for her whatsoever.

Elizabeth's little birthday party had been a great success. When everything had been cleared away and the children were safely tucked up in bed, Jean came down to the sitting room and flopped onto the sofa.

"Gosh, I'm exhausted," she said.

"Well, you should get people in to do parties and not try and do it all yourself, as usual," David ended with a sneer.

"Oh but I love it!" exclaimed Jean, somewhat unwisely.

"Yes, you love doing things for everyone except me."

"Darling, that's not fair. I always make sure you have nice meals and clean clothes, and, and—"

"Good God! You know what I mean. Even my mother used to make more time for me and do things *I* wanted, than you manage to do. Even with all the help I tell you to get, which you say you can't, but I'm sure half the village would love to come and work for Saint Jean..."

"Don't yell at me, David! If you go on shouting like that you'll wake the children,"

"Bloody children. That's all I hear these days. The whole world revolves round them, and nobody, least of all me, can get a look in. I really am thinking of going abroad, and leaving this ruddy village to stew in its own parochial juice."

"Please David, don't get cross. I am afraid I do love St Wraich, and I don't like the sort of town life you seem to want, although perhaps I could get away for a day or two next week if you like."

"Don't try, Jean, I know how you hate it. You make it abundantly clear when you do come, and therefore it isn't much fun for me. Just let me be and I'll work something out, and don't think it will include you!" and he stumped out of the room.

Jean was horrified. They had never shouted at each other like that, and she didn't know how to handle the scorn in his voice and manner. He was silent during dinner, and did not come up to bed until Jean, worn out by emotion, had drifted off to sleep. She had intended to stay awake and comfort him in the only way she knew, but slumber overcame her and when David eventually crept upstairs he was thankful to find her fast asleep.

The following morning he was cool to her, and politely informed her at breakfast that he was going up to London for a few days, packed his suitcase, and drove off, giving her cheek a quick peck as he climbed into the car to drive off to Bodmin.

To say she was shattered was an understatement. The telephone rang a minute later, and she ran in to answer it. The call was from Mrs Truckle asking her if she would like some eggs, but when she heard Jean's voice she just said, "I'll be up in five minutes."

Jean had not wanted anyone to know the problems she was having with David. After all he had lived in the village a lot longer than she had, and was revered by most of the local community mainly because they had respected his parents, although they also had taken Jean to their hearts. But when Mrs Truckle saw her face and put her arms round her, Jean dissolved into floods of tears, and the whole sorry saga came tumbling out. Mrs Truckle was appalled, but not surprised. She knew, especially from some of Tom's remarks, that David was incredibly self-centred and selfish, and it had always surprised her that Jean had been taken in by him, and apparently adored him. She had always hoped that Jean would see sense and give her heart to Tom.

Two cups of tea later Jean had calmed down, apologised for her outburst, and told her dear friend she was probably imagining David's meaning, and perhaps he was not feeling well, and she ought to have known.

"Poor David, he has gone off without me giving him anything to eat on the train." She sighed.

But when Mrs Truckle had gone she felt completely drained and sat at the kitchen table until Ellen came in and started to prepare lunch. She took one look at Jean, put her hand on her shoulder and gave it a squeeze.

"There are some daffodils just coming out in the garden. Why don't you go and pick a bunch, they'd look nice in the drawing room for your coffee morning tomorrow," she suggested and chivvied her out. Jean wandered down to the orchard and tried to compose herself as best she could.

Everything went on as normal, although Jean felt as if she had a lead weight in her heart. David did not telephone that evening, which was his regular habit, and when he telephoned the next day he had no loving words for her. She tried to sound cheerful, as if nothing had happened between them, calling him "darling" and not even mentioning the children. But he sounded so distant she did not know how to respond.

"Perhaps he is just punishing me, and it will all come all right when he comes home." She thought.

But it didn't.

"I want to talk to you. Come into the drawing room." He said, after he had dropped his suitcase in the hall.

She went meekly, prepared to crawl to him if it would settle matters. She would agree to everything he asked if only this awful situation could be solved. She sat down on the sofa, but what she heard made her wish she had never refused to do what he asked.

"I don't think, in fact I know we can't go on like this," he began, and when she tried to speak he held up his hand to silence her.

"I have decided to take up an offer of working abroad for the next few months."

When she gave a gasp he looked away, out of the window, as if to emphasise that nothing she could say would make any difference.

"You will get on perfectly well without me. You must have realized in the last few months that I have not been happy living the boring village life which you seem to enjoy. We've grown apart, Jean, and it is no good trying to deny it. I must spread my wings again; I have so many new ideas I want to put into practice, and this offer will be a new start for me."

"But how will I manage, with your father, and the children and... everything?"

"I will pay a substantial sum of money into the bank; easily enough for you to do anything you want; educate the children and so on. All I ask is that you don't try and contact me. If I don't get away completely I feel I shall go mad. I just want to cut loose and have a life of my own."

Even in all the turmoil she was experiencing, Jean could not help noticing the word that cropped up most was "I." He made no reference to what she had thought was a blissful marriage, the way she coped with the demands of the household, not to mention the children and *his* father. Meals regularly prepared and served to him, day after day, and the loving times they had shared in bed. Just this cold statement of his intent to leave them all to go on a wild goose chase to goodness knows where. And for how long? Money for educating the children? That implied years, not months. She felt engulfed by fury.

"I simply cannot understand you. I thought you loved me. How can you go off and leave all this, and the children, and me too." Jean gave a sob, holding back tears without totally succeeding.

"I really am sorry Jean, but I do need to go and find some sort of adventure, and I know I certainly won't find it in Cornwall. When I was in the Navy it was so exciting travelling round, seeing different places, and I feel completely stifled here."

"What will I tell everyone? That you have just gone off and left us and I don't know where you are? They will want to know, and what about your father? He will be devastated; or hadn't you thought of all that?" She sat down and put her head in her hands with a gesture of despair.

David shrugged, "I don't know. I am sure you'll think of something."

That night Jean lay in bed, waiting for David to come. She felt if she could put her arms round him, in the comfort of their bed, he would relent and decide not to leave them. She heard him on the stairs, and trembled with anticipation. She listened, hearing his footsteps turn into the children's room, and stay for a minute or two, then go into the spare room and shut the door. She was overwhelmed with the sense of utter helplessness, and turned on her side and wept bitterly until she fell asleep, exhausted by emotion and a feeling of loss and despair.

When Jean came downstairs in the morning, she saw suitcases in the hall, and David tucking into a substantial breakfast. He looked up, and then away as he saw Jean's tear-streaked face.

"I am sorry it was such a shock. You must have realized I was unsettled and bored with everything here in the last few months."

Jean gave a little nod but could not trust herself to say anything. He went on, "I'll just go and collect my things out of our room, and then I'll be off. Mr Crossdon is taking me to the station."

He made no mention of Jean accompanying him, and she was not sure if she wanted to. Station farewells always brought back memories of saying goodbye to her mother all those years ago. She just nodded, realizing if she spoke she would not be able to stop herself entreating him to stay.

It seemed only a second until he was down again, and helping Mr Crossdon load his luggage. He looked at her.

"Come inside a moment." When they were out of earshot of Mr Crossdon he gave her a brief and totally unloving embrace, saying, "I do not want anyone to know where I am going. I want absolute freedom. If you have any desperate problems get in touch with Ferbourne & Co, our solicitors. You've got their address and telephone number. I'll contact you before long to let you know how I'm getting on. But don't expect much communication as I'll often be in places with no contact. Take care."

With that he walked out of the door.

South Africa

Chapter 12

Polly stretched her arms above her head and gave a huge sigh of contentment. Paul put his hand out and stroked her breast; the nipples were soft now, but still warm from his caresses earlier. She smiled at him noticing his dark red hair shone with sweat.

"Was it alright?" he asked, with a tenderness she had not heard before.

"Wonderful, just dreamy. I can't bear to think you've got to go; now we've done that at last."

Paul smiled. "Never mind, it will be the first thing we'll do when I get back!"

He started to pull on his shorts, glancing at his watch as he did so.

"God, I must skedaddle. Jan is coming any moment to pick me up and drive me down to Maritzberg. You'd better put something on in case your Pa happens along," and he threw her dress at her, knowing she had not worn anything else. Everywhere was so hot. Sticky and still, with no cooling breeze like sometimes. He gave her a quick hug, longed for it to be a bit more, and ran down the path from the secluded bit of the garden where they had managed to find complete privacy to say their farewells. Those farewell kisses had turned into something more passionate than Paul had anticipated. He had always thought he would make love to Polly for the first time on their wedding night, but he had received unexpected orders from his regiment to report that afternoon, and she seemed especially willing when the kissing became more than either of them could control.

Polly dressed slowly, feeling languid, her arms aching as she bent to put her sandals on. She felt sore and tender down below, but it also served to remind her of the bliss she had just experienced for the first time. Paul was going off to serve in some unknown conflict, and would be away for some months. She already felt bereft as she watched him stride down the path. He turned to blow her a kiss and she heard Jan's old car revving up in the driveway. They were so excited at the thought of what they might be expected to do in the special group of which they were members. He wouldn't tell her, only that they would be out of the country for some time, and not to expect any communication for a while.

Polly's mother had noticed the burgeoning romance between her beloved only child and Paul de Freyburg. Perhaps mothers do sense these things, in spite of the fact that she was terminally ill herself. She had breast cancer and only had a few months left, a fact that her husband refused to acknowledge.

But other events were happening just then, which took most of her strength to manage. A gentleman called Donald Belham had written to her husband to ask if he could come and see him about some deal to do with vineyards he was involved in, and his plane from Durban was due that day. Reluctantly Polly had been made to organise the linen in the spare room, and as her father was away, to go down to the little airfield to meet Mr Belham.

"It's so hot, Mum. I'll get Minnie to mix you up some lemonade first."

She called out to their cook, "Minnie, mix Mum some lemonade from those fresh lemons I picked yesterday."

"Coming right up, Mis' Polly," said Minnie as she waddled in.

"Time you was goin' meet that plane, Mis' Polly. I'se heard it comin' over the mountain jus' now."

Polly swore under her breath, searched around for her sandals, which, as usual she had kicked off as soon as she entered the house, gave her mother a brief kiss, and ran down to the driveway. She jumped into the old jeep, revved up the engine and shot off. She loved driving the jeep. A sports car would have been better, but her father disagreed.

"Bad enough that Paul drives you round in that beat-up van of his. If you had a car of your own we'd never have a moment's peace, and I don't want your Mother worried, when she says she is not feeling well."

So she resigned herself to struggling with the farm jeep, and used it whenever she could find an excuse. Driving out onto the wide stretches of veldt gave her a sense of freedom, sadly lacking as the only child of elderly parents.

The small airstrip, which served the few properties round about, was barely three miles from Whiteoaks the van Stadt's farm. It only took Polly fifteen minutes or so to get there, and she saw the small plane on the mown strip which served as a runway. She gave a loud toot on her horn as she drew up by the shed that provided shelter for those few passengers waiting to board a plane or wait for transport. As she jumped down onto the baking surface she found herself face to face with a tall and extremely handsome man with the bluest eyes she had ever seen.

***

The heat struck him as he descended from the little aircraft. It had been a bumpy flight, and more than once Donald, (as David had decided to call himself now), had cringed as the small plane skimmed the trees below. The landing was bumpy too, and Donald had definitely smelt drink on the pilot's breath. But they had got there safely, and that was really all that mattered.

"Out you get," growled the pilot, having opened the aircraft doors and automatic steps.

Donald seized hold of his baggage, (he had left his large suitcases in the care of the hotel in Durban), and climbed down the steps onto the dusty brown landing strip. He had been told one of the van Stadts would be there to meet him, but the whole place seemed deserted. He saw a tin shanty on the side of the runway and he made for that. Two people were standing behind a desk, one white and the other a scruffy looking black man in tattered jeans. The latter glanced up and retreated a few paces to give him space in the tiny office. Donald was only just getting used to the white man's supremacy in South Africa. He had been shattered to see the signs "For use by White Persons" on nearly every public toilet and on entrances to buildings. But he had always liked being waited on hand and foot, and felt he could easily settle in a country where his word was law if he chose.

"You must be Donald Belham?" the white man held out his hand. "My name is Piet. Welcome to Draken River. Mr van Stadt told us to expect you today. I expect Polly will be along soon to pick you up. In fact I think I hear the jeep coming now. Usually with Polly, people have to wait, she's always late!"

He saw a cloud of dust approaching the airstrip, and heard a screech of brakes. The horn gave a loud blast which made him jump, and out skipped the most beautiful girl he had ever set eyes on.

"Hi, Piet," she called, "I saw the plane coming in; sorry I'm a bit late!"

She turned to Donald, giving him a glance out of deep blue eyes. Running her hand through her hair she held it out to Donald.

"Mr Belham, I'm Polly, glad to meet you. Hope the trip wasn't too hairy. Old Frank does throw the plane about a bit sometimes."

"Hallo Polly. Yes, it was a bit scary at moments. Let's say I'm glad to have arrived in one piece!"

"Well, we'd better get going. Is that all you've brought?" she asked, seeing the small grip beside him.

"Yes, I left the rest in Durban. Not sure how long I'd be staying."

They both climbed into the jeep, which had definitely seen better days, and with a grinding of the gears took off along the dirt track road.

Donald held on to his seat, trying to appear quite unconcerned at the seemingly reckless driving.

Polly looked sideways at him and grinned.

"You'll soon get used to everyone tearing about. There's no traffic to speak of, and anyway you can see another car coming for miles by the dust cloud. Usually it's someone you know, so you then slow down and usually stop and have a chat, like meeting a friend in the street. There are so few people round here, its fun to have a guest to introduce! By the way, can I call you Donald?"

He glanced at her and nodded, thinking what fun he was going to have after all.

Margery Van Stadt was resting on the stoep when they drove up to the house. It was cooler there than in the house, and she was getting to hate the long hot days, and yearn for the beginning of autumn. She saw the dust cloud approaching and heard the jeep come to a screeching halt. They both climbed out and she thought what a handsome couple they made, as they laughed at something together. She had heard that Donald Belham was a wealthy man, and she was starting to despair of Polly's relationship with Paul. It had seemed quite intense of late, but Paul was committed to the Army, and he did not seem to be unduly worried about leaving Polly. Polly was a beautiful girl, and Margery could detect the hormones raging within her, ripe for love if only the right man would come along. Particularly, she thought, before I have to leave her. She would so love to see Polly on her wedding day, dressed in the traditional white and wearing the family veil.

***

Polly had not heard from Paul for four weeks since he left, and she felt disappointed he hadn't called or even written a postcard. She was pleased to find the "Mr Belham" was not the middle-aged businessman she had expected. Moreover he was fun!

Gordon (her father) was up in the Drakensberg Mountains for a couple of days, and therefore it was up to Polly to entertain Donald. Apparently he had not ridden horses before, and expressed a desire to learn, so she saddled up her old pony and took him out for a riding lesson. This proved hilarious as Donald decided to act the fool, although he did manage to rise to the trot after an hour or so.

"Enough bullying!" he called to Polly. "Come and help me get off."

"You silly, just throw your right leg over. No! Take both feet out of the stirrups, you idiot, then throw your right leg over and let yourself down."

After a few attempts and cries of help, he said, "I can't do it, come and help me!"

She went up to him, directed his legs, and he jumped down, nearly bowling Polly over in the process. Laughing, he steadied her, keeping his arm round her for a moment. She felt so good, and it had been a long time since he had held a girl in his arms. A brief spasm of guilt ran through him as he remembered Jean, then he put the thought behind him and gave Polly a hug.

"Enough for today, I think. I'll be so stiff tomorrow when your father gets back, and I have some important things to discuss with him."

That evening, after Margery had retired for the night, Polly and Donald drifted out to the stoep and sat on the swing seat together, sipping brandy and chatting. The dark was magical, the sky huge, reminding him of days at sea, when he felt he could touch the stars. Polly, sitting beside him, felt it was completely right when he leaned over and gently kissed her. She gave a little sigh, but Donald felt it was of contentment, not sadness, and he whispered, "Thank you for a lovely day."

***

Gordon Van Stadt returned the next day to find his guest already installed as one of the family. He was as delighted as his wife to find Donald Belham such a personable young man, and was pleased to see Polly had taken to this stranger so soon after she had bid farewell to Paul, who he distrusted. Polly was his only treasured child, and he wanted the best for her.

He lost no time in engaging Donald in discussions about his vineyards, which he had started a couple of years ago, and should now be producing enough fruit for a respectable yield of wine.

Donald had seen the time approaching when wine drinking would become popular, and he wanted to sign up various vineyards, the produce to be bottled locally, and then exported all over the world through his wine business. He had spent the last few weeks in Capetown investigating the numerous farms, but they were already established wine exporters. A man who he met in the hotel in which Donald was staying suggested he should go up to Durban, and visit the vineyards just starting up in Natal, and get in on the ground floor as it were. After a few Cape Brandies he also gave Donald the names of farmers who he had heard were just planting up vines for the first time.

Donald felt he had been extraordinarily lucky to have picked the Van Stadt's vineyard for his first visit in Natal. He was entranced by the sight of the Drakensberg Mountains in the distance, the wide open spaces, and most of all, the captivating daughter of the house. Added to which Gordon Van Stadt was almost as enthusiastic as he was, agreeing with most of Donald's ideas without hesitation. With Margery so ill, he needed a new project to take his mind off a future without her.

Therefore their discussions were over quickly, far too quickly for Donald, and he was delighted when Margery suggested he should stay a few more days and get to know the vineyard and farm.

"It will be easier for you if you know the workings; how the grapes are picked and how the wines are made and so on. The big Wine Merchants like to know the provenance of each batch, and it would be a great bonus if you could say you know where it all came from, methods of production, and so on."

Discussing their guest in the privacy of their bedroom that night, Gordon suggested that Donald was a very personable young man and would do well for Polly.

"Just what I thought," said Margery. "They seem to get on extraordinarily well. You never know, it could be the answer to all our prayers."

Polly was delighted too. She had taken to Donald; in fact she felt she could fall in love with him easily, if the thought of Paul had not been in the back of her mind.

Donald had been there a week when Polly suggested taking him fishing. They had some well-stocked lakes around the farm, and she persuaded Minnie to pack up a picnic, as the lake she was aiming for was quite a way from the house.

They set off in the Jeep early in the morning when it was still cool.

Polly drove fast, as usual. Donald wondered where they were going, as the so-called roads gave way to dirt tracks, and then open veldt, until they came to a dip in the hills, and there, stretching before them, lay the most stunning vista. He could see a blue lake, rippling in the faint breeze, with a few shelter trees and bushes by the edge. Polly parked under a tree and Donald climbed out, still stiff from his ride the day before.

"How lovely," he exclaimed. They disembarked the fishing rods and picnic, and sat down on a rug to drink the cool lemonade Minnie had put in the picnic basket. Donald, who had done a bit of fishing before was eager to start, and was down by the water's edge, before Polly could suggest where they should go. She knew this lake, and parts of it were likely to hide the odd snake or two. Without saying anything to Donald she reached into the Jeep and extracted a small rifle, just in case.

They fished companionably for about an hour. There were plenty of trout, and they had two each when Donald saw a ripple in the water. Polly saw it at the same moment and shouted...

"Donald, run for the Jeep, quick!" As he hesitated she yelled...

"Run...snakes...drop everything and run!"

She lifted her gun as the snake's head appeared above the surface, black and menacing, making tremendous speed as it made for the shore, apparently gaining on Donald. Polly aimed and fired, but the snake still came on. Donald had no idea snakes could swim, much less hurtle themselves along the ground, and his heart nearly stopped as he realized the snake was going faster than he was. It was only about ten yards from him when Polly fired again. The bullet thudded into the ground just in front of the snake, and it stopped in its tracks, weaving its head from side to side. By that time Donald was safe in the Jeep, and watched as Polly stood quite still, the gun aimed and ready to fire, as the snake turned and slithered slowly back down the bank into the water. She waited, and then walked slowly backwards towards the car, keeping the gun ready to fire should the snake appear again.

When she reached the Jeep her legs seemed to give way, and Donald just managed to catch her as she collapsed, white as a sheet, but not unconscious.

"I should have known better, I remember last time we came here Daddy warned me that Black Mambas nest right beside the water in those banks. I should have taken you to the other side where it slopes into the water, Oh dear. I am sorry." She was trembling as she spoke.

"Are Black Mambas dangerous, then?"

"The most poisonous of all, and they can travel much faster than humans can run, and I should have known better," she repeated.

Donald's heart turned over at the sight of this gorgeous girl so upset, that it seemed only natural to take her in his arms. She clung to him, shaking, for a minute, and then looked up, her beautiful blue eyes glistening with tears.

"Daddy will never forgive me for nearly killing our honoured guest." she whispered with a watery grin. "Thank you for not being furious at being shouted at. We'd better drive somewhere else for our picnic."

"What about the fishing gear?" asked Donald.

"Oh, I'm not going down there again! We'll send a couple of boys up here to collect it. Jo-Jo would love to get off work for a time and come up to the lake. They will probably kill the Mamba if they see it. It almost certainly has a nest in the bank, with babies, and they will smoke them all out, rather like wasps. I read about those once. We don't seem to have *them* here, thank goodness. Snakes are bad enough!"

The next morning Donald went out with Gordon to inspect the new vines, which was just as well, as Polly felt strangely lethargic and nauseous. However by midday she was full of her usual bounce again. She put it down to the excitement of the snake episode, and did some work for her mother. However Margery had noticed, and when the same thing happened the next morning she decided to tackle Polly.

"I noticed that your period is overdue."

Polly was shattered. With all the excitement of Paul going, and Donald coming, she had not given it a thought.

"Oh God," she breathed, "It is rather late, isn't it."

Margery looked at her with concern.

"Have you—, I mean, could you have done something you shouldn't—with someone or, oh, Polly, what have you got yourself into?"

Polly blushed, recalling the passionate lovemaking the day Paul left. She had never thought of taking any sort of precautions; she would not know how to in any case. She believed 'it' couldn't happen the first time anyway, although she now realized that was simply an excuse. The idea of a baby coming before she was married in a long white gown and family veil, did not feature in her upbringing. Her mind whirled, while her mother drew in a little breath of pain. Life was extra precious to her now, and she had to think of some way to help her lovely daughter through this trauma.

"Darling, just let me be alone for a bit, and I'll think of something we can do. Meanwhile don't say anything to anyone."

She shut her eyes, and Polly tiptoed away to worry on her own.

Chapter 13

A day or two later Gordon had to go off again to Pietermaritzburg on business, and Donald, sensing Polly was a bit down in the dumps for some reason, suggested they should go on a ride up towards the Drakensburg mountains to get some cooler air. They decided to take a picnic and make a day of it.

Jo-jo saddled the horses, and as they were starting out he told them, "You'm betta look out, Msm Polly. Thems big cloud up them mountins. May be you find big rain afore you'se home agin."

Polly looked where he was pointing, but decided it would be nice to have a cool shower. It wouldn't hurt either of them. It was so dry and dusty that a spot of rain would be a welcome relief.

They mounted. Donald was becoming quite competent, having had a short outing every day, and he was now confident enough to ride a younger horse. Polly was on a spirited chestnut mare, which danced around as Minnie handed up the rucksack with their picnic.

"Have you put some lemonade in?" she asked Minnie.

"Oh Yes'm, Miss Polly, and your fav'rit chick'n sandwiches."

They rode off, waving to Margery, who was sitting in the swing seat on the shady stoep. They rode side by side, and Donald noticed Polly's mood had lifted as she hummed a contemporary tune to herself.

"Where are we going?" asked Donald after a while.

"I thought up to Bergdorf, and then perhaps to the river up there. It's usually beautifully cool as the water comes straight off the mountains. We could have our picnic there and have a swim."

Donald thought how fortunate that he had added his swimming trunks to his rucksack, and presumed Polly had packed her swimsuit too.

It was a long trek, and gradually the air became cooler as they climbed a gentle slope. It was a smooth trail, and Donald whistled quietly as they rode side by side. Polly recognised the tune and joined in, and they both felt the joy of singing together in the open air.

Donald thought they would be nearer the Drakensburg Mountains, but Polly told him it would take two days to reach even the periphery.

"In any case," she said, "we would have had to take really warm clothes if we went up there. It is literally freezing. But it won't be long," she added, "before we get to the river."

In fact, it was another hour, and Donald was beginning to wish he hadn't agreed to such a long ride; he was getting quite stiff and sore, and felt aghast at the thought of much longer in the saddle.

But as they turned a corner he realized why Polly had brought him to this location. Surrounded by large rocks and bushes, lay a perfect sward of grass, which gently led down to a wide inlet from the river; this had been created by boulders diverting the rushing foaming water, forming a perfect little bathing pool, overhung in places by long strands of greenery.

Donald gave a gasp of amazement.

"My God, this is out of this world!"

Polly smiled. "I discovered this last year. The water is a bit cold, but wonderfully refreshing after a long ride. Let's have a bathe first, and then see what Minnie has put in for our picnic."

Donald looked away as Polly began to pull her breeches down. He started to do the same and had managed to haul on his swimming trunks when Polly called out, "Are you decent?"

He saw she had changed into a modest one-piece bathing suit. It was a sapphire blue, the colour of her eyes he thought, and despite it being all-in-one it revealed every curve of her young body. He swallowed, and to cover his confusion he laughed.

"Is it safe to bathe here, or will I find a black mamba chasing me?"

Polly giggled. "Oh no. It's too cold for snakes up here, come on..." and she raced down the grass and jumped in. Donald followed her and when he hit the water he felt as if he had dived into ice. After the heat of the ride it was sheer exhilaration, and he struck out across the lake.

After a while he found Polly beside him, her hair plastered to her head in rough curls, her eyes shining with delight.

"Isn't it just something?" she asked.

"Glorious."

"We mustn't stay in too long first time. We'll have another swim after lunch. Race you to the edge!" and she struck out before Donald could catch his breath. It certainly was extremely cold, and they were both shivering as they heaved themselves out of the water.

"I'll rub you if you rub me." She handed Donald a towel and they spent the next few minutes drying each other, with good-natured banter, although Donald felt as if he would like to do far more than dry Polly's back.

"I'm starving," Polly exclaimed as she unpacked the picnic and held up a bottle of golden wine. "I smuggled a bottle of wine without Mum or Minnie seeing! We really ought to have had brandy to warm us, but I couldn't risk being spotted."

They devoured the food with all the hunger of well-exercised young, and sipped the delicious wine out of mugs provided for the lemonade that Minnie had packed. Replete, Donald lay back on the rug they had spread out on the grass, and closed his eyes.

Polly sat for a while, gazing at the mountains and thinking. She thought of Paul, and her predicament. She had truly thought she had loved him, and had given herself to him willingly. But meeting Donald had changed things. She thought

Donald was attracted to her and provided she could move 'things' along, all her worries could be solved. She felt she could love Donald more and more, and she knew her parents liked him very much indeed. He seemed to be at a loose end, with no real plans to travel on anywhere for the present. She gave a little sigh, and lay down.

They both must have slept for a short period, when a crash of thunder in the distance woke them both at the same time. Polly jumped and moved closer to Donald.

"I hate thunder," she wailed, and it seemed so natural for Donald to put his arms round her. Remembering the last time, with Paul, she stiffened, but then relaxed while he held her. He gently turned her to face him and even more gently, kissed her. They both felt a shock run through them and Polly clung even more tightly.

"Was that lightning?" she whispered.

"No, I don't think so. Just us," he laughed and hugged her. It was a long time since he had held a girl in his arms, and as he kissed her he felt familiar stirrings. He ran his hand gently up between her legs, parting them a little, feeling a slight shiver run through her. The sun was warm and the wine had been potent enough to prevent any inhibitions, and Polly was drowsy and quite incapable of resisting him as he helped her take off, first her blouse and then her breeches, laughing a little as he had to tug them over her feet. He took her in his arms again, kissing her as he divested himself of his shirt, and, gradually, the remainder of his clothes. Then they were skin to skin, and if Donald wondered why it was so easy, he was not so experienced in the way of women to realize she had been there before. She did give a little gasp as he entered her, which convinced him it was the first time, when he thought about it afterwards, but then...then it was just ecstasy under the African sky.

Another huge flash of lightning woke them, and as the first fat raindrops fell they both leapt to their feet and scrambled into their clothes. The sky was darkening and Polly knew from experience they were in for a real humdinger of a storm, as only Africa can generate. The horses were becoming restive, and they packed everything as fast as they could into their rucksacks. It became colder and colder, as the thunder roared in a way Donald had never heard in England, or for that matter in America, where he had experienced some extremely vicious storms.

"We had better find shelter if we can." Polly shivered, her teeth chattering. Neither of them had brought warm clothes in spite of Jo-Jo's warning.

"I'm almost certain there's a small farmstead up here somewhere," Polly said with a frown, her hair soaking wet and dripping. Donald hoped she was right as it had been a four-hour trek coming up, and he didn't fancy a long wet ride back to Whiteoaks.

They saddled up and Polly led the way out of the clearing and turned right down a narrow track. Donald was glad to see evidence of tyre marks, showing civilization was somewhere nearby. After about twenty minutes they heard a dog barking, and found a gate. This proved somewhat stiff to open, but Donald dismounted and heaved it until they could get the horses through. Ahead was a long white house with various outbuildings, some looking in need of repair. By that time the rain was teeming down and they were both completely soaked through. Donald dismounted and knocked on the green-painted door. He heard a noise inside and after a moment the door opened to reveal an elderly lady, dressed in an old-fashioned long dress with a pinafore.

"My, you poor things!" she exclaimed when she saw them. She nodded at Polly and said, "Come in, come in out of the rain. The boy, Tali, can help your husband put the horses in that shed over there, and then let himself in. Oh my Lordy me! You come along in, and get out of those wet clothes or you will catch your death. Oh my, oh my! What a to-do!"

The words "your husband" slid off Polly. She was trembling with the unaccustomed cold. But Donald smiled, and took the horses to the shed. It had straw in there and some hay in the manger. Tali, a strong looking native boy, found a bucket and filled it with water, and Donald showed Tali how to roll a handful of straw to give the horses a rub down, as he had sometimes watched Tom do. Thinking of Tom brought memories of Jean, which he quickly suppressed. This was his time and he must not let himself remember things he had vowed to put behind him. Shutting the barn door he left Tali drying the horses and ran through the still teeming rain to the house. He heard a huge clap of thunder and the sky was lit for a moment with a streak of lightning such as Donald had never seen before, as he reached the door and let himself in.

Polly was sitting in an armchair wrapped in a voluminous dressing gown. It was the colour of cornflowers and as she looked up at him he noticed her eyes were the same colour. Her blonde curls were tousled from the rubbing she had given them, and they stood up on her head in a cloud of gold. She looked like a doll and his mind gave a lurch as he remembered the doll he had given Elizabeth for her first birthday.

"Goodness, you look as if you've seen a ghost." She giggled.

"In a sort of way, I did; I must go and get out of these wet things. I wonder if our hostess could let me have some clothes while these are drying."

As if on cue Mrs Richards, (for that was her name), appeared with an armful of shirts and trousers.

"These belonged to my late husband. One or two of them should fit you. Go upstairs to the bedroom on the right and try them on."

He climbed the stairs and entered a large room, in the centre of which was an enormous double bed. He was so tired he felt he could have lain down and slept. But he was also hungry, and some delicious smells were coming from downstairs. He hastily drew on a flannel shirt and a pair of corduroy trousers which seemed to fit him well. He also found a set of tortoiseshell brushes on the dressing table by the window, and he ran a brush through his thick hair, which was still damp.

When he came downstairs Mrs Richards beckoned him to sit down at the table, and a large native woman emerged from the kitchen with a steaming bowl of thick soup.

"Sarah makes lovely soup," Mrs Richards told them, as she ladled it into bowls. "Now, you tuck in and it will stop any chills which you might have suffered." It certainly was delicious, and later there followed a dish crammed with chicken and vegetables, and after that some baked apples with cream.

"I am stuffed," sighed Polly, contentedly.

"So am I," echoed Donald.

As they sat round after this splendid meal, Mrs Richards told them a little of her history. She had come to live in the farm when she married her husband John. They were not blessed with children, but they worked hard and the animals were their family. Remote as it was, she told them, they did not miss company. They were happy together, and every so often people called in and were made welcome. Sadly John had caught a bad cold several years ago, and never got his strength back. For two winters he had struggled with chest infections, but one spring just when the weather was warming up, he caught his hand on a rusty nail. The resulting poison was too much for his poor health, and his diseased lungs finally gave in, and he died only two years ago.

"Didn't you feel like leaving this remote house and moving nearer friends?" asked Donald.

"No, not once," she answered, "we had been so happy here, and I have Tali and Sarah, who both look after me better than anyone could hope for, so here I stay. It is wonderful when people stop by, but I am content here with all my memories and the animals of course. And, if the storm is over tomorrow you can see my garden."

Polly suddenly sat up.

"Oh, goodness, have you a telephone? I should ring my mother to tell her we are safe!"

Mrs Richards showed her where the phone was, and they could hear Polly explaining to Margery they were being well looked after, and would be back the following day. She came back into the room,

"Mum was worrying where we had got to. Minnie was full of gloomy stories about people lost in storms! Luckily Mum is pretty sensible, and she knew we'd try and find shelter somewhere, and we were so lucky to find you!" She smiled at Mrs Richards,

It was then that the effect of the large supper and warm atmosphere got to Polly, and she gave a huge yawn.

"Oh, I'm so sorry." She smiled, "I really am exhausted, do excuse me!"

Mrs Richards rose and put her arm round Polly.

"You have had quite a day," she steered Polly upstairs, into the room on the right, saying, "I've put a nightdress out for you. Actually it is one I wore on my honeymoon; I was a good deal slimmer then!"

Polly found herself blushing. 'Husband', 'honeymoon', what had she got herself into, she wondered. She nearly blurted out the truth, but some instinct stopped her, and she just kissed Mrs Richard's velvety old cheeks and thanked her. Five minutes later she was sitting up in the huge double bed, dressed in the voluminous white gown, admiring the tiny tucks and inserts of lace and ribbons. She was wondering what memories it held of years long ago. Perhaps nights of passion, perhaps times of indecision, as she was feeling just now.

She heard a little tap on the door, and Donald poked his head round.

"Are you decent?"

Polly giggled. "Terribly. It was so sweet, she thinks we are on our honeymoon and she has lent me her own honeymoon nighty!"

"Do you mind?" asked Donald with a wry smile. He came over to the bed and sat beside her. "If you would rather, I'll go downstairs and confess everything, and ask for another bedroom."

Polly looked at him with those big cornflower blue eyes. "We simply can't disappoint the old dear," she said, and lay back, her curls spilling over the pillow.

Donald did not use the pair of striped pyjamas which had been placed on one side of the bed. The beautiful nightdress likewise was soon discarded. All Polly's doubts faded with Donald's first long lingering kiss, and if Donald had misgivings about making love to someone as young and innocent as Polly, they soon evaporated. She was as enthusiastic as he was experienced, and he led her to an ecstasy she had previously only dreamt of. Their initial fumblings under the African sky became a journey of discovery for Polly, and surprise for Donald after Jean who had been grateful for his attentions, and the girls he had paid to give him pleasure. After a while they both slept, until a huge thunderclap and streaks of lightning lit the room, as the eye of the storm passed and the elements returned renewed with raw energy. Polly clung to Donald, not entirely because she was frightened. This led to Donald comforting her, and with the natural progression of things, to yet another blissful interlude. The storm seemed designed to heighten their awareness of each other, and afterwards Polly felt that she must have been carried by the winds up to heaven.

The next they knew was a tap on the door, and Sarah coming in with a tray of tea and little shortbread biscuits for them. They dared not sit up, naked as they were, so Polly mumbled "Oh thank you Sarah. Could you put the tray on the little table?"

Sarah smiled knowingly, and did as she was told; then drew the curtains back, letting the sunlight flood in.

"A lovely day after the storm, ma'am."

They were soon dressed in their own clothes which Sarah had dried and put on the chair and before long they were tucking into an enormous breakfast. A young black girl who was serving turned out to be Sarah's youngest daughter, Tipi. She was shy but they discovered that she was Tali's brother, and there was another brother, Toji, who helped in the garden. There did not seem to be a father, and they did not like to pry.

After a few moments Mrs Richards appeared.

"Now, come and look at my garden." And she led the way out of the French windows, down a wide grass path with borders of vibrant flowers each side.

"They really loved that rain," she remarked. "Although some look a bit battered. I must get Toji to tie them up. He won't have to do any watering today!"

They turned a corner, and a beautiful vista of colourful shrubs and shady trees stretched out before them in a semicircle, creating a wonderful background to what could have been a stage in an open-air theatre. Polly gave a gasp of admiration,

"Midsummer Night's Dream!" she cried and Mrs Richards nodded.

"Yes, we used to put on plays for our friends. In fact all our friends took part, come to think of it. We had some wonderful times in those days." She might have added "when we were young."

After a cool drink on the stoep they made their farewells, promising to come again soon, and rode away, back to the house, where Polly's mother was anxiously waiting for them.

She was obviously relieved to see them again, and fascinated to hear their adventures, although, of course, there were some things they did not mention. She remembered Mrs Richards, and the fun they had all had when they were young. She gave a little sigh which only Polly heard, and she went over and hugged Margery.

***

Polly did not feel particularly well for the next few days, listless and somewhat nauseous. Donald noticed, and hoped she had not had second thoughts about their intimacy. It had seemed so natural at the time, and he was sure she had enjoyed it as much as he had. One evening after supper, when Gordon was helping Margery get to bed, they were sitting on the stoep enjoying the cool of the evening, he took her hand, and gently stroking it he asked her what was the matter.

Polly hesitated and then blurted out,

"Oh, Donald, I think I'm going to have a baby!"

***

After that everything seemed to accelerate in Donald's life. He had no idea what possessed him, but he found himself asking Polly to marry him. He did not even think what he was getting into. He only felt he had to prevent Polly from her parents' wrath, which was evident when they told Gordon and Margery the news. It was all so different from his first marriage that it did not seem wrong at all to be asking another girl to marry him. "Different name, different life," he persuaded himself, as he was plunged into pre-wedding plans.

Margery was the only person who realized the necessity of haste. She made her illness the excuse, which was readily accepted by friends. In fact she was secretly delighted that she would be able to see her daughter walk up the aisle, wearing her own wedding dress and veil, which she had lovingly kept for years.

Polly had been pregnant for seven weeks, and was still as slim as ever, although her breasts were becoming heavier, allowing her to fill the bodice of Margery's dress in a most becoming way.

David felt slightly awkward, having no friends in the country, but he had one or two contacts, and he chose a personable young man, who was to be the manager of his new South African company, to be his best man. He explained to the van Stadts that he had only an elderly aunt in England, who could not possibly make the journey, and having been the only child, with both his parents dead, (almost true); there was nobody else he could invite. This was accepted, and even welcomed, as the Van Stadts had plenty of friends.

Margery found Polly huddled on her bed the night before the wedding. She gently put her arms round her beloved daughter and rocked her as she had done when she was a small child and had got herself into trouble.

"You do love him, don't you?" she asked.

Polly sniffed, "Yes, I do, Ma. But I still wonder what I'll feel when Paul comes home again. I'm sure it is his baby, though Donald and I, you know..."

"Yes, I do know, and I also know sometimes one cannot help oneself when it comes to love. But one thing you must promise me, you must never tell Donald, and you must always think of the child as his."

"Oh Ma, I won't ever let on, even if the baby is the spitting image of Paul!"

"Well, Donald hasn't ever met Paul, and he will think red hair comes from our side of the family!" They both laughed.

Saturday January fourteenth dawned bright and clear, with the usual hint of the heat which would spread through the day. As guests had to come from some distances, the van Stadt's rondavels were all filled to overflowing and a party atmosphere prevailed from first light. Donald had been banished, along with Jed, his Best Man, to a neighbouring farm for a couple of nights, and he was surprised how much he missed Polly.

He had travelled down to Durban to equip himself with a cool white suit, and other necessities. His Wine business seemed to be flourishing, with several vincyards signed up to supply him exclusively. Satisfied, he visited a nightclub, but the girls were not a patch on Polly, so he left early to return to his hotel to compose a letter to Jean. He had written before once or twice, and had managed to find people to post them for him from all over the world.

Dear Jean, I hope you and the children are managing. Don't forget I have arranged for you to draw as much as you need from the bank in Wadebridge. I trust the children are well. I am moving all round, Africa at present, so don't know when I'll be able to write again. Please do not worry about me, and don't try and reach me, it would be pretty impossible. Life continues to be interesting, I can't say I miss St. Wraich, but I do think of you. David.

England

Chapter 14

The letter had come yesterday, dropping through the post box, just as if it was one of those catalogues for shoes or garden implements. It had a South African stamp, and David's easily recognisable writing, as if he couldn't wait to finish one word before going on to the next. Jean had been alone in the house, Ellen having taken the children out for a walk and May had the day off. She had sat down in the hall and tried to catch her breath as she had slit the envelope open with shaking fingers. It had been short and very much to the point. No personal details, the only special sentence being "I do think of you," which she had read over and over. Hearing the children returning she had hastily slipped it into her pocket, where it had lain all day. Now it was the next morning and she saw it beside her on her bedside table where she had put it the night before; it almost seemed a rebuke. Nothing whatsoever in it about James his firstborn's birthday, which was today. Had he deliberately chosen to snub them all? Of course, written in January, perhaps he would realize later and send something. Not that he had remembered last year, although she had received two letters before. Hardly letters, one was a postcard posted in Egypt, and the other about eight months ago, told her he was still travelling and was posted in India but no other details. James was five today, and would soon be asking why he did not have a Daddy like other boys. Of course Tom had been like a father to both children and they adored him.

Jean sighed and began to get dressed. Tom, she knew, would like to be their proper father, and last year he had asked her again to marry him. Just when she felt she might give in to being cherished, one of David's communications had arrived, proving he was still very much in the land of the living. She dreaded telling Tom again, as she knew that he hoped his erstwhile friend would free her from this burden of being a wife to a phantom husband. She realized that Tom felt that if David did not want to live with Jean, he should do the decent thing and give her a divorce so that she could find happiness again. And they both knew where that should be; in Tom's arms, as he had yearned for, for so long.

She had just finished dressing when what appeared to be a tornado swept into the room, followed by a smaller but equally boisterous whirlwind.

"It's *my* birthday and I'm *five!*"shouted James.

"James fife, James fife," echoed Elizabeth.

She swept them up into her arms. "How could he miss all this?" she thought, hugging them both.

"Come on, I think there are some surprises for someone who is five today!" and they all trooped downstairs.

It was a joyous day. First of all they visited Grandpa, who was very frail in both body and mind, but loved to see the children for a short time every day. He had gone downhill fast since David left, and could not really understand why his son was not there. Most days he enquired when David would be coming to read to him, and she had given up trying to explain the situation to him. He was sitting up in bed waiting for something he knew was going to happen, but he could not recall what.

Jean kissed his old furry face and said brightly, "Here are the children, Uncle George. James is five today!"

He smiled benevolently at the three of them, and they dutifully gave him a kiss. It was a morning ritual, and as he really had no idea what day it was there seemed no point in trying to explain. As small children do, James and Elizabeth totally accepted their grandfather as he was, and did not wonder why he had no presents or cards for them.

"Ellen will bring your breakfast up soon," Jean told him, and they all trooped out again.

When they reached the dining room, she let James unwrap his presents before trying to make them sit down for breakfast.

A bright red tractor, a football, and a football jersey awaited the birthday boy. There was also a card from Uncle Tom. Inside was a message which Jean read out loud, "After the milking I will come and wish you a Very Happy Birthday, and bring you a present!"

"Ooh, I wonder what it is, Mummy,"

"Well, eat up your cornflakes and then we'll be able to see." Silence reigned, except for dutiful munching. Their milk was hastily drunk, and marmite toast demolished.

All of a sudden a man shouted outside the window. "James, Happy Birthday!"

Tom was standing there, with a very small pony. It was light brown, with a nose the colour of porridge, and a dark mane and tail. Jean opened the French windows, in spite of the cold, and they all trooped out.

"James, this pony is my present to you. Happy Birthday!"

James went bright pink. He had longed and longed for a pony, ever since Tom had put him up on the back of the old horse the Truckles had kept to help cart things round on the farm. He stood there transfixed, and tentatively stroked the mealy nose, which was soft as velvet.

"Mine," he breathed.

Jean glanced over at Tom. He was looking so proud of James, just as if he was James's father, which indeed he seemed to be nowadays. The children knew him better than their own father, who was no more than a photograph in Mummy's bedroom. James had taught them everything they knew in their short lives and she felt so grateful to him for stepping into David's shoes in such a natural and unassuming manner. If he moved into their house he could not be more part of their lives than he already was now. He smiled at her as if he knew what she was thinking. Once again she was dreading telling him about David's letter.

Tom spent a large part of the day with James and the pony. He had arranged for the general farm work for that day to be carried out by his farmhand, Rob, so that he could teach James how to ride. His feet would hardly reach the stirrups, but he seemed to have a natural balance, and once up in the saddle it took a lot of persuasion to get him off. After a good amount of discussion James decided the pony should be called "Mousie," as Jean had been reading a book to them, (knowing what was coming), called "Moorland Mousie" about a pony that had a mealy nose. He could talk of little else, and fell asleep that night with a blissful smile still on his face, having told his mother, "That was the bestest day in my whole life!"

Tom came up to The Old Rectory later on that evening, his excuse being that he wished to check on Mousie. Jean accompanied him out to the orchard, leaning on the gate while Tom ran his capable hands over the pony's flanks and rubbed his furry ears, Mousie giving a sigh of contentment. Obviously all was well and he came back to lean on the gate beside Jean.

"Now you can tell me. What is troubling you?"

Jean swallowed. She might have guessed. Tom was so sensitive where she was concerned he had obviously realized something was worrying her.

"Oh, Tom, I've had another letter." And Tom put his arms round her, rocking her gently.

"Can you show me?" he asked. Jean did not have to tell him the letter had come from David, and she knew how contemptuous he felt about his old friend. She drew the letter out of her pocket and handed it to Tom. He read the cold note slowly. There were no indications of where David was living, no mention of his eldest son's birthday, and no declarations of love. It was a cold missive, designed to keep Jean at arm's length, but not letting go either. Thoroughly selfish and self centred, 'as always.' The sentiment hovered unsaid between them.

"Come inside darling, you need a stiff drink," he said to Jean. It was the first instance he had called Jean 'darling', but the time had come to speak openly of his love for her. He had stood on the sidelines so often, watching Jean hurt. David had been his best friend, but that closeness had evaporated when David left so abruptly with no explanation to any of them. He knew just what his mother thought about David. "Spoilt brat; he always was, and always will be, mark my words."

Jean sank onto the sofa and Tom brought her over a brandy. He poured himself a beer and came over to sit beside her.

"You know how much I have always loved you Jean. Can we put David behind us and get on with our own lives? I do so want to take care of you and the children. They seem like mine anyway." He grinned ruefully. "I think they see me as their dad. They know me better than their own father anyway. Of course I want to marry you, but first we must get hold of David's solicitor, and you must get a proper divorce, so that we can be man and wife in the eyes of the law."

Jean gave a great shuddering sigh, which tore at Tom's heartstrings. He realized it was too big a decision to settle just then, after a tiring day, so he put his arms round her shoulders and started to kiss her. Gently at first, but passion, which had been missing in Jean's life for so long, broke through her carefully nurtured defences and she responded to Tom's caresses with an abandon which took them both by surprise.

"I think" she murmured, with a twinkle in her eye, "we'd better go upstairs or Ellen will get a shock if she happens to come in!"

That evening was a revelation to both of them. It had all been so long in coming that Tom found it hard to hold back. Jean was nervous, but the unaccustomed drink and Tom's gentleness made their loving a relaxed yet passionate experience.

They both were overwhelmed by the unexpected joy they gave each other. And when afterwards, with Tom tenderly stroking her damp hair back from her eyes, Jean whispered, "Thank you, my darling Tom," he felt happier than he had ever thought possible.

Tom went home later, after they had decided to take steps towards a permanent split with David. Legally, they believed it could be arranged after four year's separation and David had been gone for two.

Meanwhile in the coming months they managed to enjoy each other's company. Tom's parents had a good idea what was going on. As they had always wanted Jean for Tom, they felt it was worth the waiting for an official divorce, and shut their eyes and ears to the comings and goings of the two lovers. Tom spent a lot of his time at The Old Rectory, without his farm work being unduly neglected. Ellen too, was delighted by the romance, and discussed the progress endlessly with May. The village thought their own thoughts, but would never disapprove of anything Jean got up to, and, in any case, they had seen it coming for months.

South Africa
Chapter 15

Donald decided to take Polly to Durban for their honeymoon. He had booked a suite at the Grand Hotel, the biggest and most luxurious hotel, right on the beach front. The rollers coming in were spectacular to watch, and exhilarating to dive through and feel their power battering their bodies as they plunged through the waves. Donald hired some surf boards, which were just starting to become popular, and the sight of Polly, golden curls flying, her beautiful body clad in a forget-me-not blue swimsuit, made him think how lucky he was to have won this gorgeous creature for his own. Later, lying on their big double bed, he had the same effect on her.

They spent four days in Durban, and then drove down the coast to a sleepy little place just beyond Port Elizabeth, with sheltered coves and a calm blue sea lapping the golden sand. David had rented a small cottage right on the shore, and they were cared for by a wonderful couple, who kept the place spotless, produced meals when asked and were thoroughly discreet. Polly and Donald just lived for the present and each other for a week, before they had to pack up their things reluctantly and head back to Draken River and Whiteoaks.

***

Margery was sitting on the stoep waiting for them to arrive, and they were both shocked at her appearance. She looked painfully thin, almost like a skeleton already, and so pale with no colour in her shrunken cheeks. Polly was devastated that she could have gone downhill so fast. But the fact remained she had lived for the wedding. She could let go now. It was wonderful to see her darling daughter so happy and fulfilled. She could hardly bear the thought of not seeing her first grandchild, but also she was finding it increasingly difficult to tolerate the pain of the cancer, which was devouring her body. She could let go now.

Gordon, who had at last accepted the truth that Margery's illness was terminal, had engaged a nurse to care for her in her last days. Only a week after she had returned, Polly was called in to Margery's room to say goodbye to her mother.

Margery whispered to her, "Polly, my darling. I am so happy for you."

Polly choked back tears. There seemed so much to say and no time to say anything. But she felt she must be brave and strong.

"Oh, Ma, I am so happy with Donald. He is a wonderful husband, and you never need worry about me, or the baby. We will look after Dad for you, too."

"And I know, my darling," Margery whispered with difficulty, "I will always be with you. Now I just want to sleep for a bit..." Her eyelids drooped, and Polly tiptoed out as the nurse came in.

Margery died peacefully three days later, and Donald felt this sad interlude in their lives was such a contrast to the joyous days of their honeymoon, and that the memories of those carefree days had been washed away by Polly's tears.

But life had to go on, and Donald became more and more involved in his wine business, and visiting the various vineyards with which he had signed contracts. Polly found herself in Margery's shoes, as the household organisation fell on her young shoulders. Minnie and the other staff were a great help to her, but like most native servants, they needed constant supervision and direction, and with the baby growing apace inside her, she soon became tired and rather fractious. Donald, remembering Jean's first pregnancy, tried to be understanding. But the comparison between their carefree honeymoon, and living with an increasingly bulky and tired wife, did not suit him at all.

"Can't you relax and come and talk to me sometimes?" he asked plaintively one evening. Polly felt he was being unfair, and rounded on him.

"If you did a bit more to help, it might be easier," she snapped, and they had their first monumental row, shouting all sorts of things which they did not mean at each other. Polly broke down, and Donald, feeling a twinge of remorse, took her in his arms and promised to try and help a bit more. Money being no problem, he insisted on two more servants. Luckily Minnie suggested two of her relations, and the trouble was solved for the moment. But a row is a row, and Polly had never been opposed before; Donald had also been thoroughly spoilt by his parents, and had led an easy life, usually entirely to his own satisfaction. Recalling his arguments with Jean, it all seemed frightenly familiar and not at all the life he had envisaged with Polly.

Gordon also proved to be a problem. Working the farm, never speaking unless spoken to and generally completely lost without Margery. Polly felt she had to cheer him along, devoting more time to him than Donald.

"Only while he is getting over Ma's death," she explained, when Donald remonstrated she was neglecting him.

At least the weather was getting cooler. Snow appeared on the tips of the mountains, and infiltrated down into the valleys. They even had some frost one night in the middle of June. Polly, who was getting noticeably large and cumbersome, welcomed the cool days as she dragged her way around. Donald did not remember Jean being so huge after barely eight months. But Polly assured him that she was sure it was all fluid round the baby, and he accepted that.

Just when he was sure they had at least another month to go, Polly began having labour pains.

"Much too early," she said through gritted teeth, trying to convince herself as much as Donald that this was the truth. Donald worried, but the pains receded after a bit, and he went off to a meeting in Pietermaritzburg, persuaded by

Polly it was only a false alarm. As soon as his car had driven off Polly gave a yell of anguish and Minnie came waddling into the room as fast as her fat legs would allow.

"Oh my, Msm Polly, you started the babby comin' then?"

"It seems so, Minnie," Polly groaned. "Ring for Doctor Blake, Minnie; *now*." she yelled as another searing pain ripped through her.

As far as Polly was concerned, it was a nightmare morning. Doctor Blake arrived within an hour, and after examining her he said with a twinkle, "Not much wrong here, my dear. Just quite a big baby for eight months! But you were pretty large yourself, when I helped your mother in the same situation!" He had brought Polly into the world and there was not much he did not know about the van Stadt family.

Later, remembering those words, Polly wondered briefly if she had also been conceived before her parents' wedding.

Maggie made her way from darkness into light, just as Donald drove up the drive. Seeing the doctor's car there, he raced inside, as his child emerged with a penetrating yell of fury. Donald was up the stairs two at a time, coming to a standstill at the bedroom door, shy of intruding at this very private moment. Minnie was standing by the bed as Doctor Blake bent over Polly. He was saying to Polly, "Well done, you have a little girl!" He noticed Donald and beckoned him forward. Polly was looking dishevelled, her curls damp and her huge eyes wide with wonder. She reached out to Donald as Doctor Blake cut the cord, and Minnie, having wrapped the baby in a blanket, handed the precious bundle to Polly. Donald looked at them both with amazement and for once in his life, gratitude. Their daughter was beautiful. She had Polly's curls, but they were a glorious auburn colour, and her eyes when she opened them were a deep sapphire blue. Polly almost blushed, as she realized her little daughter was the spitting image of Paul de Freyburg.

***

Donald was amazed at himself for behaving like a besotted idiot over Maggie, as they had decided to call the baby. He did not remember feeling so protective when Jean had their children. In fact he recalled being rather hurt when he was no longer Jean's Number One, when she had spent all the time looking after his son, and then his daughter, and apparently having little time for him. But Polly was soon up and about, and they engaged Laliya, a reliable African friend of Minnie's, to look after Maggie. They could both enjoy watching Maggie develop from a newborn into a bouncing baby, without any of the chores like changing nappies and dealing with screaming sessions. Maggie was a noisy infant, and liked constant attention, and as all native servants adored babies she was thoroughly spoilt by everyone. Polly started off by feeding her herself, but it was too restricting for her, and she soon weaned her onto a bottle so that she could spend more time with Donald. They were still infatuated with each other, and the temporary suspension of lovemaking only served to make it more exciting when they resumed. After the weather became warmer they often escaped up to the picnic place where they had first made love, Polly discovering new ways to give pleasure to Donald. Fortunately the new methods of birth control were now available in South Africa and all he felt he had to do was make sure Polly took her 'pills' as she should, and at that time they felt their somewhat delayed honeymoon would never end.

Donald often took Polly with him when he travelled, and if they never went to England she did not wonder why. They tried not to leave Whiteoaks for long periods, as neither of them wished to miss more than a few days of Maggie's development. When they were home they watched her for hours, and she particularly enjoyed being bounced endlessly on Donald's knee, while he sang "Ride a Cock Horse" to her over and over again.

However, Polly did have to organise the household, and that meant seeing that her father, distraught after the death of Margery, ate properly and was generally cared for. Donald ruefully remembered his own father, and how Jean had had to cope with them all. Presumably she still was, as he never had heard from his solicitors in London that George had passed away. He had left careful instructions to be told about any death or momentous event, but he had no intention of returning, at least not for a long time. Life continued in a delightful and carefree way and before they knew it Maggie was looking forward to her third birthday. She had been promised a pony and she looked out of the window eagerly for days before, watching for signs that her present had somehow materialised in the night.

"Mummy, is it my birfday today?" she would ask every morning.

"Not yet darling, another few days," Polly would tell her.

Donald had spent weeks finding the right pony. Size, colour and of course temperament all mattered. One day, visiting a stud not too far from Whiteoaks, he met a knowledgeable young man who seemed to know instinctively what was needed, and led out a small brown pony with a dark mane and tail and a mealy-meal nose. Donald immediately settled the deal, and asked the young man to bring the pony up to Whiteoaks on the twenty-sixth of July, as early in the morning as possible.

"My daughter is three that day, and she looks out of the window every morning to see if her birthday present has somehow appeared! It will be such a wonderful surpr... I say, are you all right?"

This last as the young man had turned white and staggered a little.

"Oh yes, sir," he said, "It's just that I know Whiteoaks well. I've only just returned from being in the Army overseas, and I was coming over to see them anyway. How are they all? Mrs Van Stadt was pretty ill when I left."

"I'm afraid she died just after the wedding. She was so thankful to be able to live to see Polly married."

"Ma...Married? Who to?"

"Why, me actually."

There was a short silence, and then Paul seemed to pull himself together and shook Donald's hand.

"Amazing! Polly married, who'd have thought it! When you get back tell her Paul de Freyburg is back and bringing over the pony. She'll be chuffed to hear I'm back in one piece after all this time!"

"That will be great. She never mentioned you, but I know she'd love you to stay and see Maggie's reaction to the pony, and perhaps you could come over and give my daughter a few riding lessons. Polly would be grateful too, as she doesn't have a lot of time these days. I really don't know a lot about horses anyway, except as a method of getting round the place and picnics with Polly. See you on the twenty-sixth for breakfast."

Watching him ride away Paul swallowed, gave a thoughtful sigh and went in to telephone Polly.

After the short telephone call Polly dashed up to their bedroom, slammed the door and flung herself down on the big double bed. She was unbearably shocked, but at the same time grateful to Paul for warning her. If Donald had told her casually that Paul de Freyburg was back and coming over to Whiteoaks, she might have given everything away. As it was now, she would be forearmed against the shock, and could be quite natural when she heard his name mentioned. "Oh Lord, what if Donald sees Maggie in him?" she thought, She had grown more and more as she had remembered Paul, and she was convinced her first-born was Paul's daughter. The dates were a perfect match. Luckily Donald had never seen anything untoward and had never ever questioned Maggie's parentage.

Hearing Donald's car in the drive she leapt up, ran a comb through her curls and ran downstairs to greet him.

"You'd never believe who I met today," he said, giving her a hug. "A young chap called Paul de Freyburg. He's bringing over you know what." (The last as Maggie appeared behind Polly).

"He said he knew you, and is looking forward to seeing you again. He's coming over on the day for breakfast."

"What day, Daddy?" piped up a little voice.

"Never you mind, Little Miss Know-it-all." And he looked at Polly and grinned.

Later, when they were alone Donald explained to Polly.

"I've asked this Paul chap to come and give Maggie some riding lessons after her birthday. I'm going to suggest she also learns how to care for the pony. Even with Jojo to grant her every whim, I think she should learn how to groom and look after the pony's needs as well as her own."

Quite soon Maggie woke upon a clear and sunny morning, with a touch of frost on the grass. She felt a sort of tingly feeling as she remembered that today was the day! She was warm and cosy, and any other day would have to be dragged from her bed, but she heard noises outside and she was up in a flash, kneeling on the wide windowsill. She rubbed off the frost on the windowpane, looked down and saw...a pony! The young man holding the bridle looked up to the little figure waving at him frantically. His heart gave a lurch as he saw a replica of the photograph in his parents' bedroom; curls like Polly's, standing up all over her head as Polly's used to. But they were dark red as his had been before the Army had shaved them off. The face that gazed down at him was the face in the photograph, and he felt a shudder of shock go through him. She was three today, this much Donald had mentioned, and a quick calculation had brought a thunderbolt of realisation. This enchanting mite could easily, must be, his own daughter. What had Polly been thinking of to marry Donald? Then he just as swiftly remembered he had gone away, not really bothering to write; always meaning to, but never quite getting round to it until it was too late. Poor Polly, she must have been desperate, her mother dying, and if her father had found out he would never have understood, or even sanctioned a marriage between the two of them. He had been the rough son of poor horse breeders, and she the daughter of a well-to-do family. He supposed the well-off personable young man appeared at the opportune time, and Polly had seized the moment in an agony of uncertainty and somehow engineered the marriage.

All this ran through his mind in the seconds he was waiting with the pony, before Polly, with Maggie in tow and Donald behind, opened the door. Maggie let go of Polly's hand and ran down the steps, her eyes shining, her auburn curls bouncing and her mouth (his mouth) grinning happily. She put out her little hand and stroked the pony's nose.

"What are you going to call her?" asked Paul.

She didn't hesitate. "Mousie," she whispered, "My own Mousie."

***

After Donald had telephoned him to arrange the time of delivery of the pony Paul had a good think. He could not bear the thought that Polly should be compromised by his appearance if Donald noticed his remarkable likeness to Maggie, so he decided to visit the barbers in Pietermaritzburg and change the colour of his hair. Actually, when Polly saw him that morning she could hardly contain her laughter. As he had been wearing his old Army cap when Donald first saw him, he felt it was safe in becoming a South African bleached blonde, like so many of his friends. He caught Polly's eye, and she had to cover up her mirth by bending down and pretending to buckle her sandal.

Paul was thankful that their first meeting after such a long time had passed so smoothly. He was confident enough to give her a wink while Donald was admiring Mousie with Maggie. Polly turned away, her heart bumping in the most alarming manner. She too went over to Mousie and stroked her silky neck.

"Would you like to have a little ride?" Paul asked Maggie, who, speechless with delight, merely nodded, and held up her arms for Donald to lift her into the saddle.

"You put your feet into the stirrups," Paul said.

"Of course I do," said Maggie, with scorn in her voice. "I've seen Mummy and Daddy do it hundreds of times you know!"

"Of course, how stupid of me," acknowledged Paul with a hint of amusement in his voice. "But now we will just make them fit," and he found himself trembling a little as he touched his daughter's little legs for the first time.

After that day Paul came over two or three times a week to give Maggie riding lessons. She progressed at an amazing rate, as if she had been born to it; hardly surprising considering her parentage. Polly was always there and they were careful to keep the proceedings on a light level. But Paul discovered he had not lost the love he had for her; in fact, if anything it was even deeper than before. Sometimes he turned to find her watching him, and he dared to think there was more than mere friendliness in her eyes. They recovered a little of their old banter, but often their eyes met across Mousie's neck as they walked each side, ready to rescue Maggie should she topple. Their favourite outing was to the fields where the young vines were growing. Being winter they had been pruned quite severely, and there was plenty of space between the rows for two adults and a small pony. Maggie progressed so well that one day Paul suggested that Polly should stand halfway down the row, and Maggie should ride Mousie all by herself from Paul to her mother. For Maggie this was emancipation indeed. She rode proudly and sedately down the row. Later, when she had learnt to trot, the space between Polly and Paul widened, and one day, to her utter joy, Mousie broke into a canter. Maggie's red cheeks almost matched her curls as she felt the wind in her hair for the few tense seconds as she rode between the two adults.

"Oh, Mummy, did you see me? Mousie went really fast! Can I go back and do it again?"

The weather was becoming warmer when Paul told Donald that he thought Maggie was ready to go on a 'proper' ride. Donald would have liked to have been there, but he was going up to Johannesburg early that day, for a week. He was sad not to go on Maggie's first long ride, but he knew she would be in safe hands with Paul, who he liked and trusted.

Although by then Maggie was competent enough, Paul decreed she should be on a leading rein "in case Mousie doesn't know the way." So the little party set off up the tracks towards the greening veldt. It was a safe route to take a novice, and easy to ride three abreast, and also simple enough to turn round and return home if Maggie seemed to be getting tired.

Every now and then Paul looked across at Polly, who was staring straight ahead with seeming concentration on the distant hills. Maggie chattered endlessly, oblivious of the tension between the grownups. Paul knew the route, in fact had ridden there often enough with Polly before he had left home. He murmured in a wistful voice, "Polly, remember when we came up here?"

Polly blushed a delicious rosy red.

"Of course I do you idiot. Every minute of that ride, just before you left," and she smiled a little for the first time since they had set out. "Watch it," she warned as Maggie was obviously taking in every word; and to Maggie, "Paul and I used to ride our ponies up here years ago, when we were both children, but I had quite forgotten him," she lied, while Paul put his hand up to hide a grin.

"Yes, little pitchers have large ears," and he sighed. "Now, come on, Maggie, we are going to have a little canter. So squeeze your knees right in, sit tight, and try not to bounce up and down too much."

That first canter was the highlight of the ride, as far as Maggie was concerned. Polly was not so sure, until she saw how all Paul's gradual tuition had paid off, and Maggie was completely at home in the saddle. Her little girl was flying along, completely oblivious of everything except the sheer joy of hooves pounding under her and wind in her hair.

Paul kept it short, although Maggie begged for more, and faster. "It will make Mousie too tired," he told Maggie, giving Polly a wink.

When they arrived back at the stables, though usually Paul had made Maggie watch how Jo-jo gave the pony a rub down before turning her into the field, she was obviously exhausted. "Go and find Lally and tell her to give you some milk," Polly told her. Lally was Maggie's name for her nanny,

Laliya, who had cared for her ever since she had come into the world, and adored her, without spoiling her. The adoration was mutual, and Polly knew they would not see Maggie until she was rested after her exciting experience.

When Maggie had disappeared inside the house Paul held out his hand to Polly. Silently and quietly he led Polly up the long grass slope to their special and secret place where he and she would meet before he went away. Reluctant to go with him at first, Polly felt as if her will had evaporated like a plume of smoke, leaving her helpless to decide anything for herself, much less resist this, her first, and now she realized, only love.

They looked at each other and Polly shuddered.

"What is happening? This is not right." she whispered.

"But doesn't it seem right?" Paul asked, drawing her to him in a gentle embrace. "We have never really been apart, you and I, even though other things and other people have come between."

Polly gave a shudder. "But what about Donald? I do, have, loved him. I know I was having your baby, but I sort of thought as you hadn't written, you had decided that you didn't..." and she burst into sobs.

After she had cried for a few moments she seemed to gather herself together. Paul was stroking her hair, feeling her golden curls run through his fingers as he remembered, when she confided, "Maggie is your baby. I knew she was there before I let Donald... you know...make love to me. And then I did fall for his good looks and he really is very sweet. I thought I could love him forever, and you were just a beautiful dream, which was part of me for always, but it seemed like a lovely story I had read, and I had to grow up quickly, and..."

Paul thought the tears were starting again, and he hugged her. His body was hard against hers, everything she remembered came back, only it was real this time, in the same place, almost the same time, but it was now, true, and there they were, repeating the love scene they had enacted three years ago. Both of them now more experienced, the garden not so stifling hot, more clothes had to be discarded, but still their loving had the same intensity that Polly had never found in Donald. This was true loving, each trying to give pleasure to the other, neither passive, but now using experience to enhance their passion.

Paul was overwhelmed and humbled and grateful all in one. Once again he had not planned to make love to Polly, but it seemed as natural as breathing, and gazing into each other's eyes afterwards neither of them felt they had committed any wrongdoing.

Once more before Donald returned, they were able to escape to their special haven at the top of the garden. Hemmed in by bushes, which had grown since they had first discovered it, they came together without any thought of the future. Heaven while it lasted, but the hours flew by and their idyll soon came to an abrupt end.

Donald had completed his work in Johannesburg, and eager to get home, had caught an earlier train. Alerted by the sound of his powerful car, just as they were preparing to depart their love-nest, Paul hastily snatched up Polly's clothes and said, "Quick, get these on and go on down as if you'd been for a stroll. I'll get out round the back; he won't even know I've been here."

But Polly, knowing she must be flushed from lovemaking, made for the stables, and after calming herself, and splashing her face with cold water from the stable tap, she wandered up to the house. She saw Donald before he saw her, and was momentarily overcome with guilt as she saw her handsome (and he *was* handsome), husband scooping Maggie up in his arms with joy.

"Daddy, I cantered really cantered, almost galloped, Mummy said," and she could see Donald hugging Maggie. At that moment he saw Polly, and he put his arm out to include her in his welcome.

"I hear we have a jockey in the family!" he said.

"What's a "jockey" Daddy?"

"A little girl who goes much too fast for her Daddy's liking," he answered.

They were a family again, but now it did not seem the same as it had before. Polly had to face the fact she had tried to hide from herself for so long. That Donald was the odd one out, and part, the main part, of her family was escaping through the back garden like a thief.

Chapter 16

Life carried on much as before, but it was not long before Polly, feeling unexpectedly sick early one morning, remembered she had forgotten to take her pills in all the excitement of Paul's re-appearance. Donald had made love to her the night after he had returned. Somehow she had managed to postpone it on that first night, giving a tummy ache as an excuse. When she was sick, Donald remarked with a sigh, "Well, you weren't feeling up to much yesterday, you must have eaten something which has given you a bug."

But as she felt absolutely fine later, she allowed Donald to take her in his arms and love her. Remembering her snatched moments with Paul, she almost shuddered when Donald entered her, but she hoped he would think it was ecstasy at having him back. She felt sad, remembering how she had always welcomed Donald into her arms, although she now realized he was a selfish lover, not always trying to give her pleasure, as Paul had, but taking it all for himself.

"What a life I will now have to lead," she thought, as she extricated herself quietly from Donald's arms. He, as usual, had gone straight off to sleep, without asking her if she had been satisfied. She could not help comparing her two lovers and finding her husband the one who was wanting.

The following morning Donald rose early, and she was just able to avoid rushing to the bathroom until he had gone downstairs. But three days later he heard her, and began to wonder.

"Do you think you could be pregnant again?" he asked. "What about your pills? Have you forgotten to take them or something stupid?"

Polly felt the tears well up at this last remark, said without kindness.

"I did actually run out the other day, and somehow didn't get the time to go to the chemist. But," she lied, "I didn't think it would matter, just for a few days."

"Well, it obviously did," he snapped, and flung out of the door. Polly tried to rise, which brought another bout of nausea. She retired back to bed, and curled up unhappily, her mind racing. Could this baby be Paul's again? It almost certainly was, and she found herself shivering with what could be anxiety, or perhaps even delight. She simply hoped this time it would not resemble Paul quite so noticeably.

Paul still came up to Whiteoaks twice a week, ostensibly to take Maggie for rides. Polly usually accompanied them, and when two rides had gone by without Polly appearing Paul asked Maggie if her mother was away.

"Oh no, she just doesn't feel very well in the mornings, but she's perfectly all right by lunchtime," Maggie informed him. Paul, knowing a little about the problem of pregnancy, his young cousin having recently produced a baby, was immediately concerned.

"Is your daddy here today?" he asked Maggie.

"No, he's gone off in the big car. I don't know where, he didn't even come and kiss me goodbye."

So, when they returned from their ride, which seemed shorter than ever today, Paul told Maggie he would come in and see her mother, and she must find Lally and ask her for some milk and biscuits.

Maggie dashed in, shouting for Lally, while Paul followed slowly into the sunny sitting room, where he hoped he would find Polly. Sure enough she was sitting on the wide flowery sofa, staring out of the window, her face the picture of utter despair.

She rose when she saw Paul, and, throwing caution to the winds, he enfolded her in his arms and cradled her head against his shoulder. After a moment she looked up with a watery smile.

"Paul, my love, I think we've been and done it again!"

"Does Donald know?"

"No, I don't think so. I really am certain it is our baby, but it could be Donald's if you know what I mean."

"I hope it is ours, my darling. I know you have to be a wife to Donald, but really and truly, one day I want to be your husband, lover, father to our children, everything."

"Yes, I know. I do so want that too. Oh, Paul, we have been idiots," and gave a deep sigh, but this time she had Paul's arms holding her.

***

All they could do was to carry on as normally as possible, and if Polly seemed at all dejected, Donald put it all down to her pregnancy. She loved riding, and when consulted, Dr Blake permitted her to go on gentle rides.

"No wild galloping or jumping, now, he told her, "I suggest you go out with Maggie, and keep to her pace."

This was adding fuel to the fire, as usually after each ride Paul and Polly could steal an hour or two on their own. Sometimes they would make love, and always Polly would feel herself carried to a kind of paradise which she felt she had never achieved with Donald. Sometimes they tried to work out how they could resolve the conundrum of an uncharted future. There never seemed to be an answer, but it was still wonderful to be together. When it was too cold they met in the stables, with the excuse that Mousie needed looking at for some reason, any reason, to give them an excuse to be near each other.

Jo-jo noticed their meetings, and became worried, but it was not his place to wonder what Msm. Polly got up to when she thought no-one was watching. Minnie also, was concerned. She had known Polly since she was born, and she also knew that she was headstrong, stubborn and always determined to get her own way, one way or another. Minnie had noticed how she looked on the day when Maggie was going riding, and she sometimes watched Polly coming in, long after Maggie had returned, with a flush on her cheeks and stars in her eyes. Minnie dreaded the day when Donald would notice. So far he had carried on as he normally did, seemingly delighted to see his wife, and apparently glad to see her so happy and full of the joys of living, in spite of her pregnancy.

Donald thought, (or rather, he didn't reflect unduly), that their ostensibly mutual love for each other was a glorious part of their life which would go on forever, and perhaps having another baby like his darling Maggie was a price he had to pay.

But babies do grow, and before long Polly's "bump" became a large and heavy part of her body, and she had to give up the rides "with Maggie," and just watch in envy as Paul rode off with his daughter twice a week, all the love and yearning in her eyes following the two people she loved most in the world going off without her. Paul would look back at her, and she, too, was aware of the longing and concern in his face. Often they managed to touch, as they adjusted a girth which did not need adjusting, or bent down to feel Mousie's fetlocks when there was nothing to feel. Maggie did not notice when they sometimes snatched a kiss or hugged each other. She was hugged and kissed by both of them, and it seemed quite a natural motion to a small child. Besides, the weather was getting cold again, which gave much relief for Polly, but less reason for her to be outside. The end of April became quite warm, although more snow than ever appeared on the top of the Drakensburgs. Polly had a tremendous turn-out of cupboards in the kitchen, driving Minnie round the bend, but she recognised the symptoms, and kept quiet, replacing everything when she had persuaded Polly to go and rest. Donald, too, realized that Polly was not behaving rationally, and recalled the days before Maggie arrived, when everything had been turned upside down.

"For heaven's sake, Polly darling," he said, "let's go for a little stroll. It really is a lovely first of May. Can you manage to walk as far as the stables to see if Mousie's all right? Paul hasn't been for the last few days, and Mousie is getting too fresh for Maggie to take out, I think."

They turned the corner into the stable yard, and someone came out of Mousie's stable. Obviously Paul had had the same thought. Polly's heart seemed to convulse when she saw him, and the baby within gave a huge jump as if it knew its father had appeared.

"As I haven't been for a few days, I thought I would check on the horses, as I know you're busy." He addressed Donald, but Polly knew he was saying to her, "I just had to see you." She looked at him, knowing that nothing could be said just... A spasm shook her.

Donald expressed his gratitude to Paul.

"Thanks, Paul. It really is good of you. Maggie's cold is nearly better, and she will soon be badgering one of us for a ride. But I don't think I can leave Polly at the moment."

"Shall I take Thunder, and Mousie with a leading rein, and give them both a good gallop for you?" Paul suggested.

"That would be...Heavens, what's the matter, Polly?" as Polly, wrapping her arms round her large tummy, almost collapsed with a groan.

"Oh God, I think the baby has started. I'd better get back to the house. Help me... Somehow I don't think I can walk!"

Both the men stepped forward and put an arm round her each side, helping her stagger back. But it was the left side which Polly leaned against most, the side which Paul supported. Both almost wished the short journey back to the house had been longer, pains or no pains. They helped her upstairs, and into the bedroom. What Paul would have given to have had the right to stay there only Polly knew. As it was, after gently helping her on to the bed he simply whispered "Good luck," and left, feeling slightly resentful of Donald. Actually, Paul felt, as he let himself out, I have more right to be with Polly than Donald. He went back to the stable, saddled Thunder, attached a leading rein to Mousie and trotted off, before breaking into a wild gallop as soon as he reached open country. Then, coming to an abrupt halt he dismounted, buried his head in Thunder's thick winter coat and wept.

***

Polly's baby took her time, and gave her (and those attending her), a few anxious moments. Donald could not bear it, and went out. He saw his car in the drive where he had left it earlier, and thought he would take a spin to get away from all the paraphernalia of birth. He told himself he was only getting in the way, and that was faintly true, as Dr Blake more than once told him to go downstairs and pour himself a drink. Polly would have liked to hold his hand, but more than anything she knew that, had Paul been there he would have helped her, instead of moaning that it was taking so long and couldn't the doctor hurry things along, not for Polly's sake, but because Donald himself wanted it all to be over. After he had left, Dr Blake noticed that Polly visibly relaxed.

"Ah well. Maybe some husbands are not good at these things," he thought, and got on with assisting Polly to produce, in the early hours of May the second, another beautiful little girl. This time her hair was much darker than Maggie's, but still with that telltale hint of red. A little later she heard the car, and Donald came pounding up the stairs. In spite of it being the middle of the night, Jo-jo had met him by the front door.

"Master, I tink babbies come. I did hear babbie's cries a littl' while back, you'm best go in, I'll tek car to g'rage. You go."

Donald came over to the bed, where Polly lay, her golden curls damp with exhaustion, but smiling.

"Look, we have another little girl," and showed him the tiny bundle in her arms. Donald bent over, and gazed into two bright eyes looking up at him, with a faintly stern gaze.

"I think she disapproves of me!" He smiled, and kissed Polly. "Well done, I see the red hair has got through once again. I did hope this one would have golden curls like her mother!"

"I don't know where it hails from, but I think my aunt had red hair, didn't she Dr Blake?"

Dr Blake knew an appeal when he heard one, and replied without hesitation,

"Oh yes, she was a real firebrand," which was not exactly a lie, as Annabel, Margery's sister, had been quite wild in her youth. Donald did not see the gratitude in Polly's eyes.

Maggie was allowed in to see her little new sister the next morning, and thoroughly approved.

"We'll have to get another pony for Ellie," she said.

They had had a lot of discussions on names for the new baby in the weeks before, and had decided on Eleanor, if it turned out to be a girl, swiftly changed by Maggie into "Ellie." She had been longing for a sister, and was delighted.

***

After a few weeks of living in the midst of what he called "baby worshipping," Donald took himself off on one of his trips. He usually telephoned Polly every day, telling her where he was off to next. He was fascinated by the intricacies of vine production, the tending, pruning, and general care of the precious bushes, which would eventually produce the South African wines. These were becoming more and more popular, largely due to his expert guidance on public relations, and the importance of marketing. Cape Brandy had been a popular drink in South Africa for many years, but the reds and whites were gradually taking its place, especially as they were significantly less expensive. Of course, the cheap rough brandy produced by small producers would always have its place amongst the poorer people. But those who were "on the up" were taking to wine as a more acceptable drink.

Donald found the money was flowing in, without much help from him, and became somewhat fed up with the marketing side of the business. Likewise, after he had seen one vineyard after another and listened carefully to the same spiel on growing the vines to perfection, he became bored stiff and wondered if this was all life had to offer.

Polly, meanwhile, was enjoying being the centre of attention at Whiteoaks. Her father Gordon had moved out of the house after Margery had died, and lived in a small cottage on the estate. He did not come to the house much, firstly feeling he should let the newlyweds settle in by themselves and then, when Maggie arrived, he found the noise of a child too much for his newly found peace. He liked Donald, and was thankful Polly had settled down with such a good looking young man, after she had seemingly become besotted by that horse breeder's son Paul.

However, visiting the family one day, he discovered that Paul was back, apparently friends with Donald, and teaching Maggie to ride. He had hardly recognised Paul who was now a man, rather than the callow youth he remembered. His hair had been bleached almost white by the sun, and Maggie seemed to adore him almost as much as she treasured Mousie.

But Gordon was uneasy to think that Paul was around and obviously completely accepted in the family circle. Also he noticed that Polly still had a soft spot for Paul, but did not appear to have told Donald that she had known him in the past. It was all very strange but he did not want to rock the boat, and vowed he would only tackle Polly about the situation if circumstances warranted it.

About three days after Ellie was born, he walked up to the house to meet his new granddaughter. Maggie saw him coming, and dashed out to meet him.

"Grappa, we've got a new baby! She's called Ellie, and she is tiny. Much too small to go riding yet, but Mummy says we will get her a pony as soon as she is as big as me," and with that she took hold of Gordon's hand and led him in to the nursery, where Laliya was just putting Ellie back in her cot, having changed her nappy after Polly had fed her.

"You see," Maggie explained, "Mummy has lots of milk in her fronts, and so Ellie gets her lunch that way. She's not big enough for a spoon yet," and with that riveting information she led her 'Grappa' over to the cot.

Gordon bent over the cot. Large brown eyes gazed up at him, rosy cheeks and a tiny button nose, and a mop of deep red hair. He was shocked, but managed to hide it from both the knowing eyes of Maggie and Laliya. The little mite lying before him was the image of a certain young man who lived not too far away, and had obviously been a bit more than just a friend of the family.

"Isn't she pretty?" said Maggie, with a proprietorial air, and he looked round to answer her. It hit him like a bulldozer. This beautiful child, his first grandchild, was not Donald's child any more than the baby was. It shook him to the core. He could not imagine how Donald had not seen the resemblance; He had, however, always thought Donald was a self-centred young man and he only supposed he had never visualised anyone but himself being the father of his children. He did not know how to face Polly when he saw her, but he felt it was not the time or place to probe. He just folded her in his arms and whispered,

"You have two beautiful children, Polly my pet. Your mother would have been so proud." This brought tears to both their eyes, and the moment passed. Time enough to find out the truth and this is not the time, Gordon thought to himself.

But it soon was.

***

When Ellie was three months old her hair changed colour to a wonderful auburn shade. She was beautiful, in a way that Maggie could never hope to be, and perhaps too much the centre of attention. Maggie began to show signs of jealousy, and in her distress turned to her friend Paul more and more.

"I want to go out riding on Mousie, with Paul," she said every day. Paul would have dropped everything for Maggie, but even he could not neglect his own work so much. In any case he felt it was dangerous to be too often at Whiteoaks. He had seen the looks which Gordon gave him when they met, and he realized how the two little girls bore a strong resemblance to the photograph of him as a child, and when he met Gordon he felt he must have also noticed the likeness in some way. But nothing was said, and he visited his barber in Pietermaritzburg often to keep the tell tale deep red hair at bay.

Polly managed to keep Donald's attentions to the minimum, which he found hard to understand. Polly had been so ardent in the early days, but this had dwindled during her first pregnancy, and even after Maggie was born he often wasn't able to encourage her to regain the passion she seemed to enjoy before. She always had some excuse when he expected her to pleasure him; Maggie was teething and she had been up all night; she had had a bad night the night before; it was too cold, or too hot; and so on. When he had finally managed to get her alone, the ardour on her part was missing. It seemed to him that she was making an effort, not revelling in it.

"Do you think you should see Dr Blake, and get a tonic or something?" he grumbled one night.

Polly had not realized her deception had been so obvious. It had been her fault in the first place, tricking Donald into marriage, without loving him. Yes, it had been easy, as Donald fell in love with her, just when she needed a father for her baby; and yes, she had loved the physical side of marriage, and entered into a life with Donald, never dreaming she would ever see Paul again. It was Donald's fault, she argued with herself, for making love to her in the first place. Of course, it had been incredibly convenient at the time, and as her parents were so relieved to marry her off to a respectable and presentable young man, it had all seemed providential. But she quickly realized marriage is a long-term commitment. She yearned after Paul, never thinking she would ever see him again. He became a knight in shining armour, a picture in a story book never to be seen again, but to be dreamed about, especially when she was lying in Donald's arms.

A dream certainly. But when he reappeared in her life, the dream became reality and Paul was there, flesh and blood and twice as handsome; then disillusionment with Donald set in. After she had once more tasted the transports of delight to which Paul led her, again and again, Donald's selfish lovemaking was tedious and tiresome.

Donald hardly noticed, as she was particularly careful not to refuse him, and tried to act as lovingly as before. But it was hard, and she began to make excuses, particularly after she had spent the afternoon lying in Paul's arms.

The weather was getting warmer, and Polly often arranged to meet Paul halfway between their two properties. They had a favourite place, a little dip between two hills, the grass soft, the surrounding bushes giving them privacy. Sometimes they just lay on the grass and talked, sometimes they were overcome with love for each other, and then they could not wait to divest themselves of whatever they were wearing, and give everything to each other. When it was really hot, there were only shirts and shorts to discard, and they lay, closer and closer in body and spirit, until they really seemed to become one.

"How can we go on like this?" Paul asked her, stroking her damp curls back from her forehead.

"I don't know; I've thought and thought. Donald is so possessive, and I don't think he would ever give up the children, and I know we couldn't either."

***

It was a problem that would not go away, but was solved unexpectedly at the beginning of December. There was a real heat wave. The bright South African sun was burning hot, and Donald decided not to go to Port Elisabeth as planned, but to stay at home and catch up with paperwork. Polly and Paul had already planned to meet, with Maggie and baby Ellie for a picnic in a shady grove not far from Whiteoaks.

Polly put her head round the study door, and told Donald, "I'm going to take the children out for an hour or two. It is so hot, and they need a bit of fresh air. We'll take a picnic to have in the shade. We'll be back in an hour or two."

Donald looked up.

"Wish I could come with you, but I must finish this today, so have a good time."

Polly breathed a sigh of relief, as she had been fearful Donald would want to come too. Paul adored his children, but did not have the opportunity to see them much, and had been looking forward to spend time playing with them as an ordinary father. He had arrived at their meeting place well before he saw Polly. She was riding old Thunder, with baby Ellie strapped across her chest, and a haversack on her back, and Maggie followed on Mousie, her eyes lighting up at the sight of Paul. Polly had not told her who they were going to meet, for fear she would tell Donald, and in her innocence spoil the afternoon for Paul. It was a real family outing she felt, as Paul embraced them all in such a natural manner. If only they could always be like that, relaxed and happy and free to be together. He had spread rugs on the ground and Polly unpacked their picnic. A beautiful weeping eucalyptus provided shade, and Polly took the baby's nappy off and let her kick her chubby little legs to her heart's delight. Paul had brought a big red and blue ball, and was teaching Maggie how to throw and catch. She watched them with love in her eyes when a shadow fell across her. She looked up lazily only to see Donald, gazing at them all with dawning comprehension.

"How long has this been going on?" he muttered, taking in the scene of domestic harmony, with a glint in his eye.

Polly gathered her wits together. "Oh hallo, darling, how lovely you could join us."

"Do you really mean that? It seems as if this has been planned some time ago."

"Well, we did sort of think it was a lovely day, and Maggie wanted Paul to see Mousie's new bridle and..." she ran out of excuses and was silent. Paul looked down at Ellie, kicking her little legs in the air, her face screwed up with delight. She was watching Paul and Maggie, and Donald let his eyes follow her gaze. He looked hard at Paul, and then back at the baby. The hair was different, but the face was undeniably Paul's. All the doubts which he had been feeling in recent weeks came to the surface. Polly had been so strange in the last few months. He had not been able to understand it, but the truth struck him like a hammer blow.

"When did it happen?" he asked in a controlled voice. "When I was in Jo'burg that time, I suppose. And is it still going on? It certainly looks like you are running the two of us in tandem. You are disgusting!" He glared at them, then strode off, jumped on Ginger and without bothering with the stirrups, galloped away without looking back.

Polly could not see his face, which was contorted with rage, and his eyes wept with fury and hatred. How could Polly let that...'horse breeder' touch her in that way? Much less, he could not bear the thought of what must have taken place between them. Thank goodness Paul had not been around when Maggie was conceived. But she was being contaminated now, and he must put a stop to all those cosy 'riding lessons' and send a message to the young man that he was no longer welcome at Whiteoaks. He would like to have thrown Ellie at him and tell him he could keep his own brat. But Maggie was such a bright little thing; she would be so upset if he disturbed her family circle. Certainly Ellie would not have any of his money in the future; she could go to her own father for that.

When Donald had ridden off Paul came over and flopped down beside Polly.

"What was all that about? I thought you said he was safely occupied in his study."

"Oh Paul, he knows! What are we to do?" she wailed. Paul gathered her in his arms and stroked her hair, until she calmed down a little.

"Only about Ellie I think. He doesn't seem to realize I knew you before."

Maggie flung herself on top of them both. "Mummy, what's the matter? Why are you crying?"

Polly extricated herself from Maggie's demanding little arms. "Goodness, I got a fly in my eye, and it has made my eyes water. Look, it is getting better very quickly. Let's have our picnic now shall we?"

Food, as always, took priority in Maggie's mind, and soon they were all munching the cheese sandwiches and chocolate cake which Minnie had provided. The food tasted like sawdust to Polly and Paul, but they kept up the pretence for Maggie's sake.

"Go and give Mousie this," Paul told Maggie, handing her a crust. When Maggie was out of earshot Polly murmured miserably,

"What are we going to do? He will be out of his mind with fury. I'm quite scared what he will do now, he looked so angry."

"Can you come back with me?"

"Paul, if only; He still thinks of Maggie as his own and he would never give her up. I'd better go back and calm things down. I'll give you a ring later to let you know what's happening." She began to pack up their picnic.

When they returned to the house Donald was nowhere to be seen.

"Master, he go off t'wards mountains, Msm. Polly. He go so fast, he get there an' back afore he started." Jo-jo waved his arms expressively in the air.

Polly worried he would go and do something stupid. Donald was apt to act irrationally when he was in a rage. But shortly before suppertime he appeared, sweaty and dishevelled, and silent. He kicked his riding boots off in the hall, spoke rudely to Laliya, who happened to be passing through and stumped into the dining room. He ate in complete silence, and when Polly started to say something he held up his hand to quieten her. The atmosphere was thick with reproach, and Polly felt she was chewing a thick woolly blanket, instead of the delicious roast chicken which Minnie had lovingly prepared. No hope of keeping the servants unaware of the situation. Minnie, who had known Polly since she was a baby and had always thought Donald not worthy of her "golden chile," was most concerned and had tried to make things better by cooking Donald's favourite dish. It might as well have been biltong the way he chewed his way through it. She put a hand sympathetically on Polly's shoulder as she passed.

"You may leave us now, Minnie," he barked, and she scuttled away, fearful for her darling, but unable to see how she could help.

Polly spent a forlorn evening alone. She tried to read a book, leaf through a magazine, or listen to a record of music, but thoughts kept tearing through her mind. What will we do? What will happen to us? By us she meant herself, the children and Paul, the latter most of all. When she eventually persuaded herself to go to bed she wondered if she would be sleeping alone. She was so distraught that tiredness overcame her and the next thing she knew was the door crashing shut.

Footsteps, unsteady and shuffling, came towards the bed, and as she reached for the bedside light a heavy weight crashed down on top of her. She began to remonstrate.

"Donald, be careful, you'll wake the children," as she tried to push him away.

But he was stronger than she was, and had been drinking and thinking all evening. He had worked himself into a blind rage, and now he was going to give Polly a lesson she would never forget.

He took hold of the top of her nightgown, and in his blind frenzy tore it away from her breasts, scratching her as he pushed her down. She put her hands up to stop him, but it only served to inflame him more.

"You little whore, you obviously like rough common men. Well, I can be as rough as you like, you little tyke!" With that he pinned her down as he began to ravage her. No loving words, no gentle kisses, he just forced himself onto and into her again and again, clawing at her breasts and scratching her arms until she was crying for mercy. When she began to feel she would rather die than endure another second of his unwanted attentions, he rolled off her, and snoring drunkenly, fell into a deep sleep.

Polly moved carefully away from him, easing her bruised body to the edge of the bed. She felt drained, sick, and utterly humiliated. She lay in a sort of stupor, until he gave a snort, terrifying her into action. She glanced at her husband. Husband, she gagged. How could a husband behave like that to his wife? Well, she could never be a wife to him again. She gathered her wits, and seizing some clothes she crept out of the room, closing the door gently behind her. Dressing quickly, she went into the nursery. Waking Laliya, she put her fingers to her lips to quieten her, and whispered,

"Don't ask any questions. Help me get the children dressed, very quietly. I don't want to wake the master, but we have to leave as soon as we can."

"Yes, Msm. Polly. Where we goin' this time o' night? I'se need my sleep, I do."

"I know, Lally, but I need to get the children away up to Mister Paul's house. You can come with us if you want to. Mister Donald has had too much brandy, and he might hurt them."

Laliya accepted this, with all the unquestioning faith of the native. White people did strange things, and she knew what it was like when too much brandy had disappeared down a man's throat. Her father was no exception, which was why she had welcomed the offer of a job in the big house. She never thought it could happen with white folks, but you never knew, and the master was not from this country after all.

She carefully woke Maggie, quietened her down, and dressed her in her riding breeches.

"Now," she whispered to Maggie, "we are all goin' on a night ride to Mister Pauls. Isn't that excitin'? But you must be quiet so you doan't wake yo' Daddy."

Maggie thought it was all a great adventure and crept about, helping Polly to collect things for baby Ellie, and whispering to Laliya to keep quiet. They all crept out to the stables, where Jo-jo was surprised to wake from a deep sleep to find his mistress saddling up Mousie and Thunder.

"What you'a doin' Msm. Polly?" he asked, through a fog of sleep.

"We are just going over to Mister Paul, Jo-jo. If the Master comes looking for us, just tell him you saw us leave, but you don't know where we have gone."

This was difficult for Jo-jo to understand. He would know where they had gone, so he could not tell the Master anything else. The best thing he could do was to go back to his home in the Bush, and then the Master would not know where to find him.

Polly mounted and reached down for Ellie. Laliya would walk; she knew where to go, even if they went a little faster. Polly could not wait. She could have gone to her father, but he would not have believed the "nice young man" could have raped her. He would persuade her to stay, and try to heal the breach. This she felt she could not do. She never wanted to see Donald again, ever.

England
Chapter 17

After David left Jean was completely bereft. She did not know how to explain to everybody just where David had gone, and why, and for how long. After all, she did not know herself. She occupied herself with all the usual village activities, apparently her customary cheerful self. But inside she felt drained of all feeling and emotion. For a week she cried herself to sleep, trying desperately to understand David's actions.

After a few days Mrs Truckle called in, with her usual excuse of "nice brown eggs for the children's tea." She had heard that Jean did not seem to be 'at all well', the village's explanation for any change in someone's demeanour. After greeting Jean she realized something was definitely wrong, and plunged in, with her usual bluntness.

"Now Jean dear, you certainly do look proper poorly and no mistake."

Jean swallowed. "Oh Mrs T...David's left and I don't know where he has gone, or for how long or..." and her voice tailed off.

"Come here, my dear, and tell me all about it." Mrs Truckle drew Jean to her ample bosom, cradling her until she had calmed down. She always knew David was a selfish young man and his parents had spoilt him from a very young age, but this was the limit.

Jean poured it all out to her dear friend. As the details unfolded Mrs Truckle was appalled. To go off and leave this lovely girl, mother of his two small children, devoted carer to his aging father, and keeper of a large house and garden, not to mention all the activities in the village which she was expected to carry out; it was simply too much.

"A nice cup of tea, and then we'll sort things out together," she announced.

It was so marvellous to unburden herself, and as Jean related the whole sad story, Mrs Truckle could hardly contain herself with anger towards David.

"But I will say that David has left arrangements that I can draw as much money as I need while he is away;" Jean always felt she had to stick up for David, although why, at this moment, she wondered. David had been her life for so long, and, as she confided to Mrs Truckle, he would be part of her life whatever happened.

Between them they decided to tell whoever asked, that David had gone off prospecting, and was going to be away for a long time, sometimes far into the Bush, or Jungle, or somewhere, and could not easily be contacted. Meanwhile, Jean decided to get on with her life as best she could in the circumstances.

"Where is Daddy?" James would often ask, but gradually became used to his mother's sad face and excuses as she tried to explain. His daddy's image increasingly faded, taken over by his beloved Uncle Tom, who was around far more than his daddy ever had. Tom stepped in, teaching James all about the country ways, taking him down to the farm, and letting him help milk cows and herd the sheep.

Jean, too, came to rely on Tom more and more and their relationship slowly deepened into love, such as Jean had never experienced before. She now realized what a selfish husband David had been. Tom told her he thought that after three years she could obtain a divorce, if no trace of David could be found.

"Then I can make an honest woman of you, and all the tittle-tattle in the village could dry up!" he joked.

But for Jean, strictly brought up in the Christian tradition, it was most distressing to think her marriage could be wiped off the face of the earth, just like that. It was the only time they argued. Tom's parents were old-fashioned too, and he knew it would be difficult to marry Jean if they had no proof of David's demise, or wishes. Besides, Jean had his letters. Hard, cold, and infrequent they might be, but they were proof of his existence, just enough to make Jean draw back each time he thought he had persuaded her to make a home with him.

The money was always there; almost a brake to Jean's progress in life, and old George still needed a lot of care, so her dear adoptive father would never have understood.

When Tom had finally broken Jean's defences, after James' fifth birthday, the weeks had gone by in a haze of happiness, laced, for Jean, with torment about exactly what steps she should take to regularise her relationship with Tom.

By the end of 1958 she really began to feel that there was no chance of David returning. She had not heard for nearly two years, and she felt that if David really did want her to be his wife, he should make contact with her at the very least. One day she even went up to London to see his solicitors, but they had nothing to tell her, (or would tell her more like, she thought). All they were prepared to say that he had only given instructions that she should have enough money for her needs, and nothing more.

She returned to St. Wraich in shreds, none the wiser. Tom met her at Wadebridge Station, and drove them both up onto the Moor, thoughtfully producing three large handkerchiefs, necessary by the time Jean had told him all the news.

"Mr Ferbourne more or less told me I was lucky to have as much money as I wanted, and he had strict instructions not to divulge anything about David's whereabouts. But Tom, he did say something strange."

"Tell me. Why strange?"

"He said I wasn't the only one in the dark. He wished he himself knew, and he thought the whole situation as it is, was most unsatisfactory."

"If it is unsatisfactory for him, what does he think it is for you?" Tom exclaimed, feeling a sensation of fury and impotence.

There followed a few weeks of a kind of coolness between them, but neither of them could keep it up. Their love was too strong to be thrown off course for too long, and soon they were lovers again, feeling more deeply towards each other than ever before.

Tom's parents did not condone their behaviour, but even they could see how impossible the situation had become, and were sympathetic to their liaison. Tom was in and out, mostly in, the Old Rectory, but did not neglect his farm duties, especially as his father could not manage as much as he had in the past, and the Truckles were hoping to retire as soon as Tom could sort his life out.

***

They had no warning. Jean heard the car in the drive. She had gone down to the vegetable garden to see if anything growing big enough to use the next day. Tom was coming over, and they were going to tell the children that he was going to be their proper Daddy. They knew they could not marry in the Church, as they both would have liked, but they were planning a kind of commitment to each other. The Rector, who understood their predicament, and wished he could have given them a service in Church, agreed to come to the Old Rectory, and hold a little private blessing on their union. This was planned to take place the following week, but they felt the children should get used to the idea. James, now six, would understand somewhat; Elizabeth would just enjoy a party.

Jean felt she was in a kind of trance. The thought of Tom moving into the Old Rectory, and becoming part of her little family group was joyful, and as she wandered slowly back to the house her heart gave little leaps of pleasure.

The sound of a car stopping brought her reverie to an abrupt halt. She wasn't expecting anyone, and it was sure to be someone who needed her help, it nearly always was. As she came round the corner, hidden from the drive by the ivy pergola, she could see the car. It was Mr Crossdon's taxi, which was surprising in itself.

"Who on earth could that be?" she thought, as she waited to see who opened the door. But even she could never have envisaged who appeared out of the back of the car.

If she had ever needed Tom by her side, it was at that moment. She felt an explosion in her head and numb at the same time. For there, in flesh and blood, tanned, and hair bleached by some foreign sun, was her husband David. He handed Mr Crossdon a note, and then stopped to gaze up at the old house.

"Long time since you wuz here, Mr David," said Mr Crossdon, putting the five pound note in his pocket. With generosity like that, he was not going to ask any questions; although of course they all knew that David had been missing for some time, and Tom Truckle was moving in to the Old Rectory shortly. It gave him quite a shock when he saw Mr David coming out of the Station. After all, it had been a long time, nearly three years, since he had taken Mr David to catch the London train. What a change in a man. He had hardly recognised him. Still handsome, he had filled out; his hair was the colour of the sun which had obviously tanned his skin.

"Can I take your bags in, Mr David?" he asked hopefully. He would have liked to see the reunion, and be able to relate all the details to Mrs Crossdon, who would be sure to ask.

"No thanks. I can manage," David answered abruptly. He did not want the whole of Cornwall to hear the story of his homecoming. He picked up his suitcases and, seeing the front door open, walked in.

Jean was shattered, and did not know what to do next. So many emotions washed over her. Anger was the dominant one: How dare he walk straight in, just as if he'd been to London for a few days, and then expect his life, and everyone else's to be exactly the same. She supposed it was his home, and he had every legal right to be there, but not a moral one.

She took a deep breath, squared her shoulders, and head held high walked in through the garden door.

David had dumped his cases in the hall and was in the drawing room by the big mantelpiece, gazing at the photographs of James and Elizabeth. As Jean came into the room he turned.

"Hello Jean, I'm home," he said, as he held his arms out.

Jean stopped suddenly in the doorway; she gazed at him, a golden god, more handsome than he ever had been, but her heart felt totally unmoved. The only emotion she felt at that moment was sheer, unadulterated fury.

"What do you mean, home?" she spat.

David recoiled somewhat at this unexpected greeting. He visualised a hero's return, flags out, special meals, loving family delighted to welcome him back after a long absence.

"I'm here now, home forever. I know it's been a long time, but I couldn't help that. Jean darling, it is so wonderful to see you again. Come and give me a kiss, and tell me you've missed me."

The arrogance of it astounded Jean. Now she was glad Tom was not there. Friends or no friends in the past, Jean knew only too well how Tom felt about David now. He would have given David the biggest beating he had ever had in his life, possibly even killed him, knowing the agony Jean had been through in the last two or three years.

"David," Jean spoke quietly but firmly, endeavouring not to shake like a leaf. "I know this is your home. Your father is upstairs in his room. He is old and frail, and does not realize you have been away for long. Your children hardly remember you, and I do not feel any longer that I am your wife. Of course you can move back here, but as soon as you do I will take the children and move out, and you can start caring for your father and the house and everything, just as I have all this time."

And with that she glared at him with disgust, turned and walked out of the room.

David was speechless. He remembered the welcomes his mother had given him after coming home from school or the Navy. He now realized he should have given Jean warning. It must have been a shock to her to see him after so long, and of course, he had not written much. He had left Jean in shreds, but still he had thought she loved him, and would be thrilled to have him home. She owed everything to him. Money had not been a problem. She was always busy he remembered; too busy for him as it happened. Oh, well, she would soon get over the shock and things would be back to normal.

He sighed, strolled into the hall, picked up his suitcase, and took it upstairs. When he reached their bedroom he was annoyed to find the door locked. He rattled the door knob, and called out to Jean.

"Come on darling, open up. I've brought my things up and you can help me unpack. I have got so much to tell you."

There was a sound of movement inside, and the key was slowly turned. The door opened and Jean stood there, glaring at him.

"I daresay you remember where the spare room is, or have you forgotten?"

David stepped forward, but Jean put her arm out to stop him.

"You lost the right to call this your room at least two years ago, but if you really wish to sleep here I will move my things to the spare room."

"You cannot really mean that, when I've been looking forward so much to being at home with you, and the children, and, and everything."

Jean gave a little moan.

"Please, David, this has been such a shock. You must give me time to sort things out," and she closed the door once again.

He sighed in frustration. This was not at all what he expected. He picked up his suitcase and took it into the room along the passage which he remembered had been the spare room. But obviously no longer. He saw a train set on the floor, and all the paraphernalia of a small boy's bedroom. He remembered his father was ensconced round the corner, in a suite of rooms which he had organised after his mother's death, and decided to go and see him.

Jean lifted up the telephone by her bed and dialled the Truckle's number. She felt numb with shock, and the only thing she could think of was Tom. Dear comfortable Tom, who would surely know what to do. Mrs Truckle answered.

When she had calmed Jean, and realized what had happened, she thought for a minute and then called out of the back door to her husband, who was feeding the hens in the yard. When she had briefly explained the situation, they both decided Tom would have to be told at once. He was out in the lower meadow trimming the hedge, collecting holly if he saw a nice berried branch for the Christmas decorations. As he reached up for a particularly colourful branch he saw his father waving to him. Fearing some crisis at the farm, he dropped his knife and ran to the gate where his father had stopped,

"Is everything alright, what's to do, Father?" he panted.

"Young David's come home."

Tom went white, and clutched his father's arm.

"When?"

"About an hour ago, Jean's been on to Mother. She's very upset, Tom. I think you should go and see what's up. But be careful, they are still husband and wi—"

But Tom was gone, no longer listening, but running fast as he could towards the Old Rectory.

Fortunately David was with his father when Tom arrived at the Old Rectory. He came in the back way, carefully, listening as he went. He did not want to meet David before he had seen Jean. She was not downstairs so he crept upstairs to the bedroom they had been sharing, on and off for the last few months. He gave a little knock on the door. Jean, sitting shivering and miserable on the bed recognised his tap and rushed to the door to open it. She pulled Tom inside and shut and locked it again, before turning round to face him.

She only had to begin "Oh Tom!" and he put his strong arms round her, holding her close, gently rocking her trembling body until she seemed to pull herself together and reluctantly disentangled herself.

"Mother told me. Where is he?" asked Tom.

"Please, Tom, don't start a fight or anything. It is his right to be here. But not," she gave a rueful smile, "in my bed!"

Tom had to smile too, and he felt calmer, and stronger.

"Do you want me to stay?" he asked.

"I think so. He is with Uncle George at the moment. Thank goodness May has taken the children out, but they will be back soon, and I must try and explain to them. David seems to think he can just go on where he left off. But I can't, Tom. So much has changed. They won't know him for a start."

"James might."

They heard the childish voices coming up the drive at that moment, and both made a move towards the door. Tom unlocked it and they both went downstairs.

May had taken James and Elizabeth into the kitchen for a glass of milk, while she made tea for them all. It was Ellen's day off, for which Jean was relieved. "One less to explain to." she thought. May had hardly known the Master, but Ellen had thought he was a God, and never had understood why he had left so suddenly, and she was almost the only local person who believed Jean's story. May rose from the table and glanced towards Tom. He looked very grim, she thought, and Jean looked as if she had been crying. Strange, as they going to be 'sort of' married next week. She hoped they hadn't had a bust-up and called it off. It had been ever so romantic.

"Could you make us all a cup of tea?" Jean asked her. Swallowing, she went on. "My..., Mr David has come home, so put an extra cup out. He is with his father at the moment." She looked at May warningly, and went on, "Come on, children, you can come with us to the drawing room. We...have something to tell you."

They followed her meekly, sensing as children do that something was going on. When they reached the drawing room Jean sat on the sofa, and drew Elizabeth onto her lap. Tom sat down and drew James towards him, while Jean spoke softly.

"James, you will remember Daddy?" But James looked blank. He frowned and gazing at Tom said, "But Mum, you said Uncle Tom was our Daddy now, and I love Uncle Tom. I don't want another one."

Jean thought her heart would break.

"Well, my darling, don't you remember that Daddy when you were little?"

James screwed his face up.

"Sort of," he admitted reluctantly, "but he didn't know how to ride, or milk cows."

Both Jean and Tom, even in their distress, could not help a grin.

"You see he smacked me once and I didn't like him."

This was worse than Jean had thought. She never knew David had chastised James. Of course Elizabeth had only been a year old when he left, and now she could not understand what all this was about.

"I'm hungry, Mummy. Can we have tea soon?"

The door opened, and they all looked up, expecting May with the tea things, but David stood there, with his arms stretched out towards the children.

"Look, your Daddy's home, come and give me a kiss!"

Tom gagged at this hypocrisy. He felt himself clenching his fists, willing himself not to lose control in front of the children.

"And Tom, how splendid!" David looked across at his old friend. Jean had given the children a little push towards David, but they remained firmly where they were, sensing something was not quite right.

David sat down in the armchair he had always sat in, and looked round proprietarily as if they were the guests and he the host.

"I thought you would be hard at work on the farm at this time of day, Tom." He smiled. "Have you come here for something? Can I help old chap? We mustn't keep you." Before anyone could draw a breath James piped up, "Uncle Tom lives here now. He is going to be our proper Daddy next week. He gave me a pony called Mousie, and he is going to teach Lizbeth to ride soon."

A deadly silence followed. The air was thick with feelings. Jean did not know where to look; Tom almost laughed out loud. "Brilliant James," he thought. David appeared astounded. Little James gazed at the grown-ups and wondered why no-one spoke. Then the telephone rang. Jean jumped, and Tom, who was nearest, picked up the receiver, listened, said "Right," and put it down.

"Mum," he said briefly, "wants to know..."

"Wants to know what?" David almost shouted, and Elizabeth buried her face in her mother's lap.

Tom turned to David. "Well, if you must know, she wants to know if she should come up and sort you out."

Jean pulled herself together.

"Not good for little ears," she muttered, and taking the children she opened the door and called for May to come and collect them.

May had not been too far away, hoping to hear a bit of what was going on so that she could relate it all to Ellen when she came back. She took the little hands, (James's were trembling), and pretended to be a big lion, chasing them up the stairs, always a favourite game with them.

The tense atmosphere relaxed a little. Tom stared at David with contempt and hatred. "Surely even you can see what a shock all this is to Jean and the children?" he growled.

David turned on them. "To come back to my own house, my own family, my own wife? Yes, it is a shock to *me* to find she has not waited for her loving husband to return from the wilds to her; after all this time I expected at least something of a welcome. Not to find you, my supposed friend, had moved into my bed, and taken over my family!" He spat the last, and Jean reeled from the fury in his voice.

She felt Tom's strength beside her, and she put out her hand to him, clutching it as if it was a lifeline. She said quietly, "Yes. Tom and I are proposing to live together as man and wife. We have moved heaven and earth to find your whereabouts, and even your precious solicitors could not tell me. They too, have been unable to contact you. You left me with your aging father, your two tiny children, and the responsibilities of a large house, without ever letting any of us know if you were alive or dead. Tom did not approach me until I gave him my heart, broken though it was, and he has been a tower of strength through every crisis during the time you were away." She stopped as the large form of Mrs Truckle came in.

"Yes," said that dear friend. "And there have been times when I have found her weeping her heart out for you. I wonder if you ever wept your heart out for her."

Remembering nights of bliss under African stars and all the exciting times he had been through during the last four years, David had the grace to feel a little guilty. But Mrs Truckle, ever practical, addressed Jean.

"This is David's home, Jean, and so he has a right to stay. But if you want to come and think things over, you and the children can come back with me to the farm to give everyone a bit of time to decide what will happen now. David, you stay here. You have two maids to look after you and your father, and perhaps you can let Jean have time to recover from the shock you have given her, and let her decide her future, whether it will be with you or Tom." She drew breath and then gave Jean a kiss, and quietly left the room.

There was a collective sigh, as they all came to conclusions of their own. Tom went over to Jean, took her hand, and led her out of the door, shutting it carefully behind him. They heard the children talking to May in the kitchen, and Jean, swallowing hard, called out to them.

"We are just going over to see Aunty Truckle, so get your coats."

To May she said, "May, we are going down to the farm for a bit. Mr David will be staying here, so please could you and Ellen look after him, and his father, as well as you can. This has all been a great shock to us, and we need a little time to get over it." She could hardly get the last words out, and Tom, seeing her difficulty, took over.

"My mother has asked Jean and the children to come and stay. Of course we will tell you what is going to happen, as soon as we know ourselves. I am sorry for all the upset, but I know you and Ellen will make the best of it."

They did not even stop to collect their nightclothes, but hand-in-hand, and trying to make an adventure for the children, they crept out of the back door, just as David, trying to get over the shock of this extraordinary welcome home, emerged from the drawing room.

He was astounded at the turn of events. Leaving Polly and Maggie (Eleanor did not count), had been a pretty traumatic experience. He had stayed in Durban for a few days, trying to make sense of it all. He transferred the organisation of the wine business to his manager, with instructions to carry on, and approach his solicitors with any problems. David told him he had been advised to take a complete break for health reasons, and no contact should be attempted. Any problems could be sorted in London. His young manager thought it was all somewhat strange, but then Donald had been acting oddly of late, and as long as he still had his job, which he loved, and was going to be paid as handsomely as before, he found no reason to enquire further into his boss's directives.

David's mind had then turned to his family in Cornwall. He had forgotten all the rows and dullness of his life there, and he had felt the most obvious move was to return to the arms of his loving family. After all, he vividly remembered the welcomes he used to receive from his mother. How everything used to revolve round his wishes, with no more complications than to decide what to have for his favourite dinner. Of course, she was no longer there, but Jean would be ecstatic to have him home again, and the children would welcome their father back. He would get a pony for James and begin to know Elizabeth, who had only been a year old when he left.

He had decided not to let them know he was on his way. It would be a lovely surprise for them all. If the Truckles were still about, they could let Jean have a chicken to roast, and he could go out for a beer with Tom and tell him all about his adventures, leaving out Polly, of course! He grinned to himself. Polly had been fun to start with, how could he have known that horse breeder was worming his way into her affections. It still rankled, the fact that Polly had preferred that man from all he, Donald, could give her. And Maggie; his beloved Maggie, that had been a real wrench, but he could not take her away from her home. However, he would make it up to her one day.

And now; now nothing was as he expected, and he put his head in his hands in despair. Somehow it had all gone wrong. He couldn't believe Jean would desert him for Tom of all people. But now his erstwhile friend seemed to have taken his place in more ways than one, and he must think of some means of sorting out this awful mess.

He heard Ellen come back, and a lot of talk from the kitchen regions. He sighed at the thought of explaining the situation to Ellen. He wished Violet was still there, he had always been a favourite of hers, and she would have understood.

He made himself a stiff gin and tonic, swallowed half of it in one gulp, and rang the bell. As he had hoped it was Ellen who appeared at the door. Actually May had been too scared to answer the summons. She had told Ellen a little of what she thought had occurred; Ellen had been appalled, but not surprised. She was flabbergasted though at the insensitive way David had reappeared. She had been helping Jean to prepare for her 'wedding' to Tom, and she could imagine the shock David's unexpected return must have been. She had seen Jean's anguish when he left all those years ago, and she was equally stunned by his unanticipated homecoming.

"Hullo, Ellen," he said breezily, as if he had just returned from a couple of days in London. "You see I've come back to dear old St Wraich. Not much of a welcome though! I sincerely hope you're not going to desert the sinking ship. I suppose there's no hope of some lunch."

"Yes, sir, we've got a casserole in the Aga. I will bring it in presently. You'll want to wash I expect."

It was all so normal David wanted to scream at her, but he bit his lips, murmured some thanks, and went past her into the cloakroom across the hall. He ran some icy water and splashed it over his face in an effort to clear away the nightmare. Then he made his way to the dining room, where he struggled to eat normally while May served him vegetables as if nothing was any different, and Ellen hovered in the background. After all, this was her day off but she would not have missed the drama for anything.

She had known David since he was a youngster, and Violet had often remarked how his mother had always spoilt him rotten. No wonder he wanted his own way. But she could not help wondering what he had been up to all this time. She had seen Jean's distress, and lately, her new-found happiness, and felt a tug of loyalty between Jean and the Master, as she had called him ever since his father had died.

***

For the first day or two after David's return Jean felt completely numb. Mrs Truckle understood, put her to bed with instructions to stay there, and went about coping with the children and keeping everything as normal as possible for her extended family. It was nearly the end of the school term, and therefore James was fully occupied with the Christmas festivities. He was to be Joseph in the Nativity play, and could think of little else but having the honour of leading the donkey up the aisle.

"Mummy will be able to come and see me, won't she?" he asked Mrs Truckle anxiously.

"Of course, my love. We will all be coming," she assured him.

Elizabeth just enjoyed staying at the farm and helping in the kitchen. When Tom came in from milking and called out to his mother, she put her little fat fingers to her lips to admonish him, "Be quiet, Uncle Tom. We mustn't make a noise, "cos Mummy's resting!"

"Of course not, you are a good girl to remind me," answered Tom solemnly. He managed to get out of the room before he had to wipe his eyes. Whether it was tears of laughter or sadness, he didn't know. He had been going over the situation every minute and at present could not see a solution. If only they had moved in together before David had returned it would have been a fait accompli. Now they would have to sort out the whole ghastly situation, and he really could not visualise the outcome.

After two days in bed, and remembering the Nativity Play, Jean appeared, looking pale and drawn, but once more in command of her feelings. She went across the room to Tom, and put her arms round him.

"Nothing has changed, Tom darling," she whispered, and then gave the children rather more robust hugs.

Endeavouring to sound vigorous she told them, "I must go back to the house and gather up some things. We must collect the Joseph outfit and I must talk to Ellen and May, and see what's needed there."

The Truckles were full of admiration for the strength she was showing, and all vowed to themselves they would do all they could to support her. Tom rose and put out his hand, "I'll come with you."

"Actually, I think it will be better if I go by myself." Jean visualised appalling rows if Tom came, even a fight. She knew Tom was terribly upset that his erstwhile friend had behaved so badly, and she dreaded to think what might happen when they met. She was calm enough now, had grown a shell round her feelings while she had been resting, and wanted to sort out the whole beastly situation between David and herself. The children hardly knew David, and certainly did not want to go and see him. Mrs Truckle, that most perceptive of souls, understood.

"Perhaps you could take up the cream to give Ellen," she suggested to Jean, to give her a pretext for returning to the Old Rectory.

David was sitting in the drawing room when Jean appeared. She had put the cream in the larder, and, rather relieved not to meet Ellen or May, she went through to where she guessed David might be. He looked up, obviously not expecting her.

"Goodness, back in the lion's den, Jean?"

She smiled. "Well, back to see you, anyway," and sat down opposite him looking wan, but determined.

"I just wanted to know what you planned to do. I will have to go and live somewhere. I can't stay with the Truckles for too long. They have been so good to me while you have been..." she hesitated, "away. But there is not really room for all of us at the farm."

"What about me?" It was such a predictable statement that Jean almost laughed.

"I supposed you would want to live here. After all, there is your father, and he cannot be expected to move in the state of health he is in, so I supposed you would want to care for him." (As I have done these last few years), she longed to add.

"Jean, I cannot believe this. When I left you did not want me to go, and I thought you would be delighted to see me again, and we could go on as before. What on earth has got into you to change your mind?"

"I do agree with you that I didn't want you to go. But you did, and you literally disappeared out of my life so completely, that many times I thought I was a widow. When you did deign to send me a note, it was so cold and hard that I sometimes wondered if you were actually dead, and your captors, or whatever, were forging those notes, after you had died. And do you know? After a bit I began to wish you were dead, and I could mourn you and then move on with my life." She brushed a tear out of her eye, but it was a tear of anger, not sorrow.

"And, here am I." said David, the bitterness creeping into his voice. "Thinking you would all be delighted to see me. Well, I've been wrong haven't I?"

They sat for a moment in silence. David sighed, then got up and walked to the fireplace to put another log on the fire.

"This is my home, and the children's home, and of course your home, but I can't force you to live here. I am not going to let you divorce me, so you will have to find somewhere else to set up your little love-nest with Tom." He almost snarled, and Jean recoiled at the viciousness in his voice. "Father is so far gone he won't notice if I get a nurse in to care for him. In fact you should have done that, ages ago. I really don't mind what happens to the children; they can stay with you, or come back here. Ellen and May can still look after them. James is old enough to do without a nurse-maid running after him, and I really couldn't care about Elizabeth." He drew breath then, which was just as well. Jean had left the room, disgusted at what she was hearing, determined that her children should have as little as possible to do with this self-opinionated monster.

There was still the problem of Uncle George. He was confused, she knew. But she also knew that he recognised her and especially the children, and would not be able to understand why they did not come and see him every morning.

She bit her lip and went into the kitchen to see Ellen and May, and try to explain to them what was going on.

It was an awkward twenty minutes as she endeavoured to clarify the situation, as much to herself as to them. But after a time Ellen just reached out and put her arms round Jean's shoulders and held her, as she had so many times in the past.

"Don't you fret, my dear. May and me will manage, and I daresay the Master will sort things out as he wishes. We will stay here and see to things until you can all work it out between you."

Jean gulped her gratitude. She felt blessed to have such faithful friends. She told them she would be at the farm for the present, until David had made up his mind whether he stayed or went off again. She would make sure the children came up to the house now and then, if only to see their Grandpa. But she herself could not live with David any more, in the circumstances. Nothing was said about Tom, but his name loomed large in all their thoughts.

Later that week, May was sent to collect the children, who reluctantly went back with her to the Old Rectory to see their father. Remembering Maggie, David tried his best, but in their estimation he had been a stranger too long. James had witnessed his mother's distress over the years, and he was now old enough to connect that with his father's cruelty. Elizabeth seemed stolid and ordinary compared with his mercurial Maggie, and David found he could not connect with either of them naturally. After an hour of forced jollity James announced, "I think we would like to see our Grandpa now, and then go back to the farm. You don't feel like our Daddy, and anyway, we don't like you much, so can we go." He took his sister's hand and led her upstairs. If David had not felt so put out he would have laughed.

He telephoned Jean to tell her. She was not surprised as she knew James had been dreading the visit. She felt proud of her children, behaving in such a dignified way, but sad at the same time. Then Tom came in, and roared with laughter when she told him, which put the whole affair in perspective again.

"That boy has got a lot of gumption," he said proudly, just as if he was indeed their father.

David realized that his marriage was now over. He utterly refused to divorce Jean, but came to the conclusion there was no way he could make her live with him. However, St. Wraich was his home and he wanted to stay there while he consolidated his business interests, and decide what to do next. He did not dare write to Maggie, and did not wish to contact Polly; the legal muddles would be too complicated. She would probably be relieved to find she could lawfully marry Paul. But he was not about to give her that satisfaction. He had so successfully disguised his persona, that there was no way she could find him. Donald Belham was wiped off the map forever.

South Africa

Chapter 18

Polly was in shock for several days. Paul wisely did not ask questions. Laliya was not communicative, but she helped settle the children in Paul's small house, and soon became part of the collection of servants. She much enjoyed being the centre of attention for a bit; although she could not tell them much of the reason for their arrival in the middle of the night, it leant a certain air of notoriety.

"I'se 'tink dey had big row, and Msm. Polly, she come 'n say we go now to Mister Paul wid' 'de childen." But that was enough to create big speculation.

Polly stayed quietly in bed, gradually recovering, and was pleased to hear Paul knocking on her door on the third morning. Her thoughts had been whirling round and round. She was sore in mind and body, and had needed the breathing space to heal both. She also realized she was in Paul's bed, and she began to wonder what was happening to him and the children. But she appreciated his sensitivity and when he opened the door she lifted up her arms to him in welcome.

"My darling, I thought it best to let you rest. Can you talk about it now?" he said, his voice full of emotion.

Polly swallowed. "Oh Paul, he raped me, over and over. I don't, can't..."

"It might help to tell me. It won't make any difference to us, whatever he did. You needn't ever see him again. I heard this morning he has gone. Taken all his things, and went off in his car. Minnie came and told me. She wants you to come back. She says Whiteoaks is your home anyway."

Polly broke down with relief, and Paul held her gently as she sobbed out her story. He felt like jumping into the car and chasing after Donald, and killing him at the very least. But Polly clung to him as if she could never let him go.

He felt a twinge of conscience. If only he had written when he first went off with the Army. But he had been absorbed into secret operations which took over his life, and the months had gone by. Polly had been a lovely memory, like a photograph, and he had never dreamed he would really fall in love with her again. They had been like a couple of puppies exploring life without thought of the future, and he had never visualised what an impact she would have on him when they met again. Now they knew it was a lifetime's commitment from 'this day forward'.

Polly went to see her father, and she was amazed how understanding he was, as if he had expected something like this. In fact, he had seen it coming. Much as he regretted Paul returning, he could see the stars in Polly's eyes which had not been there for a long time. He had liked Donald, but there had been a certain 'something' about him all along. Margery had been so relieved to get Polly married, and shortly before she died she had confessed to Gordon about the pregnancy, and how Donald was the answer to all their problems. To see Polly happily wedded to Donald had been such a joy to her that he hadn't the heart to express any doubts. When he first saw baby Maggie, and the de Freyburg red hair, he had worried that Donald might wonder, but all had seemed well, and they had appeared happy enough.

"Now, my pet," he declared to Polly, "Donald seemed to have done the decent thing and departed, so that you can move back into the house with the children, which will be better for them."

"And Paul?" asked Polly.

Gordon smiled wryly. "You know I always felt Paul was not our sort, but you have his children." He hesitated and permitted himself a small grin. "Oh yes. Of course I knew from the moment Maggie was born, and I saw her hair. As a matter of fact, your mother told me just before she died the true reason for a quick marriage to Donald. I couldn't really believe her until I saw Maggie's hair!"

"Oh Pa!" Polly flung her arms round her father, and they both were silent, remembering Margery and all she had meant to them.

"It will be marvellous having you back at home, and I'm sure I will soon get to know your Paul, and find the hidden talents you seem to have discovered in him!"

Paul was a little reluctant to become the Master of Whiteoaks, but Gordon decided to swallow all his pride, and welcome Paul into the family. He was impressed how mature the lad had become. Obviously the Army had brought out all his best attributes, and gradually, with the children helping, they both became friends.

Paul was very knowledgeable about horses, which helped break the ice, but at first he was not terribly interested in the vines, so there were no clashes of interest. Gordon sometimes asked him to help in the fields, which he did willingly, and as Gordon aged, Paul gradually took over a good deal of the work, becoming fascinated in the process. Polly watched the growing fondness between them, and was thankful for such a harmonious existence.

Paul and Polly lived in a haze of bliss, but Paul longed to make Polly his wife, in the eyes of the law, and the church. Without telling Polly he went to great lengths to trace Donald, to ask him to release Polly, but he could not find a hint of anyone with the name Donald Belham. After some months he consulted solicitors, and was told the marriage could be annulled after three years desertion. They were so happy together that there did not seem much point in going further, and he put it to the back of his mind.

Maggie and Ellie prospered. At first Maggie asked where her Daddy was.

"Has he gone away again?" she badgered her mother, who just hugged her and said, "I think you must believe that Uncle Paul is your daddy now. In fact we want you and Ellie to call him "Daddy." Would you like to do that darling, for Mummy's sake?"

Maggie put her head on one side and considered the matter for all of two seconds.

"That's a good idea Mummy. I'll go and tell Ellie. Can we have a 'Daddy Party,' Mummy, just to show him?"

"Oh, my sweet. That is a wonderful plan. We will keep it a secret, shall we? It can be a surprise. When can we do it?" Polly knew what the answer would be.

"Today! Can we have a cake, Mummy, and balloons?"

"I think it might take Minnie a day or two to make a cake. Let's have it on Saturday, and mind you, don't tell Ellie or she will let it out. Just let it be our secret."

"Oh Mummy," Maggie sighed with satisfaction at being allowed to be grown-up enough to keep a secret, and put her fingers to her lips. "I won't tell anyone, even Mousie."

Paul had a feeling something was being planned, as Maggie kept looking at Polly furtively, but with such a twinkle he felt it must be a celebration of some sort. Her teddy bear's birthday or similar, which had happened before. So when he came in from the fields rather late for tea on Saturday, he not surprised to notice an air of repressed excitement.

"Da...Uncle Paul, go and wash your hands," Maggie was dancing up and down with anticipation.

"Of course, my pet. I always wash my hands before tea,"

"But this is special, and you need extra clean hands."

"Why?" asked Paul.

"It's a secret, and I can't tell you, but hurry up." Maggie could hardly contain her enthusiasm.

Paul did as he was told, then went across the hall and into the sitting room. When he opened the door there was a brief hush, then....

"Happy Daddy Day!" they all shouted. Maggie and Ellie rushed forward and flung their little arms round him, (in Ellie's case, round his legs which were as far up as she could reach). "We decided you really are our Daddy, and it is a sort of naming day party," explained Maggie, and Ellie just said "Daddy, Daddy, Daddy" over and over again.

Paul glanced over at Polly with such a look of love she thought her heart would melt. He knew it was her idea, but he bent down, hiding his emotion.

"My darlings, what a lovely idea, and a party too, and balloons and such a pretty cake."

"Yes, Minnie made it, and look, she's put "Daddy" on it too!" Maggie pointed to the table.

He went over to Polly and hugged her. There were no words, and in any case, he could hardly hold back the tears as he gazed at his family.

"We really are a family now." He whispered.

***

It was another two years before they took their vows to be "man and wife forever." It was a quiet ceremony, with just the two families present. Maggie was nearly eight and growing up, and obviously the thought of dressing up to be a bridesmaid was not her idea of fun. But Ellie still loved pretty dresses, and so she was allowed to walk in front of Paul and Polly, as a flower girl, with a basket of rose petals picked from the garden that morning. It was such a contrast from Polly's first wedding that there was no comparison. Just the happiest day of her life, she felt.

Maggie had bequeathed Mousie to Ellie, and Paul had given her a larger pony, Blackie. Mousie and Blackie had ribbons woven into their manes and Jo-jo had brought them to the Church to welcome the happy couple as they emerged. They featured in all the wedding photographs, much to Maggie's delight.

Gordon had decided to give them a trip on the Blue Train as a wedding present, and he moved back into Whiteoaks to take care of the children while they were away.

They drove up to Pretoria and embarked onboard the fabulous 'hotel on wheels' for a memorable trip to Cape Town and back. They were entranced by the fairytale atmosphere of the most famous train in the world. They had their own suite, which converted into a bedroom for the night. The service was impeccable; white coated servants tending to every need, superb food, and the most incredible scenery which left them gasping with wonder. Of course they had lived all their lives with animals and the wonderful panorama of the Drakensburg Mountains, but the vistas they passed through were so stunning they could hardly bear it when dark descended, the curtains were drawn, and they could see no more.

Then, however, it was their special time, and they could hardly wait until after they had finished dinner, and the servant had pulled their bed down from the wall, to jump in between the snowy sheets and discover even more delights. Away from the children, the responsibilities of the stud and farm, and completely on their own, they both experienced the deepest feelings of belonging to each other for the first time. What a wise and perceptive choice of wedding present Gordon had given them.

England

Chapter 19

After a few weeks of mooching round the Old Rectory, trying to cope with his father's needs and running the household without Jean, David once again came to the conclusion that he felt suffocated in St. Wraich. He was sorely tempted to return to South Africa. But on reflection he could not see how he could resume any sort of life there. He tried to make friends with James, but they had no interests in common, and James patently hated him. One day he was desperately trying to be nice to his son, and remarked in a petulant sort of way, "You don't like me much do you?"

"You always make Mummy cry," answered James. "When you went away she cried a lot. Uncle Tom makes her laugh and helps her do things. Uncle Truckle said you always were a right spoilt brat. You're not like a proper Daddy, and I would like to go back to the farm now." Then, in a very dignified manner, he shook David's hand solemnly and walked out of the door.

David almost laughed. What an indictment from his own son, but he squirmed all the same. He flung himself down in his armchair and picked up the newspaper. On the first page was a huge map of America, some big news story. It seemed a pointer to his future. Why not go off again and be someone else in America. He had managed it before and not been caught. No-one wanted him here, and he had loved the United States when he had been there before. Of course he would have to go to a different part of the States, so his various contacts over there would not recognise him. But most of his South African 'adventure' had been fun, and he could see himself happily creating a new persona again. There were no ties in England now. His father would not know if he was alive or dead, and if he left Jean could come back to the Old Rectory and look after the old man again. Now that his mother was dead there seemed no-one who really cared about his wishes any more. It had always been so great when she had been there. His favourite food, his special outings, always their lives had revolved around his wishes and desires. Now no-one thought about him anymore, least of all his own wife and children. His fingers curled as he thought of the perfidy of his erstwhile best friend, stealing his family away like that.

Ellen came in with the tea things. She had seen the small dignified figure of James striding down the drive, and had tactfully removed the mug of milk and extra sandwiches she had made. "Another bust-up" she thought to herself. "Where will it all end?"

It was not long before she was told. David had hardly touched his dinner that evening, and after he had toyed with his favourite treacle tart he looked up at Ellen when she came in to clear the dishes.

"Ellen, I don't seem to be fitting in here any longer." He put his hand up as Ellen started to remonstrate.

"I have decided to travel again, and I expect Jean will come back here and look after things, my father and so on. You have been very good to stay on here, but I can see I'm not wanted." He ended bitterly.

"Oh, but Sir..." Ellen had been so fond of him in the past, and, although she could see how badly he had behaved towards Jean and the children, her loyalties were torn.

"You mustn't blame Jean," said David, rather magnanimously he thought, "I always seem to be chasing after the next rainbow! Maybe I'll settle down in a few years, but not yet."

By the following week he was gone, and it was as if he had never come back; except they all had their memories of husband, father, Master and friend.

***

Jean received a brief note from David, stating his intentions of leaving the Old Rectory the next day. He thanked her briefly for looking after his father, hoping she would continue, but gave his permission to put him in a home if the care was too much for her. He wrote that the money arrangements would be the same, and on no account should anyone try and contact him. He suggested he might be travelling to inaccessible places again. He said nothing about Tom, divorce, or anything personal which would have made it easier for Jean. He did not mention the children.

She read it in disbelief, which rapidly turned to fury. Passing it to Tom she left the room, unable to contain her distress, and not willing to create a scene in front of the children. Tom read it, his blood boiling, clenching his fists as if he could go and hit his erstwhile friend into the next county.

"If only we had not been such friends in the past. It makes it so much harder to accept that he has changed so much." Tom said to his mother later,

Mrs Truckle grunted. "He was only friends when it suited him, His parents spoilt him and that's a fact. He always did just whatever he liked, and was never denied a thing he wanted. That's bad for a child, and don't you forget it Tom, when you are bringing up his children. And your own," she added quietly.

Tom looked up, startled.

"Yes," she smiled. "Even before David came back I thought Jean was getting that look in her eye. And haven't you noticed my boy, she's not too grand in the mornings?"

Tom was shattered. He thought he knew everything that was to do with Jean, but with all the hoo-ha of David's appearance little signs had passed him by. Now he hurried out to the orchard, where he knew Jean was hanging out the washing. She was taking a sheet out of the basket endeavouring to find the ends. Her hair was brushed back, and her cheeks flushed from the effort. As she lifted the sheet he noticed her breasts, usually small and pert, had become rounder and heavier. Approaching, he took one end of the sheet and helped her peg it out. Then he let his hands fall on her shoulders, and turned her to face him.

"My darling," he started, and could not go on. Jean, who had been wondering how she could break the news to him, melted into his arms.

"How did you guess?"

"I ought to have known, but Mother gave me a hint, just now. Oh, my dearest darling, this will be a new beginning for the whole family. A wonderful joyful happening for all of us." He gave a huge contented sigh.

"I feel it couldn't have happened at a better time. The children will have something else to think about and plan for; oh, you are so clever!"

"Well, you are pretty clever yourself," she laughed.

Jean sailed through this pregnancy. They had all moved back into the Old Rectory, within days of David's departure, and dear old Uncle George hardly noticed the comings and goings. At first, when Tom called in to see him, he became a little confused. But Tom was his usual gentle self, and George accepted his presence very quickly. He took a great deal of the load off Jean's shoulders, and insisted she should rest every afternoon. Sometimes he joined her, and those became precious times, when they lay and talked of everything under the sun, and occasionally he took her in his arms and loved her tenderly, knowing they had all the time and privacy they needed.

James thrived too. He watched his mother become happy and carefree, always smiling and singing to herself. He had been scared of his father, and although David had only once smacked him, James had always felt on edge when in his company. Elizabeth, the placid one, was happier than she had ever been. The prospect of Mummy having a baby for them all was exciting, and much better than dolls. She couldn't wait, and nearly every day she would ask, "Is the baby coming today Mummy?"

Therefore it was a very happy family which Benjamin Thomas joined at four o'clock on Friday 22nd November

1963. A lusty baby, no-one in the house was in any doubt when he emerged into the world. Tom had anxiously waited downstairs, shooed there by his mother, who took charge as she always had done with Jean's babies, but when Tom heard the forceful cry of protest emanating from his infant he was up the stairs three at a time. He slowed, a little hesitant as he opened the bedroom door, but he need not have worried. Jean was flushed but grinning, his mother wrapping the wriggling baby in a shawl, and old Doctor Howard turned and gave Tom a pat on the back,

"You have a splendid son, Tom my boy. Congratulations!"

***

The day Ben arrived became more than just a birthday. It was the day they all became a proper family. James and Elizabeth had hardly known their own father, and since Tom had been living in the Old Rectory he had become their 'real' father. They had always called him Uncle Tom, and Jean and Tom wondered how it would work out when Ben came to talk, and say "Daddy." As usual with children, the problem resolved itself. As soon as Ben began to speak he made up his own name for his father. One day, when Tom came in from work on the farm, Ben toddled over to him, lifted up his little arms and shouted "Clom, Clom." He had not mastered his 'T's', and this was the nearest he could get to copy his siblings. Naturally they all thought it was wonderful, and soon the other two were calling Tom by Ben's special name.

Jean had blossomed with happiness, and had decided she would not work so hard. They found another girl, Sarah, to help Ellen, and May became the children's Nanny. One of Tom's farm hands had a son who was mad keen to learn about gardening, therefore they were able to give him plenty of work, and under Jean's expert advice he became their full time gardener.

With more time on her hands Jean looked after herself a bit more, having her hair done sometimes, and resting if she was tired, so that she was always full of fun and energy for her beloved family. Tom never wanted to travel to London, or visit the 'bright lights' as he called them, but sometimes they all went out for the day in the little car he had bought, and visited Daymer Bay, or Polzeath, and let the children dig sandcastles and swim in the rock pools. But the farm always took precedence, and outings were few and far between.

James, particularly, longed for the day when he could be a proper 'lad' on the farm. But his main interest lay in the new machinery, and one of his highlights of the year was being taken to the Royal Cornwall Show. Once there he would head for the stands of new tractors and threshing machines, begging to be allowed to 'just sit' on them.

Just before Ben's first birthday, Tom suggested to Jean that they should go out for dinner at a local restaurant, just the two of them. This did not happen very often, although they did sometimes slip out for a meal on their own, enjoying being by themselves, and Jean loved putting on a nice dress and being with Tom alone for a while.

When they reached their destination she realized that it was the same place as Tom had taken her, long ago before she had married David. Tom's friend was still running it, and had made a great success of his venture, and he welcomed them as honoured customers. He ceremoniously seated them at the same table by the window, reminding Jean of how happy she could have been if she had accepted Tom's proposal all those years ago.

After they had partaken of the delicious fare on offer, Tom leant towards Jean.

"Do you remember?" he asked.

"Of course, my darling," she answered, "I was just thinking how foolish I was last time we were here. I should have said "Yes." Think of all those years I wasted, imagining David was the one for me."

Tom drew a velvet box out of his coat pocket, and handed it across the table to her.

"Last time we came here I hoped to be able to give you this, but instead I put it away until this evening. But now, my dearest Jean, will you wear it?"

She pressed the little clasp, and the lid opened to reveal a beautiful diamond ring, with a sapphire in the centre gleaming in the light of the candle on their table. She looked up, her eyes awash with tears, which glistened like the stones in the ring.

"Oh Tom," was all she could say, as she slipped it on her wedding finger. She held her hand out to him across the table. "Look, it fits perfectly."

Tom had noticed that she had removed all David's rings some months before, and he had taken one from her drawer, and asked the jeweller to make sure his ring would fit her finger. He would tell her one day.

***

Life went on in St. Wraich as it always had, ever since Jean could remember. There were the usual village celebrations, Christmas, Easter, and the summer holidays, with the Church Fete, and Jean's birthday. The tradition of having her birthday party as an element of the Fete had faded when she was married to David. He had not liked the idea of the village helping to celebrate.

On Jean's and Penny's special days, David had always arranged some smart dinner with a few friends, who might be of some use to him. Penny had been invited, but in the later years had found something else to do, and Jean did not enjoy these occasions. She remembered those days when it had all been such unsophisticated fun, and even the day when her parents had been staying remained in her memory as a special time. Talking about those days with Tom one evening gave him an idea. As the date of the Church Fete approached Jean was too busy organising the Cake and Jam Stall to remember she was going to be thirty five in a few days time.

The day dawned misty, always a sign in Cornwall of better weather later in the day. The Fete continued to be held at the

Old Rectory, as the garden was large enough for children's races, bowling for the pig, (donated, as always, by the Truckles), and all the sideshows and stalls. As they all prepared, the sun broke through, promising a warm and fair afternoon.

Jean handed the excited children over to May, and went upstairs to change into a cool and summery dress, and run a comb through her hair. She no longer used much makeup. David always said she looked dowdy without it, but Tom thought she looked beautiful as nature had intended her, and had persuaded her that she did not need any further adornment.

She ran down the stairs, to meet the 'distinguished person' who had been asked to open the Fete. She had not been told who this was, which was rather strange, but there always seemed to be some reason why she was not let into the 'little secret'.

"We are not quite sure," and "we can't tell you," were the rather odd answers she was given when she enquired.

No-one was in the hall, so she made her way out of the garden door to be met with a sea of faces, all singing, "Happy Birthday to you!" In the foreground Tom was standing with the children, and one other rather special person, looking mischievous and full of fun... Penny!

Tom grinned, "We thought we'd revive the double birthday party you both used to share, and managed to drag Penny away from London."

Jean swooped down and flung her arms round her friend in a most unladylike way.

"Penny, how super! Oh I can't believe you're here. It is ages since you came back to have our old celebration again, Oh dear, I think I'm going to cry!"

Tom produced a large handkerchief, and an even larger grin. It had taken some planning, and a lot of subterfuge to arrange this party within, as it were, a party. But most of the village had been in it from the start. They all adored Jean, and had known Penny when she was a child, and, in any case, they loved any excuse to give Jean back something for all that she had done for them over the years. The cake was wheeled in, and the two girls cut it with much hilarity, toasts were drunk in tea and lemonade, and then the afternoon got down to the main event, raising money for the Church. Jean, with Penny's help, sold all the cakes on her stall very quickly, and then they were free to wander round, making fools of themselves, giggling like the children they had been once, and generally radiating such joy that it affected the whole afternoon.

"A good time was had by all." Never was a saying truer.

Much later, in the privacy of their bed, Jean thanked Tom for his wonderful idea.

"You couldn't have given me a more wonderful day. I'll remember it all my life," she whispered to him.

Penny stayed in St. Wraich for a few days. Her parents were still living in the 'big house', and were delighted to have their daughter at home again. She had not been back regularly, having a demanding job as a Personal Assistant to the Managing Director of a large printing firm. Also, she had lost touch with Jean when David was there. He had made it quite obvious he did not like her much and it became awkward for Jean, so she had stayed away. The ice had now been broken, and she promised Jean she would come down often from now on.

Life for Jean and Tom flowed on like a tranquil river, although there were a few moments when their peaceful existence was momentarily disturbed.

The children always visited their Grandfather at teatime, just popping in to say "hullo" or tell him little snippets about their lives. George loved them. He did not really know who they were, often referring to James as "David," but he smiled and sometimes gave them a little sweet or chocolate.

They now employed a full time nurse to care for him, especially as he was inclined to wander off suddenly; even, once, with no clothes on. Luckily he did not get very far, just to the end of the drive, where Tom, coming home from the farm, found him and gently brought him back, trying not to grin too much.

"Poor old dear, he would have been mortified if he had realized. The Rector of this Parish starkers, oh dear!"

After that, Nurse Beryl was brought in, and she quickly became part of the happy group.

One cold winter's day Jean went up to see if he had enough blankets, and to have her daily 'chat' with him. Beryl had gone to make a cup of tea, and Jean found George sitting mournfully, staring into space.

"Hallo, Uncle George, I've just come to see you are warm enough. It is so cold outside; they are saying it might snow tomorrow."

But George did not wonder about snow, or ice, or storms, He had finally left them to join his beloved Nancy, sitting in his chair, surrounded by all his own possessions, comfortable and contented.

Jean was sad, but not bereft. She knew he had longed for this day, and his belief was strong and steadfast.

James was very upset at first. He had loved his grandfather, and was old enough to remember George before he lost his memory. But Jean comforted him with the knowledge that George had looked forward to dying, that he believed it was not the end, but the beginning of a new kind of life, and no-one should be sad for him, only for the ones who had to wait for the next life themselves.

"But Mummy, how do we know where Granpa has gone?" asked James forlornly, on the way to the school bus with Jean.

"You know that window in the Church, behind the Altar?"

"The one where there a lot of flowers and birds and things, and Jesus, looking at them?"

"Yes, that is where Granpa has gone or somewhere very like that. Granny will be there too and he wanted to be with Granny again, so he is happy now."

"Will he be able to remember Granny then?"

Oh yes. When we get to Heaven, everything is perfect again, just like we wish it could be always. But you only get to Heaven," she added thoughtfully, "when Jesus invites you to come."

"Granpa got his invitation then. When did it come? I didn't see the postman today."

Well," Jean struggled manfully, "It is a sort of magic invitation, and kind of comes when your body is ready to leave this world and go on to Heaven. Usually at exactly the right moment."

"But, you get buried, don't you? That isn't very nice, not like the window."

"Darling," she put her arms round him, "your body is like the egg shells of your chicken's eggs. The real life is inside the shell, and our real life is inside our body. We just bury the shell, because the inside has gone to live with Jesus in heaven; in that lovely garden, with all the flowers and things."

"Is Jesus there?" James was not going to let it go lightly.

"Yes, He is always nearby if we need Him, in this world and the next."

James had to be satisfied with that explanation as they had reached the bus stop.

***

A certain re-arrangement of the house followed George's death. His suite of rooms was completely redecorated, slightly altered, and made into a study-bedroom for James, a new bedroom for Elizabeth, and a sitting room for the children as they became too grownup for nursery life. A new bathroom was also installed. Jean and Tom both were looking ahead to the days when one or more children flew the nest, and they could take in bed and breakfasters.

There was always a demand for accommodation for visitors to Cornwall, more and more as news of the delights of the most western county spread. Surfing became much more of a sport than just a fun thing to do with a body board. Visitors arrived with equipment which made the local lads stare with envy, and they all gravitated to the beach to watch the tanned youngsters riding in on the waves, standing up on the boards instead of lying on them.

When James reached his teens he yearned for a "proper" surfboard, and eventually, on his fourteenth birthday, he was given one by James and his mother. They all went down to Polzeath, and watched his first attempts, which were not very successful, and created much laughter and banter being shouted from the sidelines as he struggled to stand up on the board.

The surfing community was always ready to help a newcomer, and after a few hints from the more experienced lads he managed to stand, if only for a few seconds, as the wave bore him triumphantly in towards the beach. But it was a beginning, and after that he was hooked. He begged lifts to the beach off his family whenever he could, and soon was quite competent riding the waves.

As he grew older the sun and sea transformed him into a golden god, much sort after by the girls who hung around the surfing beaches. Occasionally he allowed Elizabeth to tag along, and was very protective of his young sister. When the whole family made a day of it, he took Ben out and let him ride on his board, (and fall off!) but he always made sure Ben was quite secure, so that Jean and Tom could relax, knowing the younger ones were safe with James and his friends.

If only life could go on so peacefully forever.

***

James attended school in Truro, which entailed a long bus journey every day. He also missed out on many after school activities, and several of his friends told him of the fun they had as boarders. Jean was very loathe to let her firstborn live away from home, but even she was beginning to see that James would benefit from staying at the school during the week.

"You see, Mum," James explained to his mother, "so much goes on after lessons, and all that time I spend in the school bus I could be studying, and then have time to do some other classes. There are so many, like woodwork and electronics I'd really like to do, but miss out on. Please Mum. I'd be back at the weekends, so it wouldn't be much different."

He had an ally in Tom, who eventually persuaded Jean, and by doing so further endeared himself to James.

"He would be amongst boys of his own age, in a safe environment, and you know how keen he is on machinery. He doesn't get the chance to study it, except on the farm. If he wants to make that his career, it is a good way to start."

At first, they all missed him terribly, and were inclined to spoil him when he returned at the weekend. But Tom, ever the sensible one, reminded Jean of David and how Nancy would grant David's every wish, and how he turned out, spoilt and selfish.

"Tom, you are so right, as usual," said Jean, hugging him, and after that, when Fridays came, and James returned, it was as if he had always been there. Nothing special, just queries about cricket or football, and "wash your hands, it's nearly teatime!"

Elizabeth travelled to Wadebridge every day. She had no wish to go further afield, although Jean often wondered if she should not have sent her to Glen Marten, her old school in Somerset. But Elizabeth was a real homebody, and was perfectly happy to be able to stay in St. Wraich while she grew up.

Ben sailed through Primary School in St. Wraich. He was never short of friends in the village, and loved being at home. Tom gave him some hens, which he treated as pets, and was so proud to present his mother, and even Aunty Truckle, with nice brown eggs. When one of them inexplicably died, she was given a state funeral, attended by everyone he could persuade to come. They all stayed to tea afterwards, and thoroughly enjoyed the whole proceedings. Ben confided to his mother that dying wasn't too bad after all, if you could have a party afterwards.

But soon they all discovered it was worse.

***

James was delighted to have been accepted as a pupil at the Duchy College to study farm mechanics. It meant boarding during the term, but was close enough to St. Wraich to come home some weekends. These became fewer and fewer as he got more and more involved with college activities. His only regret was the distance the college was from the sea, and therefore the surfing. When he did arrive home it was not long before he was off again with his friends to catch the latest waves.

"Off again," she grumbled to Tom. "There do not seem enough hours in the day for James! I wish he would stay here a bit more, I never get to talk to him."

"But darling, isn't that a whole lot better than mooching round doing nothing!" laughed Tom.

"What would I do without your sense? Now, what are you going to do today? Going off too, I suppose." It sounded like another grumble, so she gave him a grin. "I really could do with a little more loving attention, you know!"

"Just you wait, my girl. You've asked for it, and later you'll get it!" He gave her a playful slap on her bottom and went off whistling.

He had to plough up the bottom field that morning, and, knowing it was some way from the farm, he had taken sandwiches and a flask of tea, which he stowed behind the tractor seat. He reached the field, and spent a little while eyeing the lie of the land. It was a bit steep, and therefore tricky, but he had tackled it many times before. He turned on the radio; Radio Cornwall was always interesting, full of local news and gossip. Starting up the tractor he set off. After an hour he was satisfied with his progress. Looking back he saw good straight furrows. His Dad would be proud of him. "I'll just do another half hour," he thought, "and then stop for a mug of hot tea, and stretch my legs." There was a bit of a steep incline in the centre of the field, and he slowed down to take it easily. Putting his foot on the brake he could not feel a response. "Blast," he thought, "the wretched cog has slipped again." He tried to change gear, but the engine did not respond. The incline was approaching, and he desperately tried to steer the tractor to the left, so as to avoid the worst of the slope. But the engine seemed to have a mind of its own, gathering speed as it hurtled downwards. There was a huge bump as the machine hit a rock, disguised by the grass, and Tom felt the great contraption begin to topple. He was flung out as it went over, hitting the ground with such force that he was mercifully knocked out, and did not know the horror of tons of weight crushing him into eternity.

***

James was due home for the holidays that evening, and was looking forward to telling Tom that he was now qualified to service a tractor, and therefore could pull his weight on the farm this time. He arrived to find his mother looking worried. "I don't know where Tom has got to," she said. "I know he was ploughing the bottom field, but he should have been back by now."

"Don't worry Mum, I'll go down there and see if I can help. The wretched machine has probably broken down, and you know he hasn't a clue about mechanics, and now I can help him," he finished proudly. "I was going to have a look at it this hols anyway. That tractor played up last time I was here I remember."

He set off in high spirits, delighted he would have such an early chance to show off his new skills. But the scene that met him needed more than he could give. When he saw the tractor on its side he gasped and ran down the hill, but was unprepared for the sight which greeted him. A little way up from the great machine lay the mangled body of his beloved mentor, his uncle who in his eyes was really his father, and loved by everyone, now gone from them all in such tragic circumstances.

He approached gingerly, bent down and touched Tom gently, but there was no sign of life. For a moment he gave way to heaving sobs. Out there in the field, with no one to see or hear, he shouted in anguish. He was a small boy again, and the best friend he would ever have lay dead in front of him. But then he thought of his mother, waiting with tea for them all, and the worse horror hit him, that he would have to be the one to bring the news of her beloved Tom, who would come home to tea no more.

America

Chapter 20

He spent three days in an anonymous hotel at Heathrow, signing in as Gordon Pennyfeather, a name that came to him out of the blue as he wrote in the book. He was rather proud of it, but decided to revert to his own initials once he reached New York. He had spent a little while mulling over suitable and dignified names, and had come up with Daniel Alistair Brooke. He spent the next two days getting used to it. He went and bought a ticket in that name, having frequented one or two dubious bars in London, finding a member of the underworld who altered his passport accordingly. He also called in on his solicitors, leaving a sealed envelope with his details and other necessary papers to be unopened unless he was pronounced dead at some time. Then he settled all his bills with cash and having once more successfully covered his tracks, he left England on a night flight to New York.

He was exhausted, both physically and emotionally, and glad when the stewardess came round with a soft blanket and pillows.

"Can I get you anything else sir?" she purred. Daniel, feeling a bit randy after the generous free drinks which the airline handed out to First Class passengers, nearly said, "Yes please, you will do." Then he grinned inwardly. I mustn't blot my copy book, he thought. He put on the sleep mask and slept as they winged their way across the Atlantic. Sooner than he thought possible he was being woken with a steaming hot towel and a cup of coffee, and instructions to prepare for landing at New York Airport in twenty minutes.

"Now it begins," he thought, with a twinge of conscience at everything he had left behind, both in South Africa and

England. The cold air hit him as he stepped from the plane. He had forgotten the icy blasts which could sweep the country in the winter. He could see a scattering of snow on the ground, parts of it noticeably grubby, and not at all the view that people expected at the gateway to America. Entering the huge concourse the atmosphere changed to clinging warmth, as the heating vents poured forth the sort of environment to which Americans had become accustomed, and indeed expected. He stood waiting for his suitcases to appear on the carousel, and wondered where he should make for next. One of the billboards showed a sun-filled beach scene, with girls playing in the surf, and palm trees edging the sand. "Come to Sunny Florida" it screamed at him in large black letters.

Why not? He thought. I could do with a bit of sun, sea and..." his suitcases appeared at that moment, and he summoned a porter.

"Where to, sir?" the porter asked, heaving Daniel's cases onto his trolley.

"The check in-desk for Florida," he said.

Daniel was well used to airports, and settled down for a long wait for the flight to Miami. He found a comfortable chair in the First Class Lounge, and read the papers, drank endless cups of complimentary coffee, and took a little promenade every now and then to stretch his legs. He kept a weather eye open for people who might know him; unlikely, but one could never be too careful.

He could not help noticing a young lady sitting at the other side of the lounge, reading a magazine, and every now and then impatiently looking at her watch. Feeling bored, he walked over with the excuse of picking up another newspaper, and casually remarked, "I do hate the long time one has to wait, in order to get anywhere quickly."

She looked up, and Daniel found himself gazing into eyes the colour of the blue seas he recalled in South Africa. She put her hand up to push her long chestnut curls back.

"Where are you going?" she asked.

"Miami, for the moment," he replied, "then, well, it depends on all sorts of things."

She put her magazine down beside her, and picked up her coffee cup, which Daniel noticed was empty.

"Let me get you another?"

"Gee, thanks. I really do need it after the last few days."

Daniel walked over to the cafeteria and poured two more cups and brought them over to her.

"My name's Daniel Brooke, by the way."

"Annabel Studebaker." She took the cup gratefully.

"Why do you need this so badly, or shouldn't I ask?"

She flashed a large emerald ring at him. It was on the third finger of her left hand, which faintly disappointed him.

"I've just been buying my wedding dress," she explained without enthusiasm. "What a palaver. I really don't like it much, even now." She looked utterly miserable.

Daniel did not know what to say, but plunged in.

"Surely the dress is not that important. It is who you are marrying and your whole life together which is the important bit."

"That's just it. I suddenly thought yesterday that I don't love Brad and never will, and now it is too late, and..." she began to weep quietly.

Daniel produced his large white handkerchief and passed it over to her.

"I expect you are tired."

"Probably that too. Here I am, sobbing my silly heart out to a complete stranger. I am so sorry." And she blew her nose, mopped her eyes, looked up at him, and Daniel was lost... When he left St. Wraich he had decided he would not get entangled with a woman ever again; and here he was, barely arrived, and there she was, unbelievably beautiful, needing someone. He longed to put his arms round her, and comfort her in the only way he knew how. Not possible, even in a First Class lounge, he felt.

At that moment the tannoy announced the flight to Miami. He helped her with her bags and parcels, and allowed her to get on board in front of him. He felt for his wallet, and pressing a hefty fifty dollar bill into the steward's hand he arranged for his seat to be changed.

"How strange," he said as he sat down next to Annabel. "We seem to be seated next to each other."

"That's nice."

The three-hour journey passed surprisingly quickly for both of them. Plied liberally with drinks, Annabel related her troubles to Daniel, not asking for sympathy, but, as she said, "to get my head round things."

"Sometimes," she confided, "it is easier to talk to strangers, and I really needed to talk to someone."

Daniel understood her parents were keen on this young man. He was of impeccable family, with a large property, (real estate as she referred to it), and plenty of money. The families had adjoining land, and she had known him "forever."

"It kinda seemed the right thing to do, and at Christmas when Brad proposed in front of the whole family. I did not know where to look or what to say; so I said "Yes," and now I really think I should have said "No." Oh Daniel, I don't know what to do," and she began to sob again.

Fortunately, being in First Class, they had seats on their own, with no close fellow travellers to see and hear Annabel's distress. The stewardess silently produced a box of tissues and another brandy, and left them to sort out whatever it was troubling them. Daniel longed to be able to take her in his arms to comfort her, but he tentatively handed her a tissue, and then put his hand on her arm.

"Just cry it out, then we'll talk," he advised.

The storm subsided, and Annabel gave him a watery smile.

"What you must think of me, blubbing like a schoolgirl."

"I think you are even prettier when you weep," he answered softly, giving her hand a little squeeze.

They sat in companionable silence, until Daniel looked at his watch.

"We land in about twenty-five minutes," he said. "Is anyone meeting you?"

"Well, as a matter of fact, no. I have come on a much earlier flight than fixed. I couldn't bear to look at any more clothes. The thought of wearing them on honeymoon made me feel ill. Anyone meeting you?"

"No, I'm quite alone and fancy-free. Let's pretend we are a couple and go off to a hotel somewhere. So we can talk some more," he added quickly, just in case Annabel thought he was trying to seduce her or something.

"Ok, I guess we could go to the Silver Springs Hotel. It has nice comfy armchairs we can relax in, and maybe have a swim in the pool." She hesitated. "It is rather expensive, I'm not sure..."

He grinned. "Don't worry. No money problems. If you travel First Class you don't ask the price!"

The Silver Springs was, indeed, a luxurious hotel. It looked like something out of the movies. He caught himself smiling. ("I'm becoming American already," he thought). The air was balmy compared to New York, and the sun shone with all the promise of the poster fulfilled.

The porter took their bags, and Daniel went over to the large and imposing Reception desk and booked a suite, and they went up in the lift (elevator, now) to the sixth floor.

"I thought this would be quieter than the lounge," he told Annabel. "Please don't think...."

"No, of course not. Good idea though. We could have lunch sent up a bit later."

"What time do you have to leave, Annabel? I am a completely free agent, and I'd like to stay here for a few days and look round."

"No-one is expecting me for a couple of days. I'd really like to show you round Miami, if you would like that."

Daniel smiled.

"I would like that very much. If you don't mind, this apartment has two bedrooms. We both could stay here. Shall we have all our luggage sent up?"

"Why not." Annabel agreed with alacrity, a little stirring of anticipation in her belly. She felt so at home with this gorgeous, polite and understanding Englishman, as if she had known him all her life, and could tell him anything.

Daniel thought briefly of St. Wraich, cold, wet and grey, and that was only the weather. Maggie lingered in his consciousness, but faded equally quickly. This was the country to be in; lively and exciting, the sun reflecting his mood. He was in his middle years with a future still ahead, and with him a stunning girl as companion. The world seemed to be at his feet, waiting for them to explore together.

Annabel found herself coming under his spell. He seemed like a small boy at times, with a new toy. At others he took charge in a satisfactorily masculine way, and she realized that he was invading her bruised heart as well.

They spent some time in the lovely blue waters of the hotel pool. Lying next to each other on the sun-loungers after a swim, they never stopped talking. Quite early on Annabel confided to Daniel that she was going to break off her engagement to Brad. She realized now he would never be the man for her. (Now she had met the man who would, she thought).

"What about the dress?" Daniel asked with a grin of mischief.

"Oh, I daresay I'll find a time to wear it," she said, rather shakily.

They became such friends that Annabel telephoned her parents to tell them she was staying on in Miami with some people she had met, and would return home in a few days. She rang Brad and had a difficult and non-conclusive conversation with him. She realized she would have to break off their engagement face to face, but postponed the confrontation. Daniel was stealing into her heart, and she wanted to keep him all to herself for the time being.

Daniel, too, felt the brush of Cupid's wings and the excitement of a new love; another rainbow.

The hotel boasted an orchestra, which played every evening. Couples danced to the evocative music, and Daniel and

Annabel joined them on the dance floor, smooching a little to the lilting sounds of the sentimental tunes being played. On the third evening Daniel held Annabel a little closer than before, and lowered his head to rest his lips on her temple.

"This feels so right," he murmured, as he kissed her gently. She did not resist. She had never really fallen in love. Brad had merely been there like a big brother, and even after he asked her to marry him, he had never been at all romantic. But now, now Daniel was wooing her, slowly and languorously, as they shuffled round the tiny dance floor. She felt as if all her insides were melting, as he caressed her back. When the music stopped he did not immediately let her go, (as Brad always had), but gave her a little extra hug.

"What do you think you would say if I asked you to marry me?"

She hesitated, only a fraction.

"I think I would say "Yes please, as soon as possible!" she breathed. She could hardly speak; it was all rather sudden, and yet she had been expecting it, wanting it, ever since they had met in the Airport lounge.

They bought the ring the next day. Daniel realized Annabel came from a family who would not think much of a man who leapt into bed with a girl before asking for her hand in marriage, and so they still slept a few yards apart in the separate bedrooms. It was hard for both of them, and all resolutions were nearly broken once or twice.

"You are sweet to want to wait," Annabel remarked next morning.

"I really don't want to, at all. I'd adore making love to you all night, right now, but I think in the circumstances...There are quite a few loose ends to tie up first."

***

The Studebakers lived some way out of Miami, on a lovely stretch of land reaching down to the sea. Annabel went home after three days, dreading a confrontation, both with her parents, and Brad.

Brad lived a just up the coast, and arrived shortly after he heard Annabel was home again, expecting to greet his future bride, and settle down to finalising wedding plans.

She met him as he drove up in his little sports car, looking eager and pleased to see her again.

"Hi there!" he jumped out of the car and turned expectantly, with his arms out, to welcome her. She went towards him slowly, and allowed him to hug her, but she almost felt distaste, as he crushed her to his side. Not that many hours ago, she had parted from Daniel, and she could still feel the warmth of their parting embrace.

"What's this, now? Not feeling well? "Brad looked puzzled as he drew away.

"Brad, we must talk. Before we go indoors, now."

"You sound serious, my angel, what's happened?" he asked, turning to retrieve a little parcel out of the car.

"Perhaps this will cheer you up," and he handed it to her.

She looked down at the package, and slowly pulled at the pretty ribbons. A small box revealed a lovely delicate crystal necklace, lying on a deep blue velvet cushion. It was so beautiful, and she felt tears pricking her eyes.

"I don't know, Brad," she said quietly. "It is so lovely, but I can't accept it."

"Why ever not?"

"I don't quite know how to tell you, Brad, but you see..."

"See what?"

"I've... I've met someone else," she blurted out. "Oh Brad, I still think you are a dear, and I love you, but I have discovered I don't love you in the right sort of way."

"And this....person. You love him in the right sort of way?" Brad almost sneered. "How come? Suddenly you go away for barely a week, to buy your wedding dress, and somehow find another man. Annabel, we've known each other all our lives; how do you tell, when you know me so well?"

"I know. When this happens to you, you will know. It is like a sort of thunderbolt and you can't stop it. However many people you hurt you know you could never live with anyone else."

Brad bit his lower lip.

"I know. I've known all my life that I wanted to marry you. I thought you felt the same and now suddenly...."

He turned to get back into his car.

She made to hand back the little box.

"Oh, keep the ruddy necklace. Maybe one day you will look at it and wish..." he swallowed hard, and with a roar of the powerful engine, was off down the drive in a cloud of dust.

Annabel's parents came out to welcome Brad, having left them to greet each other as they felt young lovers should, and were astonished to find their daughter standing in the drive with a small box in her hand, gazing mournfully at the departing car.

"What has happened? Why has Brad gone off? Have you lovebirds had a quarrel?"

"Sort of," she said quietly. "I've just told Brad I can't marry him."

There was a stunned silence.

"But...you cannot do this. What on earth...?"

Annabel looked at them, and then rushed inside, leaving them with no explanation. They had always thought of Brad as the son they had never had, and they could not imagine what had happened.

"Best leave her." Marlon said to his wife with a sigh. "Probably only a lover's tiff. Wedding nerves, don't you call it?"

Stephanie shook her head.

"It seemed more than that, it appeared pretty serious. Guess I'd better go in after her and find out. Maybe sort something out before it goes too far."

She found Annabel standing gazing out of the window, her eyes bright with tears, but otherwise composed.

"Dearest child..." she started.

"Mom, I am not a child, and I know my own mind. I am not going to marry Brad."

"But, Annabel, the wedding is all planned, and I am sure you can make it up. You were so happy when you left for

New York. Bringing back your wedding gown, and getting so excited before you left. What has happened?"

"Someone else has happened, Mom. I met the most fantastic man in the world, and he is planning to see Poppa and ask for my hand, and...and all those proper things men should do. He's English, and very rich, so you needn't worry about him being after your money, or anything."

She paused for breath, and went on. "His name is Daniel Brooke. He is just about the only man I would ever marry. I told Brad I didn't love him enough, or in the right way. You must know what that is, Mom; after all you and Poppa love each other and got married for love. Didn't you?" she finished deliberately.

"Well, yes, darling. But we had known each other for a long time. Our families were friends for years, and we grew up together. We thought you and Brad were repeating history in the most delightful way. Do we know anything about this...this Daniel Brooke?"

"Only that I love him, and he loves me; and no, Mom, he hasn't slept with me, in case you are thinking I've got to get married for any reason."

Stephanie swallowed, and speechless, she went downstairs to relate to Marlon their conversation.

Three days later Daniel telephoned, very polite and apologetic for causing such an upheaval, and asked if he might call the following day to see Mr Studebaker. Marlon took the call, and was icily courteous, arranging for Daniel to present himself at noon. Marlon told him not to contact Annabel beforehand, but he did invite him to stay to lunch. Marlon felt he could always show him the door if he proved to be the bounder he was expecting.

***

At exactly noon a new Chevrolet drew up, and Marlon, watching by the study window, saw a tall well-built man alight. He opened the rear door, and leaning in, drew out a beautiful bouquet of flowers. As he walked towards the house Marlon's first impression was of a mature good looking person, well-dressed in an understated way, with tidy fair brown hair and a reliable face. Marlon was relieved, as was Stephanie, who was watching from her bedroom window, and she went downstairs to welcome Daniel.

When he was shown where to go by Ada, the maid, he found himself in a lovely sunny room with flowers everywhere.

"Oh dear," he exclaimed, "I am so sorry, I should have brought chocolates!"

They all laughed, and the ice was broken. After a few moments Stephanie excused herself "to see how lunch was coming along," and Daniel and Marlon looked at each other.

"I am so grateful to you sir," Daniel began nervously. He had never had to do this before. A picture of his own father swam into his mind, which he hastily suppressed.

"I realize," he went on, "that this is all rather quick, and that my appearance has somewhat upset a great many plans. But I wondered if you would very kindly give me permission to ask Annabel to marry me?"

It was not a shock to Marlon, but it did surprise him to be so formal. Perhaps this was the English way of doing things, and none the worse for that. He held out his hand.

"Daniel, I have only just met you, although we are in no doubt as to Annabel's feelings. If you swear to look after her, as we have done since she was born, then you have our blessing."

Marlon could hardly believe his own words. He had been prepared to prevaricate, to play the heavy parent; but somehow Daniel had overridden all his doubts in the first easy instant, and he thought that this man was probably right for Annabel after all.

After that it was sunshine and light and laughter for the remainder of the afternoon.

***

Daniel had decided to chance fate and use the time shrewdly after Annabel left to travel home from Miami. He contacted several Real Estate firms with a view to purchasing a house in or near Miami. This proved easier than he ever thought, as the type of dwelling he was looking for, spacious, one story with attractive grounds, seemed plentiful, and he was given the details of several. He spent a happy day poring over photographs and plans, finally deciding on three which he felt would be suitable. He then prudently decided to wait and see the sort of reception he would receive from the Studebakers before finalising any sale.

The one he particularly liked and he hoped Annabel would feel the same, was just north of Miami. It was on the coast, but a highway ran between the property and the beach. When he viewed "Summervale" as it was called, he immediately put down a deposit. The residence was shielded from the road by a thicket of shrubs, which completely insulated the house and garden from any noise of traffic, or prying eyes. The house was light and airy, with enormous windows, most of which faced the huge spreading lawns at the back. These led down to a stream which formed the boundary at the rear, the water glinting in the sunlight. Several large mature trees provided welcome shade. Someone had made an effort to create a flower border, which was now looking neglected and weedy. But overall the garden formed a peaceful background for an elegant residence, suitable for a new bride. He could not wait to show it to her.

He then moved his possessions into a hotel near the Studebakers, and after a couple of days he telephoned Annabel's parents.

Daniel was swept into the preparations for the wedding. As it had already been arranged, they all decided it would be more sensible to adhere to the same plans, only, as they all laughed, with a different bridegroom. He found Annabel grow more enchanting every day. Her parents were frankly amazed at her enthusiasm and gaiety, as before she had just gone along with every suggestion, in a lacklustre sort of way. They now realized there had been nothing exciting for their daughter about marrying Brad; it had almost seemed like a brother and sister moving in together. But with Daniel it was a different matter altogether. It was obvious how much she had fallen in love, and was revelling in every little detail of her marriage.

After a few days Daniel suggested they should go and look at the property he had found. He did not want to complete the purchase until he knew Annabel liked it. This was also a new venture for him. Always before, the house had already been there. It had been (was) his own house in Cornwall, and Polly's own in South Africa. Now he was buying a house for his bride, and it was exciting. He felt a young man again, just starting out with a wife on his arm and a future to look forward to.

He drove Annabel in his Chevrolet, and when they reached the road along the beach, he slowed down.

"We are nearly there! Now!" and he swept in through the white gates, through the dense mass of shrubs, round the bend in the drive, and drew up in front of the wide steps leading up to the front door. Annabel gasped.

"Oh, darling, it is gorgeous. Can we go in and look? Have you got a key?"

"The answer to all those questions is yes!" He went round to her side and helped her out, which involved a few kisses and hugs. They went up the steps hand-in-hand like a couple of children exploring forbidden territory. Daniel unlocked the large front door, leading into a spacious hall. There were various doors leading out of the lobby, and he led the way through one of them, throwing it open wide. Annabel stepped into a large and beautifully proportioned room, with huge windows which drew her forwards. Outside the green swards stretched invitingly downwards, and the old trees cast their shade, creating welcome shadows in the hot day.

"Oh," she could only breathe, "Daniel, it is gorgeous. Almost too beautiful for a couple starting out. Can we really have it, for our own?"

"No," he said, startling her out of her reverie. Then, noticing her expression of disappointment, he put his arms round her.

"My darling, *we* can't have it. It is my wedding present to *you,* if you would like it. Would you accept it with my undying love?"

Annabel found she could not speak, but smiled with gratitude and happiness, and they stood for a long time, arms round each other, overcome by the love which they had both found for each other.

Later on, planning in between kisses, Daniel told her that the house came fully furnished. It had belonged to a couple who had gone to live in New York, and did not want the hassle of moving their furniture.

"We can, of course, throw everything out, and start again," Daniel told her, "but I thought we could move in and then change anything we wished as we went along."

Annabel was only too happy to go along with that idea, especially as the former owners seemed to have had very good taste. She was so thrilled to have such a gorgeous gift from her future husband and she couldn't wait to show it to her parents. It was further proof of Daniel's perfections as a son-in-law.

Chapter 21

Daniel married Annabel under the shade of the acacia trees in the garden. Seeing his bride come down the steps on the arm of her father, dressed in white, with a veil demurely hiding her shining eyes, he thought that this was his real wedding. The others had been shams. Jean had virtually been his little sister, and Polly...well, best not to think of Polly. She had somehow bewitched him under the African stars, and he had often wondered since if she had pretended he was Paul in order to please her parents, who had obviously considered him 'a good catch.' The only good thing that had come out of that union was Maggie, and he tried not to think of his darling mop-haired child. One day he would meet her again, and try and make it up to her. Meanwhile, the music was starting, and his one and only love was walking towards him across the lawn.

They spent the first two nights of their honeymoon in Key Biscayne. The festivities had seemed to go on forever, and Daniel, sensing this would be the case, had decided not to travel for a day or two, to give them a chance to relax and recover. The Carlton Hotel was situated on the barrier island of Key Biscayne, with golden sands and the sparkling ocean stretching before it. It was dark when they finally drove up to the imposing entrance. Neither of them fancied a large meal, or even more champagne, and therefore they were shown straight up to the sumptuous suite which Daniel had reserved.

Still faintly intoxicated from the excitement of the wedding, not to mention the wines they had been drinking all afternoon, they melted into each other's arms. Daniel said gently;

"Do you want to wait or..." Annabel gave a nervous giggle.

"I don't think so. I've never...never done 'it' before. But..." Daniel put his arms gently round her, and kissed her, and gradually nature took over. The room whirled a bit, as they fell onto the big bed, and somehow, slowly, languorously, they divested themselves of their clothing. It was the first time Daniel had seen Annabel's breasts. Her bikini had always covered them before, and now he buried his face between them, kissing her nipples softly, teasing them into ardour. Annabel had never seen a naked male in her life, having had no brother, and she felt faintly apprehensive. She had seen diagrams, of course, but the sight of Daniel aroused was a shock. But as he caressed her, stroking her thighs and letting his fingers explore places she had not known existed, she too, became eager and passionate, and they came together in the most natural way, reaching a climax of excitement together, when the whole world seemed to explode about them, and they clung to each other as if that would be the last thing they would do on earth.

Daniel was astonished by the feelings which swept over him that night. He remembered Jean, anxious and compliant; Polly too eager, avid almost, as if she wanted to devour him. But Annabel seemed absolutely perfect, and he felt he had reached the end of his rainbow at last. They gazed into each other's eyes in wonder at finding themselves in such heaven together.

They did not see much of Key Biscayne before they left for what Daniel called "their real honeymoon." They flew to Hawaii, where they spent two weeks exploring the beaches, and, more importantly, each other. They had a little cottage right on a beach, with golden sands and hardly any other inhabitants. One evening, when no one was about, Annabel threw off her bikini, and plunged in the rough surf quite naked.

"This is wonderful!" she shouted. Daniel watched her for a minute. She looked utterly beautiful, her hair tousled by the waves, her perfect body tanned, and her eyes shining with delight. "Come on, darling, come and join me!"

Without hesitating Daniel stripped off his shorts and gasped as the breakers hit him as he plunged in the surf. He swam towards her and caught her round the waist, drawing her to him. They held each other for a moment, then, "This is too much!" he shouted above the roar of the waves, and picking her up he carried her to the beach. As he reached the edge he stumbled, and laughing they found themselves collapsed on the sand, and in a while, entwined as they were, there could be only one outcome.

They both, in their own private memories, recalled that moment for the rest of their lives. It was their marriage, a pledge of love to each other, a promise given as binding as any in the nuptials, and a private vow without words to be man and wife together for the rest of their lives.

***

Annabel and Daniel settled into their new lives as if they had been together forever. If Annabel sometimes wondered why her beloved husband never mentioned his past, she was far too contented to worry much. Every now and then Daniel would mention England, and when she asked he gave vague answers, so casually that it did not seem to matter. She did gather he had loved his mother, but both his parents had died long ago. He had an elderly aunt, suffering from senile dementia, and in a home. He also implied he had inherited a sizable income, which he had put to such good use in the wine business, that money never need be a worry. They sailed through the golden days of summer, reveling in their new home. They decided to build a swimming pool in a part of the garden hidden from the drive by shrubs. The sea was not far away, and sometimes they strolled across the road and frolicked in the surf. But the road was a fairly busy one, and Daniel determined that there should be no risk to Annabel if she wanted to swim. They employed a fairly large staff to look after the house and garden, and Annabel's natural flair for design soon showed itself, both in the house and grounds. She loved having plenty of flowers for the house. She designed a flower bed especially for cutting, and another, which could be seen from the main living room, for pleasure. Nearly every morning Ned, the gardener, would arrive at the side door with bunches of roses, sweet peas, gladioli, or whatever was at its best, and Annabel would take time to arrange vases of flowers all over the house, flooding it with perfume from the blooms. Long after, Daniel would always remember the scent of those flowers wafting about him if he walked into a room where flowers had been arranged.

They spent their first Christmas in their new home, delighting in being able to invite Annabel's parents over for the day. Stephanie and Marlon would have preferred to have had the newlyweds to their house, but Annabel was so excited at showing off her new domesticity, they drove to Summervale laden with gifts for everyone, including the gardener. An air of anticipation permeated the house for days, as Annabel went crazy with preparations. She was determined to show how capable she had become at running a household.

Daniel, wisely for once, kept disappearing to his den with the excuse of investigating his latest investments, and so there were no arguments as he recalled happening in the run-up to the festive season, with Jean particularly. Thinking it over he felt a twinge of guilt. Jean had hardly any domestic help compared to Annabel, and the children were forever getting under her feet. Looking back, he recalled she had always been tired.

But his feelings of remorse did not last long. He only had to listen to his beloved Annabel singing as she arranged the decorations, to feel that this was his first perfect Christmas.

Christmas day dawned warm and sunny, but when Daniel woke he could hear noises coming from the bathroom. Annabel was obviously being very sick, and he jumped out of bed to go to her. She was leaning over the basin, retching desperately.

"Oh, darling, don't come near me. I'm being..." and at that moment she heaved again. Daniel seized hold of a damp facecloth, and putting his arms round her shoulders he gently wiped her face.

"My poor sweet. Feeling better now?"

Annabel could only nod, as he helped her back into bed, and fetched a basin to place beside her. He collected a damp cloth and a couple of fluffy towels, and plumped up the pillows behind her back.

She looked at him wanly.

"Today of all days. What could we have eaten last night? Oh darling, you are a honey. I'm so sorry to start Christmas Day like this. Actually I feel a lot better now; I think I must have gotten rid of whatever it was."

"I think that you have just given me a wonderful gift today."

"What do you mean, darling? Didn't feel very wonderful to me!"

"Do you remember, you haven't been feeling very special for the last few days? I noticed yesterday you picked at your food early on, and then ate a huge lunch."

"Yes, but..."

Daniel put his hand lovingly on her stomach.

"I think there may be a little present for us both in there."

Annabel looked up at him and then, bursting into giggles, she threw her arms round him and exclaimed,

"A baby! Oh my darling, do you really think I might be having one?"

"Can't tell of course, without seeing the doctor. But I remember," he just caught himself in time, "Some of my friend's wives having much the same symptoms when they were pregnant. Your mother would know, I'm sure."

Stephanie did, of course. Christmas Day had a special glow to it that year. She did counsel caution of course, until the pregnancy was confirmed, but the signs were so classic, they all felt it must be true.

In the usual manner Annabel recovered enough to enjoy the day, and her parents were suitably impressed by all her arrangements, from the Christmas tree in the living room to the traditional lunch. Not that it was traditional to them, as Annabel, knowing Daniel's origins, had researched English customs, and there was roast turkey and all the trimmings, and a Christmas pudding ablaze with burning brandy. This was brought in with great ceremony by Katie, the amply proportioned native cook, who by now was part of the family.

As a surprise for Daniel, Annabel had taken immense trouble to track down Christmas crackers, as these were not easily obtainable in America. They ended lunch toasting the President, and the English Queen, wearing silly paper hats and laughing a great deal. They all felt as if it was the best Christmas any of them had ever had.

***

Annabel thrived, once she had recovered from the first three months of feeling "queasy," as she described it. Daniel was solicitous to her, experiencing feelings which he had never even thought about with the other pregnancies. He felt so much love for Annabel that he wanted to share all the ups and downs. He began to feel this was the only baby to whom he had ever been a father, forgetting the times when Jean and Polly had pleaded for understanding when they did not wish to do something he had planned. The whole experience made him wonder if he had really loved the other two, as husbands should love their wives. It was faintly disturbing, and occasionally he wished he could unburden his whole history to Annabel. But, perhaps wisely, he held back from confessing his past.

He felt he could not ever have understood the joy of placing his hand on Annabel's tummy and feeling his child kick for the first time. At that moment he almost believed in God, and sent up a little prayer for the safe delivery of this tiny being which they had made in such a wonderful way together.

The last weeks went slowly by. It was the cool season, and more comfortable for Mother and baby. Annabel was huge, and waddled from room to room, wishing away the time. They had both planned the nursery, giggling together over "pink" or "blue," eventually deciding on a cool aquamarine, with a dado of shells.

"The way it's kicking, I'm sure it will be a surfer," grumbled Annabel, as they gazed, arm in arm, at the cot, already for its occupant. A nurse was engaged as Annabel did not want to go to hospital.

"I want to be with you the whole time, and in our own bed as long as possible." She announced to Daniel, who was worrying about the possibilities of complications.

Daniel quietly arranged for a private ambulance to be standing by in case of an emergency.

Stephanie and Marlon were amused, and grateful, for their son-in-law's care of their daughter. Especially so when he invited them to come and stay for a few nights over the birth.

"I am sure Annabel will want her mother near, and I could do with male support," he joked.

The last few days of Annabel's pregnancy were trying to say the least. She could hardly waddle from one side of the room to another, in spite of the nurse encouraging her to keep moving.

"I think I've got a football team in there!" She said one evening as they sat out on the terrace, sipping lemonade. "I hope it doesn't go on too long,"

Daniel leant across and took her hand.

"I can hardly bear to think this is the result of so much pleasure," he mused softly.

She gave a little puff, and grasped his hand tightly.

"Oh darling, I think it's starting."

He got up to go and find the nurse, but she pulled him back.

"Don't go yet. I want a little more time with you alone before everyone else starts rushing round."

"I love you, my darling. I'm sure everything will be fine. Just take a few deep breaths like Nurse Bamford told you, and try and relax."

She glanced sideways at him. Poor sweet, he was doing his best to calm down, but she knew he was in just as much a panic as she was. He caught her eye, and they both burst into slightly hysterical giggles, until another spasm hit her, and she doubled over with pain.

"Perhaps you'd better...." And Daniel needed no more urging. He was off into the house shouting for the nurse and his mother-in-law before Annabel could breathe normally again.

Daniel was glad to have Marlon there during the next few hours. His father-in-law recalled the time Annabel was born, and managed to calm Daniel's anxiety when the time seemed to drag on interminably.

"First ones always take longer, I'm told," he consoled Daniel. "Of course, we never did have any more; but it wasn't for want of trying!" He added, trying to inject a little humour into the tense atmosphere. But Daniel wasn't listening to his father-in-law. He could not believe that he was feeling like this. After all, this was his fifth, so to speak. But he had never felt so worried, so involved. He had never suffered for the other two, merely been rather annoyed that his life was being disrupted by females. Now... now it was his beloved Annabel who was suffering, and he suffered with her.

Stephanie came out of the bedroom and called him.

"Daniel, dear, Annabel just wants you for a minute. She's doing very well but..."

Daniel did not hear the rest; he dashed across the hall, and into their bedroom before Stephanie could finish.

He saw her lying on the pillows, her hair damp with sweat, her face racked with pain, but with a kind of determination in her eyes.

"Darling" she whispered, holding out her hand. "I just wanted to see you for a minute."

"My love, I've been aching to be with you. I do hope it is not too frightful."

"Pretty grim. But listen darling. Dr Hammond thinks there are two babies!"

Daniel reeled, and turned to the doctor standing the other side of the bed.

"Two? Do you really think so?" he choked.

"Well yes," Dr Hammond confirmed. "We had our suspicions earlier, when I examined Annabel last week. But I am sure now. As far as I can gauge, there are two healthy babies. We've given Annabel a small dose of something to rest her at the moment, but then she will have to get on and double your family! It shouldn't be too long now."

Daniel leant over and kissed Annabel.

"I always knew you were the best." He whispered, and giving her another gentle kiss he left the room to tell his parents-in-law.

Not much longer afterwards the two men heard the unmistakable wail of a baby, and as Daniel leapt up listening, and after what seemed an age, there was another. He and Marlon clasped each other's hands in a gesture of joy, and in that moment Daniel felt more part of a family than he had ever felt in Cornwall. Marlon seemed almost like a father to him, and an unbidden prayer of thankfulness flooded through him.

A little later he crept upstairs and hesitantly knocked on the bedroom door. Stephanie opened it. The nurse and doctor were leaning over the bed, placing two little bundles in Annabel's arms. She looked up, her eyes shining as she saw Daniel.

"Look, darling."

Two little faces, two little snub noses, two rosebud mouths, and four bright little eyes, and above them the dearest face of his wife, shining with pride and joy.

He really only had eyes for her. He bent over and kissed her tenderly, and put a finger out to stroke the little fists escaping from the wrapping.

"They are beautiful, like their mother," he said. Then, remembering, he asked,

"What are they?"

"Both very healthy girls," said Dr Hammond. "Your busy life starts here and now!"

***

They called the babies Judith and Rosamond. They had both decided beforehand names of boys and girls, and just chose the first on the list. Annabel wanted to add their parents' names, and managed to extract the name of his mother from Daniel. He seemed a little reluctant, but Annabel thought it was because she had been so ill before she died, and the name would be too much of a reminder, but eventually he seemed happy for Judith to have the name Nancy, and Rosamond, Anne, her own mother's second name. Needless to say it was not long before they became Judy and Ros.

The family thrived with all the usual ups and downs of any normal folks.

Daniel and Annabel liked nothing better than watching their two lovely daughters grow and thrive. The garden became a huge playground. The babies learnt to swim at an early age, and were a particularly contented pair. They were identical, except for colouring. Judy had Annabel's chestnut curls, and Ros's curls were fairer, resembling Daniel. Just as well, as without the difference in hair colour, no one, sometimes not even their mother, could have told them apart. The daughter of a friend of the Studebakers, who had trained in London, was engaged as their Nanny. As her family also lived in Miami, she already had a good many acquaintances in the area, and was happy to be living in such a lovely house with a young family, near enough to her own home. Fiona was a bit scared of Daniel, but she adored the twins, and after the first month of caring for them, she felt she really belonged and was part of the family. She had her own suite of rooms and could swim in the pool whenever she liked, although she was tactful enough to disappear whenever

Daniel and Annabel were on their own. She hoped one day she would find such love and contentment as she saw they had in each other's company.

With Fiona firmly in charge of the twins, Daniel and Annabel managed to go on various vacations, round the States. They visited California, Washington DC and parts of rural Pennsylvania, but Daniel would never stay long in New York. Even in Washington Annabel found him acting strangely, as if he might meet someone he did not like. She asked him once, and he said he had met someone once he did not like there, many years ago, and did not want to renew the acquaintance, an explanation which seemed to satisfy her.

They enjoyed their little honeymoons, as Annabel called them. Away from the family they had plenty of time to gaze into one another's eyes, and reflect how lucky they were. But they were always pleased to return, welcomed by the twins and the rest of the household, usually with homemade banners of "Welcome Home" made by Fiona and the children, and hung on the bushes as they drove in the gate. It became a little ritual, which Daniel would always remember.

After returning from one of these trips, Annabel felt a familiar twinge of nausea one morning. She could not disguise the rush to the bathroom from Daniel, and when she crawled back into bed he was grinning.

"I don't know why you are looking like that," she remarked, and threw a pillow at him. He caught it deftly, and reached out for her, pulling her to him in a swift embrace.

"Something we've done? Or rather, not done?" he smiled.

"Somehow, the latter I imagine, I forgot to take my pills a couple of weeks ago. I did not think it would matter for a day or so, but somehow I suppose it did!"

Annabel glanced sideways at her husband, and saw him grinning.

"It is just wonderful" he said, "I was hoping we'd have another sometime, it will really be fantastic to have another baby."

He could not believe he was saying this, and equally, that he meant it with all his heart. He truly felt he had his dream life, with someone he adored beyond all imagining, and children he loved; a real family. He could not but help comparing his family in Cornwall with the blissful existence he had now, and find them wanting. 'I never really loved Jean,' he thought. 'Mother thrust her at me, and she was willing, but I never felt towards her, or Polly, as I do towards Annabel.'

Annabel's third child was a boy, to everyone's delight. They called him Henry Daniel Marlon, after a bit shortened to Harry. He was a delightful baby, thoroughly spoilt by the whole family, but mostly by the twins, who treated him like a large doll and tried to help care for him. Fiona was forever rescuing him from the twins' clutches. They liked nothing better than helping to bath Harry, completely fascinated as they were at Harry's anatomy.

"Do you know," Judy told her mother, "Harry has a worm growing out of his tummy."

Annabel could hardly keep a straight face.

"All little boys have those," she told them. "That is why you are called a girl and he is called a boy. Jesus made boys different from girls in lots of ways and that is one of them. But," she added hastily, "We don't talk about it, as everyone knows anyway."

Luckily they accepted the reason as Annabel changed the subject as quickly as she could, before she caught Fiona's eye and they both collapsed with mirth. When Daniel heard the story he nearly had a fit he laughed so much. The twins were a constant source of amusement to him.

Occasionally Daniel had to fly to New York to make sure his investments were behaving themselves. He had a firm of accountants who kept his accounts, and due to the new computers and what became known as the Internet, he could gradually work more from home. But he enjoyed these little trips. He would buy presents for the children and special gifts for Annabel. He never felt the need of female company these days, with his darling wife waiting for him at home.

He had everything he felt he desired at Summervale, and when he returned and drove into the driveway, and saw his family waiting for him, he sent up a little prayer of thanks for his good fortune. The only blemish on his paradise was his past, and most of the time he forgot he had one.

The family thrived, and Marlon and Stephanie also felt they were fortunate in their son-in-law, even if he was not the one they had expected. Although they did sometimes wonder what Daniel's background had been, their thoughts never lasted long. Annabel was supremely happy, Daniel was obviously rich and generous with it, the children were perfect in their eyes, so what more could they wish for? They were included as part of the family, and always welcomed when they drove over to call. It almost seemed too good to last.

Annabel and Daniel decided that they had completed their family, and took precautions not to increase it. Although, as Annabel laughingly remarked, "If we are meant to have any more, it wouldn't really be the end of the world, would it?"

Sometimes she wished she did not have to be tied to remembering pills, and in fact, once or twice forgot to take them, but luckily she did not become pregnant again. All she wanted was her three lovely children, and most of all, her beloved Daniel.

They had huge fun too, as a family. The children were old enough to be taken on holidays, with Fiona always coming along to take them off to the beach, or zoo, or nature trail, when their parents wanted time to themselves.

***

One year when Harry was four, they decided to take a trip to Pennsylvania to see how the Amish people lived. Daniel felt it would be good for them to see that life could be lived simply with no motor cars, amid rolling countryside lovingly cared for by whole families.

They decided to fly up, as the children had never been in an aeroplane, and it would be an extra treat for them. Particularly Harry, who was beginning to enjoy anything that went "vroom, vroom."

They flew into Philadelphia Airport, and hired a car to drive up to Lancaster. Daniel had meticulously arranged every detail, and they found themselves staying in a small cottage, which he had rented for a month. It was 'playing houses' all over again, and they all enjoyed the informality of shopping and cooking for themselves. A lovely woman, dressed in the customary Amish way, complete with apron and head cap, came in every day to help, and told them a great deal about her culture. She offered to show them a traditional Amish farm, which belonged to her brother, and they spent a cheerful afternoon making friends with the family and partaking of the simple meal with her folks, and helping afterwards to clear it away, and sing lovely old hymns with them. They all voted it to be the highlight of the holiday.

The horse-drawn buggies and the quaint clothes fascinated them all, and they were sad when it was time to fly back to Miami.

Daniel planned to go to New York for a few days after the holiday. He would drive the hire car there having taken Annabel and the children to the airport, and then he would fly back a couple of days later. It all seemed better than him having to fly up from Miami, when he was so close. He saw them onto the plane, happy and tanned after their country vacation, and waved as the plane took off. He hated leaving them, even for a day or two, but Annabel was particularly anxious to get back as the twins' school term began the following week, and she had a lot to prepare.

He reached his hotel in New York before dark, and settled in, idly turning on the television in his bedroom as he passed the set. The news had just started, when a news flash came up, usually something quite undramatic which the TV people deemed to be newsworthy.

"Reports are just coming in of a plane crashing as it tried to land in a thunderstorm in Miami"...

Daniel felt the whole room twirling as he sat down hard on the side of the bed. Without hesitating a moment he reached for the telephone by the bed.

"Get me Miami Airport," he almost shouted at the operator. The line was busy, and he spent many frantic minutes trying to get through. Eventually a voice answered,

"East Airlines, can I help you?"

"That plane which crashed. Was it from Philadelphia?" he asked.

"To whom am I speaking?"

"Sorry. This is Daniel Brooke, My wife and children were flying into Miami this afternoon, and I wondered..."

"Please hold the line sir, I will put you through to someone who can help you."

Daniel waited with his heart pounding, and his mind praying as he had never prayed before. He almost jumped when a man came on the line. "Mr Daniel Brooke?"

"Yes. D...Daniel Brooke speaking."

"I very much regret to have to tell you that, according to our records, a Mrs Annabel Brooke, and her three children, and also a Miss Fiona Carslake, the Nanny, are confirmed as passengers on the plane which crashed coming in to land at Miami late this afternoon.

"Regret?"

"Sir, there were no known survivors to the crash." Daniel gasped in such agony that the official asked,

"Sir, are you all right? Are you alone?"

"Yes, yes. Thank you."

Daniel sat for a minute cradling the telephone receiver in his hand. He felt blank, numb, and unable to think of anything. Perhaps it was all a mistake. Perhaps it was a later plane. Perhaps they had mixed up the names, or muddled the passenger list. Perhaps... He knew it was no good. His whole life had disappeared in an instant. He put his head in his hands but the longed-for oblivion did not come to relieve him of his shock and despair. After what seemed an age he put a call through to the Studebakers. Marlon answered. Daniel could only sigh.

"Daniel, my boy." Marlon's voice was quiet and calm.

"You've ...you've heard?" Daniel could hardly speak.

"We are just about to go to the airport to see what we can find out. Give me your number and I'll ring you as soon as I know anything."

"No, I'll jump on a plane and get down as soon as I can. I'll call you..."

"No." interrupted Marlon. "We will meet you at the airport. I can find out which plane you are on and we will meet that. Oh, my boy..." He finished with a break in his voice.

Daniel flew into Miami three hours later. As they approached the airport he inadvertently glanced out of the window, and wished that he had not. He briefly saw the wreckage, now burning gently, debris spread all along one of the runways. Not much was left of the plane; it had obviously burst into a fireball, and he realized with horror, tinged with relief, the end must have been almost instantaneous.

Marlon and Stephanie were waiting for him by the barrier. No words were said, or expected. They all embraced in the silence of sadness, and automatically made for the exit. As they passed the chapel they noticed a small knot of people inside. Some were sitting with their heads in their hands; some were standing, hopelessly lost. They saw a priest there, with his arm round a young girl, trying to give some comfort. But there was no comfort and the Studebakers guided Daniel out of the airport, and into their waiting car. Jan, their chauffeur, quietly enquired of Marlon whether they should proceed home.

"Do you want to stay; talk to anyone here?" Marlon asked Daniel.

"I imagine you have done all...all that?"

"Yes, my dear boy. There were no survivors whatsoever. It was just a huge explosion as they landed, and no one had a hope of surviving the fireball which resulted."

He nodded at Jan and the car quietly glided off with its cargo of mourning occupants.

They did not go to Summervale. The Studebakers both felt it would be too much for Daniel to face just then. They took him direct to their house, and gave him a strong whisky. He sat silently, with the drink in his hand, not really knowing what he was doing, or what was happening. Presently a meal was served, but only picked at by all of them. Food tasted like sawdust, and most of it went back to the kitchen.

"I suppose," Said Daniel at last, "I should go home and..."

"We think it would be best if you stayed here for the night. Then tomorrow we can go to Summervale and sort things." Marlon was firm, and led Daniel up to a bedroom, gave his shoulder a tender squeeze, and left him alone to his sorrow.

***

The next few days were a blur of agony in Daniel's life. Every movement was an automatic response to events. As the husband and father he had to view the few pathetic belongings of the victims for identification purposes. A necklace of Annabel's, a toy car of Harry's; nothing at all could be found which could be detected as belonging to the twins. It seemed as if they had been wiped from the face of the earth, as indeed they had, but the sheer enormity of it overwhelmed him, as nothing else had. He was beyond weeping, until he went back to Summervale.

Marlon had already informed all the staff, and it had caused much mourning and distress when they heard the terrible news. When Daniel summoned up courage from heaven knows where, to return to the house, they met him in the hall, with tearful faces and meaningless comments, which meant little to him but seemed to comfort them. He took each of their hands in turn, and then slowly went upstairs to their bedroom. It was only there, with the door shut, that he let go. He lay on the bed, which had held so much pleasure and laughter, and wept with complete abandon. Every emotion seemed to hit him then; fury, love, despair, hopelessness. His world had dissolved in that one great fireball, leaving a void that he could not begin to fill. After a while the healing power of sleep overcame sorrow, and he sank into blessed oblivion.

For all their sorrow, Marlon and Stephanie were strong enough to help Daniel through the next few days. Stephanie held Daniel's hand when they first entered the nursery, and gazed at the children's toys and clothes. Daniel picked up a small teddy bear which had been one of Harry's favourite possessions and held it to his cheek.

"I think you should keep one or two things," Stephanie suggested, "and let the rest go to charity, One of Annabel's preferred charities was "Save the Children." We could pack them up and they will come and collect them."

Daniel could only agree; he had no will to do anything. He chose the teddy bear, and two other small soft cuddly animals which he knew the twins had loved. Stephanie arranged for their maid Sarah to place everything else in boxes, ready to be collected. Sarah was reluctant to be given this work, but she felt she could not let the Master down. She tearfully wrapped each toy in paper, recalling the times when the twins had received each one, and how they had rushed to show her their newest acquisitions. She had felt such love for them all, even when there had been tantrums and childish scenes. Often they had run to her for the comfort of her ample frame, and she would cuddle them back to good humour.

Stephanie also took on the work of sorting and packing up Annabel's clothes.

"What would you like me to do with all the jewelry?" she asked. Daniel looked so stricken that she wished she could have thrown the lot away.

"Oh dear, I don't know. Could it go to relatives or something? I couldn't bear to have it. I might find it in a drawer one day, and everything would come back, and...." He rushed out of the room into the garden, where he sat on the grass with his head in his hands.

Stephanie wisely left him, gathered up all the necklaces, bracelets and brooches, and placed them in a small case. One day perhaps, Daniel would feel like going through them. But she felt it was all too personal for him, especially Annabel's wardrobes of clothes. They would have to go to a charity too.

About a week later, they were all sitting round after dinner, when Marlon brought up the subject of the future. Daniel had just returned from Summervale, where he had spent the day. He had been trying to steel himself to sort Annabel's personal treasures. A programme from a concert they had attended together, a crushed rose which he remembered giving her for a corsage once, and some private photographs of them in Hawaii on their honeymoon. He gazed and gazed at the latter with tears running down his cheeks, recalling the exact moments they were taken and how precious they seemed now.

Marlon steeled himself to put into words what they were all thinking. "Daniel, my boy. You know you can always have a home with us, for as long as you like. But I think the time has come to decide what you are going to do about Summervale. The servants will want to know especially. They will have to start looking for other employment if you are not going to keep the house."

Daniel tried to concentrate.

"I too, have been thinking what on earth I am to do now. I really do not want to go on living there. The place has too many memories...." He gave a gulp, and went on,

"You and Stephanie have been marvellous coping with so much, and you've been such a huge help to me. I can never repay your kindness." He held up his hand as Marlon began to say something. "This is such a difficult time to make any firm decisions, but I think I must get right away, and try and sort out my life. At the moment I cannot think what or where, and I hope you will understand and won't think I am deserting you."

"Of course not, we quite understand, don't we Steph?" He turned to his wife who nodded. "Yes, we all need space to get over this. But I hope you realize this will always be home for you, and we love you for being part of our family, and giving Annabel such happiness in the short time you were together." She put her hand out in a gesture of affection to Daniel.

Daniel would have liked to leave there and then, but he had so many ends to tie up first. He put Summervale into the hands of the same Real Estate firm from which he had originally purchased the property. He made sure the staff found work, and paid them handsomely. They all felt incredibly sad, as they were aware they would be unlikely to find such a happy household again. They had adored the children, and to see the Master walking round the garden on the last day reminded them poignantly of how he must be suffering.

He also had to go and visit Fiona's family, who lived just the other end of Miami. He had met them once before, when they had come for an invited visit to Summervale. Fiona had a younger sister who was obviously devastated, and all Daniel could do was to mouth platitudes, and tell them how invaluable Fiona had been to them all, and how they had loved her.

"We could never have done without her, and she was very much part of our family. The children thought the world of her, and....and I'm sure..." he faltered, "I'm sure she was playing with them when it....it happened." He choked and could not go on. But they understood and were comforted and touched that in all his sorrow, he had made the time to come and see them.

He booked a flight to England in the name of Gordon Pennyfeather. He thought he might as well go back as he had come. He still had all his papers with his old name, David Bretton, and David Bretton he would be when he arrived at Heathrow.

England

Chapter 22

James grew up that dreadful evening, when he found the body of Tom Truckle, lying mangled by the tractor. Never again would he ever feel a child. He started to run back to the Old Rectory, but he decided to make for the farm instead. Mrs Truckle was, as usual, in the big old kitchen, just finishing cooking their tea. One look at James and she realized something was wrong. His hair was wild, and his eyes raw. His hands and legs were covered in mud and grass, and he was shaking like a leaf.

"What is it, my pet?" she asked anxiously.

"Oh Auntie Truckle," James blurted out their childhood name for Tom's mother. "Tom is...down in the bottom field. He's...he's fallen out of the tractor, and I think he's..."

"Oh, my Lord," exclaimed Tom's mother. "I'll go and call Father; he's just in the garden. Sit down a minute," and she rushed out. Mr Truckle was there in a trice and quickly extracted the facts from James. He remained amazingly calm, but Mrs Truckle realized it was for James' sake. He spoke quietly to his wife and, collecting one of the farm hands, went down to see what had happened to his son. He sent his man back to collect a gate and one of the boys, and stayed with the mangled body of his son until the makeshift stretcher arrived, and they could all lift Tom carefully onto the gate and carry him back to the farm.

Meanwhile, Mrs Truckle knew what had to be done, even though it was her son, she had to be the one to tell Jean.

Taking James back with her, she let herself in, and found Jean, anxiously waiting in the sitting room. It had been ages since she had sent James to tell Tom it was time for supper, and she felt in her bones something was wrong, badly wrong.

One look at her dear friend confirmed her fears, but did not prepare her for the worst moment in her whole life.

"There's been an accident, my dear," Mrs Truckle began, when James, unable to contain his grief a moment longer, blurted out, "Tom has fallen out of the tractor, Mum. We think he is dead."

Jean felt a knife-like pain shoot through her, and she gasped.

"Don't say that, James, how do you know? There must be some mistake. He has knocked himself out, or... or something."

"Father has gone down to see, dear. But from what James has told me, I'm afraid you must prepare for the worst. My pet, come here," and she folded Jean's limp body in her comforting arms.

It wasn't long before Mr Truckle arrived and confirmed the worst. By that time Elizabeth and Ben had appeared, and the whole family felt numb with shock. Tom's body was taken to the farm to wait for the doctor to confirm his death. Dr Howard had been visiting in the village, and so came almost at once, but he could do nothing except give Jean a pill to help her over the next few terrible hours. As always, the Truckles were a tower of strength. Their only son was gone, their pride and joy, but all their sympathy was for Jean and the family Tom had left behind, and most especially for James. Tom had been more of a father to him than his own, and in James's eyes Tom had been the one man he looked up to and respected more than any other. Now the boy had become a man, and also head of the family.

He became a rock for Jean in the next few weeks. He asked for, and was granted leave from the College, and set about learning the financial arrangements which his own father had left in place. At least his mother (and the children for that matter) would have no money worries. He discovered the truth of Ben's parentage, and was pleased his mother should have some tangible remembrance of Tom. Ben had so many characteristics of Tom that it was a great comfort to them all in the months to come.

Someone, (solicitor? friend?) suggested that Jean might like to move, and start again somewhere else, with no memories. But as she confided in James one evening, memories were all she had now.

"Mum," said James, "I know from what I can gather, that Dad is still alive, and I thought I would go and talk to these solicitors he has in London, to see if I can find out where he is and what he is doing."

"I can't stop you, dearest, but you might not like what you find," warned Jean.

"It is all so mysterious. Mind you, the things I have discovered, going through old papers and things, well, I haven't liked much."

"He was a nice young man, and I thought I loved him," confided Jean. James was a young man himself now, and Jean could talk to him as an adult. He had left college and was a qualified farm mechanic. Mr Truckle was hoping he would take over the farm, but he was beginning to carve a name for himself as a reliable trouble shooter when it came to machines breaking down all over Cornwall. One of the reasons he wanted to go and see the solicitors was to ascertain if enough money was available to start up a business. He badly wanted a van for his equipment, and cash to stock a workshop.

"Certainly," said Jean, "You should go. But your father made it quite plain he did not want anyone enquiring after him. It was all very peculiar, and he was pretty brutal when he was last home."

"I remember, and I didn't like him at all. He seemed cruel to you, but it didn't seem to matter then, because you had Tom."

"Yes. But Tom was a sort of rock. I could not have faced your father when he last appeared if it hadn't been for Tom's support. You know, years ago, they were best friends.

"No, I didn't know, Tom never said." And now it is too late for him to ever say anything again, he thought.

***

James did not get very far with the solicitors, except to ascertain that his father was still alive, he was abroad, and had left instructions not to be contacted in any circumstances, except in the case of death of any of his family.

James nearly choked. As far as he was concerned his father had no right to call any of them "his family." Mr Ferbourne was sympathetic, but firm.

"Naturally he was informed of his father's death, but we had no further communication on that matter."

James asked if they knew his whereabouts, but if they did, they did not divulge any details. At least he discovered that money was available.

"How much do you need?" Mr Ferbourne enquired.

"Enough to set myself up in business," and James went on to explain his plans. He produced a creditable business plan, and Mr Ferbourne, after perusing it carefully, remarked thoughtfully, "Chip off the old block. Your father was always businesslike in all his financial dealings."

"I have no wish to be like my father!" James blurted out.

"Perhaps not. But he had a gift for making money, which will be useful to you. There is no reason why you should not have all you need to set up your machinery repair business. I will arrange for the sum to be transferred to your bank account next week."

James returned to Cornwall with mixed feelings.

"You see, Mum, I sort of want to make it on my own, and if I use Father's money I feel I'm beholden to him and of all people..."

"Dearest, the money is there for all of us. In any case, I worked just as hard as your father when he was starting, and he said, even then, that I deserved the money as much as him."

"He said that?"

"Yes. He wasn't an ogre then, you know. I realize now he was simply a spoilt little boy, who had had his own way ever since he was born. His mother gave him everything he wanted, and the whole household revolved round his wishes. Somehow he did want to share his success with me, but I know he would want you to succeed, and would not begrudge you the funds to help you get started."

"But he treated you so badly, Mum."

"Yes, in the end he did. He never really wanted this sort of village life and I loved it, and our differences drove us apart. I think he loved my love for him, and when Tom made me see what real love was, he didn't like it. I know, and now you are old enough to understand this James, that he found amusement in London."

"What do you mean, amusement?"

"Well, glamour girls for a start. Sometimes his clothes smelt of cheap scent when he came home."

James was appalled at these revelations. He went quite white and sat down.

"How...how awful for you, Mum."

"It was sort of gradually awful. But I was falling in love with Tom, and perhaps that helped. Of course if your father had been faithful and loving to me I would never have turned to Tom. It began for me as hero-worship for your father, and of course he revelled in that. He and Tom were such friends, quite inseparable really, but your father always wanted to be a little bit superior to everyone else."

"I always think of Tom as my true dad. Father didn't want to do country things, did he?"

"No. And that was half the trouble. He was in no way content in St. Wraich, always rushing off somewhere else. He was never satisfied with country life, whereas I always loved being here. If only I had married Tom when he asked me, and not been bowled over by your father's undoubted charms, perhaps it would have been better for everyone."

"Did he ask you, then? Tom I mean?"

"Yes. Then your father came back having just launched the credit card, and was so excited, and wanted someone to share it all with, and I happened to be there, all starry-eyed and eager."

James went to bed that night full of these disclosures. He lay awake mulling over all that his mother had told him, feeling a new respect and love for his strong mother. He recalled all the happy times they had spent with Tom, but he could not remember anything very much about his own father. He felt it was sad that all the memories he had were negative ones.

***

It was exciting planning his business, and the whole family was involved in choosing the new van. Mr Ferbourne had come up trumps, and instead of the proposed second-hand vehicle, he was able to buy a brand new truck, properly fitted out with shelves and spaces for all the necessary equipment. Choosing the colour of the van became a family affair, and after much discussion a soft green with yellow lettering was decided upon. Then his name was edged with black, which looked distinguished. Ben decided it should be launched, like a ship, and Jean found an old bottle of wine. James was worried that the bottle being smashed on the van would scratch his pride and joy, so Mr Truckle was asked to open it, and they all drank a toast to "The Repair Shop," as James had decided to call the enterprise.

He already had a lot of work as farms were beginning to become almost completely mechanized. His reputation as a reliable mechanic spread, and he had more work than he could deal with on his own. A friend of his joined him and they acquired a second van, and also a large workshop was built on the Truckle farm, to which they could bring machines which needed repair in a specialized location. James took on three keen young lads and taught them all he knew, and they became a united team, all working at an occupation they loved.

James could not believe four years had gone by since he acquired their first van. It seemed to him to be the perfect life. They were busy, but he always insisted on enough free time for all of them to relax, see their families, and most important, to enjoy the surfing when the tide was up and the sea beckoning. The result was a happy hard working and loyal firm.

But, as always, the silver lining had a cloud.

Jean had not felt well ever since Tom's accident. She was so completely shattered by his unexpected and violent death that everyone expected it would knock her for six, at least for a time. But she did not pick up as her family anticipated, and Mrs Truckle noticed how terribly thin she had become, in spite of the little offerings of eggs and cream to try and tempt her. It was if the will to live had dissipated with Tom's demise.

She picked up a little when James started his business, and did her best to help him at the beginning, particularly with the accounting side. But when the initial enthusiasm had worn off, she began to slide backwards again.

Mrs Truckle, her dear friend and surrogate mother, tackled her one day over a cup of tea in the big farm kitchen.

"Jean, my dear, I do think you ought to go and let Dr Howard look you over, and perhaps give you a tonic or something."

"I suppose I should some time. I have been feeling rather under the weather lately," she admitted.

Alerted by Mrs Truckle, Dr Howard saw Jean the following week. He gave her a thorough examination, and told her he would make an appointment in Truro to be X-rayed.

"One or two little things are giving me concern," he told her. What he did not tell her was that he had felt a definite hard lump under her armpit, in her right breast. Looking at her, with only her bra and panties on, he had been appalled to see how thin she was. Ever since Tom's death she had, quite naturally he thought, looked drawn, but now he could see how the weight had gone. Jean had always been somewhat over plump. Now she looked like those returning prisoners of war, skin and bone and little else, and he swiftly arranged for an X-ray.

Elizabeth, who was working in a solicitor's office in Wadebridge, insisted on taking her to the hospital in Truro. The X-rays were all done in a short time, although she was asked to wait in case they wanted to retake any of them. They sat in the waiting room for about half an hour, and then Jean was asked to come back in. They took a few more pictures, and after a bit were allowed to go home.

"They didn't seem worried, did they Mum?" said Elizabeth in a comforting way as they drove home.

"Oh no, not a bit. I'm sure there's nothing wrong."

But there was.

Jean was diagnosed with Breast Cancer. The 'little lump' turned out to be what was regarded as a 'nasty', and had to be removed. Apparently the radiologist did not believe the cancer had spread, and Jean began a series of treatments to make sure that the tumour was well and truly zapped. She went through all the stages of losing her hair, nausea, and generally feeling a lot worse. But the healing worked, and she was delighted when her hair grew back all curly, and she was announced clear.

It was a kind of renaissance. She felt full of life and was happy for the first time since Tom had died. James was established. Elizabeth had a good job, and was becoming interested in one of the solicitors in her office, Robert Anderson. Jean noticed the little smile whenever she mentioned his name, which was often. He gave her a lift home one day, and when he met Jean he seemed everything Jean could have wished for her daughter; perhaps a little dull and pedantic, but obviously only had eyes for Elizabeth, and Jean began thinking of white dresses and flowers for the Church. Meanwhile Ben was growing taller and so like his father that it often broke her heart to look at him. He took after Tom in his ambitions as well, the farm being his one interest, and Mr Truckle confided in Jean that he hoped to retire as soon as Ben was old enough to take over. "He's a real farmer like his dad." He said.

Jean wondered if the Truckles would come and live in the Old Rectory with her when that time came. There was plenty of room, especially if Elizabeth married and had a home of her own. Ben would want to live in the farmhouse, although he was too young to live there on his own for the present. She found her imagination running away with her a little too fast.

James showed no sign of finding a wife. He had lots of girl friends, some more serious than others, but none lasted more than a few months.

During one of their conversations after supper, he told her, "You see Mum, I just haven't come across anyone who measures up to you yet!"

It was a sort of tease, but he really meant it. The girl he chose to share his life would have to be the one Tom would have approved of, and so far he had not met her.

South Africa

Chapter 23

"Mummy, look at my legs! They are getting too long for Blackie."

Maggie had grown so much in the last few months. No, Polly reminded herself; it was more than a few months; over five years since she and Paul had married. The time had passed so quickly for her, in a blissful cloud of joy. They had all thrived, with the children growing up surrounded by love and security.

Maggie was twelve now, and had been attending the secondary school in Mooi River, making lots of friends and enjoying life. Obviously she was growing too large for her beloved pony Blackie. Paul had noticed it too, with the professional eye of a horse breeder, and was in the process of purchasing a new mount for Maggie. The gelding he had in mind was just thirteen hands high, and had been schooled by a friend of his whom he trusted. But it was to be a surprise for Maggie's birthday in three weeks time, so Polly put her head on one side and told her, "I'm amazed you have grown so much. Goodness Maggie, we will certainly have to get a bigger pony soon," and left it at that.

"Do you think," Maggie went on, "our real Daddy will come back for my birthday, and give me a bigger pony, like he did Mousie, when I was little?"

They still occasionally had conversations like this, particularly after Maggie had caught sight of a photograph of her father, which she found one day in a drawer in the sitting room. She had not told her mother she had seen it. She sensed the subject was taboo, although she did not quite know why. Every time she mentioned Donald, Polly felt a jolt of remorse. She did not yet feel that Maggie was old enough to explain her true parentage. One day she would, but to spoil Maggie's innocence now would be cruel. Maggie realized it hurt her mother to talk about her 'real Daddy.' She thought that Polly would like both Ellie and her to think of Paul as their own Daddy.

Recently Maggie had started at the big school in Pieter Maritzberg, and as a result was growing up fast, both in mind and body. She travelled there every day by train, but they had plans for her to board later, when she was a little older. She made friends easily, and often was invited to stay with other girls at weekends. Likewise her friends came to Whiteoaks, and they would go riding up towards the mountains.

"I remember, when I was about your age," Polly told her, "I used to go off with friends and find somewhere to swim and have picnics."

Polly told her about the black mambas, and warned her not to go bathing in pools she did not know about; but on the whole she trusted Maggie's innate common sense, remembering the freedom she was given at that age, and trusting her to be sensible. Most of the girls who came to stay lived in the countryside themselves, and they were all aware of the lurking dangers of snakes and other wildlife.

Polly was glad to see no boys were invited. Maggie was more than content to have only girls around with whom to giggle, and, although the odd boy was mentioned in passing, he seemed to be a different one each week.

She was thrilled to have the new horse for her birthday, and flung her arms round Paul to thank him.

"He is perfect!" she cried after the first ride. "She has such a gentle mouth, and goes like the wind."

Paul thought she looked perfect too, her dark red curls flying in the wind, pink cheeks glowing from the excitement, and eyes shining with delight. "My eldest daughter, I wish she knew I was her real father." He thought.

The rides with friends at the weekends became a little longer after the acquisition of Pippin, as Maggie called her new horse. Ellie, on Mousie, quite often tagged along, but she was not as mad about riding as Maggie, and usually had her head in a book, rather than venture outdoors.

Maggie shot through adolescence, taking almost everything in her stride. She was shattered by her first period, but Polly explained it was all part of growing up.

"But I don't want to grow up if it's like this," wailed Maggie, doubled over with a bad spasm. "Do I really have to go through this every month? Oh Mummy, it's dreadful, and I did so want to go swimming this morning."

Polly was stricken too, at the sight of her lovely daughter, holding the hot water bottle to her tummy, and moaning.

"Well, my pet, they don't call it "Eve's Curse" for nothing. Every woman gets it, but when you get to be about fifty it stops. I still have it, and you'll get kind of used to it. Anyway, sometimes the first time is the worst."

"But what's the point?"

Polly drew a deep breath. It was a conversation she had dreaded, and long ago she had decided she must be honest when the moment came.

"All the time we grow tiny eggs in our tummies. They live in a special place called the womb. If we don't need to make a baby, every month they are washed away with the blood in the womb; that makes it all nice and clean for the next lot."

Polly felt she was floundering, but Maggie was hanging on every word, so she had to continue.

"When we get married, one of the eggs grows into a baby, and while it is growing we don't have the curse. All the goodness in the womb goes towards helping the baby grow, until it is ready to be born."

"How does the egg know it is going to be a baby?"

Polly swallowed.

"Well, men are slightly differently made. They have a little place where they grow things called sperm. After you are married your husband can let the sperm into you, and it finds an egg to fertilize, and that is the beginning of life."

Maggie seemed completely bewildered and thoughtful, but did not ask any more questions. Polly noticed she gazed at her boiled egg the next day at breakfast with some misgiving before she swallowed hard and cracked open the top.

Maggie had been given biology lessons at school, and gradually the subject of reproduction was covered, although human reproduction was only lightly glossed over, in hopes that parents would fill the gaps. Living as they did amongst animals, Maggie felt the whole process was completely natural, although she was extremely miffed that only humans seemed to get 'the curse'. She watched the dogs getting excited when their bitch came on heat, and was mounted by one of the dogs, and eventually give birth to five adorable puppies.

"It's really all worthwhile, when you see the result," she solemnly informed a slightly bemused Paul.

***

"Two completely different little people," Paul remarked to Polly one day, as he and Polly were sitting on the stoep discussing their daughters. But everything was so perfect there did not seem much point in rocking the boat by telling their children of their true parentage.

"Not so little," replied Polly. "Have you noticed how big Maggie is growing? I'll have to buy her some bras soon!"

Paul swallowed, "Terrifying, I think it only seems yesterday they were running round in nappies."

They decided to have a little holiday in Durban, just after Maggie's thirteenth birthday. They all four drove down, and stayed at a hotel on the beach. While Paul taught Ellie to surf, Polly took Maggie shopping, much to her disgust.

"Why can't I stay and surf too?" she grumbled.

"You can do that later. But now we have got to buy you some necessary garments. I am sure most of your friends have bras by now, and it is definitely time you had some too."

"How awful." Polly felt Maggie's reaction was typical of her tomboy daughter, but in the end it was quite entertaining. Being measured wasn't much fun, in fact Maggie found it embarrassing, but choosing the garments proved to be interesting, and at last Maggie emerged feeling trussed up like a chicken. She could not wait to remove the new restricting garment, and get into her swimsuit, and dive into the surf. She felt quite grown-up all the same, and vastly superior to Ellie, who was still flat as a pancake. Maggie was never a prude, and was happy to show her new undergarments to Paul, who professed great admiration, albeit with a lump in his throat.

Later that evening, in the privacy of their bed, Paul confessed to Polly,

"I can hardly bear to wonder where the years have gone, and our first love has produced someone who is now wearing bras!"

Maggie and Ellie were the greatest friends, although when Maggie had to move on to the Pieter Maritzberg School, leaving Ellie in the little primary school, their closeness lessened. Ellie was undoubtedly a bookworm, whereas Maggie was out, (usually on Pippin) as soon as she got home from school.

One day Maggie casually announced that Johnny was coming by that afternoon.

"Who is Johnny?" asked Paul, as he finished his breakfast one Saturday.

"Oh, a boy in my class."

"Johnny who?" Polly said as nonchalantly as she could, without daring to catch Paul's eye.

"Johnny Maitland. He lives in that big house in Kopje."

Polly knew there was a family called Maitland. She seemed to remember her mother talking about a David Maitland, as being a 'suitable' escort for her, way back when she was seventeen, but as it happened they had never met. Obviously he married and had a son called Johnny. She breathed a sigh of relief. At least this Johnny seemed to come from a respectable family.

"Do you know what time he is coming?" she asked Maggie.

"About teatime I think." Maggie shouted over her shoulder as she rushed out to the stables. But later Polly noticed when she came in she brushed her hair carefully and waited round, every now and then pretending not to look out of the window.

At precisely four o'clock a young god appeared, riding a nice grey horse, which he tethered to the hitching post, and, smoothing his hair back, rang the doorbell. Maggie rushed to open it, greeting him shyly,

"Hi Johnny. Nice to see you. Come in. We've got lemon buns for tea."

"Good oh. I like those," and they went into the living room, Johnny politely holding the door for Maggie. She seemed tongue-tied for once, then pointed to the golden-haired youth,

"Mum, this is Johnny."

They all sat wondering what to say next, until Paul broached the subject of horses. It proved to be the key to unlocking whatever made Johnny tick, and soon they were both munching lemon buns companionably and discussing breeding and rearing stock. Maggie hung on every word, and Polly watched, thinking how fortunate they were, that Maggie's first boyfriend should be so suitable.

Eventually she could see Maggie becoming rather restless, with Johnny so obviously under Paul's spell. She interrupted when a pause occurred.

"Don't you think Johnny would like to see Pippin? You could both go for a ride up to the vineyards, and have a good gallop."

Can I go too?" Ellie asked. She had been sitting quietly in a chair by the window gazing at Johnny, Polly noticed, with an air of wonder.

Maggie was torn between wanting to go off with Johnny on her own, and her fondness for her sister.

"I don't think Mousie would be able to keep up," she said, as kindly as she could, and got up.

"Come on, Johnny, let's go."

Ellie swallowed her disappointment, and turned back to her book.

For the next few months Johnny became a regular and welcome visitor to Whiteoaks. Now, every day, Maggie found herself hanging about the house, wondering if he would come and feeling enormous disappointment when he did not turn up. When she saw the familiar figure riding up to the house, her heart seemed to give the most extraordinary lurches, before she rushed down to greet him.

Occasionally Maggie rode over to the Maitland's house, Five Elms, but she did not enjoy those visits much. Although the Van Stadts were an old and well-respected family in Natal, the de Freyburgs were considered almost white trash. They liked Maggie, but felt Johnny could do a lot better for himself than a child brought up by a horse breeder. They were kind to Maggie, but she sensed an underlying reticence to make her a part of the family, as hers had done to Johnny. Never having been snubbed before, Maggie felt uncomfortable when she was at Five Elms, and much happier when Johnny came to Whiteoaks.

"Do you really think," Mrs Maitland said to her son, "that Maggie is quite the girl for you?"

"What do you mean, Mum?"

"Well, her father ran off in mysterious circumstances, and her stepfather is not, well, not one of us, as you might say."

"What on earth does that matter; I'm not going out with her parents. For heaven's sake, Mother, don't be so old-fashioned. Anyway, it's not serious. I just find Maggie such fun and a lot nicer than most of the stuffy girls at school." Johnny stormed out, leaving his mother staring after him with perplexity.

"I couldn't seem to get through to him, but I don't think he is too besotted, thank goodness. We must just make sure he meets a few nice girls soon." She told her husband later.

Meanwhile Maggie proceeded to grow up into the most vivacious young lady, captivating hearts wherever she went, and never without invitations, but remaining loyal to Johnny.

They became a couple and were invited everywhere as such; so much so that Maggie began to become a bit bored with always being in the same crowd.

They both graduated, and enjoyed the School Dance for graduates, but Maggie found other young men crowding round her claiming the next dance with her.

"Just who did you come with, this evening?" Demanded Johnny, after missing three dances with her.

"Oh Johnny, I'm sorry, but I'm having such fun. You go and ask Mary over there, she dances awfully well. I'll have supper with you later."

Johnny looked over to the lump sitting on a chair, looking as if she wished she were anywhere but there. Johnny swallowed, and thought, 'I'll show Maggie she is not the only girl on the planet,' and strode over to Mary.

"My name is Johnny Maitland. Can I have this dance with you, or are you waiting for someone?"

Mary leapt to her feet delightedly.

"I love dancing, thank you so much," and when Johnny tentatively put his arm round her ample waist, they seemed to glide across the floor. Johnny felt Mary was made of thistledown, she was incredibly light on her feet, and needed no help as she let herself be guided by Johnny. The moments fled by, and when the music stopped Johnny felt he did not want to let Mary go.

"Would you like a cool drink?" he asked, "and then perhaps we could have another go on the floor? Or are you booked up for the rest of the evening?"

"That would be lovely, and no, I am not really with anyone."

"Who brought you then?"

"George Masters, but he seems to have disappeared."

Johnny was pretty appalled, as he had seen George a little while ago behind one of the pillars, entwined with a flighty young student called Hattie, but he did not say anything to Mary.

They were a threesome for supper. Maggie was a little shattered to find Mary was being included, but she did not view her as a rival. She was so plump, and to Maggie, somewhat unattractive, but obviously Johnny found her good company, and it allowed Maggie to have a good time with lots of other boys.

At the end of the evening, as Johnny was collecting Maggie to take her home, they saw Mary looking forlornly round for George.

"I can't seem to see him anywhere," she said, with a rueful grin. "It is an awful imposition, but do you think you could drop me off home? I think it is on your way."

Maggie noticed, with slight concern, that Johnny immediately acquiesced.

"Of course, Mary. My car is just round the corner. Can you walk in those heels?"

Maggie was getting annoyed. She was wearing heels too, her first-grown up pair, and Johnny had never noticed hers.

"We can both walk, Johnny," she said shortly, and strode off towards the car. Mary felt somewhat embarrassed and quickly slipped into the back seat before Johnny could ask her to sit in front.

She gave him directions to her home, and tried to be as inconspicuous as possible.

They drove along in a slightly charged silence, until they came to a pair of large gates on the left.

"Turn in here, Johnny," said Mary, "I've got a sort of remote device which opens them," and sure enough they swung gently open as the car approached. They crept up a broad graveled drive which led to a wide open space. An imposing and elegant house, lit by the car's headlights, loomed up before them.

"Here we are! Thanks so much for the lift." exclaimed Mary. She was out of the car and up the steps before Johnny could escort her.

"Whew, that's some house," Johnny's eyes were shining.

Maggie agreed, somewhat taken aback by the obvious grandeur. "I had no idea Mary lived here. But she seems awfully nice, doesn't she?"

She looked sideways at Johnny, whose arms were resting on the steering wheel. After a moment he nodded.

"Amazing," was all he said as he drove off.

Maggie was not expecting a kiss at the end of the evening, but she was faintly disappointed when Johnny opened the car door for her, and gave her a brotherly hug.

"That was a lovely evening. Thank you, Johnny," she said, before turning to go inside. Something had died between them, and she strongly suspected the reason was Mary.

"Did you have a lovely evening?" Polly asked her the next morning, when Maggie came down to breakfast.

"It was OK; I had masses of boys dancing with me. But I did something awfully stupid, Mum."

Polly's heart gave a huge leap, as she thought of all the things Maggie could have got up to last evening.

"I was dancing with lots of boys, and when Johnny asked me for a dance I told him to go and dance with Mary Fairbairn, and he danced with her an awful lot. She's so fat Mummy, but I must say, she is an extremely good dancer. Then we took her home, and she lives in a huge house, and, and I think Johnny has fallen for her. He hardly spoke at all on the way home. Oh Mummy, I don't think he loves me anymore," she wailed.

Polly put her arms round her and gave her a hug. The ordeal of first love was so intense she did not know how to comfort her.

"My darling Maggie," she held her tight as she spoke. "Sometimes people fall in love with someone who doesn't feel the same. When you find you both love each other equally, then that will be the right person forever,"

"Like you and Daddy Paul, you mean?"

"Yes, just like me and Daddy Paul. We knew the very first time we met. I don't think Johnny is old enough to know who he loves just yet, so he is just falling for all the girls he meets. It will probably be a different one next week. It may even be you again, but I think you will know just exactly the second you meet the person you want to spend your whole life with."

"But...but what about you and Daddy Paul?"

"Just like you and Johnny, I thought I loved your daddy, but then Daddy Paul came back from the Army, and I knew that very second that he was the one."

Maggie sighed. It was a lot to take in. Love seemed to be so complicated. She decided she would go and talk to Pippin, and perhaps have a gallop to get it all out of her system.

***

"Someone on the telephone for you." Johnny's mother called up the stairs. She put the receiver down when Johnny answered, but not before she heard "Mary Fairbairn here." Goodness, the Fairbairns, no less. She had heard of them, immensely rich, and owned a vast tract of Natal. If Johnny had become involved with their daughter she could not be more pleased. Perhaps he would now forget that Maggie.

England, then South Africa

Chapter 24

James's firm was doing so well, that he felt he could get away for a break somewhere.

"Where do you think I should go, Mum?" he was sprawled on the sofa leafing through travel brochures as he spoke.

"Depends what you want to do. I mean, do you want to climb mountains, lie on beaches or what?"

"I just want good weather. It has been such a beastly autumn I really would like some sun."

"What about South Africa? I've heard it is warm out there in our winter, and there is so much to see, although the farming is pretty primitive, I'm told."

"Mum! You must be joking! I don't want to see a single farm machine for a month!"

He spent the next few days gazing at all sorts of possible destinations, deciding in the end to fly to Cape town, and maybe take a train up to Durban, or even further if he had time, and simply soak in the sun and culture.

"Wish you would come with me," he remarked to Jean, but she did not feel up to a long journey, flights and strange hotels. She had not been feeling too good lately, and tried not to wonder if the dreaded cancer was returning. But she remained outwardly cheerful, and no one but Ellen noticed.

So one dreary day in early November James set off with great excitement. Having never been further than London the whole journey enthralled him; even waiting hours in Heathrow for a delayed plane did not dampen his spirits.

It was strange to land in blazing sunshine, and quickly shedding his coat, he stuffed it in his holdall. He felt it stranger still to see so many black people walking round, usually offering to carry his bags for a small reward.

He stayed a few days in a modest hotel, and took the tourist trip up to the top of Table Mountain. It was one day when it was not covered by mist, (or the tablecloth as it was called locally), so that the view was everything he could have dreamed of, and more. He visited a vineyard, but was not particularly interested in the wine producing process. He enjoyed a good beer over a glass of wine any day.

After a week he bought a ticket for the train to Durban, but arranged to stop off at a delightful sounding spot called Port St. Johns. This proved to be the rest he needed, as there was nothing whatever to do there except find a completely isolated beach, and swim and lie in the sun. Along the almost deserted coast he found pretty coves, and hardly any visitors, and more than once he stripped off and swam completely naked in the blue sea. Once, when he emerged, he could not resist rolling in the sand from sheer joy, and then dived in again to rinse it all off. It gave him a feeling of absolute bliss, a sensation he would remember for the rest of his life.

One balmy day he was lying on the warm sand when he saw a vivid rainbow curving over the sea. One end seemed to bury itself so near he felt as if he could reach out and touch it, and remembered his mother reading them a magical story called, (what was it?), oh yes..."Where the Rainbow Ends."

He resolved if he ever found a girl to marry, he would bring her there for their honeymoon. This led him to review his prospects with the girls he knew, and he came to the sad conclusion that he knew of none with whom he would share this experience.

Reluctantly he left Port St. Johns after a week for the bright lights of Durban. The comparison was astonishing. The beaches there were wide and crowded, and the shops bustling. He stayed in a hotel right on the centre beach, and enjoyed some of the best surfing he had ever had in his life.

A bit scary at times, as the waves were higher and stronger than Cornwall. He was just about to pack up for the morning on his third day there, when he saw two girls paddling out towards a real monster of a wave.

"Hi! Great waves today!" They called out as they ran past him.

"A bit too big for me," he joked, and at that moment the younger girl, who had dived in first, was apparently caught in a current and started yelling "Help, something is pulling me out!"

James, with the experience of Cornwall, recognized a strong undertow, and swiftly realized the girl would soon be engulfed in the huge wave approaching. He paddled towards her and caught hold of one of her outstretched hands. It nearly slipped from his grasp, but he kicked his legs towards her to get a better grip, and hauled her swiftly to him, as they dived through the wave and came out the other side, none the worse, but somewhat shaken.

"Oh God, thanks," she panted, as he guided them both towards the shore. Her waiting sister waded forward to help them,

"Are you both okay?" she asked anxiously.

James looked up for the first time. He was already breathless from the exertion, but somehow now felt a different kind of breathlessness. For a moment the sun caught the older girl's tousled curls, turning them all colours of the rainbow. She shook the sea water out of her hair and bent down to attend to her sister. In the background a vision of the St. John's cove seemed to hover over her; he swallowed hard and said in a voice cracked with seawater and effort, "I think we had better get your sister further up the beach, the tide seems to be coming in rather fast."

"Heavens, yes! Thanks so much for rescuing Ellie. By the way, my name is Maggie."

"I am James." Reluctantly he turned to Ellie.

"How do you feel? Can you walk now?" He put a hand under her arm, while Maggie took the other one, and together they helped Ellie up the sand until they reached a dry place above the tidemark, and all collapsed in a heap with exhaustion.

After a while Maggie got up saying, "We'd better be going; parents worrying and all that. Thanks again so much."

Before James could gather his wits they had both left him lying on the sand. He tried to shout something, anything, after them, but his voice was still croaky from the water he had inhaled and he could not make them hear. They disappeared behind some huts and were lost to view.

The rest of James's holiday seemed flat after that encounter. Everywhere he looked for auburn curls. Sometimes he thought he saw them, but they were never the right ones. When he rushed up to the surprised owner he became almost used to saying, "Oh sorry, wrong person!"

He left Durban, flying to Johannesburg, (which he hated), and took a plane to see the Victoria Falls, (which he found marvellous), but everything seemed flat, and he could hardly wait to get home to Cornwall.

If only he had asked her surname; if only he had found out where she lived; if only...Then he decided that one day he would come back and he was sure he would meet her again. The vision of the cove hovering over her surely meant he would find her again somewhere, sometime.

***

"Lovely to see you again! Did you have a wonderful time?" Jean greeted James as he walked in through the door.

"Oh Mum, it was great. Marvellous waves; about twice the size of Cornish ones. I've got loads of photographs to show you, but at the moment I could do with something to eat. The aeroplane food was lousy and I'm starving."

"Actually, I know Ellen made some pasties this morning. She thought you'd be hungry when you got back so come and tuck in."

Jean watched her son as he demolished a couple of large pasties. He was tanned and relaxed, but she detected an impression of hurt inside somewhere. She wondered what had happened out in South Africa. She was sure she would know soon, as he had never hidden anything from her.

Sure enough, that evening, after supper he told her. Elizabeth had gone out with Robert, and Ben reluctantly left to do his homework. Jean looked across at him. "What's up, James?"

"Well, I met the most marvellous girl, and..."

"And what?"

"Just that. I don't know her surname, and I...I couldn't find her after, after..."

"After what, James?" Jean nudged him gently along.

"Well, I'd better tell you the whole story, Mum."

South Africa

Chapter 25

Maggie was unnaturally quiet and thoughtful, but later they all put it down to the accident Ellie so nearly had in the surf. When the two girls reached the hotel, Polly and Paul were waiting, slightly impatiently.

"We thought you were never coming," Paul grumbled.

"We so nearly didn't," Maggie said rather shakily. "Ellie got into an undertow, and was being dragged out. It was awful," and she could not help herself trembling. While Polly was comforting her, Ellie gave a graphic description of the rescue.

"A terribly nice man managed to get hold of me, and drag me out of the wave. It was huge, Mummy, I don't know what I would have done if he had not been there. He nearly got dragged out too, but he was awfully strong, and kept hold of my hand."

Ellie, having got over her fright, was rather enjoying being the centre of attention, but Polly noticed how white and shaken Maggie seemed to be.

"Ought we not to thank this young man?" asked Polly.

"We don't even know his name," said Maggie, mournfully.

"Except it was James, and he was English I think; he was very nice to talk to," Ellie went on. "I do wish we'd found out where he was staying, then we could thank him properly. Though of course, we did thank him afterwards, so perhaps that's all right, isn't it, Mummy?"

"I'm glad you did that." Paul was looking at Maggie. She was in a dream world, and he thought perhaps she would have even happier if they had remembered this James's full name.

Later that evening, when they were in bed together, he said to Polly, "I really think Maggie looked as if a thunderbolt had struck her, didn't you?"

"Yes, I thought that too. Obviously this James made a deep impression on her. I wish we could meet him."

But they went back to Whiteoaks the next day without even catching a glimpse of Ellie's rescuer.

* * *

Maggie had left school, and was looking forward to getting herself some sort of job with horses. She had helped Paul, and knew a fair amount about breeding and schooling. She rode in a number of horse shows, often winning cups for jumping, but she felt there was more to life than being at home, sometimes showing the beautiful animals Paul bred. She began to get restive, always the vision of a tall young man called James materializing in her dreamier moments. Several young men, vied for her attention, and she was sweet to all of them, but one was never singled out to be special.

"Bees to a honey pot!" Exclaimed Paul one day, when three young men turned up one day to take Maggie out. She had quite forgotten she was going out at all.

Maggie was talking to Polly one morning in the garden, "I think that I should do some sort of secretarial course, and even take a trip overseas. I feel sort of, well, stuck here." She paused. "Of course I love being at home, but I seem to be getting in a rut."

Polly swallowed. It seemed only yesterday that Maggie was born, and now here she was, wanting to spread her wings and fly the nest.

Polly bent to pick up a weed to hide her sudden dismay. "I do understand, we must find out what is the best thing to do."

Surprisingly, it was Paul who came up with the best idea. He suggested Maggie should go to a secretarial college in London. She would be able to explore Britain, learn shorthand and typing, and even perhaps get a temporary job for a few months to earn enough money to travel a bit. She could then spend a few weeks touring round Europe before coming home. After that she could decide if she wanted to become a full-time secretary in the horse breeding world, or even with a trainer of racehorses.

"There are lots of openings for secretaries in the equine world. In fact I've sometimes longed for one myself to take care of all the paperwork."

"Would you mind me going off like that?" Maggie asked anxiously.

"Of course, we would miss you so much," said Polly. "But we do think you should see more of the world, and Ellie too when she is older. We have been facing the fact that you will both want to fly the nest at some time, and the time has now come for you to go off, Maggie, and see something of the great wide world!"

Maggie was relieved that her mother, and Daddy Paul, as they still called him affectionately, had understood her longings, and hugged them both.

"Thank you so much, it really is super of you to understand."

Ellie was very envious of Maggie, and got quite upset when all the attention seemed to be centred on her sister. But Maggie tried to make it up by including her in the shopping expeditions to Durban to search for suitable clothes, a suitcase, rucksack and toiletries required for a journey to the other end of the world. Of course Ellie was given a new dress and shoes as well, which delighted her, as she nearly always had hand-me-downs.

"I'm not going away forever, only a year at the most, and if I hate it I'll come straight home." Maggie told her.

When the moment came to say goodbye, and go through the doors to the departure lounge at the airport, Maggie clung to them all, especially Polly, and if she had been given a choice she would have thrown her ticket in the air and come rushing back to her waiting family. She gritted her teeth, determined not to break down, handed her boarding pass to the waiting official, and strode determinedly through the barrier. Once past, she allowed herself a quick glance back. Paul had his arms round her mother and Ellie, and they were all trying to smile. But she knew, as soon as she was out of sight there would be tears. She gave a last gulp herself, lifted her chin, and strode forward to begin her new life.

***

They had done a lot of preparation and Maggie was able to take a taxi straight to her digs when she finally reached London. She had rented a room in a boarding house near her work, which the college authorities had recommended. It was three floors up, and Maggie, tired after the long journey, regretted not finding out before. Her luggage seemed incredibly heavy as she carried up her cases one by one.

"Can I help you?" A nice looking girl of about her age leant over the banisters.

"Oh, thank you, I could do with a hand. I seem to have an awful lot of baggage."

They soon had all her luggage up in the room, and Maggie smiled as she thanked her helper.

"Thanks so much. That was kind of you. My name is Maggie; Maggie Belham, that is."

"I'm Susie Graystone, and I've got the room opposite yours. Anything you want, just bang on my door. Would you like a cup of tea before you start to unpack?"

"That would be lovely. I feel so dry after the flight."

"Have you come a long way?"

"From South Africa. It was a long flight. I thought we'd never get here."

Susie's room was a comfortable mess, and they sat down on an old sofa by the window, chatting companionably and drinking cups of tea, until Maggie said, "I must go and unpack. I really have enjoyed the tea, thanks so much. When I get straight you must come over to my room soon."

She looked round her new home, and thinking of Susie's room, she decided she would get some bright cushions and a nice rug to liven up the dreary furnishings provided by the landlady. She unpacked, and after placing her teddy bear on the bed, and her photographs on the chest of drawers, she felt it all seemed friendlier. She heard a bell sound from downstairs, and Susie knocked on her door.

"Dreaded supper," she called.

Maggie opened the door.

"You have to come down to meals, unless you've told the Dragon you are going out," Susie explained, as they made their way down the three flights of stairs.

Maggie was introduced to the other lodgers: Two other girls, three men of indeterminate age, and one old lady, who turned out to be the Dragon's mother. The Dragon was actually called Mrs Cotton, and obviously ruled her boarding house with a firm hand. But Maggie, observing the manner of the other boarders, realized that more than likely she was kind enough under the somewhat strict exterior.

Supper was ample and satisfying, if not exactly cordon bleu, and was quickly over. Conversation ebbed and flowed, and Maggie kept quiet, terrified of doing the wrong thing her first evening. She was dead tired in any case, and could hardly drag herself upstairs. The time change was beginning to hit her, and she just managed to unpack her pyjamas and change into them before falling into bed. When Susie softly knocked on her door there was no reply, and Susie could hear gentle breathing. She opened the door quietly, and saw Maggie curled up under the bedclothes, obviously fast asleep. She shut the door thoughtfully, deciding that her new neighbour was one of the nicest people she had met since she herself had come to London from Cornwall, three months ago.

Susie was employed by a picture gallery, and Maggie could not wait until she was qualified to take a job, and earn enough money to share a flat with her new friend. They spent many evenings planning where they would live. Maggie wrote home telling them all about their plans, and sounded so happy that Paul and Polly were able to relax, and stop worrying about their eldest daughter.

England

Chapter 26

Jean tried to hide her obviously increasing ill health from others. Shortly after James returned from South Africa she visited dear old Dr Howard, who was still practicing, although his wife insisted he should give up seeing most of his patients. He had an assistant now, a young man who took the weight of the work, and Dr Howard only looked after a few favoured patients. The National Health Service was beginning to take over, and young Dr Tremayne knew all the ins and outs of the new arrangements. He had 'surgeries', whereas Dr Howard had always visited the sick, and continued to do so.

He saw Jean in church at Christmas, and was not at all surprised when, later in January, she asked him to pop in to see her. She was painfully thin, and when he had given her a brief examination he realized he would have to break the really sad news to her that the cancer had returned, and nothing much could be done except to relieve her pain when necessary.

And then David came back.

***

David had spent several days in London, sorting out his affairs. He heard from Mr Ferbourne that James was now in business as a farm machinery mechanic. Beyond that Mr Ferbourne could not enlighten him regarding his family, and he decided he should go down to Cornwall and see how Jean was getting on. He reminded himself he still had a family, even after the terrible loss of his beloved Annabel and the children. He was sure Jean would welcome him, in spite of the harsh words they had exchanged when he left. After all, she was his true wife, and he had never sought a divorce. Once they had been happy, and he was her husband.

He did not let anyone know he was on his way to Cornwall. He took the train from Paddington to Bodmin Road and a taxi to St. Wraich. It felt so strange, not to be met by Mr Crossdon. Now it was a morose individual called Robbie, who hardly spoke. He recalled the days when Mr Crossdon used to welcome him and transport him to the Rectory, filling him in with all the latest village news as they drove to St. Wraich. He sat in the back, gazing out at the familiar landmarks; nothing much had changed in the years since he had left. Soon they were driving through the gate, and drawing up by the front door.

He paid Robbie, adding a handsome tip, and picking up his suitcase he stood there uncertain what to do next. Should he ring the bell, or simply open the door? It was his home in spite of everything. But he did not want to give them too much of a shock. Ten years was a long time to be away, after all.

Jean was lying on the sofa, with her eyes closed, when she heard the car draw up to the front door. "Who on earth could that be?" she thought. She got up wearily, and made her way to the hall. Ellen had beaten her to it, and was just opening the door. They confessed to each other afterwards that they got the shock of their lives.

Standing there, a little hesitantly, was a ghost from the past; older, a little grey, but astonishingly recognizable all the same.

"Master David!" exclaimed Ellen.

"David." whispered Jean, holding on to the chair beside her. She was visibly shaken, and David felt he should, perhaps, after all, have let them know he was coming. Jean looked so thin, and white with shock. He put his hand out to steady her, and she drew back a little, as if she could not bear his touch.

"I'm so sorry to scare you," he started, when Ellen took charge.

"Master David. Who'd have thought it after all these years? You'd better come in and I'll bring a cup of tea. You go and sit down Jean love, I'll help you," she finished as Jean looked as if she was about to faint.

David followed meekly as Ellen put her arm round Jean, and led her to the sofa. Not a word was said, and Ellen left to get the tea.

David cleared his throat.

"I'm sorry to arrive like this, without letting you know," he hesitated. "The truth is I really did not think."

"You never did," said Jean wearily. She looked at him properly for the first time since he had come in the door.

"I suppose there is some reason for this ...intrusion."

David sighed deeply.

"I have been through quite a lot since, since I saw you last. I just felt I must come home, and at least explain it all to you, and try and make it up to you somehow. I know you always were a generous person. Please can I tell you? I know it has been hard for you, but I have learnt such a lot of lessons, and realize how badly I have treated you. Will you listen for a bit?"

Jean had never heard David so humble. It was not like him. "What could have happened to him?" she thought. He looked different, too. Not as arrogant as he had been, older, and perhaps wiser, she surmised.

"Wait 'til Ellen has brought in the tea." she answered.

David gazed out of the window at the garden. It was looking fairly unkempt. "She must be finding it too much for her," he thought.

After Ellen had brought in the tray of tea, and somewhat reluctantly left, Jean leant forward to lift the teapot.

"Here, let me do it," David could see the shock was still affecting her, and she was shaking too much to lift the heavy pot.

He poured them each a cup of the steaming brew, added two sugar lumps to Jean's cup and handed it to her. She could not help being touched that he should remember she had a sweet tooth.

They sipped in silence. Then Jean leant forward a little.

"I think you can see I am not well," she started, and held up her hand to stop him interrupting.

"I have cancer. While you have been away I have had a pretty tragic time. Tom and I became a couple, and then," she drew a sharp breath, "then Tom was killed." It was such a bald statement of the facts that David's heart was pierced with anguish for her.

"Oh. I'm so sorry." It was so unlike David to be sorry for anyone except himself that Jean looked at him properly for the first time.

"Much the same thing happened to me," he said quietly. His voice broke and he could not go on. They sat in silence for a while.

Jean was just about to say something when they heard a noise in the hall, and the door burst open.

"Whose suitcase is in the hall, Mummy?"

"Darling, this is..." she looked appealingly towards David to explain. He held out his hand.

"You must be Elizabeth? I don't suppose you remember me? But a long time ago I was your daddy."

"But, Tom was our daddy." She went over to Jean and sat on the sofa beside her.

"Mummy, who is this person? I don't remember him. Are you sure? I don't understand."

"Dearest, I am sure. But I feel tired now. I will explain it all to you later." Jean's voice sounded exhausted. David intervened.

"It has all been a bit of a shock to your mother, Elizabeth. We'll clarify everything to you later. Perhaps you should help your mother up to bed for the moment."

As soon as Jean was comfortable, lying down with an eiderdown over her, Elizabeth went to seek clarity from Ellen.

"Oh love, what a shock for your poor mother..." she started. Elizabeth interrupted,

"But Ellen, who *is* he?"

"He's your real father. That's who he is. Gone away for years without letting your poor mother know where he'd gone. Why, she couldn't even get married again as she didn't know where he'd disappeared to. And now he's come back, large as life, and twice as stupid, I don't wonder."

Elizabeth was none the wiser, but she could see Ellen was in a 'state' (as she called it), and she would not hear any sense from her today. She would just have to wait until her mother recovered to hear the details.

"Who are you?" she heard Ben enter the sitting room, thinking to find his mother. She listened.

"I am David. And who are you?"

"My name's Ben. How do you do." Elizabeth almost laughed out loud at Ben's efforts to be polite. "Mother would be proud of you," she thought.

After a brief silence, she heard her father ask Ben if he had just come home from school. Ben, never at a loss, immediately launched into a description of his day's activities. Halfway though she heard the back door open, and Ellen calling to James, who had just come in from work.

"What!" she heard him shout. Ellen obviously was trying to calm him down, but he thundered into the sitting room, and brushing Ben aside, shouted at David.

"What the devil do you think you are doing here? I suggest you go as soon as possible. Have you seen our mother?"

"James, calm down. Yes, I have seen your mother. I'm afraid I gave her rather a shock."

"I should think so, bursting in on us like this. What do you want?"

Elizabeth hurtled down the stairs, desperate to calm things down before her mother heard it all.

"James," she intervened. "Do calm down. You are doing Mummy no good at all getting into a fury. Ben, go and see if Ellen knows that there will be one more for supper. That is," she addressed David, "I suppose you'd like to stay?"

"Well yes, Elizabeth. I had thought I would be staying. After all, it is my home too, you know."

Elizabeth could almost feel James' fury boiling over beside her, and put out a hand to calm him.

"Yes," she said, "I will get the spare room ready, and James, you carry Daddy's case up for him."

James looked as if he was going to refuse, but Elizabeth, though younger, was firm, and he turned away to do her bidding, muttering under his breath as he did so.

"You must understand," she said to David, "after the last time we all thought you had gone forever, and, and Tom became our father. Ben has known no other."

"Yes, I do understand. I gather Tom was killed; your mother briefly mentioned it."

"I don't know how to say this, but Mummy and Tom loved each other and Tom moved in here, and we all thought of him as our father. It is a shock for all of us, you coming back like this."

"I do see I should have written, but I know none of you would have welcomed me, so I thought I'd just come. I didn't know that Tom had been killed. How did it happen? Or would you rather not discuss it?"

Elizabeth swallowed.

"It was a tractor accident. It toppled over and killed him and James found him. Mummy has never got over the shock. She had cancer before, but it seemed to get better, and they were so happy together. I think the shock started it up again."

David gave a great sigh, and put his head in his hands. Elizabeth watched him anxiously. She hoped she had said the right things. After a bit he looked up and she could see his eyes were shining with tears.

"I have had a great tragedy too," he said, 'so I think I know much of what you all felt, and are feeling. I'd like to stay here for a few days if you think that would be all right and perhaps your mother and I could talk things over, and maybe comfort each other a little."

After he had gone up to the spare room, Elizabeth went to find James. He was out in the barn, gazing at a collection of tools, and she did her best to explain the situation to him.

She could see he was boiling with rage, and his hatred barely contained. He had been that much older than Elizabeth, and she remembered how he had always hated his father.

Now he couldn't bear the thought that this man had come back into their lives.

"Do you think he will want to stay here?" he muttered, his shoulders drooping with despair.

"I have no idea. But I should think he will want to be here for a bit. I sort of gathered he felt it was his home he was coming back to…"

"Yes, but he really doesn't deserve to think that. I wonder what Mummy will do. She can't be expected to move, not just now."

"She was very shocked to see him."

"I imagine she was shattered. We'll have to rally round and make sure he doesn't take advantage of her. He used to be an awful bully, I remember."

"James, I can't believe it. He seems quite gentle to me."

"Well, I just can't accept he has changed that much. But I hope for Mum's sake, you are right."

"Anyway, you had better come in and get ready for supper. Mummy is coming down, so Ellen tells me, and I think she will want some support."

"OK." James made a face, and went back inside with her.

It was a slightly strained atmosphere round the dining table that evening; David noticed Jean picking at her food like a bird, tiny pieces of food finding their way to her mouth. James glowered most of the time, ate heartily and excused himself on some pretext as soon as he could, bending to kiss his mother as he left. Elizabeth was polite, a natural hostess, and Ben chatted as if nothing was amiss.

Ellen appeared every now and then to clear the plates or bring in the next course. She obviously would have liked to stay and listen, hesitating to leave hoping she would hear some tidbit to discuss later with May. The latter would be extremely sorry to have missed all the drama of the master's return, but it was her day off and she had gone to Truro with a friend to buy a new coat. Ellen would have a lot to tell her when she returned that evening.

"We'll have coffee in the sitting room, Ellen," said Jean, when they had all finished. "Ben, you must go up and finish your homework."

Elizabeth, always the tactful one, soon made herself scarce with some excuse of ringing a friend, leaving Jean and David comfortably ensconced in deep armchairs each side of the fire facing each other.

David started first. "Do you feel up to talking?"

Jean gave a little sigh. "I think we've got quite a lot to talk about, don't you?"

"I was so very sorry to hear about Tom, and before we go further I'd like to say that I am so glad you had a few happy years together. I always thought he loved you."

"Yes, he did. In fact he asked me to marry him before you did!"

"Goodness! I didn't know that. Why didn't you?"

"I was in love with you. Or at least I thought I was, and Aunt Nancy longed for us to be married. I sort of thought it was the right thing to do. But you wanted the bright lights, and I wanted St, Wraich, so..."

David was overcome by the sadness in her voice, which matched his own feelings.

He sighed. "Can I tell you some deep dark secrets, which I would never share with anyone but you? But I think you are the only person who would understand, and hopefully not condemn me."

"Oh, David, do you really want to? Please don't feel you..."

"Yes, yes I do. I think it will explain my being here. Coming home to you, and this place and everything"

She poured out another cup of coffee for each of them, handed one to David, and curled up in the chair.

"Go ahead. After losing Tom nothing could upset me so much again."

David got up, and bent to kiss her gently on the top of her head before returning to his chair. This little gesture perhaps shocked Jean more than anything which had occurred that day. He seemed to find some difficulty in speaking, but then swallowed and went on. "I went out to South Africa first and started up a wine business with the help of a vineyard owner. Somehow the very pretty daughter caught my heart, and to cut a long story short, she became pregnant and I married her."

Jean caught her breath, but he continued.

"We were quite happy for a bit, but an old boyfriend of hers turned up, and I discovered that the second baby I thought was mine, turned out to be his, and she was obviously really in love with him, so I left."

"But why didn't they trace you?"

"I had a different name, and made sure there was no way I could be traced. Not that they wanted to, I am sure. They were glad to see the back of me."

"Then you came back here."

"Yes, but I didn't get much of a welcome, did I?"

"Not much." She smiled ruefully.

"After that I decided to lose myself in America. I flew out with another name, and this time I met a lovely girl. Jean," his voice crumbled a little, "I think I know what you felt for Tom. I found the love of my life, and I married her, and had a family." He put his head in his hands, and tried to compose himself.

"We had a fantastic marriage, Jean. You must know how wonderful it can be when you have the right person to share your life. That is why I am so glad you found it with Tom. Annabel and I had twin daughters, and then a little son Harry," his voice completely broke, as he struggled to get the words out.

Jean went over to him, kneeling beside him to put her arms round him. She held him gently, and after a time he heaved a huge sigh.

"Oh my dearest Jean, you are the only person I could ever tell."

"Go on," she said tenderly. "Did you have to leave them?"

"No, they left me in a sort of way." He was silent and Jean began to think that was all.

Then he gave a deep shuddering sigh, as if he could hardly bear to go on.

"We went on holiday. All together as a family for the first time. Annabel and the children flew back early, and they were all killed when the aeroplane crashed flying in to Miami. My whole family wiped out in a fireball. Oh, Jean, it was ghastly. I saw the wreckage as my plane landed. There wasn't a thing left." He slumped back in the chair completely exhausted with the memory of that dreadful night.

Jean was appalled. She could barely imagine the tragedy. Tom's accident had been dreadful enough, but this... She could hardly abide to think of the shock it must have been for David, and presumably this...Annabel had had a family who must have been equally devastated. She would not ask any questions now. They had both suffered and all the details could come out later. Meanwhile she felt immensely tired and ready for bed. David, who had never noticed these sorts of things before, looked at her and said gently, "Time for bed now, I think. I am sorry if I have worn you out with my sad tale. You have had so many problems yourself."

They both made their way upstairs, weary and exhausted after all the revelations. David put his hand on her shoulder as he reached the spare room door.

"You know, you really are such an understanding person. I had rather forgotten. Thank you so much." And, with that surprising statement he went in and closed the door behind him.

***

James heard his parents go up to bed with mixed feelings. He had not been listening, but as he had been in the study next door he would have heard any raised voices, and could have instantly gone to his mother's defence. But they had not shouted once to his surprise, and when they came out of the room he froze, ready to rush out and protect his mother. He fully expected his father to bully her. In the past when he was a child, he remembered his father's cruelty to him, or so he thought. There had been times when he had adored the man who seemed larger than life, and always exciting. But quite soon he had noticed the unkindness shown to them, his mother most of all. She did not seem to notice it, but he, James, did; listening at half closed doors long after he was supposed to be asleep; worried his father might hurt his mother; longing to protect her from any unkindness; loving her so much. He decided he would find out in the morning, she was tired now.

David came down for breakfast just as James was leaving for work.

"We must have a chat this evening, when you get home from work," he said to James.

James was halfway out of the room.

"Yes, I think we need to," he said shortly.

David did a lot of telephoning that morning, and later took a taxi to Wadebridge, where he collected a new car. He then called in to see Elizabeth, at the solicitor's office where she worked.

"Would you like a lift home?" he asked. But Elizabeth was going out with Robert Trevanion. He was duly introduced to the young man, who seemed exceptionally dull, but obviously very fond of Elizabeth, so he went to the Malsters Arms Pub in the High Street for a pasty and a pint, before driving back to St. Wraich.

He arrived at The Old Rectory just as the school bus from Bodmin was delivering Ben, who was immediately entranced by the new car, and had to be shown all over it. They were pouring over the bonnet when Jean, who had heard them chatting, came out.

"Goodness, what's this?" she asked.

"He's bought a new car, Mum, just like that!" Ben enthused. "Isn't it super? I bet it goes like the wind."

"I'm sure it does, but just now you are supposed to be doing homework, so scuttle in. You can examine all the details later." But David noticed she smiled as she said it.

Later she remarked to David, "We must think of some name Ben can call you by."

"What about "Uncle David" or just "Uncle?""

"We'll ask him. Come in and have some tea. I think Ellen has made your favourite chocolate cake."

"What a treat. I'm surprised she's still here."

"Still very much part of the family. I don't think she will ever leave voluntarily. Actually she has been, and is a tower of strength to me."

James wandered in later, and gazed for a minute at his father, seemingly settled in the comfortable armchair in which Tom used to relax after work. A kind of flashback hit him with a jolt; he blinked and then sat down.

"I saw a new car in the drive."

"Yes," said David, "I bought it this morning. I must have some transport."

"Where are you going?" James could not conceal the hope in his voice.

"Oh, nowhere in particular. But I thought your mother could do with a little drive out now and then."

"So you're staying?"

"James," his mother's voice was stern, and a little shocked. "Of course your father is staying. This is his home after all, and after what he has been through..."

He looked at his mother with bewilderment. How could she bear to forgive his father after he had deserted her so cruelly? He had never wished for Tom to be there so much as he did just then. The void he had left seemed to widen to a chasm. What would the man he always thought of as his father have done, he tried to guess. He gave a shrug, and sloped out of the door.

Jean gave a rueful smile "I'm sorry David, he will come round, I'm sure he will. He adored Tom, as we all did, and it will take a little while to..."

"Don't worry, Jean. But perhaps I should not have come back. It has upset everyone."

"Except Ellen. She is delighted." Jean grinned, and then gave a little groan, which she hastily suppressed. "Sorry, sometimes I have a bit of a spasm."

"Have you seen a doctor about it?"

"Oh yes. I've got lots of pills to take. I'm afraid, David that it is just a matter of time now. And I haven't got much of that."

David swallowed. He never dreamt when he came back to St. Wraich that he would be losing everything again so soon. No wonder James was in such a state, and so resentful of his presence, particularly at this time.

"If there is anything I can do...."

"No, David. I went to see a cancer specialist last week, and he merely confirmed my fears. It is the secondary cancers which are pretty vicious. I had it once some years ago, but they managed to cure it, and I was able to have some lovely years with Tom. After he d...was killed, I suppose the shock started the bad cells growing again. At least the pain is not too difficult to control."

David tentatively put his arm round her shoulders.

"Oh my dear." It was all he could say.

***

Jean died the following week. No one knew she was so near her time. Even Dr Howard told David and James he was surprised she went so soon, and everyone thanked heaven she had not had a long period of suffering. James blamed David for upsetting her, but Elizabeth, the sensible one, told him not to talk about things he knew nothing about.

"After all, they loved each other once. We wouldn't have been here if they hadn't. And I do know they made it up this time. Mummy told me Daddy had endured a dreadful tragedy when he was away, and she was able to comfort him."

"What happened?"

"I don't know. Mummy wouldn't say. I think she might have explained to us if she had had more time. But she did tell me not to ask him. I think some children died or something pretty awful like that."

"Serve him right."

"Oh James, why must you be so vicious to him? He was so fond of Mummy in the end, and you can see he is dreadfully upset that she has died so soon after he got back."

"I suppose so. But I can't forgive him for going off and leaving us in the first place. Actually he was often horrid to me when I was young, and I saw him being beastly to Mummy often enough. I hated him, and longed for Tom to be our daddy." And uncharacteristically he bent forward and brought his hands up to his face. Elizabeth put her arms round her dear brother and held him closely. She had done her own weeping in the privacy of her bedroom, and felt that she was now the mother figure, there to comfort and manage the bereft household.

Ben had gone about with his teeth clenched, his grief held close to his heart. Elizabeth wished he would cry it all out. She felt it would come in time, and she hoped it would be soon. Her fiancé, Robert Trevanion, was a marvellous comfort to her, and a tower of strength with all the funeral arrangements. He was the only person who was not mourning, although he had been very fond of his future mother-in-law. Jean had spoken to him in a professional way before she died, and they had gone through everything necessary. She had not wanted her children to have to arrange her funeral, and of course she had not known then that David would be there.

The church was packed, with some parishioners unable to get in, and having to stand outside. As Jean had wished, the hymns were joyful and however sad the occasion, the service uplifting. A great many of the village knew that David had returned, and a lot of speculation had gone on as he followed the coffin in with Elizabeth, and sat in the front seat with the family. As they followed it out at the end of the service they noticed James put an arm round Ben, who was desperately trying not to weep. He succeeded until the coffin was lowered into the grave, and then the tears came. Elizabeth took over, holding him tightly, knowing this was the best thing to happen. Not exactly the right moment, but it had to come. Once started Ben could not stop, Robert produced a large hanky, putting his arms round them both, and Elizabeth loved her fiancé more at that moment than she had ever done before. They both led Ben back to the house, where the village was gathering, and Ellen and May were dispensing cups of tea, sandwiches and cake. Seeing all his friends Ben blew his nose and strode forward to meet them.

David tactfully kept in the background and let James do the honours as host. Many of those who attended did not remember him, and those who did were a little shy at approaching him. He sought out a few of the older ones, and chatted to them as naturally as he was able. They were obviously dying to know what he had been doing during his absence, but he managed to deflect their enquiries by talking about Jean in such a loving way that they began to wonder again why she had become so attached to Tom. It was such a conundrum that they shook their heads and decided to let it be for the time. It would all be explained sometime. Meanwhile Ellen's sponge cake was too well known and delicious to waste time talking, when they could have a second slice, "if you please."

After they had all gone home the family gathered in the drawing room, exhausted both mentally and physically.

"I think the service was lovely," said Elizabeth. Robert's arm was round her shoulders and she leant back into his comforting embrace.

David cleared his throat. "Just what she would have wanted."

"How would you know?" asked James, rudely.

"Shut up, James," Elizabeth sounded distressed. "After all, Daddy did know Mummy before..."

"Before Tom," David interrupted. "Yes, in those days we all loved each other. And before you ask, I am so glad your mother enjoyed a few years real happiness with Tom. I know I treated her badly, James, but she forgave me, and she told me that one day you would forgive me too. I hope you will understand soon."

"I'm sorry," James could not manage to call David "Dad." "I think, or rather I know, you hurt her so badly she used to cry every night after you left, and I can't easily forgive you for that."

Robert felt they would go on forever in this unpleasant bickering if someone did not intervene.

"Does anyone have any chores to do, because I will lend a hand if so? Otherwise I ought to be getting home."

It was the right moment to end the discussion, and they all got up. Elizabeth went out with Robert; Ben sighed and said he had some homework to do; James said he must go and do some paperwork. "I've got so behind the last few days," he said.

David was left on his own. He poured out a whisky, gravitated to the armchair he had always used in the past, and sat down to think, and remember, and consider the bleak future which stretched before him.

Chapter 27

Maggie, I've found a flat! Can you come and see it...now!" Susie sounded breathless. "It is not too far away, hop on the next bus, Number Thirty-nine, and get out at Hatherley Gardens. I'll meet you. It only takes about ten minutes. I'm in a phone-box just by the bus stop; do hurry!"

They had been talking about finding a flat, but Maggie had no idea Susie was actively looking for one. However she sounded so excited, Maggie dashed up to her room seized a coat and handbag, and rushed out to find the Number Thirty-nine bus just approaching the stop. "Fate," she thought as she boarded. "Please can you tell me when we get to Hatherley Gardens?" she asked the conductor as she paid for her ticket.

Actually she need not have worried, as long before the bus slowed down she could see Susie jumping up and down on the pavement. Alighting she was engulfed by Susie's arms. "I'm so excited; I can't wait to show you. Super you got here so quickly."

She led the way down the road until they came to a pretty three story house, unusually for the area detached from the others. It was painted white, with a blue front door, and window boxes filled with flame coloured begonias outside the ground floor windows. Susie put her hand up to ring the bell.

"Susie, we can't afford something like this;" Maggie was dismayed. Perhaps Susie thought she had more money than she had. They had always shared everything as friends, and she had made it clear that she had only a little to live on.

"Wait and see!" exclaimed Susie. At that moment the door opened and an elderly lady appeared.

"Oh good, you managed to find your friend, Susie," she said, beckoning them to come in. "I'll lead the way. Susie you shut the door, there's a good girl. Now," turning to Maggie, "you must be Maggie Belham. And Susie tells me you come from South Africa?"

"Yes, yes I do. I'm doing a secretarial course."

"Now we will have some tea, and I will explain everything to you."

Maggie noticed a tray of tea on the table in front of a high armchair, and their hostess took a seat and poured each of them a cup, and gestured to Susie to hand round a tray of little cakes. She was elderly with white hair, cut short with a delightful wave, which refused to be tamed, and was inclined to fall forward as she spoke. She had such a twinkle in her eyes that Maggie immediately felt quite at home. She had never known her grandmother, but she felt this lady was her idea of one.

"First of all," she said, "my name is Eleanor Graystone, and I am Susie's great-aunt. As you can see, I am becoming quite ancient, and I am finding this house too big for one person."

"Oh, Mrs Graystone, you don't look at all old." Maggie could not help interrupting.

"Well, quite often I feel it, my dear. Now, Susie and I have hatched a plot!" They both smiled at each other conspiratually.

"I only heard last week that Susie was looking for a flat to share with a friend, and suddenly I had an idea. I could turn the top floor into a really comfortable flat. It has room for two small bedrooms, a bathroom, tiny kitchen and sitting room, just right for two girls. Also that would mean I would have someone living in the house. You have no idea how lonely it is when one is on one's own. I would still have my big bedroom and bathroom on the second floor, and this lovely room here with the kitchen."

Susie looked at Maggie, "Don't you think it is a wonderful idea?"

Maggie felt it was the most wonderful idea she had heard of for a long time. But she was still worried about the cost. As if she was reading her mind, Mrs Graystone added, "Susie and I thought if you could both pay me half what you are paying at the boarding house, and find your own food and so on, that would be fair."

Maggie thought it was more than fair. To be able to live in such a lovely neighbourhood, in a comfortable house with such a dear person, it would be heaven indeed. Her face was wreathed with smiles.

"Oh Mrs Graystone, it is like a dream. I would just love to come and live here, and of course you must let us help you in any way we can."

"You had better come and look upstairs. You may not like the rooms when you see them!" But it was said in jest. They all trooped up the two floors to view their prospective new home. The bedrooms were, indeed, small. But each had a big cupboard along one wall.

"I will, of course," said Mrs Graystone, "get two decent beds and chests of drawers and so on for you. Also a nice chair each I think. After all, I'm letting it to you furnished!" The last was said with a twinkle.

The bathroom was tiny, but Mrs Graystone suggested replacing the bath with a shower, which would make more room. "Also you can use the washing machine and dryer in the utility room downstairs when you need," she suggested,

Maggie glanced at Susie. She looked like Maggie felt, as if all their dreams had unaccountably come true.

The sitting room was quite spacious, with a big bay window which flooded sunlight into the room. It had an attractive carpet, three comfy chairs, and a small table with four matching chairs neatly pushed under it. On a cupboard stood a brand new television.

"Oh Great-aunt Eleanor, I really think you knew we'd be coming, and you've secretly been getting all these things for us!" Susie exclaimed.

"I did hope you would. I promised your father I would not advertise it until I had suggested it to you first. I did not know then that you had a friend you wanted to share with. And such a nice friend too." She smiled at Maggie.

They sealed the contract with another cup of tea, and the girls decided to move in when they had given a month's notice to their landlady. By that time Aunt Eleanor would have installed the rest of the furniture.

Maggie and Susie caught the bus back to their digs, full of plans for the future. "It really is a sort of dream come true," they agreed.

The next four weeks fled by. Mrs Graystone had the greatest fun she had had in a long while, choosing paint for the rooms, (pale colours for the bedrooms, and a neutral shade for the sitting room), and having the bathroom altered. Then she bought new beds, and bed linen; carpets for the rooms, and bright cushions for the comfy armchairs she had found in a sale. The two girls remonstrated with her, telling her that they did not expect luxury. But she told them the whole exercise was bringing her enormous pleasure, and if there was anything special they would like they must let her know.

"It is so good of you to spoil us like this, Mrs Graystone," Maggie told her one day when they had gone over with a few of their personal belongings. "I can't tell you how grateful we are to have such a *wonderful* place to live, after the dreary rooms we are in at the moment. They always smell of boiled fish!"

"My dear, I am having fun. Just knowing that you two will be floating in and out and sometimes popping in to see me is a delightful thought. I would be so pleased if you, too, would call me Aunt Eleanor, and please drop the Great, it sounds so incredibly ancient!"

It was a sunny spring day when the two friends brought over the last of their clothes, and took possession of two shiny bright keys. Aunt Eleanor had secretly placed a bottle of wine and two glasses on the table as a surprise, but Susie looked at them, and then down at her aunt, who was waiting anxiously at the bottom of the stairs.

Susie leant over the banisters. "My darling aunt, you don't think we are going to drink the flat's health without you, do you?" and she went downstairs to collect another glass, insisting her aunt should come up to "wet the flat's head," as she said. They spent the next half hour enjoying the wine, while the sun shone through the large windows as if the day was joining in their happiness.

"How are we going to leave this every morning?" mused Susie. "It really is our dream flat, isn't it, Maggie?"

Mrs Graystone was not surprised to see tears in Maggie's eyes.

"I'm so sorry, it is all so perfect, and I just wish I knew how to thank you." she gulped,

"It is enough thanks to know you are happy here, and when I hear your voices upstairs, I won't feel so lonely."

Maggie went over to her and hugged her. There was no need for words. She had missed her own family so much; until that moment she had not realized how much. But she had found another family to be her own in this country, and she felt safe for the first time since she arrived in London. "Someone to care," she thought.

***

They soon settled down happily, hating to leave their nest, but revelling in returning to their home after work. One or other, and sometimes both would pop in to see Mrs Graystone every day. They would do errands for her, or have a little chat, telling her what had been happening that day. Sometimes tea would be laid out for three, with homemade cakes or scones, warm from the oven, and they would stay a bit longer, talking.

One weekend they planned a little dinner party in the flat, and invited Aunt Eleanor. They had quite a few friends, but they wanted their first dinner party to be only for her, as a "thank you" for the flat. It turned out to be a pleasantly merry evening. They could not believe someone approaching eighty could be such fun.

Gradually they built up a group of friends, and with two such attractive girls there were quite a few men among their acquaintances. One particularly, John Partridge, attached himself to Susie. He was a charming young man and was duly introduced to Aunt Eleanor, who thoroughly approved.

"I don't think you need worry," she told her nephew George when she made her weekly telephone call to him. "He is absolutely the type you and Marcia would like, so keep your fingers crossed!"

Although Susie and John became a pair, Maggie still floated between her admirers, never attaching herself to one over the others. She did her best, as Susie was longing for her to have a real relationship like she and John had, but none of them lit that essential spark.

"You see," she said to Susie when they were having a heart to heart while they washed their hair, sharing the wash-basin in turns. "I just know I will feel something extra when I meet the right person, and no one has given me that sort of glowing feeling yet."

Susie understood. She had known that moment she had met John, and as the feeling was mutual, she wished she could do the same for Maggie.

But Maggie always had a vision of a god-like young man diving through the waves to rescue her sister. She often wondered if she would, (could), meet him again, and kept the memory close to her heart.

Susie was going home to spend her holiday with her parents, and John was to come down for a few days to be introduced. Susie hoped he would be asking her father for permission to marry his daughter. John came from a traditional family, and he would not dream of asking Susie to marry him, without first obtaining permission from her father. This attitude impressed Aunt Eleanor, but was frustrating for the girls.

"Do you think he will actually ask Daddy for my hand?" Susie asked Maggie.

"I think it is lovely, and so romantic, and I think you should wait for him to see your father, and then I bet he gets down on one knee to propose!"

Susie threw a cushion at her, and they both collapsed in giggles. Aunt Eleanor heard them, and smiled. It was lovely having young people in the house after all these years.

Susie could not bear the thought of Maggie in the flat all by herself while she was away, and after consulting her mother and Aunt Eleanor, decided to ask Maggie to join her in Cornwall for her two-week holiday.

"But what about Aunt Eleanor? We can't leave her all alone." Maggie looked worried.

"That's just it. She is invited too. We have a huge house, and Aunt Eleanor always comes down for a few weeks in the summer, so if you didn't come, it would be you all alone, and I couldn't bear that. So please, do come."

Maggie was delighted to accept. She had heard so much about Cornwall from Susie, and the promised surfing was an additional attraction.

The excitement started when they all took a taxi to Paddington. Aunt Eleanor had insisted on treating them both to First Class tickets on the Cornish Riviera, a new train which travelled all the way from London to Penzance. It was a long journey, but comfortable. One of the unexpected pleasures came when Aunt Eleanor announced they would have lunch in the Dining Car.

"And you are not to worry, girls, this is my treat."

"But you are already paying for our tickets," said Susie, while Maggie held back, a little embarrassed by the generosity shown to someone who was not even "family."

"My dears," said Aunt Eleanor, "I always travel like this. I do not travel often these days, and so I spoil myself when I do! You are helping me, with all my luggage and things, and it makes the start of my annual holiday such a joy to have you both with me. So of course we will all go and have lunch, and really begin to enjoy ourselves."

So they did. After a splendid lunch, served with the countryside whizzing by, it seemed no time at all until they were able to see the sea lapping the shore just below the train. They went in and out of tunnels, tiny beaches materialized, then a long stretch of surf breaking onto a shingly shore.

"Is this Cornwall?" asked Maggie, entranced by the views speeding past.

"Not yet," Susie stirred herself from her reverie of John, "We are still in Devon. After Plymouth we go over a huge bridge, and we usually all shout "Cornwall" when we get halfway across! Sort of family tradition!"

Sure enough, after a great many passengers alighted at Plymouth, the train proceeded slowly across a huge bridge over the River Tamar, which, Susie explained, was the boundary and they all three duly shouted "Cornwall" as the train reached the halfway mark. Luckily no one else was in the carriage.

After that the train seemed to crawl, stopping at several small stations, before Susie said, "Time to get our luggage together. Only about five more minutes!"

The train slowed and came to a halt in front of a long platform. As they descended a whirlwind of welcome and activity surrounded them. Someone had organized a porter, and their bags were quickly scooped up and carried off to a large car. Finally Susie was able to extricate herself from the arms of a tall lady, and introduced her; "Mummy, this is Maggie. Isn't it great she could come too?"

Susie's mother put her hand out, enclosing Maggie's with a warm clasp.

"Yes, I am very glad you could come and join us. We usually have a crowd staying at this time of year, but only one or two this time."

She hugged Mrs Graystone. "Aunt Eleanor. How lovely you could come too. I do hope they haven't worn you out on the journey down?"

Somehow they all piled in the big car, and it wasn't long before they turned in at large wrought iron gates, and were driving up a lengthy drive, which reminded Maggie of the night Johnny had driven Mary Fairbairn to her house after the School Dance. But the house at the end of the drive was completely different from the Fairbairn residence. It was incredibly ancient, and made of grey stones, all diverse shapes and sizes, with old slate tiles covering the roof. Some form of climbing plant trailed over the walls, softening the effect of what could have been a very grim building. A huge front door was open wide, although no one was there. It was as if the house itself was welcoming them, without the need of people.

"Welcome to Greystones!" Susie helped her mother out of the car. Maggie turned back to do the same to Aunt Eleanor.

"Are you named after the house, or the other way round?" Maggie asked Susie later.

"It is a bit muddling. But my great-grandfather found it years ago. It was much smaller, and called "Greystones" for obvious reasons. He was so amused to find a house with almost the same name as his, that he bought it for holidays. He made it a lot bigger as his family grew, and my father loves it so much we now live here all the time."

"You are lucky to live in such a gorgeous place."

"Yes, and you can hear the sea, if the wind is in the right direction." She opened the window of Maggie's bedroom. "Listen."

Maggie leant out and Susie put her arms round her shoulders.

"Oh yes, I can just hear it. And Susie, I can smell it too. Can't you?"

They both laughed. It all seemed too perfect.

"Tomorrow we'll go and surf at Polzeath. Mummy will lend us her old car, and we will hire you some surfboards. I never thought to ask, but can you surf, or will you need some lessons? There is a surf school there."

"Gosh no! Last time I surfed was in Durban, and the waves were huge, and Ellie nearly got swept under one of them. It was awful." She stopped, suddenly remembering a man called James. In her mind she saw him so clearly she felt herself blushing. But Susie simply thought it was the memory of her sister, and gave her a hug.

"They are not huge here. Not unless there has been a big storm or something. Anyway, they have lifeguards usually, so I shouldn't worry."

"Oh, I'm looking forward to it. I love the sea."

While they had been upstairs, there had been quite a commotion downstairs. Susie's brother Jonathon had arrived. As he explained to Maggie later, nothing could keep him away from Greystones in the summer. He was at Cambridge, studying law, but they had long vacations, when they were supposed to study, but what better place to study than Greystones, especially when he could slink off to the beach when the sun was out and the surf was high.

Maggie took to him at once. Being Susie's brother he had the same sense of humour and fun. The first dinner they all had together that evening was full of laughter, Aunt Eleanor joining in with great interest. She loved to hear all their adventures. Jonathon knew about the flat of course, but he had never seen it, so plans were made for him to visit London and see it all.

Later, when the grown-ups had gone to bed, the three of them sat up late, putting the world to rights, and generally planning what they would do with themselves the next day.

"Do you know, Maggie is a surfer? She last rode the waves in Durban of all places."

"Goodness, I hope you won't find the Cornish waves too tame?" Jonathon looked at her.

"Not at all. I was a bit scared in Durban to tell the truth, and it was a long time ago anyway. Funnily enough, a chap from Cornwall rescued my sister when she got into difficulty."

"I wonder who it was. Did you get his name? We might know him."

"I think," said Maggie, trying desperately not to blush, "it was James something or other; beginning with a "B."

"It could be James Bretton," said Jonathon, "he used to be a lifeguard when we were younger; he has a farm machinery repair firm now. They live in The Old Rectory at St. Wraich."

Maggie found she could not breathe, let alone speak. "I really think that might be the name," she eventually managed. Susie noticed her hesitation, but wisely kept quiet, resolving to do her best to find James Bretton, and discover if this was the man who so obviously set Maggie's heart racing.

That evening Maggie went up to bed in a haze of anticipation. She wondered if the man they knew as James Bretton really was the one she had met in Durban. She could not help feeling the coincidence was too much, and if by some chance she did meet him, he would not be the same James, and the disappointment would be hard to bear. And there again, if it was, perhaps he would not be the wonderful person she imagined. After all, she had only met him so briefly, and in such strange circumstances, how could she fall in love with a man to whom she had hardly spoken?

Her mind went round and round in circles, until she fell asleep, and dreamt of huge waves engulfing her, and no one there to save her.

***

A glorious day welcomed them the next morning, and Jonathon decreed that the tides were just right for some surfing. They packed up a picnic lunch of rolls, cheese and ham, with some crisp juicy apples, and bars of chocolate.

"We can buy something to drink from the cafe on the beach," Jonathon told them, "and possibly an ice cream. Maggie, you have no idea how good Cornish ice creams taste. I dream of them all term!"

"I believe you," she said with a laugh. "Susie has been going on about them all summer in London!"

They piled into Jonathon's car, with his and Susie's surfboards lashed onto the roof.

"We will hire one for you, Maggie, and also a wetsuit."

"What on earth is that?"

"They are a sort of all-in-one garment, which keeps you warm, and gives you a certain protection."

"I think they do have them in South Africa, now I come to think of it. But of course, I expect the water is warmer there," Susie explained to her brother.

Polzeath was not far away, and they were soon unpacking all their suits and boards, and directing Maggie to the little shop which hired equipment. Kitted out she sallied forth with the others. The waves were quite tame compared to Durban, but when they paddled out Maggie discovered the ride back to the shore was longer, and really much more enjoyable than the violent surf she had experienced in South Africa. Also she found a certain skill was required in choosing the right waves. Some petered out early on, some had adverse currents, but if she decided to ride the right one it carried her in with great style. She followed the other two, who she soon discovered were knowledgeable enough to recognize the perfect wave.

"Now!" one of them would cry, and they all jumped up on their boards and rode in together, collapsing in the shallows with laughter.

The beach was fairly crowded, as it was the holidays, so they had to make sure they did not collide or run into other surfers, or the children paddling at the edge. Maggie kept her eyes open for a head of golden curls; she was sure she would recognize him if she saw him, but she saw no sign. However, she enjoyed herself hugely, and tucked into their picnic with an appetite she had not experienced in London.

They lay on the rocks, replete after their lunch, and chatted. Susie thought how lovely it would be if her brother and Maggie would fall in love and get married. She even got as far as a double wedding. She and John, Jonathon and Maggie, what fun that would be.

Jonathon, on the other hand, was wondering if he dare bring his latest girlfriend home. She worked in a restaurant off the King's Road and was "not quite our type," as he knew his mother would say. But, gosh, she was hot stuff, and he found himself blushing at one or two memories.

Maggie sighed deeply. She had been fantasizing about meeting James again, and how they would look into each other's eyes and...

"Time to get out in the surf again, before the tide goes out too far." Jonathon's voice pierced her dreams.

The days flew by, and the sunshine never seemed to end. The evenings were so warm that on more than one occasion they built a barbecue, and cooked sausages and chicken legs, eating them in their fingers after dipping them in the most delicious sauce made by Aunt Eleanor.

All of a sudden Maggie realized they only had two more days left before returning to London. Aunt Eleanor would be staying for another fortnight, but she and Susie had to get back to work.

"Let's go and swim in the moonlight," suggested Jonathon. He was always full of ideas, some madder than others. It was a full moon that night. The day seemed to slip seamlessly into night as the sun set and the moon rose. They drove to a small cove which Jonathon had discovered. Lazy waves were rolling in, their tips tinged with silver as the moon's rays caught them. It was, and felt, incredibly romantic. John was with them, and he and Susie wandered off. Jonathon and Maggie lay on the sand chatting.

"I don't know what to do, Maggie."

"Why, Jonathon?"

"I love this girl, you see." He started. "I don't think my parents would approve though. She is "not our sort" as they would say, but she is wonderful, and I can't get her out of my mind."

"Oh Jonathon, how awful for you. My mother had the same problem."

"Goodness, do tell me. I mean, if you can."

"I don't think she would mind. She fell in love with a boy who was not to her parents' liking as you might say. He went off in the Army, and she married my father. Then Paul came back, and my mother realized she had loved him all along. I don't quite know what happened, I was only about three at the time, but there was a most awful row, and my father pushed off. Then after a bit my mother married Paul, and they are terribly happy and in love after all these years. I sometimes wonder if my sister Ellie is Paul's child, but there has never been any sign I have a different father. My daddy was super, and he gave me my first pony, and I missed him terribly at first. So you see; at least I don't suppose you do see. I'm afraid I haven't been much help." She rolled over and looked at Jonathon.

"Well, yes, I think you have. It has made me decide to bring her home and see how we all get on. I may think she is a disaster down here. She is very much a town girl, and I can't see her doing this, but, gosh, I do love her terribly."

At that moment there was a slight commotion. A couple of chaps dived into the sea a few yards up the beach, and swam strongly out, carving a silver streak as they went. Maggie looked up, annoyed to be disturbed. One of them called to the other, and they raced a wave which was rolling in. The one in front had his head half under the water, and surfaced a few yards from Jonathon.

"I'm so sorry to disturb you," he said, shaking the water from his head. Maggie tried to stand up and felt the whole beach tipping. Her head was whirling, and she could not breathe properly. A strong arm caught her and at the same moment said quietly, "Maggie?"

Maggie looked up. It *was* James.

"James?" she whispered, unable to speak properly. Jonathon rose and exclaimed, "Good heavens! James Bretton! I haven't seen you for ages!"

James tore his gaze away from Maggie, although he did not let her hand go. "Jonathon Graystone! What are you doing here?"

"Same as you, I imagine. Enjoying the moonlight."

"But what are you doing in Cornwall?" He turned back to Maggie. "I thought you lived in South Africa."

"I do. But I'm over here doing a secretarial course," Maggie felt so breathless she could hardly answer.

James thought, "I was going over to look for her next month. Miracles do happen!" He actually said, "How amazing. How is your sister?"

"She's fine. Still at school. She was awfully grateful to you for saving her. We tried to find you to thank you properly."

"I tried to find you too."

They looked at each other, completely oblivious of the others. His friend Dick came in from the water to discover why James was still on the beach. Susie and John returned from their stroll, (Susie looking somewhat dishevelled, but no one noticed). Jonathon was the only one who, naturally courteous, introduced everyone to each other. The whole story of the Durban encounter was related. Jonathon was not the only one who noticed that James had not let go of Maggie's hand, as if he was terrified she would disappear again. One of his arms had crept round her shoulders, and it seemed the most natural thing in the world to them both to leave it there.

"Why don't we all go back home and find something to eat?" Susie wanted to prolong the evening for Maggie's sake now, as well as her own. "Can you and Dick come?" she added.

James looked over at Dick.

"Sorry, I must get back. Early start tomorrow, but my house is on the way to Greystones, so you can drop me off and go on, James."

James did not take much persuading. Somehow, Maggie would never know how, Dick got in the back of James's car, and she found herself sitting in the front. She looked over to the Jonathon's car, where the other three were sitting.

"Should I...?"

"You'll be OK here," said James, with a grin.

They left Dick at his cottage, and drove on towards Greystones. After a while James slowed down, and then stopped the car.

"I think we should have a little talk," he said softly. He twisted to face her, and she was glad of the darkness which surrounded them, as she felt the all too familiar blush spreading over her cheeks.

"First of all," he whispered, "I am going to do something I've been longing to do ever since I saw you in Durban," and he gently took her face in his hands and kissed her.

She was not surprised, or shocked, or reluctant. To be honest she had longed for that too, although she had never visualized quite the time or the place. After the first surprise of feeling his lips on hers, she reciprocated, and the next few moments they were lost in a world of their own. If it had been daylight when they drew apart they would have seen the love in each other's eyes. As it was, the dark seemed to intensify their feelings.

"This is the most marvellous night of my life," James murmured. "Fancy finding you after all this time in Cornwall; on a beach too. It might have been meant."

"I'm sure it was meant. When Susie asked me to stay in Cornwall, I sort of had a dream I might run into you, especially when Jonathon said he knew you."

"Why didn't he contact me before? We seem to have wasted nearly two weeks. Two weeks of this," and he kissed her very thoroughly again.

"We'd better get back," said Maggie, when she could disengage herself.

"Yes, I suppose so. Now, I can take the day off tomorrow. What about spending the day together?"

Maggie woke up the next morning with a feeling of blissful excitement. She had told the others, after James had left, a little of what had happened in Durban, and had gone straight up to bed in a sort of dream. They had not said anything, but when she had left the room they looked at each other and burst out laughing.

"Talk about 'love at first sight'," Jonathon was the first to recover.

"I think it is sweet," Susie remarked. John just looked at her and winked, making her blush and Jonathon threw a cushion at John. It seemed such a happy episode in their lives. They were all young, and incurably romantic. Their dreams were part of their lives.

***

James asked Ellen if she could pack up a really nice picnic lunch for two people. She looked at him knowingly.

"Now James. Who might you be taking out on a workday? I know the sun is shining, and you love a good surf. Or are you entertaining some businessman in the office?"

James knew he could never pull the wool over Ellen's eyes, even though she was getting on in age.

"The girl I told Mum about. I have met her again, and Ellen, she is just as wonderful as I thought she was when I met her in South Africa."

"So your Ma knew about her then. Tell me, James, is she, er, *dark*?"

James threw his arms round Ellen's ample form.

"Oh, you old silly. Of course not. There are masses of white people in Africa you know, and it wouldn't have mattered anyway."

"Glad to hear it. Now then, move out of my way and I'll pack you up something nice."

She did too.

Maggie came down to breakfast in the morning with her head in the clouds. Susie could see she was in a dreamlike state, especially when she started to put salt on her cornflakes.

"Wake up, Maggie!" she cried. "I don't think you'd like those cornflakes much!"

Maggie giggled. "Goodness. Oh dear. I don't know what has happened!"

"Love has happened, it makes one do the silliest things. I know, I've been there!"

They both fell about laughing, and when Aunt Eleanor poked her head in through the door to enquire what the joke was, they told her. Somehow, one told Aunt Eleanor everything, without embarrassment. She was thrilled to hear the romantic story of Maggie meeting James in Durban, and longing to meet him again.

"I just never thought it would be here, in Cornwall. And the lovely part of it Aunt Eleanor, is that I have discovered he felt, feels," she corrected herself, "the same."

"He is coming to pick her up this morning so you will be able to meet him." Susie told her aunt.

"That would be nice. Mind you call me if I am not around when he comes, Maggie."

James's car roared up the drive at ten-thirty, and Maggie was breathlessly waiting in the hall. As he came up the steps she put her hand out to Aunt Eleanor, who was hovering nearby.

"Here he is. Oh dear. What if I don't feel the same in broad daylight?"

There was a hoot of mirth from Susie, who by strange chance had just come into the hall. Then the door bell rang and they all jumped.

"Go on, answer it!" Susie could not contain her impatience.

Maggie opened the door, and at that moment realized she had not, and never could have, doubted her feelings. When she saw his face, all the love came flooding back, causing a vivid blush, which James found entrancing. They stepped towards each other, were quickly aware of the others present, and stopped, rather foolishly gazing at each other.

"Hullo James."

"Hullo Maggie, hullo there, Susie."

"James, this is Mrs Graystone, Susie's great aunt, who is staying here."

"How do you do, James, I have heard quite a bit about you. At least, only this morning. It seems remarkable that Maggie should meet you after all this time, here in Cornwall." Aunt Eleanor said with a twinkle.

"How do you do, Mrs Graystone. Yes, it is wonderful, isn't it? I do hope you don't mind if I take her off for the day? We have such a lot of catching up to do."

They were waved off as if they were going on a long journey, as indeed they were.

James took her through Camelford and up to a hill he called "Rowter," although the sign post said "Rough Tor." From there one could see for miles. It was a gorgeous day, clear and sunny. There did not seem to be a soul about on the moor, and after climbing up the hill, James found a sheltered spot, out of the wind, which he explained was always blowing up so high. He placed a rug on the grass in front of some rocks, and took off his rucksack.

"Ellen, our cook, plus maid, plus friend, plus everything else, packed us up a lunch," he told Maggie.

They sat down, and quietly gazed at the vista spread before them. Little fields, and farms, and gorse-strewn moors stretched for miles. Even the coast was just visible.

"It is the most wonderful view I have ever seen." Maggie feasted her eyes on the panorama. "It is awful to think I have got to go back to London tomorrow, and leave all this for the streets and lines and lines of houses."

"And me?" teased James.

She turned to look at him. "And you," she said softly.

He put his hand out and she took it, and for a moment the world seemed to stop.

"My God, I love you," James pulled her to him, and then they were lost in each other.

"I ought to ask your parents first, but Maggie, my darling Maggie, will you marry me?" James kept his arms round her as though he thought she might disappear.

She closed her eyes for a minute, willing herself to see her mother and Paul, knowing with all her heart they would love James. She was sure they would approve, and encourage her to accept. It would, of course, mean living in England. She would miss her home in South Africa so much, but they could travel over there. Flying was so much easier these days. But there was no question of saying "No" to James. Separation from her beloved family or never seeing James again, she had only one answer in her mind, and she knew her family would understand.

This all passed through her mind in a flash, and she looked up at James, waiting anxiously for her answer.

"Oh yes please," she whispered.

They did eat the delicious lunch which Ellen had provided, but quite a long time later. James was overcome by her acceptance, and sealed it with more than one kiss. By mutual and unspoken agreement they did not make love, although they both wanted to. It seemed too early, and as James said, "We have all the time in the world." Maggie was so overwhelmed by finding the man of her dreams, she wanted to relish every moment of courtship, and not hurry any part of getting to know him.

When the sun went down, they packed up the remains of their picnic, and drove back to Greystones reluctantly.

"Next time you must come to the Old Rectory and meet my sister and brother, and Ellen too. Yes, and my father. But better wait till we have more time. I will come up to London as soon as I can for a day or two. Then when you have some time off, you can come down here again. Oh darling, I'm going to miss you every day we are apart."

***

Maggie did not write to tell her mother about James. She hugged the knowledge to herself. "Plenty of time later," she thought. The days in London dragged after she returned. Some evenings James telephoned, but not very often. He told her his father was usually sitting near the telephone, and he had not told his family either about their meeting. It seemed as if it was a private thing between them, to be cosseted and nurtured without anyone else becoming involved.

However, before long James managed to arrange a couple of days off and Maggie decided to miss one or two classes. She was nearly at the end of the course, and it did not seem to matter if she attended or not, so long as she let someone know. She was in a haze of excitement, mingled with anxiety. Perhaps it was all a holiday romance, a dream that would shatter when they saw each other again.

But it wasn't. As soon as they met, they both knew it was for real, and forever. James had bought a ring from the jewellers in Wadebridge, a pretty circlet of diamonds and emeralds, and as they walked in the park he asked her again to be his wife.

"Because, my darling," he said, "I can't imagine living with anyone else but you for the whole of my life."

Maggie looked up at him with such love that his heart turned somersaults. "I can't imagine life without you either."

He took the little velvet box out of his pocket and handed it to her.

"Will you wear this for me? I hope it fits, but if it doesn't we can easily have it altered."

She opened the box, and gave a little gasp as she saw the ring nestling inside.

"I thought it would go with your hair," he murmured quietly. Then he caught hold of her left hand and slipped it on the fourth finger. It fitted perfectly, and they both gazed at it in wonder.

"Next time it will be a wedding ring!" he said with a laugh.

Chapter 28

Maggie finished the course about four weeks later, and was able to plan to visit Cornwall again. Aunt Eleanor had had a beastly cold, and decided to spend a few weeks in the West Country to recover before the winter months set in.

"We will both travel down together and then you can help me with my suitcase." She suggested,

"That would be a lovely idea. James is going to meet us at Bodmin, and he can drop you off at Greystones."

"You are going to stay with James's family then?"

"That is the idea, Aunt Eleanor. I hope you think that is all right?"

"Yes, of course, dear; but you must always feel you can come to Greystones if you feel the need. Promise?"

"How kind you are. I think I will be all right. James has a sister and brother, and his father; I'm longing to meet them."

"Well, just remember, we are not far away if you need us."

This time the journey seemed longer. There was still the beautiful scenery flying by the windows. They still had a delicious lunch in the Dining Car, and the view as they crawled over the Tamar Bridge was just as stunning, but how she longed to be in James's arms again. She was collecting their luggage together far too soon, to Mrs Graystone's amusement.

But at last the voice of the guard was saying "Bodmin Road Station, Bodmin Road Station next stop," and they were slowing down, and there was the beloved figure of James, peering anxiously at the doors opening, and the passengers alighting. His face lit up as he saw them, and before a moment was gone she was engulfed in a huge hug, and he was greeting Mrs Graystone as courteously as he could while clinging to Maggie as if he would never let her go.

They drove to Greystones and had to go in and have a cup of tea. After a brief half hour James was obviously impatient to get home, and farewells were said.

"Whew! They are sweet, but they do want to hear all the news, don't they?" Maggie was almost making small talk. Privately she was rather apprehensive of meeting James's family. He grinned at her.

"Don't worry, they won't bite you." It was as if he knew her innermost feelings and she smiled.

"Please James, don't read my mind quite so well!"

After a bit he slowed down.

"This is St. Wraich." She gazed out of the window. He was driving very slowly, and Maggie could see pretty cottages scattered about, little roads leading everywhere and gardens spilling out, with flowers just past their best, but still bravely blooming. There was a big chestnut tree just in front of the old church. James told her it had been grown from a conker brought back by a soldier from the First World War. Two or three old men were standing there, leaning on their sticks, putting the world to rights.

"It is a kind of meeting place," James told her, "everyone says "meet you under the tree," and you know it is there."

Soon they were driving through a wide gate, and up a short drive to an old ivy- clad house. The front door was already open, and an elderly lady in an apron was waiting there.

"This is Ellen," James introduced them.

"The provider of delicious picnics!" said Maggie.

Ellen smiled. "Well I do know James likes his food."

The ice was broken, and Ellen stood back to let them into the hall.

"I believe Elizabeth and Ben are in the sitting room, so perhaps you had better go straight in," she suggested.

Maggie felt a little niggle of nervousness. "Meeting the family," she thought, "I hope they like me."

James took charge, and opened the door. Elizabeth was by the window, and Ben was curled up on an armchair, from which he rose rather quickly and nearly toppled over. Maggie put an arm out to steady him and he smiled.

"Sorry, my feet got in the way," he said.

Maggie commiserated, "Isn't it awful, feet always seem to have a life of their own in armchairs."

The ice was broken, and Elizabeth came forward and introduced herself, and soon they were all chatting as if they had known each other all their lives. Ellen brought in a huge tray with tea things, and Ben hurried out and collected the plates of sandwiches and cake. They all sat down to chat, and enjoy, (certainly in Ben's case), more than one slice of Ellen's delicious sponge cake.

"Wow! I wish you'd come every day. Ellen puts on a huge tea when we have guests!" Ben exclaimed.

They were talking away as if they had known each other all their lives, when they heard a car drive up.

"That must be Daddy," said Elizabeth. Maggie noticed a slight silence, as if they were wondering what their father would do when he came in. Ben stuffed a last mouthful of cake into his mouth, and made as if to leave by the French window. James seemed to stiffen and stepped forward to be at her side when his father came into the room. Only Elizabeth seemed completely relaxed as the door opened.

David walked in, wondering what James's girlfriend would be like. James had been extremely reserved about her, although David could see the love shining out of his eyes when he had told them she was coming to stay. She was standing the other side of the room with James holding her hand, as if to protect her from the monster. There was a little gasp as she looked over to him.

"Daddy?"

Suddenly time collapsed as they each recognized the other. There was an electrifying silence, as those in the room tried to understand what was happening.

"Maggie...! How did you...?" David was the first to recover.

"P-pictures. I s-saw a photograph, and took it out of the drawer. I wanted you to come back so much." She seemed to crumple.

David and James both stepped forward at once. Utterly bewildered, James was more hesitant, and it was David who put his arm round Maggie's shoulders, producing a handkerchief. But James pushed him aside, pulling Maggie into his arms as if for protection.

"What on earth do you mean? Maggie's name is Belham; she could not be your daughter. Maggie, you must be dreaming." James turned to her, his face white.

Maggie looked up at him with bewilderment, rousing in him even more protective feelings for her.

"I told you my father had disappeared when I was quite small. I never knew what had happened, but I always hoped he would come back, and give me another pony when I grew out of Mousie and..."

"Mousie?"

"My first pony. Daddy gave him to me."

"I called my first pony Mousie too. But this is silly." He turned to his father.

"What *is* all this nonsense? You couldn't be Maggie's father, I don't understand."

"Nor do I." Elizabeth looked completely mystified. Ben was quiet for once, totally transfixed by the drama. Nothing like this had happened to him before, and he was fascinated.

"Let's sit down and I will try and explain." David sighed, as he realized his entire secret life was about to unravel. He did not want to hurt Maggie, who he had adored as a child, and he dreaded to think what effect the revelations would have on the others, especially James. In the last few months he had been slowly building a trust between himself and his son, but it was so fragile, and what he had to tell them would bring the whole edifice tumbling down.

"When I left your mother here," he nodded to James and Elizabeth, "we were very unhappy. We had such different ideas about life. Your mother was happy in St. Wraich, and although we still loved each other it was not enough. I wanted to spread my wings; she was happy to look after you children and live a quiet life, and really unknown to us both, she actually loved Tom, but she did not recognize it at the time. So I pushed off to South Africa, changed my name, met your mother, Maggie, and married her."

There was a gasp from Elizabeth. "But Dad, you were already married. You and Mummy never divorced, did you?"

"No, we didn't, but it did not seem to matter somehow. I never thought I would come back, ever."

"Well," Maggie intervened, "Why did you leave *us*?"

"Your mother fell in love with Paul, and, I think you are old enough to understand this, Ellie is Paul's child."

"Oh." Maggie seemed to shrink into the chair.

The consequences had taken a little while to sink in, particularly to James. Elizabeth, who had a quicker mind, gasped.

"So...That means James and Maggie are half brother and sister, I suppose."

James went white and clasped Maggie's hand. "You...you bastard!" He shouted at his father." You are a destroyer of everyone's lives."

"Why?" asked Ben, in a small voice. He rather liked David, who had been so kind to him after Jean had died.

"It means that James cannot marry Maggie now." explained Elizabeth.

The words sounded a death knell for two people, who had been, were, very much in love and had been planning a future together. Maggie went deathly white as she realized what this meant for her. She looked down at James's hand, clutching her own like a drowning man reaches out for rescue. There was no hope for either of them. An empty landscape stretched before them, devoid of happiness or any lasting life together.

She felt numb. "I suppose I had better leave. I will telephone Aunt Eleanor. Can I do that?" she asked Elizabeth, who seemed to be the only person in the room with any sense.

"Yes, yes of course. Come into the hall. You can phone from there."

Maggie withdrew her hand from James, who was still clutching it. She could hardly bear to look at him. She glanced up at her father, who was looking stricken. She even felt a little sorry for him, but her overriding feelings were for James and herself. She followed Elizabeth into the hall, and dialed the Graystones, hardly knowing what she was doing.

"Can I speak to Mrs Graystone senior?"

"Speaking."

"Oh Aunt Eleanor, I can't explain now, but can I come over and spend the night?" Her voice was breaking, and Mrs Graystone, visualizing a lover's tiff, was not unduly worried.

"Yes, of course, my dear. The family are away, so there is only me here. Come over straight away."

"Oh thank you, I'll do that. As soon as I can get a taxi. Thank you so much," she repeated, and putting the receiver down she stood still for a moment, trying to recover her wits. Elizabeth put her arms round her, and tried to comfort her.

"You don't need to get a taxi, I'll drive you. Ben will go and collect your suitcases." She beckoned to her young brother who had come into the hall, mainly to get away from the strained atmosphere in the sitting room. He nodded his head and ran upstairs.

"Elizabeth, I must see James for a minute; I can't bear to go without saying goodbye," Maggie murmured.

Elizabeth fetched James, saying, "Be gentle with her; don't explode till she's gone. She is trying to be so brave, you must be too."

She left them in the hall and went back to find her father still gazing out of the window, tight-lipped and silent.

James took Maggie in his arms.

"Darling, this can't be good-bye. Somehow we must sort it out. We love each other too much for parting."

"I know, James. It seems totally wrong, but perhaps we do love each other just because we are brother and sister. I think I will go back to South Africa, and talk it over with Mum and Paul. Oh darling, darling James..." she could not go on, and he held her tightly until Elizabeth appeared with the car keys.

She reluctantly dragged herself away, not looking back in case her resolve broke, and got into the car.

Elizabeth maintained a tactful silence as they drove to Greystones.

"Thank you so much for being so understanding." Maggie kissed Elizabeth when they arrived. Aunt Eleanor had heard the car, and was waiting at the front door. Elizabeth helped her up the steps with her cases, and was soon on her way. Mrs Graystone took one look at Maggie, and said, "Supper on a tray in the drawing room, I think; but first, a strong drink."

Maggie nodded miserably. "I'll tell you about it after I've had that!"

And she did.

***

Mrs Graystone was appalled. The terrible coincidence of James' father also being Maggie's was almost too much to bear. As Maggie poured out the whole sorry saga she could hardly believe it. The fact that these two lovely people had met at all was fate, and she could only give her sympathy, no solution. They were brother and sister, and there could be no getting round it.

"I thought I would go home now," Maggie told her. "I can hardly bear to be in the same country as James. I might meet him again, and Aunt Eleanor, I don't know how we would resist being more than brother and sister, if you know what I mean." Mrs Graystone nodded.

"Luckily we haven't..... We were keeping all that till after we were married." At last she burst into tears, and rushed from the room, up the stairs to her bedroom.

Mrs Graystone had supper alone that night.

Needless to say Susie had been devastated with Maggie's decision to return to South Africa. She could not believe the revelations that James was her half brother.

"It is like a bad dream." She said.

"If it is, I just wish I could wake up," Maggie sobbed. She sometimes wondered where all the tears came from. Susie was appalled at Maggie's weeping. She had always been so full of fun and laughter. Now she seemed to be fading into ghost of her former self, a handkerchief seldom far from her face.

But as the time came for her to board the plane she flung her arms round Susie.

"You have been marvellous to me. I'm sorry I have so miserable. If you ever see James please tell him I will never forget him. He was, is, my life, and one day we will be together. Don't know how, but we will." She lifted her chin, gave Susie a small smile, and went through the doors of the boarding lounge.

***

Maggie spent the whole of the flight home wondering whether she should tell her mother the reason for her return. She decided not to enlighten her with the circumstances of her and James' relationship. She felt it would stir up too many unhappy memories. She would just say she had fallen in love with someone, and it just did not work out. While she had been packing up in London, she had sent them an airmail letter telling them she was coming home early and letting them know the time of her arrival.

They were all there to meet her, and their greetings were all that Maggie could have wished for. There were no questions, simply delight that she was home again. And if Polly noticed how thin and drawn Maggie had become she did not say anything. "Plenty of time later," she thought to herself.

Later that night, in bed, she remarked to Paul,

"Maggie is terribly thin, isn't she?"

"I thought so too. I also think she is dreadfully worried about something."

"I don't think we should probe too hard though, do you?"

"No. I think she will tell us in her own time. We must just love her as we always have. I am sure, now she is home again, she will recover from whatever is troubling her."

"As usual Paul knows what to do." Polly thought.

South Africa

Chapter 29

With Paul's help, Maggie found work with a Racing Stable. They bred wonderful racehorses, and there was a great deal of secretarial work involved. It was just the kind of career she had envisaged. She was able to ride some of the beautiful horses in the stables, which made the cataloguing of their ancestry all the more interesting. She thought of James constantly, and with love; sometimes he seemed painfully near, and she wondered then if he was thinking about her too at that particular moment.

Polly and Paul tried to find nice young men who might interest her, but she just pushed Ellie forward. Ellie was growing up too, and was never averse to going out with someone who had been destined for her sister.

"But Mummy," she said when Polly remonstrated, "Maggie asked me to take her place. She did not feel like going out."

Paul found a replacement for Maggie's horse Pippin, who Ellie had annexed while Maggie was away, and was really too small for Maggie now. The new horse was a beautiful grey mare, and Maggie transferred all the affections she had left, to her.

"What are you going to call her?" Paul asked, after she had ridden her round the paddock.

"She is so beautiful, there is only one name for her."

"What is that?" They were all dying to know, as they watched Maggie have another canter round, and Paul thought how graceful his daughter looked.

"Beauty!" she announced.

Beauty was also a brilliant jumper, and Maggie started entering Horse Shows, and winning quite a few rosettes. Her admirers increased, particularly a young man, Freddy, who did not live far away, and seemed to ride over more often than the others.

"He really is as bit of a nuisance, I don't want to see him quite so often, even if he is exceptionally good with Beauty." She remarked to Ellie one day.

Ellie laughed. "It is not Beauty he comes to see, you idiot."

Maggie shrugged her shoulders.

"Well, I'm not interested. You have him, Ellie, if you like. I mean, he is pretty good with horses, but I'm not a horse."

Next time Freddy came, Maggie made herself scarce, and Freddy found himself helping Ellie to school Beauty.

"I'm sorry, Maggie is busy today, and she cannot come out with you. She said I could ride Beauty if you were there to make sure I was OK."

Freddy tried not to show his disappointment, and actually found Ellie great fun. Next time he came he seemed pleased that Maggie was not there, and gradually Freddy and Ellie became friends. Ellie confessed to Maggie that, although she was not in love with him, he was a great person to have around.

Susie often wrote to Maggie. She told her she missed her terribly, especially as she and John were getting married in the spring, and she had so wanted Maggie to be a bridesmaid.

I suppose you couldn't fly back? She wrote. *It would be such huge fun to see you again. But of course I am asking the Brettons, and I don't suppose you want to bump into any of them again. Did you know Elizabeth married her Robert last year? She asked me, but I couldn't get away that weekend. She told me James is still on his own. He will hardly speak to his father, I hear. Elizabeth told me there is an awful atmosphere in the house. Also your father is not well, they think heart problems, but he will not tell them, and pretends all is well. I just wish everything had worked out for you, and send my love, as does Aunt Eleanor. She is in tremendous form, and helping me with dresses, veils etc. WISH YOU WERE HERE! Lots of love....Susie XXX*

England and South Africa

Chapter 30

There was a terrible atmosphere in the Old Rectory after Maggie had gone. Elizabeth tried her best to keep everyone going, for Ben's sake, if nothing else. James was no help at all. He went round with a black look on his face, growling to anyone who spoke to him, and refusing to speak at all to his father. In the end Elizabeth took him to task, and cornered him as he was going out. She seized a coat and rushed after him.

"James, hang on, I want to talk."

"What about? I'm in a hurry."

"No, you are not. In any case, we must talk. You can't go on like you are. It depresses everyone, and at least you could be civil to Ben and me."

"Well, I don't feel like being civil to anyone."

"I'm sure you don't, but you must try. I want to get married, and I want us all to be happy. Please James, I do hate this awful atmosphere." She could not help the tears rolling down her cheeks. James had never seen Elizabeth cry; at least not since their mother died, and he was shocked.

"Oh Elizabeth, I'm so sorry. I do see I'm being awfully selfish. I'm just so miserable. I can't think of anything but Maggie. I love her so much." He put his arms round Elizabeth, and hugged her.

They heard Ben returning from school, and James produced his large handkerchief. By the time Ben came into the garden to find them they had recovered, and the damp handkerchief was back in James' pocket.

"Just seen Robert's car coming up the drive." Ben announced, and Elizabeth fled to greet him.

"Can you help me mend my bike?" Ben asked his brother. James had always helped Ben, whom he adored, but had been inclined to neglect lately. They went out to the garage together, and Elizabeth noticed thankfully that they seemed to be chatting amicably. Life was getting back to normal, she hoped.

David had not felt well since Maggie had left. He had so longed to explain to her that he had really loved her mother, at least until Maggie was a toddler. But there had been so little time. Maggie had left so peremptorily, that he had had no opportunity to explain. He had had a short letter from her, saying that it was not his fault that she and James had fallen in love. She also wrote that she did not want any contact with the family, and she was going home as soon as she could get a flight. She sent her love, "for what it is worth," and signed herself Maggie, without any other endearments. He had kept the letter in a box with the mementoes of America, and tried to go on living.

***

Whether it was all the shocks of the last few years, or just fate, but when he finally gave in and visited the doctor the verdict was much as he had feared.

His heart was failing. The diagnosis could not have been worse, and he had very little time. Dr Howard had passed the case on to his younger partner, who after numerous tests confirmed that David's heart was beyond repair. But Dr Howard had delivered David, and cared for all his childhood illnesses, and now visited him often as a friend. As David had very few friends nowadays this was welcome, especially for Elizabeth.

She was just beginning life as wife to Robert. They lived in Wadebridge, so she was able to pop out to St. Wraich and keep an eye on David. James was no earthly good, as he still blamed David for his troubles and his mother's troubles, and even Maggie's misfortune at being his daughter.

For poor Ben, just leaving college, the atmosphere in the house was hardly happy, and he spent most of his time out of it, with friends. Elizabeth worried about him. It was three years since Maggie had left and, with no mother in the house, his elder brother should have become his mentor. Instead James was worse than useless,

"Couldn't you make an effort?" she grumbled to James one day, after he had been particularly short with Ben. "You are the only one Ben has to turn to, and I'm afraid you are driving him out of the house, and into the arms of some rather unsavoury characters."

"How do you mean, unsavoury characters? He is too young for that sort of thing, Isn't he?"

"Oh James, don't you notice anything nowadays? Or are you still so wrapped up in yourself you can't see what is happening under your nose?" she said in exasperation.

"I'm sorry, Elizabeth, I do feel completely numb these days. I still can't get Maggie out of my mind."

"Then it is really time you did. Spare a moment for Ben now and then. I can't be here as much as I'd like to. I feel my duty is to Robert now. I love him, like you loved Maggie, and I know I do not want to have to worry about all of you as well. Besides, I don't think Tom would have expected you to behave like this."

The shaft went home. James sighed.

"Oh dear. I'm sorry Sis. I've been a selfish bastard and I'll try and spend time with Ben and give you a break."

James realized after that conversation how self-centred he had been, expecting Elizabeth still to cope with the Old Rectory needs as well as her own house, and her new husband Robert.

He made an effort to be civil to his father, and started making friends with his young brother.

Ben had always looked up to him with a kind of hero worship, and it was not hard to involve him in surfing expeditions, and days out. He sat Ben down and endeavoured to find out the sort of career he was considering. As it happened he was not Tom's son for nothing, and he longed to be a farmer, and had plans to take over from the Truckles when he was old enough.

"You see, I've always wanted to be a farmer, and even more so after Dad was killed. It seemed to me that it was right for me to carry on as soon as I could; but I'd like to learn to do it all properly, if you see what I mean. Do you think you could help me, Tom?"

James swallowed, aching with remorse.

"Of course I will. What about applying to study at the Duchy College where I went."

But I don't want to study engineering like you."

"There are courses for all sorts of things there. Engineering was just one of them. I'll make an appointment for an interview, and we will go together and find out what they can offer which would suit you."

"Oh would you James? Thanks so much," and to both their embarrassment Ben flung his arms round his brother and hugged him.

James had never felt so guilty in his life. He had been so wrapped up in his own unhappiness; he had not noticed Ben, struggling to grow up with no father or mother to guide him. He quickly changed words to deeds, and before long Ben was blissfully getting down to learning everything about modern farming methods at the College, and the old ways from his grandfather, Mr Truckle. He did not have time to hang out with his previous "mates," for which Elizabeth was profoundly thankful.

James also began to notice the deterioration in David's health. In spite of all the little delicacies which Ellen cooked, he became thinner and very gaunt. His friends were very few. Most from his childhood had left St. Wraich, and since he had returned he had not had time to make new ones. Most of the village people had accepted his return, and greeted him warmly if they saw him, but he did not feel like going out much, except to wander forlornly round the garden, or to visit his parent's grave in the Churchyard. Tom and Jean were buried together in another spot, and he felt it would be wrong to invade their privacy.

He longed, with an increasing desire, to be reunited with Annabel and the children. He had told Dr Howard of his life in America, and the reason for his return. Dr Howard had listened and kept his own counsel. He felt perhaps that David had suffered enough to remonstrate with him.

David confessed to him. "I have asked Elizabeth to place the little box, which contains all that I have left of that family, in my coffin. I feel it will bring us all closer."

Dr. Howard nodded his wise old head. "I am sure you will be all together sometime, one way or another. I know you loved Jean in your own way, but you were both young, and you both found your true partners in the end."

David died peacefully in his sleep a few nights later.

South Africa

Chapter 31

"Do you think I should wear my blue dress?" Ellie was gazing at a selection of frocks, which were tossed onto her bed as she pulled them out of the cupboard. Maggie had come in to see if she was ready to go out with the young man waiting downstairs.

"Really Ellie, what a mess! Jan is waiting for you. For heaven's sake, get a move on."

"Oh well, perhaps that yellow one suits me best. Could you help me, Sis? The buttons are so fiddly."

"Anything to hurry you up; come here and turn round."

Ellie meekly obeyed. Maggie gave a little sigh. "Tell me, is Jan so special why you are getting in such a tizz about?"

"He is rather yummy, isn't he? Yes, I think he could be 'special' as you said."

"But, don't you know? I mean, it sort of hits you when it is the right one."

"Well, how do you know? You don't seem to have found anyone yet! Must rush..." and she was off downstairs like a whirlwind before Maggie had to think of an answer.

She sat down on the bed, feeling as if she had been crushed by a sledgehammer. She had built up a wall of denial, refusing to think about James, or Cornwall, or even Susie very much. Ellie had flitted from boy to boy, never showing emotion about any particular one; until now. This evening she had reminded Maggie of herself, so long ago it seemed, when she was getting ready to go out with James. The whole period in her life came flooding back. Shattered, she rushed out to the stables, threw a saddle on Beauty, and rode off at a gallop towards the mountains. Paul, coming back from a meeting with a horse dealer, saw her. He called out, but she did not hear, (or did not want to), so he shook his head and went inside. Polly was in the sitting room.

"Did you see Maggie just now, dashing out of the house as if the devil was after her?"

"Yes I did. I wondered what was up. No one has telephoned or anything. Do you think Ellie has upset her in some way?"

They discussed it for a bit, and decided to wait until she came back, then perhaps she would tell them.

Later they heard Beauty's hoof beats in the stable yard, and Maggie came in, looking completely drained. She managed a watery smile before taking the stairs two at a time, and shutting her bedroom door. Paul and Polly looked at each other.

"Well," Paul grinned ruefully. Best leave her, I think."

Maggie came down to supper, and the meal passed in unusual silence. Eventually she turned to her parents.

"I'm so sorry, I..." and she burst into tears.

Her parents were shocked. It was so unlike Maggie who was always so steady and cheerful. Admittedly she had been quieter since she came back from England, but that was now nearly three years ago, and she had seemed more positive of late. Polly went over and gathered her in her arms.

"Darling, hush now, don't cry. Can you tell us, it might help?"

Maggie swallowed. Paul gave her a large hanky to mop her eyes, and she sat down opposite them.

"I don't know where to begin, or how to tell you." She said, with a sniff. "But I'll try."

She sat down in a chair opposite them, and sighed deeply.

"When I was in Cornwall I met Daddy." Polly gave a gasp, but Paul put out a hand and restrained her. "Let her go on," he said quietly.

"I don't know how to tell you this, Mum, but he has another family. I should say "had," as they are a bit older than us. They have been living in Cornwall all the time he was here." She stopped, clutching Paul's handkerchief as if for support.

"Do you remember when Ellie nearly got swept out to sea, when we were in Durban some years ago?" Paul nodded.

"The man who rescued us, do you remember us talking about him?"

"Yes, of course. We tried to find him to thank him." Polly was speechless, but Paul had answered.

"Well, it is hard to believe I know, but he was Daddy's son, James." Maggie almost choked as she spoke his name.

"I met him again in Cornwall, and..." She could not go on for a moment. Then she took a deep breath, determined to tell the whole truth to her mother and Paul.

"I...We fell in love. James asked me to marry him, and I said "Yes." He bought me this ring," she pulled out the chain which was round her neck, where she had worn the ring as close to her heart as she could keep it.

"Then I was taken to his home, and discovered Daddy was his father too. So of course we are half brother and sister. I just came home."

She finished with a break in her voice and put her head in her hands.

Both Polly and Paul were aghast. They had kept Maggie's true parentage from her, knowing how fond she had been of Donald. They looked at each other, and felt their hearts were breaking. They had put their beloved elder daughter through such suffering, when telling her the truth would have saved them all such a lot of heartache. Polly started first.

"Darling Maggie. We have kept something from you all these years because we thought we might hurt you by telling you. Now we must try and explain a bit of the past which I, and I know Paul, would want you to know."

"Oh Mum, are you sure you want to tell me if it is so secret?"

Polly swallowed.

"Many years ago, when Paul and I were barely out of our teens, we fell deeply in love. My parents did not like, or approve, of Paul very much. We used to escape and kiss and hug each other. But then Paul was going away in the Army. We hid in our favourite bit of the garden to say "goodbye" and somehow we...we went a bit further than cuddles, if you know what I mean." Polly allowed herself a small smile at the memory, and clutched Paul's arm tightly.

"Paul went off, and it was all so secret I did not know where he was going, or if I'd ever see him again. After a short time I realized I was going to have a baby. Suddenly Donald appeared on the scene. I didn't exactly plan to marry him, but he fell for me, and I'm ashamed to say I let him make love to me, and then told him I was pregnant. When he asked me to marry him I was relieved that I would have a father for the baby. Your grandparents were very enthusiastic, my mother particularly, as she was dying of cancer, and wanted to see me settled. Daddy liked him too, as he was interested in the wine business, so I was sort of swept into the whole wedding scene." She was silent for a minute, and then as Maggie started to say something she held up her hand.

"No, darling, let me finish. I am not proud of all this, but I must go on. Of course he thought the baby was his, and when you arrived we all made him think you were premature. Though you were a bit big for that; but somehow he never realized. He adored you, and I know you loved him dearly."

"Mummy, do you mean Daddy is not..."

"No, my pet. Paul is your true father, and he loves you, and always has done. But when he returned from the Army, I was married to Donald, and he very honourably chose to let Donald think you were his daughter."

"What about Ellie then, who's...?"

"Paul is Ellie's Daddy too. I'm not ashamed to say that I never stopped loving Paul, and when he came back we stole some precious moments together. One day your father found all four of us having a picnic..."

"Yes, I sort of remember that picnic. Daddy went storming off, and later that night we all escaped to Paul's house. I never understood why, only that it was rather exciting, but I missed Daddy for a long time."

"Well, as I was saying, he recognized the red hair on Ellie, and she did resemble Paul, especially when she was a baby, that he couldn't miss it, and he suddenly went wild."

Paul put his arms out to Maggie, and she rose and went to him and was enfolded in the biggest hug she had ever had from him.

"Darling Maggie. You mustn't blame your mother. I don't think she will mind if I told you that Donald raped her that night after the picnic. That is why she escaped with you and Ellie, and came to me."

Polly went on. "After that Donald just took off. We never could find out where he'd gone. I wanted to divorce him, so I could marry Daddy Paul, but we just had to wait three long years before we could legally wed."

Maggie extricated herself reluctantly from Paul's arms.

"Now I know! He went back to Cornwall for a bit, then out to America. Something tragic happened out there, and when he returned James said he was a changed man. He was devoted to Jean, James' mother, who died a few years ago, and then he just went on living in the Old Rectory, (James' home), which is where I met him. It was such a shock; oh Mum..." and she put her head in her hands.

Paul had been thinking. Something was niggling him. He and Maggie came to the same conclusion at the same moment. He spoke first.

"Maggie, do you see now. You and James are not related at all! You can marry him now; there is nothing to stop you both becoming man and wife."

"Oh Daddy Pa...I mean Daddy," she grinned, all trace of tears gone, "Is that really true?"

"You bet! What's more my darling Polly, you and I are legal too!"

There was laughter and a little sadness for the wasted years. Ellie came in, and had to be told the whole saga. She was completely fascinated by the romance of it all. Much better she said, than a story book.

Maggie became strangely quiet.

"I can't help wondering," she looked up at her mother, "if maybe James has got married to someone else by now."

Polly thought for a minute. "There is only one way to find out, and that is to go back to England."

"I could write to Susie. I owe her a letter, and she would know I should think. Even though she is married she still goes down to Cornwall sometimes."

That evening Maggie wrote a long letter to Susie, explaining most of what had happened, and the momentous news of her true parentage. Almost as an afterthought she asked if Susie had any news of James and his family. She posted it next day, by airmail, and could hardly contain herself waiting for Susie's answer.

This came by return, as if Susie realized she would want to know as quickly as possible.

Dearest Maggie,

It was lovely to hear from you and amazing to hear about your real father. I could hardly believe it when I read your letter. It is like one of those novels we used to read!!! Funnily enough we were down in Cornwall last week, showing off our baby. (Did I tell you I had a bouncing boy last month?) He is called Edward, known already as Eddie, and is huge.

Well, while we were there we met James Bretton. His father is desperately ill with heart problems, and James had escaped the Old Rectory for an hour or so to get some fresh air. He said his father probably would not last more than a few days. I suppose it does not really matter to you now, as he is not really your father, and of course that means you are not related to James after all. He does not seem to have any girl friends, so I'm sure he'd love to see you again. You did seem to have quite a "thing" going when you were here. Do come and stay with us. Or Aunt Eleanor. She has let the flat, but she still has a spare room. Just send a telegram, and jump on a plane.

See you soon, and lots of love from us all, Susie XXX

Maggie did not exactly jump on a plane straight away... But she did send a telegram, and very soon she was in the air, winging her way to England, and, she hoped, eventually to Cornwall.

England

Epilogue

James shook his head in disbelief. He looked again, but could not see the dark red curly hair which had caught his attention a minute before. "Must be dreaming," he thought, and turned back to the coffin being lowered gently into the grave. The last words were said. Not read; the Reverend Catherine had officiated at too many funerals to need to have a book in her hands. She quietly finished the prayers with the words "All prayers are answered, all sins forgiven, Amen." And besides the Rector perhaps only Elizabeth knew what it meant, having heard a little of the story of David's life abroad from her mother, as she lay dying.

Now the villagers drifted away, intent on being the first to find a chair in the Old Rectory, and partake of Ellen's special sponge cake before it was all gone. Only the family lingered for a moment before turning to walk back to their home. James, deep in thought, did not turn when he felt a small hand slipped into his.

"Coming, Elizabeth," he whispered.

"It's me..." a dear unforgettable South African inflection seared into his consciousness, and he whirled round.

"Maggie." His voice croaked with emotion. "Why are...? How did you know your father had died? When did..?"

She put her fingers on his mouth to stop him saying any more.

"It can wait. But first of all, and best of all, he was *not* my father in any case."

"What do you mean? I don't understand. Maggie, is this a dream? That is our father down there, and you've come, and now you tell me..."

"My darling, darling James. We are not brother and sister at all."

She gave a brief explanation. Still encircled in James' arms she said hesitantly, "We can...at least, have you met someone else? Oh, Lord, have you?"

"No, of course not. I never could even think of it after you." He tightened his arms round her as if she was a ghost, and then, feeling her long remembered figure, he bent his head and kissed her gently, holding her closely as if she might suddenly disappear again.

"James, are you coming?" Elizabeth's voice interrupted them. "You must come and help with all these people. Ben and I are..." she stopped suddenly as she saw who was with James.

"Good heavens, Maggie. How very kind of you to come all the way over to say farewell to your father."

James gave Elizabeth a brief explanation, and Maggie took Elizabeth's hand and squeezed it.

"I know this must seem awful, but I did not actually know he had died until I got to St. Wraich, and one of the villagers told me he was being buried, so I thought I would come. After all, I thought he was my Daddy for a long time. I didn't mean to give you all a shock. I was going to slip away, and come back after it was all over. But I saw James, and, well, it was like a magnet drawing me to him."

"Magnet, or no magnet," the ever practical Elizabeth broke in; "You must both come and help. Ellen and May are being rushed off their feet. Oh, if only St. Wraich did not like a good funeral!" and she hurtled off.

James and Maggie looked at one another and burst into hoots of slightly hysterical laughter, suddenly stifling their joy as they realized it was supposed to be a solemn occasion.

"One thing," James turned to Maggie. "We must get this straight. My darling Maggie, will you marry me, as quickly as possible?"

She looked up at him with a grin. "Yes, yes please."

***

Maggie and James were married under the trees at Whiteoaks. Elizabeth and Robert had brought Ben, and Ellen, to be with James at his wedding. The sun shone for them, and if Paul's and Polly's eyes strayed to the path which led to the hidden dell where they first found love, no one noticed. All thoughts were with the radiant bride and the handsome groom; except perhaps Ellie, who caught Jan looking at her with longing, and had rather strange feelings of her own.

All too soon Maggie was being hugged by all her family, before she and her husband took off for their new life together. They spent their first night in Durban, and it was all they had longed for during the months and years they had been parted.

But their real honeymoon began the following day in Port St. Johns, watching the rainbow curve over the Bay, and never really ended.